OUT OF CONTROL

It was silly to get too worked up about men. The sad, awful truth was, the more you wanted them, the less they wanted you. It was a cruel formula, but she'd learned to live with it.

Davy McCloud turned her formulas upside down.

"Why are you scared?" he asked. "I thought you wanted this."

Margot tried to smile, but her shaking mouth wouldn't cooperate. "You make me feel shy," she whispered. "That's all."

He kissed one knee, then the other. His lips were exquisitely warm and soft. His hands slid down her thighs. A deep, melting sweetness shivered through her legs in their wake.

"Are you trembling because you're scared, or because you're turned on?" he demanded.

"Both," she admitted.

BOOK YOUR PLACE ON OUR WEBSITE AND MAKE THE READING CONNECTION!

We've created a customized website just for our very special readers, where you can get the inside scoop on everything that's going on with Zebra, Pinnacle and Kensington books.

When you come online, you'll have the exciting opportunity to:

- View covers of upcoming books
- Read sample chapters
- Learn about our future publishing schedule (listed by publication month *and author*)
- Find out when your favorite authors will be visiting a city near you
- Search for and order backlist books from our online catalog
- Check out author bios and background information
- Send e-mail to your favorite authors
- Meet the Kensington staff online
- Join us in weekly chats with authors, readers and other guests
- Get writing guidelines
- AND MUCH MORE!

**Visit our website at
http://www.kensingtonbooks.com**

SHANNON McKENNA

OUT OF CONTROL

KENSINGTON BOOKS
KENSINGTON PUBLISHING CORP.
http://www.kensingtonbooks.com

KENSINGTON BOOKS are published by

Kensington Publishing Corp.
850 Third Avenue
New York, NY 10022

All Kensington titles, imprints and distributed lines are available at special quantity discounts for bulk purchases for sales
promotion, premiums, fund-raising, educational, or institu-
tional use.

Special book excerpts or customized printings can also be created to fit specific needs. For details, write or phone the office
of the Kensington Special Sales Manager: Kensington Publishing Corp., 850 Third Avenue, New York, NY 10022. Attn.
Special Sales Department. Phone: 1-800-221-2647.

Kensington and the K logo Reg. U.S. Pat. & TM Off.

ISBN 0-7582-0563-5

First Trade Paperback Printing: April 2005
First Mass Market Paperback Printing: April 2006
10 9 8 7 6 5 4

Printed in the United States of America

Chapter

1

San Cataldo, California

A poke in the eye, that's how it felt.

Mag Callahan curled white-knuckled hands around the mug of lukewarm coffee that she kept forgetting to drink. She stared, blank-eyed, at the Ziploc bag lying on her kitchen table. It contained the evidence that she had extracted from her own unmade bed a half an hour before, with the help of a pair of tweezers.

Item #1—Black lace thong panties. She, Mag, favored pastels that weren't such a harsh contrast to her fair skin. Item #2—Three strands of long, straight dark hair. She, Mag, had short, curly red hair.

Her mind reeled and fought the unwanted information. Craig, her boyfriend, had been uncommunicative and paranoid lately, but she'd chalked it up to that pesky Y chromosome of his, plus his job stress, and his struggle to start up his own new consulting business. It never occurred to her that he would ever . . . dear God.

Her own house. Her own *bed.* That pig.

The blank shock began to tingle and go red around the edges as it transformed inevitably into fury. She'd been so nice to him. Letting him stay in her house rent-free while he bugswept and remodeled his own place. Lending him money, quite a bit of it. Cosigning his business loans. She'd bent over backwards to be supportive, accommodating, womanly. Trying to lighten up on her standard ballbreaker routine, which consisted of scaring boyfriend after boyfriend into hiding with her strong opinions. She'd wanted so badly to make it work this time. She'd tried so hard, and this was what she got for her pains. Shafted. Again.

She bumped the edge of the table as she got up, knocking over her coffee. She leaped back just in time to keep it from splattering over the cream linen outfit she'd changed into for her lunch date with Craig.

She'd come home early from her weekend conference on purpose to pretty herself up for their date, having fooled herself into thinking that Craig was only twitchy because he was about to broach the subject of—drum roll, please—the Future of Their Relationship. She'd even gone so far as to fantasize a sappy Kodak moment: Craig, bashfully passing her a ring box over dessert. Herself, opening it. A gasp of happy awe. Violins swelling as she melted into tears. How stupid.

Fury roared up like gasoline dumped on a fire. She had to do something active, right now. Like blow up his car, maybe. Craig's favorite coffee mug was the first object to present itself, sitting smugly in the sink beside another dirty mug, from which the mystery tart had no doubt sipped her own coffee this morning. Why, would you look at that. A trace of coral lipstick was smeared along the mug's edge.

Mag flung them across the room. Crash, tinkle. The noise relieved her feelings, but now she had a coffee splatter on her kitchen wall to remind her of this glorious moment forevermore. Smooth move, Mag.

She rummaged under the sink for a garbage bag, muttering. She was going to delete that lying bastard from her house.

She started with the spare room, which Craig had commandeered as his office. In went his laptop, modem, and mouse, his ergonomic keyboard. Mail, trade magazines, floppy disks, data storage CDs clattered in after it. A sealed box that she found in the back of one of the desk drawers hit the bottom of the bag with a rattling thud.

Onward. She dragged the bag into the hall. It had been stupid to start with the heaviest stuff first, but it was too late now. Next stop, hall closet. Costly suits, dress shirts, belts, ties, shoes, and loafers. On to the bedroom, to the drawers she'd cleared out for his casual wear. His hypoallergenic silicon pillow. His alarm clock. His special dental floss. Every item she tossed made her anger burn hotter. Scum.

That was it. Nothing left to dump. She knotted the top of the bag.

It was now too heavy to lift. She had to drag it, bumpity-thud, out the door, over the deck, down the stairs, across the narrow, pebbly beach of Parson's Lake. The wooden passageway that led to her floating dock wobbled perilously as she jerked the stone-heavy thing along.

She heaved it over the edge of the dock with a grunt. Glug, glug, some pitiful bubbles, and down it sank, out of sight. Craig could take a bracing November dip and do a salvage job if he so chose.

She could breathe a bit better now, but she knew from experience that the health benefits of childish, vindictive behavior were very short-term. She'd crash and burn again soon if she didn't stay in constant motion. Work was the only thing that could save her now. She grabbed her purse, jumped into the car, and headed downtown to her office.

Dougie, her receptionist, looked up with startled eyes when she charged through the glass double doors of Callahan Web Weaving. "Wait. Hold on a second. She just walked in the door," he said into the phone. He pushed a button. "Mag? What are you doing here? I thought you were coming in this afternoon, after you had lunch with—"

"Change of plans," she said crisply. "I have better things to do."

Dougie looked bewildered. "But Craig's on line two. He wants to know why you're late for your lunch date. Says he has to talk to you. Urgently. As soon as possible. A matter of life and death, he says."

Mag rolled her eyes as she marched into her office. "So what else is new, Dougie? Isn't everything that has to do with Craig's precious convenience a matter of life and death?"

Dougie followed her. "He, uh, sounds really flipped out, Mag."

Come to think of it, it would be more classy, dignified, and above all, final if she looked him in the eye while she dumped him. Plus, she could throw the panties bag right into his face if he had the gall to deny it. That would be satisfying. Closure, and all that good stuff.

She smiled reassuringly into Dougie's anxious eyes. "Tell Craig I'm on my way. And after this, don't accept any more calls from him. Don't even bother to take messages. For Craig Caruso, I am in a meeting, for the rest of eternity. Is that clear?"

Dougie blinked through his glasses, owl-like. "You OK, Mag?"

The smile on her face was a warlike mask. "Fine. I'm great, actually. This won't take long. I'm certainly not going to eat with him."

"Want me to order in lunch for you, then? Your usual?"

She hesitated, doubting she'd have much appetite, but poor Dougie was so anxious to help. "Sure, that would be nice." She patted him on the shoulder. "You're a sweetie-pie. I don't deserve you."

"I'll order carrot cake and a double skim latte, too. You're gonna need it," Dougie said, scurrying back to his beeping phone.

Mag checked the mirror inside her coat closet, freshened her lipstick, and made sure her coppery red 'do was artfully mussed, not wisping dorkily, as it tended to do if she didn't gel the living bejesus out of it. One should try to look elegant when telling a parasitical user to go to hell and fry. She thought about mascara and decided against it. She cried easily; when she was hurt, when she was pissed, and today she was both. Putting on mascara was like spitting in the face of the gods.

She grabbed her purse, uncomfortably aware, as always, of the 9mm Beretta that shared space with wallet, keys, and lipstick inside. A gift from Craig, after she'd gotten mugged months ago. A pointless gift, since she'd never been able to bring herself to load the thing, and had no license to carry it concealed. Craig had insisted that she keep it in her purse, along with an extra clip of ammunition. And she'd gone along with it, in her efforts to be sweet and grateful and accommodating. Hah.

If she were a different woman, she'd make him regret that gift. She'd wave it around at him, scare him out of his wits. But that kind of tantrum just wasn't her style. Neither were guns. She'd give it back to him today. It was illegal, it was scary, it made her purse too heavy, and besides, today was all about streamlining, dumping excess baggage.

Emotional feng shui. Sploosh, straight into the lake.

By the time she got to her car, the unseasonable late autumn heat made sweat trickle between her shoulder blades. She felt rumpled, flushed and emotional. Frazzled Working Girl was not the look she wanted for this encounter. Indifferent Ice Queen was more like it. She cranked the air-conditioning to chill down to Ice Queen temperatures and pulled out into traffic, the density of which gave her way too much time to think about what a painful pattern this was in her love life.

Used and shafted by charming jerks. Over and over. She was almost thirty years old, for God's sake. She should have outgrown this tedious, self-destructive crap by now. She should be hitting her stride.

Maybe she should get her head shrunk. What a joy. Pick out the most icky element of her personality, and pay someone scads of money to help her dwell on it. Bleah. Introspection had never been her thing.

She parked her car outside the newly renovated brick warehouse that housed Craig's new studio, and braced herself to see Craig's tech assistant bouncing up to chirp a greeting. Mandi was her name. Probably dotted the *i* with a heart. Nothing behind those big brown eyes but bubbles and foam. She had long dark hair, too. Fancy that.

There was no one to be seen in the studio. Odd. Maybe Craig and Mandi had been overcome with passion in the office in back. She set her teeth and marched through the place. Her heels clicked loudly on the tile. The silence made the sharp sounds echo and swell.

The door to Craig's office was ajar. She clicked her heels louder. *Go for it. Burn your bridges, Mag, it's what you're best at.* She slapped the door open, sucked in air and opened her mouth to—

She rocked back with a choked gasp. The panty bag dropped from her hand.

Craig was dangling by his wrists from the pipes in the ceiling, suspended by one of his own ties. Naked. Blood streamed from his nose and mouth. Her brain picked out random details to focus on with preternatural clarity. The tie knotted around his wrists, cruelly tight. Beige silk, tasteful accents of gold. One of his favorites.

His bloodshot eyes rolled when he saw her. His mouth worked, but no sound came out. Fine hairlike things protruded from his naked body. Needles. He was stuck full of them. They were everywhere.

She lunged forward, a hoarse croak that felt more animal

than human jerking out of her throat, and stumbled to an abrupt stop.

Slim legs sprawled wide on the floor, one shoe on, one shoe off. Gartered hose. Bare, pale, skinny bottom. Mandi. She lay terribly still.

Mag's horrified gaze locked with Craig's. His desperate eyes flicked to a point behind her, to her left. She slowly turned her head.

A flash of awful pain, fire, and ice combined stabbed into her neck, down into her arm, up into her head, where it proceeded to explode.

Fireworks were overtaken by blackness. The world was gone.

"She has to die, Faris."

Marcus's voice on the cell phone Faris clutched to his ear seemed soft with puzzled regret, but he knew the cold steel beneath it very well.

Faris stared at the naked girl lying on the hotel bed. Her coppery hair was snarled against the pillow. He stroked the curve of her belly, the indentation of her navel. Her translucent skin was so soft and fine.

He was so gifted. He deserved this. Her love would fill that hollow ache that tortured him whenever Marcus had no jobs for him to do.

"No," he whispered.

"This was meant to be a murder-suicide, Faris. You were supposed to recover what Caruso took from us. Not ignore my orders and wander off to indulge yourself."

"But the scenario is almost exactly what you wanted," Faris protested. "Caruso's jealous girlfriend burst in on what will look like kinky sex. She shot him and his lover with her gun, threw it into the nearest Dumpster like the panicked amateur she is, and disappeared."

"Faris." Marcus's voice was ominously soft. "That's not what we—"

"I know where the mold is," Faris broke in. "I'll get it for you now. What difference does it make if she disappears or dies? She's the obvious suspect. The police have no reason to look any further. Let them waste their energy looking for her. They'll never find her."

"Faris." Marcus's reproach was palpable. "That's not the issue. My trust is the issue. I invested a huge amount of energy and money in your training. I made you the best of the best. And like a spoiled child, you say no?" He paused. "Perhaps you're less worthy than I thought."

Faris's fingers traced the poignant hollow beneath her rib cage, where her vital organs lay protected only by smooth muscle, silky skin. Normally, Marcus's anger would distress him to the point of vomiting, but with his red angel at his side, he felt untouched by it. Almost . . . free. "I've never asked for anything for myself before," he said, in a dreamy voice. "I always do everything you say. Always."

Marcus's sigh was sharp and impatient. "We can't risk our plans over something so banal. Women are expendable. No one knows this better than we. Be reasonable. I will give you ten of her. A hundred."

No. There was not another one like her on the face of the earth. His red angel. Faris's fingers feathered down to circle her hip bones.

"I am shocked at your attitude. The Callahan woman is worthless as anything but a prop. Finish the job. I want to hear the tragic conclusion of the Caruso/Callahan saga on the eleven PM news tonight. Failure is unacceptable. Do we understand each other? Faris?"

Faris broke the connection and turned his attention back to the girl. The cheap synthetic bedspread was not worthy of her. She should be lying on an altar of crimson velvet, draped with cloth of gold.

He checked her pulse, fingers lingering over the tender skin of her wrist. He prepared a dose of a drug that would keep her unconscious for two more hours and slid the needle tenderly into her arm.

He considered tying her to the bed, just in case he was delayed, but he was reluctant to start off their love affair by scaring her.

He wanted to be tender with her. Indulgent. Two hours was plenty of time to recover the mold for Marcus. A few minutes with Faris's needles, and Caruso had been very forthcoming about where he'd left it.

This was a pathetically easy job, in fact. Almost beneath his dignity. If all went smoothly, he would not even have to torture her.

He hoped not. Faris was a master at the art of torture, but he preferred that she love him. If he had to torture her, things would be much more complicated. Women took things so personally.

Faris lingered by the bed, hating to leave her so soon after he had found her. He groped for his snake pendant, the symbol of his order, and lifted her head to place it around her neck, arranging it carefully between her perfect breasts. His most prized possession. He stroked the soft skin, the lush curves. There. Better. It was tangible proof of his commitment. It would protect her until his return. She looked perfect.

This ecstatic emotion made him giddy. Strong enough to bear even Marcus's anger. He left the room, imagining how grateful and admiring she would be when he came back to wake her.

She owed her very existence to him. Every moment of her life was now his. She should be grateful to him for every breath she took.

A detailed and highly sensual fantasy of all the ways she would express her gratitude kept him pleasantly entertained as he drove.

Chapter

2

Seattle, Washington, eight months later

*D*ragon sinks into the ocean . . .
Davy McCloud's body flowed through the form, unencumbered by conscious thought, in harmony with the ancient sequence of movements. Grab with dragon claw. Sink down to pull his phantom adversary to the ground. Breathe low and soft, to pull qi down into his vital organs and circulate it. His body was fluid and relaxed, his attention focused, mind, body and spirit in perfect equilibrium. Qi focused out through the eyes.

He was the dragon, the cloud where it formed, the ocean where it lived. Balanced on air. Suspended in space.

The door of the dojo made no sound as it opened, but his heightened senses felt every minute change in temperature and air currents. He recognized her energy without even turning. He knew the way it felt in the back of his head. Like the ringing of a zillion tiny bells.

Seconds later her scent hit him. Spicy. Ginger or clove.

Woodsy, like cedar, with a hint of orange. Mouthwatering. It strengthened as she approached the tatami where he was practicing, and damned if he wasn't making a tiger claw now, a downward ripping movement instead of the softer, circular dragon claw. He corrected himself instantly and took a split second to gather his concentration.

Dragon stretches out his left claw . . . she must have just finished teaching her aerobics class at the Women's Wellness Center, the all-women gym next door. He'd heard the pounding music ease off a timeless infinity ago, which the tracking mechanism in his brain identified as about fifteen minutes. Deep into that remote no-man's-land in his brain, he'd barely registered the high-pitched chatter of the women heading out of the gym into the pedestrian mall towards the parking lot, buzzed on endorphins.

And here she was. In his face. In his space.

Dragon stretches out his right claw . . . what the hell was she doing in here? He'd been so fucking careful to avoid her, and now his breathing was hard, too tense and dynamic, too high in the chest. His heart beat fast, thudding against his ribs as if he were afraid.

Concentrate, goddamnit. He softened his breathing, but that just let still more of her warm female scent into his lungs. Damp sweetness. Perfumed soap, shampoo, or whatever other female goop she smeared on her body, activated by the heat of exercise. If he turned and looked at her, her perfect skin would be glowing with a pearly sheen of sweat.

He did not look. He did not even look at her, and still his groin tightened. It made him furious with his own body.

Dragon grabs the rainbow . . . the bright pink spandex workout gear she was wearing jarred the corner of his eye as he turned. Distraction was just another challenge to face and overcome, he reminded himself. So were surges of irrational anger. He knew the drill. Dispassionately observe his reaction. Let it go. Move on.

He should welcome challenges to his concentration. It

was just a mind game. Ideally, he should be able to maintain perfect focus even if the sky fell around his ears. *Dragon stretches out his left claw . . .*

Yeah, but the falling sky didn't have that sweet, spicy smell that punched through his defences like armor-piercing rounds.

He spun around, leg extended, and couldn't help but note again that she was wearing the hot pink two-piece leotard, a seductive French-cut thong. One of his favorites. He'd memorized her workout gear in the six weeks since she'd started working next door. Every last piece.

Vaguely perverted of him, once he thought about it.

But he shouldn't be thinking at all. At this point, no more than twenty-five percent of his concentration was focused on the form. The other seventy-five was hyperconscious of Margot Vetter watching him as he practiced in the twilit, silent dojo, making him as self-conscious as a teenage boy. He'd taken off the cotton jacket of his gi, and his bare torso dripped with sweat. If he could smell her from this distance, she could smell him, too, and after teaching two karate classes back to back, it wasn't pretty. A nose full of ripe, sweaty male animal.

Stop it, forget it, cancel it out. He sank down into the opening pose once again, grimly determined to get through it. *Crane flies into the sky . . .* leap, land lightfooted in left cat stance, right hand scooped under left into *crane cools his wings . . .* and it was fucking useless, with those tiny bells ringing, shooting his concentration to hell.

He finished the form, just because his own nature would not permit him to leave a thing unfinished once he had begun it, and sank down into *crane guards its nest*.

Wasted effort.

Nothing should knock him off balance when he was in that meditative zone. Nothing ever had until Margot Vetter had shown up at Women's Wellness next door to teach the aerobics classes. He was thirty-eight years old, and he had a stupid-ass crush on the woman.

Which is all it could ever be. He'd known it since the evening that Tilda, his tenant who ran the Women's Wellness Center, had introduced them. A night spent tossing in bed until all the sheets were ripped off the mattress and wrapped around his sweating body. Imagining Margot twined around him, on top of him, bent over in front of him. He'd given up on sleep halfway through the night and gone to the computer to do what any man with a functioning brain should do when contemplating getting involved with a woman. A comprehensive background check.

The results of that check had put him in a foul mood for weeks.

He took a deep breath, and let it out very slowly before he turned.

"No shoes on the tatami," he said.

"I'm already barefoot," she said. "I left my flip-flops at the door."

Her husky alto voice brushed over the nerves on the surface of his skin. His hairs prickled, and his groin was heavy, and he was angry at himself for being angry, embarrassed for being embarrassed. His gaze traveled rapidly over the length of her body: slim bare feet, graceful ankles, turquoise leggings clinging to long, muscular legs, the hot pink spandex leotard hugging every lush curve. She was tall, broad-shouldered, wide-hipped. Not too skinny, with that round ass that stuck out a little in back, and the soft, lush swell of her belly. Head high, back straight. An uppity, hip-swaying walk that could hypnotize a man into driving up onto the sidewalk and into a parking meter.

Which he had nearly done the first day he'd caught sight of her.

The sports bra top that went with the thong contained big, soft-looking tits. One of these days he would have to stroll through the gym next door under the guise of a neighborly visit and look in on one of her aerobics classes, just to monitor that bra's performance. But he would have to see those breasts bare and unbound to truly believe them. Until then, he would remain skeptical about God's existence.

Wrong. No. Wouldn't be going there, wouldn't be doing that. He'd slammed the door on that possibility weeks ago, but still the images spun through his mind, and now the heaviness in his crotch was solidifying into an official hard-on. The thin cotton trousers that he wore to practice kung fu would be no help in preserving his male dignity. He was so screwed.

Her eyes were a ragbag of bright colors; irises rimmed with indigo that faded to bluish green and then to gold around the pupil. They met his so directly, he had to fight the impulse to drop his gaze and stare at his own feet. Jesus. Next he was going to start to stammer and blush.

The charged silence was driving him nuts.

"What are you doing here?" he demanded. Embarrassment made his voice harsher than he'd intended.

She sucked her full, rosy bottom lip between her teeth and chewed on it. "I'm . . . I'm, uh, sorry to have interrupted you."

He shrugged. Waited.

"Your kata looks great," she offered. "You've got amazing technique. I'm no expert, but . . . well, wow. It's just beautiful."

Courtesy demanded some polite acknowledgment of this remark, but all he could manage was a grunt and a nod. She waited in vain for him to pick up his cue. He clenched his teeth and concentrated on clamping down on his body's physiological response. The biofeedback equivalent of trying not to think about a pink elephant.

Her cheeks flushed pinker. "I, ah . . . I had a couple questions for you, actually. I heard you're a private investigator, and—"

"Who'd you hear it from?"

She looked taken aback at his curt tone. "That blond guy

who teaches the kickboxing classes here. He told me that you—"

"Sean," he said. "My brother. Never could keep his mouth shut."

A perplexed crease appeared between her straight dark brows. Probably wondering how he could possibly be related to Sean, the quintessential calendar pinup male with the flirtatious charm to match. There wasn't much resemblance between the two of them, other than the dirt-blond shade of their hair and their bizarre background.

"Oh." Her voice was cautious. "Is it some big secret, then?"

The thought of Sean chatting Margot up made his jaw clench. The fact that his reaction was stupid and irrational made him even angrier, like an endless feedback loop. "I'm phasing that business out. I'm still licensed, but I'm not taking on any new clients. As Sean knows damn good and well."

"Oh." Her voice was subdued. "Why are you phasing it out?"

He crossed his arms over his bare chest and longed for his jacket, which was draped over the weight rack all the way across the room.

"Boredom. Burn-out." He made his voice curt and dismissive. "I'm moving on to other things."

Her eyes dropped. She took a step back, chilled.

It was working. He'd put her off. She wouldn't be back. Exactly what he'd intended. All according to plan.

So why did he feel like such an asshole?

"I see. Sorry I bothered you, then," she mumbled as she turned away. "I won't take up any more of your time—"

"Wait," he heard himself say.

She turned back slowly. Her face looked pale in the fading twilight. Her hair was cinched into a clip, a wild explosion of spiky wisps up top. Those hollows beneath her high cheekbones were new. She'd lost weight in the last few days, and her pallor confirmed what he'd suspected the minute he saw her. That dull, dark brown hair color was false, like her name, her driver's license, everything about her.

She looked different tonight. Fragile. An image of Kevin flashed through his mind, triggering a dull ache of pain. His younger brother, killed years ago when he ran his truck off a cliff. Davy had been in the Persian Gulf at the time, but he'd dreamed of his brother the night before he got the news. He'd seen a shadow lying over Kevin's face.

Margot Vetter had a shadow like that hanging over her tonight.

He was deviating from his script. The woman was trouble he did not need. A walking, breathing question mark. He had enough to deal with, with the new business he was starting up.

Margot Vetter's checkered past was not his business, no matter how curious he was. He didn't need to know what she was running from, what responsibilities she was evading. With his constant efforts at self-mastery, he'd be damned if he would let his dick drag him into the snakepit of somebody else's bad decisions and rotten judgment.

No more rescue missions, either. He'd tried the hero routine years ago, with Fleur, and had fuck-all to show for it.

Unless you counted the scars.

Margot jerked her shoulders, impatient with the long silence. "So?" she demanded. "Wait for what? Why are you staring at me?"

He played for time. "Why do you need a detective?"

Her full lips tightened. "What do you care? It's irrelevant, since you're no longer in the business. And I would hate to bore you."

"I'm not bored. And I'll decide what's relevant."

She grew three inches in a breath. "Will you? Gee, that's arrogant."

Arrogant. Huh. Women had thrown that at him before,

but he just shrugged it off. There were worse things a woman could call a guy.

"Just tell me." He concentrated on his command stare, which he'd used to great effect as the sole authority figure for three unruly younger brothers. He'd developed it further in the army, and honed it to perfection as a martial arts master. All the force of his will, blazing out through the eyes. Legend held that a true master of the dragon form could terrify his enemies into submission with a single glance. He hadn't made it to that point yet, but he did all right, for the most part.

Didn't work worth a damn on Margot Vetter, though. She just wrapped her arms over her tits and glared right back at him. "I don't have time for idle curiosity, buddy. I've got a body sculpture class to teach in"—she consulted her watch—"three minutes. So go on back to your karate moves, and don't stress yourself about—"

"Kung fu," he said.

She gave him a death ray stare. "Excuse me?"

"I was practicing kung fu, not karate," he clarified.

She rolled her eyes, turned her back and marched for the door.

He lunged ahead of her to block the exit, without thinking, and she shrank back, startled. "Hey! How'd you do that?" she said sharply.

The sheer variety of colors in her eyes was distracting. "Do what?"

"I didn't even hear you move, and whoosh. You appeared right in front of me." She stabbed his solar plexus with her finger and yanked her hand back at the shock of contact with his skin. "You scared me!"

"Uh . . ." He groped for any kind of response. "Dragon spirit, maybe."

Aw, shit. He regretted the words the instant they left his mouth.

"Dragon who?" She regarded him with deep suspicion.

"According to legend, a practitioner of Shaolin can, uh, use the spirit of the dragon to misdirect his opponent into thinking an attack is coming from the opposite direction," he said lamely. "Theoretically."

Margot's pointed chin lifted. "Oh. I see. Are you going to attack me, then? Since when am I your opponent?"

"You're not. You're absolutely not," he assured her. "I just said that, without thinking. It was stupid. I didn't mean to imply . . . wait. Please. Don't go yet." He moved to block her as she sidled around him.

Her brow furrowed. "Hey. Are you deliberately trying to creep me out, or are you just naturally weird?"

He thought about it, and rapidly concluded that he did not want to creep her out. "Just naturally weird, I guess."

She rolled her eyes. "OK, that's enough," she announced. "Out of my way. I've got stuff to do." She dismissed him with a commanding wave of her slender hand.

"Meet me after your class. You can tell me about your problem. Over dinner. If you want." He blurted out the unpremeditated, ill-considered words, and held his breath for her response.

Her eyes widened, defenceless in her surprise. She wrapped her arms across her chest, and her cleavage deepened. She had a sprinkle of red freckles on her tits. He dragged his gaze away from her chest.

"Who said I had a problem?" Her voice was belligerent.

"People who go looking for a detective always have a problem," he said. "Tell me. At least the short version. Please."

Margot stared down at the floor for a long moment, and let out a long, unsteady sigh. "Well . . . it's just that I've got some sicko stalking me, and it's freaking me out." The words came out in a quick, nervous rush. "I just wanted to tell someone. You know. To get another point of view. I'm chasing myself in circles, thinking about it."

"What happened?" he demanded. "What's he done so far?"

She twisted her hands together. "I started finding red rose petals on my doorstep, which was strange, but whatever, right? Secret admirer, whoop-di-doo. It's happened off and on for the last two weeks. Then I got burgled six days ago. Don't know if that's connected. But then the other day . . ." Her voice trailed off. She swallowed.

"What?"

The rough impatience in his voice made her flinch. "The dog. I found a dead dog on my porch. Throat slit. Blood everywhere."

A cold, dark hole yawned open, somewhere deep in his gut. "What did the police have to say about it?"

She hesitated, and shook her head. "I, um, didn't call them."

"Why not?" he demanded. Though he knew damn well why not.

The shadow over her face deepened by imperceptible degrees. Her eyes flicked away. The faint, bluish smudges beneath them made her look haunted. "Look, uh . . . never mind, OK? I shouldn't have bothered you in the first place, and I'm late for my class, and you're not in the business now anyhow, so thanks for your time, but I have to—"

"Tell me the rest of it over dinner," he urged.

She gave him a long, searching look. "You know . . . something tells me that wouldn't be such a fabulous idea."

Here it was. His chance to back off with his dignity more or less intact. You win some, you lose some, and God knows it was just as well.

"Why not?" he asked baldly.

She looked flustered. "I have to pick up my dog at the kennel—"

"I can wait," he said. "Do you like Mexican?"

"Sure, when I can get it, but there's no point in flapping my jaw about my personal problems if you don't—"

"I've changed my mind about not taking on any more cases."

Startled silence stretched out after his words. Her subtle shadow weighed on him, teasing him like a painful dream that slipped out of reach of conscious thought, leaving sick dread lingering in its wake.

It was a familiar feeling. The cases that he gave a shit about always haunted him. But the haunting didn't usually start so quickly.

Her throat moved as she swallowed. "Actually, I wasn't proposing to hire you. The plain truth is, I'm too broke to pay you. I just wanted to bounce it off somebody. My dog is tired of hearing me talk about it."

"So bounce it off me," he said. "While we eat."

She bit her lip, her eyes big and apprehensive. "Your vibes are really intense, McCloud. And it's been a long day, and I'd just like to relax and hang out with my dog tonight. So thanks for the dinner invite, but no thanks. And you can get out of my way now. Any time."

"I'll tone my vibes down," he said. "I'll get takeout while you get your dog, and meet you at your place."

She shook her head rapidly. "Not. You will do no such thing."

Her withdrawal made him feel desperate, as if a boat he should have boarded was pulling away without him. She tried to slide between him and the wall. He blocked her with an arm in front and one behind.

"Wait," he pleaded. "Just a second."

"What the hell?" She lashed out.

He snagged her flailing hand out of the air before she could smack him with it. "Calm down," he urged. "This is serious. I want to—"

"Don't you dare touch me!" She flung her knee up.

He spun sideways in an automatic reflex to protect his balls, and ended up pinning her against the wall. It happened so fast, and suddenly his nose was full of her scent, her soft hair tickled his mouth, and her lithe curves were pressed against the full length of his body.

She was trembling. Scared of him.

He let go instantly and backed away, horrified. "Jesus. I'm sorry. I didn't mean to do that. I swear."

She stared at him, panting. She put one hand over her mouth, then pressed both hands against the hectic blush that stained her sharp cheekbones. He prayed for her not to look down. Tried to hold her gaze like a tractor beam, willing her, *don't look down, don't look*—

She looked down. He was busted. Heat surged up into his face.

"Holy cripes," she whispered. "You freak."

"I'm sorry." He held up his hands. "I didn't mean to grope you. I don't know what got into me."

Her gaze flicked back down to his crotch, and she snorted. "Oh, I think I could maybe take a wild guess."

He floundered around in his mind for a justification for his bizarre behavior, and found none. "I just didn't want you to, uh, go away mad."

She shook with a burst of dry laughter. "Smooth, McCloud. Very smooth. I've got a little social tip for you. Remember to take your anti-psychotic meds on schedule from now on, OK?"

The glass window with *McCloud Martial Arts Academy* stenciled on it rattled in the door frame with the force of her parting slam.

Chapter
3

Mikey was going to make her pay for leaving him at the pet hotel. The extent of his hurt and outrage was evident in the rigidity of his small body as she carried him up the steps to her porch. She braced herself against sick dread as she peeked into the shadows to make sure that something horrible wasn't draped over her doormat.

Nothing today. Snakey the Sicko Maniac was taking the day off.

Air came slowly back into her lungs as she unlocked the door. She flipped on the urban blight light, a naked dangling bulb specifically designed to highlight water damage and plaster cracks, to say nothing of undereye circles and assorted facial blemishes. She loathed the thing, but her nice lamps had been smashed in the break-in. She was stuck with the urban blight light till she got her act together. Though the way her life was going, that day seemed to get more distant all the time.

She set Mikey gently on the floor. He shook himself and sniffed around with remote puzzlement, as if to say, *What is this place? I scarcely remember it . . . or you.* He turned his back on her and limped, slowly and pitifully, towards the kitchen.

Of course, he'd always limped, since the day she'd found him. She'd found him half-dead on the side of the road seven months ago, after her flight from California had finally landed her in Seattle. A car had fractured his back legs. The vet had recommended putting him down immediately, but she'd never been known for her propensity for following sensible advice. She'd nursed him through it with her own intuitive version of dog physical therapy, taking on the task of saving Mikey as if he were a symbol of everything in life worth saving. And if she pulled it off, things would eventually be OK for her again, too.

Silly and superstitious, maybe, but it didn't matter, since Mikey the Wonder Mutt was his own reward. Smart, devoted, and the most shameless manipulator she'd ever known. His hitching gait made her heart hurt. He was probably playing it up to make her feel bad, but she knew from experience that aches and pains were worse when you felt depressed and abandoned. Why should it be any different for Mikey?

Besides, if he was faking it, she forgave him the ploy. He was a little dog. Old, too, in dog years. He had to use what weapons were available to him. Now there was a concept she could relate to.

She peeled off her clammy workout gear as she trailed into the kitchen after Mikey, and ran a basin full of water with a capful of laundry soap. Mikey climbed into his basket, did his compulsive three and a half turns, and flopped down with a dejected sigh.

She let out a dejected sigh herself as she dunked her spandex into the suds. A quickie shower in her mildewy bathroom was next, after which some sloppy sweatpants, her big Superman T-shirt, and she felt almost human. She rummaged for her comb in the basket on her dresser. Her fingers closed around the heavy gold snake pendant.

She pulled the thing out and tried to stare down the sense of dread it gave her. She wished the thief had taken this instead of her laptop. It was worth more money, and she would have been grateful to be rid of it. She should pawn the nasty thing. The money would be tainted, but she'd get over it. Vet bills had to be paid somehow.

She knew why she hung onto it, though she didn't like to admit it. The pendant was the only key she had to the nightmare puzzle her life had become. It was like a magical talisman. If she got rid of it, she might be trapped in this lonesome gray nowhere forever. No way out.

Whoops, don't go there. She couldn't let herself think that way, even briefly. The only way to keep her sanity was to stay focused on the present moment. Breathing in, breathing out, and grateful to be alive.

She headed into the kitchen and hunkered down next to Mikey's basket, fully prepared to grovel. He'd curled up into a ball, graying muzzle buried between his paws. Eyes tight shut. No wags, no licks, no yips, no friendly interaction of any kind. It was the doggie deep freeze.

"Hey. Mikey. Don't you want some dinner?" she asked.

Mikey was far above such obvious bribery. He didn't twitch so much as a whisker. Margot got up and rummaged through the cupboard for the dog treats. She waved one in front of his nose.

He opened one slitted eye and gave her his patented "as if" look.

"This isn't fair," she told him. "I'm leaving you at that kennel to protect you from Snakey, you ungrateful little snot. I can't afford it, either. I'm still in hock to the vet for your last fight. That dog was ten times your size, but did you think about that before you got mouthy?"

Mikey indicated with a snuffling grunt that dogs will be dogs, and she could stick her budget problems where the sun didn't shine.

"Besides, you owe me," she reminded him. "You'd be roadkill if it weren't for me, fur-face."

No go. Mikey wasn't coming down off his high horse tonight.

Margot sagged down next to his basket and concentrated on petting him the way he liked best, a gentle stroke from brow to nape with an extra against-the-grain rub around the ears on the upswing. He allowed her touch, but refused to respond to it. She ran her fingers through his silky hair, careful to avoid the shaved spots around his stitches. A relic from his run-in with a bad-ass stray in the park.

Mikey was a scrappy little guy. She admired that about him, even when it cost her money. He didn't know when to shut his big mouth. A lot like yours truly, so it's not like she could point fingers.

She was whipped, but she really should work on her web design business, or plod away at her private amateur murder investigation.

The thought zipped through her mind before she remembered that she no longer had her laptop. The rat bastard thief had it now.

Gah. She was squeezed dry tonight anyhow. Nothing left but pulp. Up before dawn to get Mikey to the pet hotel before her waitressing shift, then she schlepped downtown to do a lunchtime body sculpting class and aerobics class at a health club that catered to corporate types, and then the evening classes at Women's Wellness. She was woozy, too, after a week on the new crash diet. The kennel fees and vet bills had bitten deep into her already lean grocery budget.

And yet, her butt still hadn't gotten any smaller. Go figure.

Time to start foraging. It took character and a sense of humor to make a meal out of what was left in her kitchen. She heaved herself to her feet and opened the cupboard. Crumbs in the bottom of the cornflakes box. Whatever she might still be able to scrape out of the Skippy's jar. There was a third of a bag of peeled baby carrots in the fridge, and she was hungry enough to actually eat them tonight, not just tell herself that she should. God, it would be great to just pick up the phone and order in something wickedly high-caloric and delicious.

That made her think about Davy McCloud's offer of Mexican food. A whoosh of something potent and scary shivered up her spine.

She'd been checking the guy out ever since she'd started teaching at Women's Wellness. Your typical stern, taciturn Nordic warrior type; studly, gorgeous and as cold as ice. Apparently uninterested in her, but oh, so fascinating. The lure of the unattainable, and all that crap.

She stared at the black pepper and the teabags while the images played through her mind; McCloud's powerful body moving over the tatami with the swift, lethal grace of a thrown spear. He was so well-proportioned, you didn't notice how huge he was until he was right in your face—and then, whoopsy daisy, it was too late.

He was way too big for her, though. Big guys made her nervous. On those rare occasions that she did indulge her baser instincts—that would be way back in prehistory when she still had the nerve—she picked mellow, scrawny guys who made her laugh. Guys she could put into a hammerlock, if need be. Craig had fit into that category.

Her mind shied away from poor Craig. She focused her attention back on the far more appealing image of Davy McCloud's half-naked body. Nobody could put McCloud into a hammerlock. She had a tough time imagining him laughing, either. The thought of those piercing eyes made heat rush into her face—and various other parts of her body.

Strange, to have such a raw sexual reaction to a guy she barely knew. She'd been off men for months. Waking up naked and bewildered in a strange hotel room after witnessing a brutal murder could do that to a girl. Real libido crusher. Turned those hormones off like a faucet.

And God, she would really, *really* rather not think about that tonight, or she'd start feeling slimed, and have to take another shower.

A hot, juicy sexual fantasy starring Davy McCloud and her trusty vibrator would be a fab distraction. He was pure fantasy, though, and she'd better not forget it. With his angular face, his grim mouth, his hair cropped off into that sweat-stiffened brush cut, he looked almost military. Too severe for her. Once his hard-on was taken care of, she would drive a guy like that bonkers with her smart mouth.

Must be the old opposites-attract cliché. His attitude of rigid discipline and authority rubbed her the wrong way. Made her want to goad him. Like, *hey, who died and made you boss of the universe, pal?*

Then she'd strip him naked, rub him down with oil, knock him onto his back and ride him off into the sunset. At a hard gallop.

Whew. She opened the fridge, fished a carrot out of the bag and chomped it. Might as well give all that extra saliva an honest job to do.

She should cut herself some slack. Lusting over McCloud was a lot more fun than fretting about Mikey's big, hurt eyes when she left him at the money-sucking pet hotel, or feeling like she was going to urp with dread every time she peered into the shadows of her own porch. It was better than worrying about Snakey lying in wait for her in the dark. Or obsessing about what had happened to poor Craig and Mandi.

She grabbed the Skippy's jar and the bag of carrots and flopped down next to Mikey's basket, curling up tight around the cold, sick ache in her belly. Sometimes curling up helped. A little bit, anyway.

She ran a carrot around the rim of the jar and crunched it with grim determination. She needed a new brilliant scheme, but Snakey was hogging all the RAM in her brain. There wasn't enough room left on the hard drive to run the kapow! knock-your-socks-off creative solutions program. She'd just started to drag herself out of this tar pit a few weeks ago, when she'd landed a job in a new graphics design firm in Belltown. The fake references she'd bought for her new identity had eaten up months of meager savings, but it had seemed well worth it at the time.

It had lasted exactly ten glorious days before the studio had burned to the ground. It was like she was cursed.

Screw this. She was going to hunt down this joker who was playing tricks on her, and rip his limbs and any other loose appendages off his body. Then she would spring Mikey from the joint, clear her name, and get her act definitively together. The details were fuzzy, but that was the plan. Having a plan was a good first step, right? Right.

She stared at the phone, tempted for the gazillionth time to call Jenny, or Christine or Pia, her best girlfriends from her old life. Just to let them know she was alive, and that she missed them.

Fear and guilt squelched the impulse. She couldn't put her friends in danger, after what had happened to Craig and Mandi. Loneliness was not a good enough excuse. No matter how awful it got.

She wished she could talk to Mom. Mom had been gone for eight years now, almost nine, carried off by lung cancer. Maybe she was floating around in the ether somewhere, keeping an eye on her luckless, clueless daughter. A vaguely comforting thought. If a wistful one.

She must have been insane to go over to McCloud's gym today. Desperate to unload at least a highly edited chunk of her tale of woe onto someone who wasn't a dog. Mikey was a good listener, but not much for feedback. The kickboxing teacher, Sean—she could hardly believe that laughing, dimpled clown of a guy was the scarily gorgeous Davy McCloud's brother—had waved aside the no-money issue like it was no big deal. Besides, she'd been trolling for an excuse to get a good long look at Davy McCloud up close. Food for fantasy. She needed it bad. The nights were long when a girl was scared to go to sleep.

It was a damn shame he was so big. Couple of cans short of a six-pack, too. The bizarre things he said. Dragon spirit, her big ol' butt.

Mikey lifted his head to growl. Every hair on Margot's body stood up. Then she heard the sharp, commanding *rap-rap-rap*, and the terror that had spiked inside her eased down, leaving her wobbly.

Snakey would never knock like that. In fact, Snakey wouldn't knock at all. He would slither through a sewer pipe like a foul vapor. Slide out the bathroom drain with a wet-sounding pop.

Oh, ick. Nice job, lame brain. Now she'd grossed herself out.

Rat-tat-tat, there it came again, crisp and businesslike. Mikey clambered out of his basket, barking. Margot looked down at herself as she followed him towards the front door. Boobs flying wild and free under the Superman T-shirt. Hair damp and snarled and all over the place. Her face, naked of all cosmetic enhancers or concealers, left to fend bravely for itself in the unforgiving urban blight light.

She couldn't be more at a disadvantage if she'd deliberately tried.

Mikey's toenails skittered on the linoleum, his limp forgotten. Margot lunged for her comb in the bedroom and dragged it through her hair as she peeked through the peephole. Yep. Him. Her heart went ka-thud. She peered out again, studying the sculpted lines of his jaw, that grim but incredibly sexy mouth. The grooves around it were evidence that he knew how to smile. Maybe he only did it in the dark when no one was around. Emotionally blocked, no doubt. Strong, silent types usually proved to be dull, stolid types, in her experience.

She'd told him to get lost. He was too big, too strange, too serious for her. Too curious, too. She couldn't trust him with her bizarre story.

She should be furious. She was going to have to fake it. That took energy, and where the hell was she going to find it, under a rock?

Rat-tat-tat-tat. Would you listen to that, his exalted Highness was getting impatient. That gave her the boost she needed to yank the door open and glare balefully out at him. "I said no, buddy."

Davy looked around her porch. "Is this where you found the dog?"

Her fake anger evaporated into nothing. She gulped, and nodded.

"Any other incidents?"

There was a brisk, businesslike tone in his voice, as if he'd flipped a switch and a whole big mechanism was starting to crunch and grind.

"Hey." She stuck her hand through the door and waved it in front of his face. "Did you hear what I said? Thanks, but no thanks. And how did you find me, anyhow? I'm not listed in the—oh. My. God."

He held up a big paper bag. Fragrant steam rose from it.

"Enchiladas," he said. "Tamales. Chile rellenos. Barbecued pork tacos. Chicken in mole sauce. Shrimp in butter and garlic. And . . ."—he lifted his other hand—"a six-pack of ice cold Dos Equis."

She clutched the doorjamb. The scent of rich, spicy food almost made her faint. But damn, she should have at least as much pride as her own dog. Mikey never compromised his principles for food.

She swallowed, hard. "Uh . . ."

Not quite a smile, just a teasing hint of one, changed the landscape of his lean face. "If you blow me off, I'll toss it into the Dumpster while you watch," he warned. "Just to spite you."

"That's sick and wrong," she told him.

"Yeah, sure. I was counting on getting here before you had dinner. I know how I feel about dinner after teaching two classes in a row."

"Five, actually," she said.

His eyes widened. "Five? Wow. Intense."

"Two gyms," she admitted. "Five classes. Some days I do more. Hush up, Mikey. He's got Mexican. Don't bite him till we get some."

Mikey rose onto his hind legs and sniffed at the bag. He smelled McCloud's shoes, his ankles, and yipped a shrill order.

"Mikey just invited you in," Margot said. "He likes shrimp."

A slow grin spread over his face, activating a bunch of gorgeous smile lines and a startling flash of heated sensuality that sucked the air right out of her lungs. "Mikey's invitation isn't enough. I want yours."

She forced herself to drag in some air. She was out-maneuvered.

"Oh, come on in, already," she grumbled.

Faris's stomach rolled with anxiety as the door closed behind McCloud. He forced himself to exhale, to think clearly. He had to be patient, to remember how desperate she was, how defenseless and alone. Marcus had ordered him to search her house and tap her phone to monitor who she was in contact with, and so far, the answer had been no one. She'd been all alone in her dilapidated little rented house on Capitol Hill, waiting for him to complete her. Until tonight.

He crept through the darkness to his vantage point, in the middle of the overgrown rhododendron near her kitchen window. He'd hacked out the hollow space in the center and removed the branches that blocked his view two weeks ago. This was not the first time Faris had noticed Davy McCloud. He'd seen the man watching Margaret leave the gym where she taught, his face disfigured by lust.

But Faris couldn't compromise his anonymity by charging into Margaret's house and hacking McCloud into bloody pieces. Marcus would never forgive him if he lost control like that.

Besides, McCloud was well connected in the community. Ex-military, a respected private investigator, ties to the local police, brother in the FBI. Discretion was called for. Faris would organize something special for him. Quiet, untraceable, personal. And very, very painful.

Faris watched through the window with hot eyes. He'd been so hurt when she fled the hotel room without waiting for him.

He'd forgiven her, though. In spite of the trouble she'd caused. The mold Caruso had hidden was the key to Marcus's plan, and stupid Faris had let the one person who could have revealed its location slip away. Marcus had been so angry. Faris still shuddered at the memory.

The situation was delicate now. It had taken a tediously long time to find her, and time had run short. Marcus was impatient. Faris wouldn't let her play him for a fool again. He loved her, but he could be very stern if he had to be. Very cruel. Marcus had taught him how.

He choked up with emotion when he thought of carrying her unconscious body in his arms, her head lolling against his shoulder with childlike trust. He'd heard somewhere that if you saved a person's life, you were responsible for that person for as long as she lived.

He'd spared Margaret's life, so it was up to him to shield her from the predators drawn by her exquisite vulnerability. Like sharks to blood.

He could not allow Margaret's attention be distracted from him now. He was herding her into his trap so gradually that when the time came, she would be exhausted. Grateful and relieved to fall into it.

She didn't need work, or money, or other people. She didn't need to drive through dangerous traffic, to be surrounded by dirty-minded men at that graphics firm. She did not need to slave into the night on that computer, straining her beautiful eyes to build a business that had no future anyway. She did not need that worthless, crippled old dog.

He was stripping it away from her, piece by piece. When it was all gone, she would understand. She just had to give herself to him. That was all. He would be her universe, her reason to exist.

The rest was just noise and clutter. She would learn.

Chapter

4

Margot flattened herself against the wall to make room in the narrow corridor as Davy McCloud's big body overwhelmed her space.

He looked into what doubled as her living room and bedroom, his eyes resting on the folded quilt on the floor that currently served as her bed. Her futon had been slashed to ribbons in the break-in, along with her new couch, both bought with the first paycheck of the short-lived job at the graphics firm. His eloquent silence made her twitch.

"Did you just move in?" he asked cautiously.

She grabbed the bag out of his hand and hefted it as she headed for the kitchen. Mmm, nice and heavy. "Seven months ago," she told him. "My stuff got wrecked in the burglary."

"Tell me more about that burglary."

She spun around, and he stopped short to keep from bumping into her. So close, she could smell his shower soap, feel his body heat.

"I appreciate your interest, but I don't want to talk about

it," she said. "Big fat downer. I want some food, and a beer. Do you mind?"

She forced herself to stare back into his eyes, counting the seconds to center herself; one thousand one, one thousand two, but somewhere along the way she got waylaid and stopped counting.

Wow. That subtle downward slant of his eyelids was so sensual. Almost exotic looking. And how could a blond guy have such dark brows and lashes? It just wasn't right. There should be a law.

She'd been floating in a gaga, timeless nowhere for who knew how long when he nodded, finally breaking the spell. "OK. Let's eat first."

That wasn't the deal she'd proposed, but she was too rattled to argue the point. She laid containers out on the table as McCloud put away the beers. She turned to see why cold white fridge light was still flooding the kitchen, and found him frowning over his shoulder at her.

"There's no food in here," he said. "Nothing but canned dog food."

She lifted an eyebrow. "Whoops! You've found me out, McCloud. I love dog food. It's fab on Triscuits. Try it. Beer from the bottle OK?"

"Fine. Can I give your dog some pork?"

"Just don't give him anything spicy," she said.

McCloud crouched down and held out a succulent chunk of pork. Mikey accepted it delicately, his small body quivering with delight.

"Huh," she said. "So you're hungry after all." She took a shrimp out of the pan, drained the butter and knelt down to offer it to Mikey.

He turned his head away, the very image of cool disdain.

"Oh, come off it," she snapped. "You big poser. You love shrimp."

Mikey held firm. Margot held the shrimp out to McCloud.

"Here," she muttered. "You give it to him. He's not speaking to me."

McCloud proffered the shrimp. Mikey gulped it down and sneaked a sidelong peek at Margot to see how she was taking it.

Being scorned by her dog in front of Davy McCloud took all the stuffing right out of her. She flopped into a chair.

"He hates me now," she said miserably. "Ever since the dead dog, when I started leaving him at the pet hotel. He thinks I'm punishing him. He won't eat, just to make me feel bad. He's already too skinny."

McCloud offered another chunk of pork to Mikey. "He doesn't hate you," he said gently. "He's just letting you know how he feels. You know he loves you. You're afraid this stalker's going to hurt him?"

She shrugged angrily. "If this weirdness escalates, that's the next logical step any normal sicko maniac would take, right?"

He looked dubious. "Is there such a thing as a normal sicko maniac? And could anything like this be called logical?"

She waved that away. "Don't be cute," she said wearily. "I've watched way too many horror flicks in my time, and I figure the maniac has probably watched some of the same ones. The only thing that would suck worse than having my own dog hate my guts would be to come home and find Mikey . . . like that."

He popped open a beer. "You're doing the right thing by your dog," he said. "Once you straighten things out, he'll forgive you. For now, you need dinner." He pressed the bottle into her hand. "So let's eat."

The food was spectacular. They ate steadily, not bothering with conversation, stuffing empty containers back into the bag until what had originally looked like a ridiculous amount of food was reduced to smears of sauce that they scraped out of the containers with the extra tortillas. Mikey made out like a bandit with the pork and shrimp. Nothing beat pigging out on fat, protein and flavor after a long dry spell.

Margot took a long swallow of beer to wash down the lovely burn of hot pepper in her throat, and sighed. "Delicious. I'm stuffed."

"Good. Now you can tell me about the break-in. And the dog."

She tried to think of a way to put him off gently, being as how he'd just been nice enough to feed her an awesome dinner. "Look, if you're trying to drum up business, I told you, I can't afford to—"

"How about you let me worry about that?"

She studied his impassive face, wary of a trap. "There's no such thing as something for nothing," she said slowly. "You don't know me at all, McCloud. Why do you even care?"

His broad shoulders lifted and dropped. "I can't help it. You made me curious. It's my only vice."

She giggled nervously. "No sex, drugs or rock 'n roll, then?"

His bland smile made the words sound silly and frivolous to her own ears. What a ditz she must seem. His waiting silence had such a calm, patient quality. He looked like he could wait for hours and not get restless or bored.

She probably revealed more by holding back than she would by spilling her guts. McCloud was the meticulous type that fed every twitch of the eyelid and slip of the tongue into the database in his mind and then, crunchity-crunch, churned out conclusions that she could neither predict nor control. She might as well distract him by throwing him a few random facts. Like chunks of meat to fend off a wolf. She was a piss-poor liar anyhow.

"I told you most of it." She avoided his eyes. "The rose

petals started two weeks days ago. The break-in was six days
ago. Three days ago the dead dog showed up. That's how
long it's been since I slept."

"What kind of dog? Did you know it?"

She shook her head. "It was hard to tell, under all that
blood. No collar. A big dog. Shepherd mix, maybe."

He nodded, and gestured for her to go on.

"I found it when I woke up," she went on. "From the
amount of blood, I figure whoever killed it must've done the
deed right here on my porch, while I was sleeping. How
creepy is that?"

McCloud reached behind himself and took another beer
out of the fridge. He popped it open with an effortless twist
of his enormous hand and placed it in front of her.

"What, are you trying to get me drunk?" she demanded.

The corners of his mouth twitched. "You need to un-
wind."

She rolled her eyes and took a swig. "Bad idea, McCloud.
If I unwound, I'd drill myself six feet into the ground. It
wouldn't be pretty."

His dimple flashed. She suddenly wished she could make
him grin again. A big, crazy out-of-control grin. She pic-
tured him laughing so hard that he rolled on the floor.
Gasping and snorting while she tickled him, maybe. The
silly image triggered a funny jolt of longing.

"Go on," he urged. "How about the break-in?"

She yanked herself back into focus. "I came home from
work one night and found the place trashed. Furniture
slashed, everything torn off the shelves. Books, dishes, the
stuff in the fridge, the cupboards. But the only thing they
took was my laptop. And my sketchbooks."

"Sketchbooks? What was in them?"

She widened her eyes. "Um . . . sketches?"

Her sarcasm didn't make the slightest dent in his focused
calm. "How about jewelry? Money?"

She shook her head. "Don't have any." Except for the evil

snake pendant, of course, but that entailed talking about unspeakable stuff, and the wretched thing hadn't gotten stolen anyway. Worse luck.

"Could they have been looking for something?" he prompted.

His tone was neutral, but her stomach still lurched with guilt. Here it was, the blank wall beyond which she had to start fudging with half-truths. "If they were, I can't imagine what for. I haven't seen anybody lurking. Haven't gotten any love notes. Haven't been asked on any dates. Haven't pissed anybody off . . . that I know of." She hoped the quaver in her voice sounded scared, rather than guilty.

He nodded calmly. "Vindictive ex-husbands?"

"Never married," she said promptly.

"Ex-boyfriends?"

She thought about Craig, and swallowed over a hard, hot lump in her throat. "No one who'd be that mad at me."

"How about angry women? Involved with any married men lately?"

"Hah. I'm no masochist," she snapped.

"Blackmailing anyone?" His tone was supremely casual.

"Excuse me?" She jumped up and pointed to the door. "Out!"

Mikey chose that moment to jump up and leaned against McCloud's knee, trembling with the force of his wags. Traitorous little stinker. He was determined to undermine her.

McCloud's fingers tangled gently into Mikey's hair. "I'm just being methodical," he said. "Don't take it personally."

Margot sank back into the chair. The urge to tell another human being her troubles—no, not just any human being, but Davy McCloud in particular—was almost overwhelming.

She'd always believed in following her instincts, but this wasn't instinct prodding her. This was fear and exhaustion, tricking her into making what was probably a fatal mistake.

She blew out a tense, explosive breath. "No married men," she said tightly. "No men at all for a long time."

"How long?"

"None of your damn business."

"Actually, it is. In this context of this particular conversation."

She picked at the label of the beer bottle. "Nine months, almost."

"Why'd you break up with him?"

Because someone slaughtered him and pinned the blame on me.

She wondered if the truth would shock that inscrutable look off his face. She gave him her flintiest stare and steeled herself to lie.

"He was cheating on me," she said coldly.

Actually, that was literally true, she reflected. Irrelevant, but true.

He just nodded. "How long have you been in town?"

"Seven months," she said. "I don't know many people here."

"Where did you live before?"

"I don't see how that's relevant," she snapped. "Oh, wait—you're the one who decides what's relevant, right?"

He smiled, but his eyes were watchful. "You said it, not me."

She took a deep breath. "L.A.," she lied.

"Do you have any reason to believe that someone from L.A.—"

"No." She shook her head, too rapidly. "Absolutely not."

His eyes narrowed. "There's a story behind that." His tone put the phrase halfway between a statement and a question.

Oh God. If you only knew. "Not really. Just ancient history." She smoothed out her face, tried to look calm while screaming panic built. She was out of her league. Wasting the guy's time for no good reason.

"You didn't call the police. Not for the break-in. Not for the dog."

There was no accusation in his tone. She felt it anyway, and flushed. She shook her head and waited for the other shoe to drop.

Minutes ticked by. Mikey rolled blissfully on his back, legs in the air, tail flopping as McCloud petted him. Her heart started to pound.

The words burst out of her. "Oh, come on, already. Aren't you going to ask me why not?"

His watchful eyes flicked up to hers. "You going to tell me?"

"No," she said.

"No point in asking, then, right?"

He was unfazed, petting Mikey like nothing was out of the ordinary. "So . . . that's that?" she faltered. "No further questions?"

He lifted his shoulders in a faint shrug. "I recommend that you call the police. You've got a serious problem. They've got resources that I don't have. In any case, I can't help you unless you tell me what's really going on." He paused thoughtfully, and added, "Then again, neither could the cops. So whatever. If you want to talk, I'm listening."

"Believe me," she said. "You don't want to know."

"Oh, but I do."

The laser brightness of his eyes made her mind go blank. "You'd be sorry," she heard herself say.

"Probably. I never said it was smart. Like I said, curiosity is my vice. It's a lot more compelling than drugs or rock 'n roll."

"You forgot about sex," she said without thinking.

His eyes flicked over her body. "No, I didn't."

The speculative look in his eyes sent a shiver down her spine. As if lying to him wasn't bad enough. Now she was flirting with him. Whoa, Nelly. Her inner devil slut was getting the upper hand, big-time.

She broke eye contact with great effort, and rubbed the back of her stiff neck, groping for a swift change of subject.

"Looking over my shoulder all the time is giving me knots in my neck," she murmured.

"I could give you a back rub," he offered.

She laughed right in his face. "Hah! I just bet you could."

"I wouldn't grope you. Seriously. I'm very good at it."

She marveled at how the urban blight light accentuated all the stark planes and angles of his face, casting every stunning detail in sharp relief. It figured. Only Davy McCloud could possibly look good in that light. "An offer of a massage is never innocent," she told him.

He shook his head. "Don't judge me based on your past experience. I'm not average. I mean what I say, and I keep my word."

She blinked. "Oh. Gosh. Excuse me for not recognizing your lordly qualities and your incredible moral superiority."

He inclined his head in a gracious nod. "You're excused."

She simply could not tell if he was joking or not. The guy was unreal. He kept a completely straight face. God, she was sick of playing the cast-iron bitch, never trusting anybody. Hell with it. Being touched by Davy McCloud would be super deluxe. She was going for it.

"Oh, whatever," she said. "But if your hands stray anyplace south of my thoracic vertebrae, I'll have Mikey bite you in the butt."

The threat didn't have much oomph, being as how Mikey was sprawled on his back, silently pleading for his belly to be rubbed.

McCloud leaned down and stroked him, his hand tracing one of the shaved patches. "What happened to him?"

"He got mouthy in Washington Park with a big, mean stray dog," she told him. "He never learns."

McCloud nodded, and got to his feet. He slid his hand beneath her hair and curved it around the back of her neck. Just that gentle touch alone made a delicious sensation ripple across her skin, all the relaxing comfort of heat, all the stimulating refreshment of coolness.

"Do you want to lie down?" he asked.

She slanted him an eloquent glance. "Yeah, right, and take off my shirt, too? Get real." She fished in her pocket for a hair tie, and wound her hair into a lopsided ponytail. "There. Go for it. Dig deep. I'm tough."

He was fabulous. Neither a timid, irritating massage that just tickled the surface of knotted muscles nor yet a macho, insensitive attack upon them. His touch was slow, sure, sensual. His hands commanded her muscles to release tension, and they obeyed him, in level after level of helpless yielding and softening. Melting.

She wished that she'd lain down after all. Sure, it would have been stupid, but letting him into her house had been stupid, eating his food had been stupid. Letting him touch her body was downright idiotic. What was one more level of stupidity in the grand scheme of things?

Time slowed, stretched, and collapsed slowly back in on itself in great, pulsing waves. She forced her eyes open when she realized that his hands were cupping the curve of her waist. "You're south of my thoracic vertebrae, buddy, and heading straight into no-man's-land."

His hands lifted away from her body. "Sorry."

She missed the warm contact instantly. "Don't sweat it. I know how it is," she mumbled. "One vertebrae just leads to another, and hey presto, before you know it you're giving me a foot rub."

He started in on her shoulders again, with a muffled crack of laughter. "I think I'd get distracted along the way," he said.

She had to struggle not to moan. It had been so long since she'd been touched at all, let alone with any real tenderness or skill.

Maybe she never had been. She'd never melted like this for anybody. Dangerous thought. Delete, delete. "My head's going to float right up off my neck," she said. "I didn't know my neck was that tense."

"After teaching five classes, it would be strange if it

weren't." His fingers caressed her neck. Lovely heat lanced down into her chest, her belly, her thighs. "I see now why you're in such great shape."

"Look who's talking," she murmured. "If you're ever short on cash, you could set up a booth and charge the ladies to massage your bod."

"Oh yeah?" His voice was wary.

"Sure. Say, fifteen bucks for a two minute fondle. Strictly PG-13, above the waist, of course. I'll sell the tickets, if you give me a cut."

His hands stopped moving. She babbled on, dazed and thoughtless. "The gay guys would go for it, too. We'd rake in the dough."

"I'd let you do it for free," he said.

His voice was devoid of irony. Her eyes popped open in alarm.

She looked back over her shoulder. The hot glow in his eyes brought her feminine instincts to high alert. She pulled away.

She and her big dumb mouth. Sexy banter with a guy she barely knew, but no nerve to back it up. Bad girl. Very immature.

"Um, sorry," she said warily. "That was hot peppers and beer talking. I actually didn't mean to flirt."

He gripped the edge of his sweatshirt and peeled it over his head.

"Holy cow." Margot's voice shook. "What the hell are you doing?"

He let the sweatshirt drop to the floor. "How can you set a price for a two minute fondle if you don't do any product testing?"

She was at a loss for a snappy comeback. "I was joking! Are you familiar with that concept? Do you take everything dead seriously?"

"I take things however I feel like taking them."

She examined each and every possible interpretation of

his words as she stared at his body. Usually blond guys were white and pasty, with bluish undertones like skim milk. McCloud's body was gold-tinted.

It glowed with power, wildly out of place in her dingy kitchen. His physique had the nervy, sculpted look of an Olympic gymnast. Every muscle knew its job, and did it superbly. Nothing missing. Nothing superfluous. Total freaking perfection.

The intensity of his eyes held her motionless. He put his arms behind his back. "I won't touch you. No groping. Word of honor."

His words made her abruptly conscious of her female body. How naked and soft and vulnerable she was under her scruffy loungewear.

She stared down at what the damp chill in her apartment did to his dark nipples. He had goose bumps. That was a good sign. It proved he was human, at least. He looked so warm and supple and strong.

Oh, Lord. She could just eat him up with a spoon.

She took a step back, and wobbled as her hip bumped the table.

"OK," she said. "Enough funny stuff. Showing off will get you nowhere. Put your damn shirt back on before I hyperventilate."

A ghost of a smile touched his stern mouth. "Touch me."

The command in his deep voice resonated through her body. Her hand lifted, drifting in the air between them. He moved closer without seeming to move at all, and her hand was splayed against his hot chest.

Her hand moved of its own accord, fingertips brushing over lean contours, ridges of bone, soft skin, the vibrant power of the muscle beneath it. His tight nipple tickled her palm. Her hand pressed against his solar plexus, felt his heart throb. She glanced at his crotch. His hard-on pressed against his jeans. His face was flushed and taut, eyes hazy. The thick muscles of his shoulders were rigid with strain.

"No hands, huh?" Her voice was wondering. "You meant that?"

"Anytime you want that to change, you let me know."

His breath was quick and heavy. His heart thudded against her hand. He was more power than she knew how to handle, like being perched on a racehorse spoiling for a run. Behind the wheel of a Ferrari, charged up and ready to let 'er rip. Vibrating with raw energy.

Her hand shook where it touched his hot skin. He was as exotic and alien as an undiscovered country. She was dazed. Paralyzed with shyness. Something cynical snickered way in the back of her mind. *Poor Margot, forced to pet a hunk's gorgeous pecs, yeah, break out the violins.*

Her mouth was inches from that alluring hollow in his neck. She could just lean forward and . . . taste him. And for as long as it lasted, she could forget the whole scary, sordid mess of her life. She would think of nothing but him. Lose herself in him. God. She ached for it.

"I don't know you," she whispered. "Not the first thing about you."

"No," he replied. "You don't."

And he left it at that. No attempt to wheedle or cajole. No bullshit.

His blunt honesty was seductive. She wanted to grab him, twine herself around him and just soak him up. All that heat, all that power.

And that would be it. She would get nailed tonight, by a great big gorgeous guy about whom she knew absolutely nothing except that he rarely smiled. Which wasn't much of a recommendation.

Mikey liked him, her inner devil slut whispered.

Yeah, like that counted worth beans. Mikey would fawn over any clown who fed him barbecued pork, excluding her own wretched self. McCloud would think she was a tramp for putting out so fast, and then she would hate herself for

OUT OF CONTROL

51

being used, blah blah blah. She couldn't do this to herself.
No way. She was hanging on by a thread as it was.

She lifted her hand to his mouth and pressed her forefinger against his soft, warm lips. "We've got to stop."

He rubbed his cheek against her hand. His glinting blond
beard stubble rasped her skin. The sensual, animal gesture
made her heart turn over with hungry longing. "How come?"
he asked.

She forced herself to pull her hand away. "Because I say
so."

She nudged the sleeping Mikey off his sweatshirt with
her toe, plucked it off the floor and held it out to him, dog
hairs and all. "Put this back on. Right now. No back talk."

He sighed, and pulled it over his head. She manufactured
a glare and had it fixed in place by the time his head
emerged. "I appreciate the striptease, and it's sweet of you to
entertain me, but it's time for me and Mikey to start winding
down. How much do I owe you for dinner?"

His face tightened. "Get real."

Margot yanked open the freezer and pulled out her dwin-
dling stash of grocery money out from under the ice cube
tray. "I figured you'd give me a hard time about that." She
rummaged through her stash of takeout menus until she
found Luisa's. "Let's see . . . tacos, enchiladas, rellenos,
tamales, mole and shrimp . . . that's about fifty bucks, plus
eight or so for the beer, so let's call it twenty-nine a head—"

"I'm not taking your money."

"I don't like guys to pay for my stuff." She threw the
words at him.

"Too fucking bad."

She flinched. "Hey. Watch it. No nasty potty mouth in my
space."

His eyebrow quirked. "I've heard you swear."

"Yeah, maybe, but you haven't heard me use the f-word. I
never do that. Do I, Mikey? You ever hear me say the f-word?"

Mikey wagged in cheerful corroboration as Margot discreetly counted her stash. Twenty-three bucks. Yikes. She held it out to him with stoic calm. "I prefer not to be obligated to a strange man," she said.

"Put it away," he warned. "Before you piss me off."

She hid her relief as she stuck the money back under the ice cube tray. She turned back to him, twisting her hands together. "Um, well . . . thanks very much for dinner, then. It was scrumptious."

"You're welcome."

She waited for something like *well, it's late, so I guess I'll be hitting the road,* but he just stood there until she started to wonder what was so damned interesting about her face. It had looked normal enough the last time she'd checked. "Good night," she hinted.

"Why are you freezing me out?" He sounded genuinely curious.

She plastered the baleful glare back on. It took more effort this time. "You know, there was a reason why I said no when you invited me to dinner back at your gym," she said. "It's the same reason I don't let guys pay for anything, not my meals, not my drinks. Because they start to act like you're acting right now, see? Like I owe them something."

He shook his head. "I never meant to—"

"So get a clue. Good night. Thanks for dinner."

"But I know you're attracted to me," he said stubbornly.

"So? What if I am?" she yelled. "I'm swamped! I've got money problems, I've got pet problems, I've got Snakey the Sicko Maniac sending me presents from the Crypt. I don't need man trouble, too!"

"I'm not—"

"I don't have the time or energy for a boyfriend! I can't even handle my relationship with my dog right now!"

He lifted his hands in a placating gesture. "I'm not suggesting—"

"I don't do one night stands, either. I can't deal with no strings sex. So where does that leave us?" She answered her own question just as his lips moved to respond to it. "Nowhere! Nothing more to discuss! So? Buh-bye, OK?"

He pulled out his wallet, took out a card and laid it on the counter. "Call me if you get any more presents from the Crypt."

He headed for the door. Not hurrying, not embarrassed, not pissed. She almost wished he would slam it. It would make her feel like she'd gotten past his guard, scored some sort of a point against him.

He didn't. She hadn't. The door clicked softly shut behind him.

The dark pressed hard against her windows now that she had only the gently snoring Mikey for company.

She felt so flat as she brushed her teeth and set the alarm clock. Let down, after all that fizzy tension. Nothing to do but try to get some rest, but she tossed and twisted on her thin pallet.

She felt hot, restless. Tormented by an ache of sensual yearning.

All she needed to make her misery complete.

God, how she wanted her life back. To be Mag Callahan again, with her nice little house on the lake, her web design business that had finally been humming along after years of patient struggling. Her sharp wardrobe, her wine rack, her stained glass lamp, her orthopedic mattress, her Social Security number, her credit cards. Her future.

She wanted her girlfriends. To watch chick flick DVD's on her big squishy couch while pigging out on chips and margaritas with Jenny and Chris and Pia. She was even nostalgic about the problems she used to stress about. Dates, or lack thereof. Panty lines. Calories. PMS. Tax write-offs. Ants in the kitchen. Mold on the bathroom grout. Hah.

She wanted to cancel out the ugly memories in her head.

She felt so small and powerless. Sex was unthinkable under those conditions, but that didn't stop her longing to be touched.

Wrecked as she was, she couldn't even remember how it felt to be confident enough to take on a guy like McCloud. Maybe she never had been. He was so damn big, after all. Ultra-macho. She'd always made a point of staying away from those types. They were way too problematic.

She had to let her sexual imagination run hog wild to encompass the idea of sex with Davy McCloud. The farther from reality, the better. Along the lines of . . . a barbarian queen and her captured enemy warrior. Yeah. That was just silly and improbable enough to work. Him wearing nothing but a sword belt and a raggedy loincloth over his manly parts. Chained hand and foot, eyes hot with helpless fury. Fresh out of battle, all jacked up and desperate. Yummy. This could be really good.

And herself, sporting lots of cleavage in a teeny weeny chain mail bikini top. A filmy skirt slit up to both thighs dangling from her jewel-studded belt. She dreamed her hair back to its original coppery red, grew it out to instant hip length, slathered on makeup; shadowy bronze tints that made her look feverish and slutty. Like the covers of those fantasy novels she used to devour, except that she was the one brandishing the sword looking tough, and he was the one on his knees, clutching her thigh. The image was so silly, it made her giggle.

Big mistake. The laughter shoved her almost over the edge into tears. She rolled over, pressing her hot face into the pillow, and slid her hand into her panties. She was wet already, squirming around a damp glow of arousal. She didn't even need the vibrator. She was teetering on the brink of a screaming orgasm just thinking about his eyes.

She shut her eyes tightly, caught her clit between two fingers, and clenched her trembling thighs together. She had to get some relief from this ache. It scared her. Her whole damned life scared her.

The barbarian queen wasn't scared. She had the power to enforce her slightest whim. Armies at her beck and call. Lucky her.

Exotic images formed, broke, and reformed in her head. McCloud on his knees, his eyes furious. Unable to hide his excitement under that skimpy loincloth. She imagined touching him as she caressed herself, her hands sliding over his tense, straining muscles, his hot face.

He was slick with sweat, trembling. She slid her hand beneath the loincloth, grasped his hard penis and stroked it boldly. He jerked, gasped, arched back in a helpless spasm of pleasure.

Images blurred and shifted in her mind, the myriad possibilities pulling her in every direction. The fantasy refocused. She stood over him naked, legs wide, his face cupped in her hands. Telling him with her eyes, *get to work, soldier, and make it good for me if you know what's good for you.*

And it was. Oh, it was. She'd never had a fantasy so clear, every nerve alive and thrumming like it was actually happening. His strong tongue thrust and lapped, sliding up and down her slit and suckling her ravenously, and the glorious feeling was building, higher and hotter, almost there, almost . . . there . . .

The tension dropped a notch, and left her dangling. Unfulfilled.

She was furious. This was bizarre. She'd never been so turned on in her life. It made no sense at all that she couldn't make herself come.

Onward, take two. Segue to the lavish, curtained bed, the light of a flickering fire. He was stark naked now, tied with silken cords to the carved posts. First she went the kinky route and had a bunch of her sexy barbarian ladies-in-waiting teasing and tormenting him to prepare him for the main event.

That lasted about a nanosecond. She sent the silly bitches packing. Poof, they disappeared.

This one was for her alone. Every last drop of him.

The silent room was charged with desperate tension. The only sounds were the crackling of the fire and the low, strangled moans of the man beneath her. He writhed, cords standing out on his neck, muscles hard and flexing with desperate tension against his bonds, but she was merciless. She gripped his penis in her oiled hands, sliding her hands up and down his shaft, swirling and squeezing her fist around the swollen head. Hypnotizing even herself with the rhythmic caress.

It was time. She straddled him, guided his penis to the soft, swollen opening of her sex, and flung her head back with a moan of delight as she forced herself over the thick, throbbing club. Taking him, claiming him. She stared down into his eyes, silently demanding that he acknowledge her supremacy.

He would not. He bucked and writhed, pounding up into her body, but his eyes stared back up, glittering bright and wild and absolutely unconquered.

And the orgasm kept eluding her. She would get so close, heart pounding, ready to fling herself into that well of dark oblivion, and suddenly, whoosh, gone. It evaporated, and he gazed up at her, eyes gleaming with wicked amusement. He was doing this on purpose.

Damn him. This was insane. This was her own fantasy, in the privacy of her own mind, and he had no right to mess with it.

But it was more than a fantasy now. It was more like a trance, or a waking dream with its own crazy momentum. She was helpless to guide or command it. She reached for the knife hidden in the sumptuous bed hangings. Held it in her hand just long enough to make that sly gleam in his eyes fade, to be replaced by wary uncertainty.

She reached back and cut the silken cords that bound his

ankles . . . one, two. She leaned over him, dangling her breasts in his face, and sliced through the cords that bound his wrists. She rocked back, letting his penis slide inside her, as deeply as it could lodge. She laid the knife in the pillows at the head of the bed, well within his reach.

It was all up to him. She stared down at his astonished face.

The paralyzed part of her mind locked behind the swirling dream images was aghast. Was she out of her skull? Did she not deserve even the artificial luxury of running the show in a silly sexual fantasy?

The fantasy thundered on. He gripped her waist with his big hands and rolled her over, a guttural snarl sounding deep in his throat. He pinned her beneath his big body and thrust deep, driving her hard.

Unleashing his passion unleashed hers too, and sent her soaring.

When she regained her awareness, she was still clenching around the pulses of residual pleasure. Dazed, gasping for breath.

And still alone in her bed. Alone in her wrecked life. Aching for the loss of something she'd never even had.

What an idiot. Torturing herself with fantasies. She fought back the tears. She'd cried enough for a lifetime already.

Chapter

5

Marcus Worthington was in a killing mood.

Years of meticulous conditioning that Marcus had instilled into his younger brother, Faris, wiped away as if by a vicious computer virus.

All that Callahan bitch's fault.

He would be glad when the woman was safely dead, though disappointment could drive Faris over the edge. Few people were aware of Faris's unique abilities, and the tremendous risks involved. So far Marcus had always prevailed in a battle of wills. Still, it worried him.

The only thing that calmed Marcus when he was so agitated was puttering in his lab, playing with what Priscilla, his late father's fourth and worst wife, was pleased to call his "toys." She would learn soon how wrong she was about him. Just as his father had learned. The wife that had preceded Priscilla had learned as well. They all had, in the end.

But Priscilla would get a very special lesson.

Marcus teased the gelatinous mold of Dr. Driscoll's hand

out of the cast. His whimsical choice of livid, corpselike green coloring for the hand amused him, insofar as he could be amused in his current mental state. He adjusted the light to better admire the fingerprints. The loops, whorls and arches were so well reproduced, even the minute pattern of sweat glands on each ridge were duplicated.

Not perfectly, but well within the parameters of the sensor.

He pressed the hand against the Krell Systems Biolock Identipad Sensor. His own database was loaded with the same template as the Calix Research Laboratories, thanks to Caruso's evil genius.

Negative. The machine beeped in protest. *No match found.*

It worked just as the Krell sales staff had promised that it would. Proof against fraud because of a complex, multi-system battery of "live and well" detection, a combination of ECG, pulse oximetry, temperature, electric resistance, and detection under the epidermis.

The Biolock Identipad wanted all five fingers, and moist, multilayered skin. It would settle for nothing else. Kudos to Krell. It was one of the most costly biometric systems on the market. Caruso himself had designed it. Marcus felt a twinge of regret that he'd been so quick to have the man killed. Craig had been useful. He'd been the one to recommend making a gummy hand with each mold, to test which image was the clearest. Marcus always followed his instructions to the letter.

But Craig had begun to play power games. Playing hide and seek with the mold of Priscilla's hand. Talking about "full partnership."

Marcus sprayed the inside of the negative mold with a light lubricant, and painted a thin coat of Caruso's wizard's brew of liquid gelatin inside it. He let it set, pressed his hand into the impression, let it bind, and slowly lifted it out. He repeated the process, taking exquisite care to match the print patterns, so as to fool the ultrasonic and electric field sensor features that tested for the print pattern in the underlying dermis. Fortunately, his and Driscoll's hands were of similar size. The half-glove of gelatin was almost invisible.

He flexed his fingers, and pressed his hand to the Identipad.

Two seconds, and the monitor flashed. *Match Found.* Keith Driscoll, PhD, Laboratory Director, Calix Research Division. A photo of the chubby scientist appeared on the monitor screen, smiling broadly.

Marcus smiled back. Driscoll had the highest security clearance, surpassed only by Priscilla Worthington herself. This was well worth the trouble he'd gone to. He'd finally lured the older man up to his quarters, after months of flirting. Driscoll was a married father of three, but his preference for young men was well documented in certain circles. Marcus's innate practicality forbade him from hiring someone else for the job. Why risk having some muscle-headed male prostitute botch this when he, Marcus, was sexually attractive enough to handle the job?

As it happened, he didn't even have to go through with it. Not that it would have been a problem if he had. Driscoll's middle-aged pudge did not repel him. Marcus's sexuality was atypical. Power excited him. He was indifferent to the secondary details: youth, beauty, male, female.

Driscoll had drunk a martini spiked with Rophynol, and conveniently passed out. Marcus had taken multiple molds of the man's hand at his leisure, bundled him into his car, and left him naked and senseless on his own front lawn.

Word was Driscoll's wife had since taken the youngest two children back to Boston with her, and that the oldest one, studying at UCSF, would no longer speak to him. Driscoll had not looked Marcus in the eye since that night. He looked pale. Thinner. What had once been cheerful, rosy pudge was now sad, grayish sag.

Marcus studied Driscoll's smiling face on the screen, enjoying the warm glow of pleasure that exercising power gave him.

A loud rap sounded upon the door. Marcus barely had time to toss the plastic cover over his project before the door burst open.

Priscilla marched in. She was thicker about the waist and ankles than she'd been ten years ago when she'd met Marcus's father, Titus Worthington, owner and CEO of Calix Pharmaceuticals. Priscilla had been a researcher in one of Calix's experimental labs. She'd dazzled the old man with her beauty, brains and forceful personality, but her face had hardened over the years. With her dark hair dragged into a bun and her white lab coat, she looked like a Gestapo prison warden.

She was shadowed by her hulking bodyguard, Maurice. She'd hired Maurice shortly after Titus's death, and moved into her own residence as well. Priscilla was nobody's fool.

Her eyes brushed over his various projects with unconcealed scorn. "Playing in the sandbox, are we, Marcus?"

Marcus's hands clenched into fists, his nails digging into the delicate Driscoll glove. "Just fiddling with some new designs."

She sniffed. "You've fiddled for years. You're relatively intelligent, after all. With three PhD's, don't you think it's time to stop fiddling and do something useful?"

Like plan your disgrace and ruin, perhaps? "I'm working on patenting some of them," he said vaguely. Let her think he was a vacuous idiot. He no longer cared. Her days were numbered anyway.

"Where on earth is the domestic staff, Marcus?" she demanded. "This place is becoming a sty. The terms of Titus's will gave you and Faris the right to reside at Worthington House for life, but remember that the place does not actually belong to you. And it never will."

"I'm well aware of that," Marcus said. He had, in fact,

dismissed the staff months ago in preparation for the Blessed Event, which required utter privacy, to say nothing of the obtrusive presence of several armed professionals. He'd never dreamed it would drag out so long. He was tired of the dust and cobwebs himself. Another inconvenience to lay at Margaret Callahan's door. Bitch.

"If the place falls to ruin, I will take legal action. And now, if you can drag your attention away from your toys, I have a real job for you."

Marcus's stomach tightened, but his smile simply widened. He'd always been good at masks. "Of course."

"Dr. Driscoll will be leaving his post as lab director. He's going back to Boston, for health reasons. His place will be taken by Dr. Seymour Haight, who is flying in from Baltimore tomorrow. His plane stops in Seattle for one night. The next day he'll fly to San Francisco."

Marcus nodded. Priscilla enjoyed humiliating him by giving him assignments more suited for a low-ranking social secretary. It was all she thought he was fit for. That, and holding Faris's leash, of course.

"I want you to organize his welcome," Priscilla went on. "Arrange for lab security to have his enrollment data entered into the system. Highest security clearance. And have Driscoll's deleted immediately."

"Of course." He was glad he had avoided having sex with Driscoll after all. The event would have lost all its power, all its meaning.

"Arrange for housing, and a limo to pick him up at the airport."

"I'll need his flight info and contact numbers," Marcus said.

Priscilla waved her hand vaguely. "Ask my staff. Melissa or Frederico should have the contact data. Tell them to arrange a dinner date for him with me that evening, too. The rooftop restaurant at the Halsey Crowne, that should be nice.

Oh, yes, another thing. Where on earth is Faris? I haven't seen him lurking about in weeks."

"He's mountain climbing in the north Cascades," he said. "He loves climbing. It's good for him. Keeps him emotionally balanced."

"Climbing? Unsupervised?" Priscilla's brows snapped together. "Titus and I only permitted Faris's release from Creighton Hills on the strict condition that you would monitor him constantly!"

"Faris is under control," Marcus soothed. "He's taking his meds regularly. I talk to him several times a day on my cell phone."

"I don't care! Get him back here immediately! I cannot risk any embarrassing incidents, particularly not after Driscoll's little scandal! The one useful function that you serve around here is to keep an eye on Faris. If you can't even handle that much responsibility—"

"I'll have him come home immediately," Marcus assured her.

"Do that," she said crisply. "I am leaving myself this week to spend a month in our lab in Frankfurt. I won't have time to orient Dr. Haight myself, beyond our dinner date. Please do what you can."

Such as that is, being the all-too-clear subtext.

"Of course," Marcus murmured.

She swept out the door. Maurice's hulking form shadowed her.

So much for Driscoll. Marcus peeled the glove off his hand and tossed the ragged, transparent scrap into the waste bin. He took the corpselike rubbery hand, grabbed a pair of scissors, and began cutting it into pieces, imagining that the hand was Priscilla's. Heard shrieks in his mind with each snip of the blades. Chunk after chunk after chunk.

He was back almost to zero. Access to the holy of holies required the tandem cooperation of Priscilla Worthington and the lab director. Priscilla's mold was still lost, and Seymour Haight was an unknown.

But Faris was in Seattle. Something had to be improvised, and quickly. There was no time left for the careful planning he'd done to obtain Driscoll's mold. And Priscilla was leaving. It was now or never.

The obvious solution was to obtain a new mold, but seducing Priscilla was not an option. She loathed him, for one thing, and for another, even Marcus's own practical attitude towards sexuality had its limits. Priscilla's rabid security staff would not let poor Faris anywhere near her. And though she did indulge occasionally, Priscilla was far too intelligent and self-protective to be taken in by a hired gigolo.

Craig Caruso had managed it, though how he'd found the courage to have sex with that cast iron bitch, Marcus would never know. Perhaps the ten million dollars Marcus had promised had kept his dick hard enough to perform the task. Marcus shuddered at the thought.

His buyer had lost patience, after eight long months of waiting. The plan was falling apart before his eyes. Years of his life, millions of his own private money, invested in this perfect mating of profit and revenge. All blocked, because of Margaret Callahan.

He had to light a fire under Faris. He wanted this to end.

Sean's truck was parked right in the middle of the driveway, leaving no room for Davy's own vehicle. It wasn't the first time. His youngest brother was careless and distracted. He also liked to make his presence felt. Usually Davy just blew it off with a philosophical sigh.

Tonight, his nerves on edge, it bugged the living shit out of him.

He parked up the street from his house and sat there for a while, staring through the trees at the lights from Mercer Island, rippling on the dark waters of Lake Washington.

Struggling to pull himself together. It had been way too long since he'd gotten laid.

Humiliating, to reduce it to that, but he was a grim realist about the effects of protracted celibacy. Six months, not that he was counting, since Beth laid down the law. He'd liked Beth a lot, and appreciated the hell out of her fine qualities, but he hadn't been up to buying her a ring.

He'd tried to make that point clear from the outset, but Beth hadn't gotten it. Women never did. They insisted on taking it personally and getting their feelings hurt, every fucking time. He wished he could put the whole sex melodrama aside and focus on other things, but his body had other ideas. He hadn't been able to strike a truce with it yet.

Then again, this wasn't the prodding of generalized horniness. Steffi, the previous aerobics instructor at Women's Wellness had been a honey-blonde with a body worthy of a centerfold spread, but she'd never inspired him to babble or grope. He'd casually considered having sex with Steffi—it had been clear that she was more than willing—but she was so damned bouncy. And her nasal voice had grated his nerves.

Steffi had left a while back to do a season of dinner theater on the coast. It had been weeks before he'd noticed she was gone.

But he'd noticed Margot, her replacement, instantly. Margot's voice did not grate. It was low, rich and smoky, like fine Scotch. Margot glided, swayed, sauntered like a female panther. No bouncing.

He slammed out of his truck and stalked into the house. The open door swung in the breeze. Every light in Sean's path towards the fridge had been flipped on and left burning. A murmur of voices from the back porch indicated that Miles, their protégé, student and future employee, was out there too, helping suck down Davy's beer.

He slapped the porch door open. "The next time you pull a shit parking job like that in my driveway, I'm slashing all your tires."

Sean froze in the act of lifting the bottle to his lips. "Shoot, Davy, that would be really counterproductive of you, being as how it would take that much longer for me to move my truck and park it according to your rigid specifications."

"The delay would be worth it if I actually managed to make an impression in your thick skull, smart-ass."

Miles put his beer down and got awkwardly to his feet. "Uh . . . should I, like, go? I'll go take the bus, if this is a bad time—"

"Sit down, Miles," Sean said. "This is business as usual."

Miles dropped back into his chair and hunched down into his habitual vulture shape of which they were both trying to break him.

Sean studied his brother, a frown between his eyes. "You've got that puckered-butt, hollow-eyed look of a guy who hasn't gotten laid in months. For God's sake, grab a beer, and chill. We brought Chinese."

"I already ate."

"Where?" Sean demanded. "You haven't gone out in ages."

Davy let the screen door slam loudly as he grabbed a beer out of the fridge. As a rule, he didn't rely on chemicals to change his state of consciousness. Fuck it. He put the beer back, grabbed a glass, and pulled out his emergency bottle of single malt.

Sean was still waiting for an answer to his question when Davy stretched out in one of his deck chairs. His eyebrows quirked when he saw the whiskey in Davy's hand. "Mr. Pure, imbibing strong spirits? How depraved. So? Where did you eat? With who? Let's have it."

He inhaled, and braced himself. "Margot Vetter."

Sean's dimples came and went as he struggled not to grin. "Oh! Awesome. Guess we're going to have to start calling before we drop by. It's about time, man. I was starting to worry about—"

"Why didn't you tell me about the stalker?"

Sean blinked. "From the tone of your voice, I take it you

haven't gotten lucky yet. Guess we can't all be as slick as I am at seduction."

"Focus," Davy snarled. "Just answer the goddamn question."

"I didn't want to give you a chance to think it to death," Sean said bluntly. "And I thought it would be a hell of a lot more effective if she asked you in person. Dewy eyes, long lashes going blinkety-blink? Full, trembling lips? Heaving bosom? And it was, wasn't it?" He studied his brother, and repeated in a sharper tone. "Wasn't it?"

Davy studied his brother over the rim of his glass. "Just how well do you know her, anyway?"

Sean's tilted green eyes were unusually cool. He waited a very long time to reply. "You mean, have I put the moves on her?"

Davy waited to inhale. Seconds ticked by. Miles looked worried.

Sean stretched out his long legs and propped his boots up on the porch railing. "I tried, sure. Any straight guy with a pulse would try. Except for you, of course, but we all know that you're, ah, special. She just wasn't into me. It's like when I got that crush on my high school French teacher. She just sort of pats me on the head while I pant and drool." His shrug was elaborately casual. "I think it's you she likes."

Davy's chest jerked in a convulsion that vaguely resembled laughter. "Hah. Not."

"Really. I've seen her scoping you. God knows why a woman would prefer your charms to mine, but babes are unfathomable."

"Stop busting my balls," Davy growled. "What did she tell you?"

Sean heaved the heavy sigh he always affected when Davy refused to play along with his bullshit. "I ran into her in the parking lot the other day. She'd locked her keys into her car. She was crying."

Davy was taken aback at the thought of Margot crying. "Her? Over car keys?"

"I thought it was weird, too. She looks like the type that would kick the tires and yell at the car. Anyhow, I galloped to the rescue with my Slim Jim, but when I got the car open, she just gave me this blank look, not responding to my devastating charm. I asked her what was wrong, and she said, 'Oh, nothing,' you know the way women do when they're about to go sit in the dark and eat a half gallon of ice cream?"

"Actually, Sean, I've don't know that I've ever inspired a woman to eat a half-gallon of ice cream," Davy said, with rigid patience.

Sean rolled his eyes. "Little do you know. You just don't pay attention. Anyhow, I coaxed it out of her. The burglary, the dead dog, yuck. It sounded creepy, so I told her to talk to you. I know you're phasing out the P.I. stuff, but she's scared. Broke, too, but you're not hurting for money, and it'll keep you from getting bored and stealing hubcaps on the street until we get our business launched. You could hold off on billing her. Or better yet, do it pro bono. That would be righteous and studly of you. Women dig that."

Davy regarded his brother with slitted eyes. "Are you trying to fix me up? Don't."

Sean looked disgusted. "Self-absorbed prick. You think this is all about you. I was just trying to make Margot stop crying. She's afraid this sick fuck is going to hurt her little dog."

"Great," Davy said sourly. "Heart-wrenching."

"Yeah, actually. It is." Sean scowled at him as he took another swig of beer. "And what if I was trying to fix you up? What's the crime? You're not making discernible progress on your own. You haven't shown signs of life since the Ice Princess gave you the boot. The chick with the blonde bun who never let her hair down, what was her name?"

Davy winced. "Beth. She wanted a ring."

Sean pantomimed wiping sweat from his brow. "Thank God you bailed. I always felt like I had my foot shoved into my mouth when that woman was around. Oh, and speaking of girlfriends, I talked to Connor. He said it's in your best interests to bring a date to the wedding, because Erin's got a flock of man-eating bridesmaids, and Erin's mama likes to matchmake. If you go alone they'll be unleashed upon you. A tornado of jewel-toned taffeta. Watch out. They see you in a tux, man? You're dead meat."

Davy hissed in dismay. He'd deliberately avoided thinking about his brother Connor's impending wedding, but it was bearing down on him now like a runaway train. "Fuck me. You bringing someone?"

Sean's grin was gleeful and wicked. "Hell, no. Bring 'em on, six, eight, ten at a time. My idea of paradise. Marooned on the lost planet of horny bridesmaids. Yum."

"Cindy's gonna be a bridesmaid, too," Miles volunteered. "She's wearing red. She's awesome in red. That's why I'm crashing at Sean's condo tonight, because Cindy has an appointment with the dressmaker for a final fitting tomorrow at eight in the morning. And I'm driving her."

Davy and Sean exchanged pained glances. Miles's hopeless devotion to their future sister-in-law's younger sister Cindy made them both nervous, but all they could do was to build up the kid's muscles, reflexes and self-esteem, and hope to God that his brain would eventually trail along behind.

Davy sipped his whiskey and let it burn down his throat. "Bridesmaids are bad news," he reflected. "Beth was a bridesmaid at her cousin's wedding. It was right after that she got all intense about commitment. Women start tossing back the champagne and thinking about the big M, and whammo, you're in a world of hurt."

"You should think about the big M yourself," Sean said. "You have to do your duty by the family DNA. You're not getting any younger."

Davy closed his eyes. "Connor's got it covered. They're probably procreating already, the way those two go at it."

The silence that followed suggested that Sean had the same quiet ambivalence about their brother's wedding that he had. Not that they weren't happy for Connor. He was so far gone in love with his bride-to-be, he was practically incapable of coherent speech.

Which was fine. Great. Extreme, out of control happiness was exactly what they wanted for their brother. But the thought of the wedding left him with a dull pang of loss. Connor was moving into a new phase of life. Leaving his brothers behind. It made him feel vaguely restless and empty, when he thought about it, so he tried hard not to.

Stupid, yes, and selfish. They loved Erin. She was perfect for Connor. Smart, brave, pretty, sweet. She'd shown her quality in that crazy thing that went down with Novak a few months ago. She'd earned her membership to the McCloud clan a thousand times over.

No, Erin wasn't the problem. It was just going to be . . . different.

Sean blew out a sharp sigh, like he was shoving away unwelcome feelings, too. "I just had a brilliant idea. Bring Margot. She'll create a force field to protect you. And she'll add to the scenery, big-time."

"Forget it," he growled. "Not happening. Lost cause."

"How come?" Sean demanded.

Davy gritted his teeth. "Drop it, OK?"

Sean's eyes narrowed. "Oh, Christ. Don't tell me, let me guess. You flubbed it, didn't you? I dropped a golden opportunity in your lap, and you blew it. You chump. No wonder you never get laid."

Davy stared at the lights that gleamed on the dark, rippling surface of the lake, declining to rise to the bait. He had nothing to say for himself. He hadn't shared the results of Margot's background check with his brother. Her mysterious secrets were none of Sean's business.

Of course, by that token, they were none of Davy's business, either. He brushed that unhelpful thought aside. "Don't you have someplace to go tonight?" he asked. "Some girl or other?"

"Miles and I might grab an action flick at the viddy store," Sean said. "I'm experiencing a brief, restful lull from my usual erotic activities. Keeping myself pure until the wedding."

"It's only two more days," was Davy's dour observation.

"A fucking eternity," Sean said. "I want to be charged up for the bridesmaids. Mow me down, ladies. Use me up. Wring me dry."

"I don't know about the viddy," Miles said doubtfully. "I've got to get up really early. I have to—"

"Be Cindy Riggs's personal slave, gofer, tutor, chauffeur, yeah. We know," Davy cut in.

Miles rocked back in his chair, his eyes wide and startled behind his round glasses. "No way! We're just good friends. She didn't have a ride to her fitting, so I told her—"

"I've seen how good a friend she is." Davy mimicked Cindy's light, breathy voice. " '*Miles, do you like my new push-up bra? Miles, would you help me with my zipper? Miles, would you do my calculus homework? Miles, who should I go out with, Rob, Rick or Randy?* '"

Miles's mouth set into a hard, angry line. "It's not like that."

Sean cleared his throat in the silence that followed. "Uh . . . maybe Miles and I should hit the road. You sound like you need a serious time out. We'll take the Chinese with us, if you don't want it."

"Yeah." Miles sprang to his feet. "Let's go. Like, right now."

Davy lifted his glass in silent apology as Sean and Miles left. Waves lapped rhythmically at the pebble beach below the porch in the silence they left in their wake. Usually it was a restful, meditative sound. Tonight, it struck him as soggy, depressing. Repetitive.

He was ashamed of himself. He had no right to criticize poor feckless Miles. He'd done stupider things himself for a woman. Would've done them again tonight, in fact. All night long, if Margot had let him.

The evening ticked by, impossibly slow. He wandered from room to room, discarding books and magazines. He surfed the net, the tube, but nothing was remotely interesting. It all seemed empty. The silence was so thick, it clogged his brain, but any music he put on irked him.

Evening stretched into an endless night. He finally wandered into the bedroom and dragged his jeans off to give his relentless boner some air. He sprawled out on the bed, but instead of sleep, he slid right into a series of erotic waking dreams about Margot. Kinky stuff, charged with anger and power games. Struggling against ropes, staring up into her bright eyes as she taunted him, showed him how helpless he was.

Very weird. He wondered what the hell that was about. Bondage games had never remotely entered his mind in terms of bed play. That was for bored people who needed to shock dulled senses to life. And God knows he went to great lengths in his life to avoid feeling helpless.

There was nothing dull about his senses. The dream memory of writhing beneath her beautiful body was vivid to the point of pain. He covered his face with one hand and gripped his stone-hard cock with a growl of frustration. There was no reasoning with his hard-on tonight, with the memory of her slim, strong shoulders beneath his hands so fresh in his mind. The fine texture of the skin on her neck. The look on her face, when she was thinking about letting him take her to bed.

His heart had beat so hard it almost exploded out of his chest.

If she'd kissed him, he would have gone for it and fucked her anyway, in spite of all the question marks. Everything about her turned him on, even her clumsy lies. They didn't come to her easily. It was almost endearing. The woman couldn't tell a decent lie to save her life.

The way his mind had couched that passing thought sent an uneasy chill down his back. He shrugged it aside.

Years of interviewing witnesses had made him expert in the study of body language. Margot was prickly and defensive because she was afraid, not guilty. She was no scam artist. She would crash and burn if she ever tried that line of work, the way her feelings were plastered on her face. She was proud, tough, principled. Impulsive. Scared to death, but more scared of the cops than she was of her bloodthirsty stalker.

Something even bigger and nastier lurked in her past. It would be a challenge to get past her wall of thorns. Challenge stimulated him, though after the Fleur debacle, he made a big effort to avoid challenges in his love life. He tried to keep things simple. Uncomplicated.

"Tried" being the operative word, women being what they were.

Curiosity burned him like acid. It wasn't his problem or his responsibility, but he wanted to nab this asshole who was terrorizing her. The more he thought about it, the more it pissed him off. He wanted to pin the sadistic fuckhead's balls to the wall.

He rolled up off the bed, restless and jittery, and wandered into the bathroom. He set the shower running, and stared at himself through the mirror fog. He wasn't vain about his body. It never occurred to him to be. It was a tool, a resource to be maintained. It was useful to have strong muscles and quick reflexes. Women tended to say yes when he made advances, and that was convenient, too. Up to a point.

He stared at himself, trying to see what Margot saw in him. Wanting her to want him. His pulse spiked, and his dick stood higher.

He stroked himself experimentally. He didn't much go for the shallow relief of jerking off. It was wasted energy, and he disliked the flat, let-down feeling it gave him after. But six months, for fuck's sake?

No one was perfect. No one was watching.

He stepped under the pounding water, soaped up his hand and gripped himself. His mind hit the reverse button and ran him right back to that moment where Margot's slender, cool hand was pressed against the center of his bare chest, her multicolored eyes wide and fascinated. Midnight blue fading to bright aqua, and a ring of golden brown around the pupil, like whoever put her together couldn't make up his mind and just kept on tinkering. That red, sulky-sweet mouth slightly open, cheeks flushed. Taut nipples poking the thin fabric of her worn T-shirt.

If things had gone how he wanted, her mouth would have curved into a sultry smile, and she would have pulled the T-shirt off and displayed herself to him. Eyes bright with that *what-are-you-going-to-do-about-it* look that drove him right out of his head.

No hesitation there. A sweep of his arm to clear the dinner stuff out of his way, and he set her on the table, shoved her onto her back so he could pull her sweatpants off, hands lingering on every warm detail of her lush hips and ass. She unbuckled his belt with frantic urgency.

Her words echoed. *". . . don't have the time and energy for a boyfriend . . . can't handle no strings sex . . . where does that leave us?"*

Good question. A dangerous idea took form in his mind, parallel and independent to the sexual fantasy that churned on unimpeded.

Maybe they could work out the perfect deal.

He didn't want a girlfriend any more than she wanted a boyfriend. He was tired of the frustration on the woman's part, the guilty discomfort on his. He hated one night stands, too. Often squalid and empty, always a health hazard, and he disliked waking up with someone with whom he had nothing in common but sex. Sneaking off before the woman woke up was bad, as if he'd stolen something, but the coffee, the groping conversation, her hopeful eyes—that was worse.

He didn't want no strings sex. He wanted carefully chosen, clearly agreed upon, precisely negotiated strings. A civilized, sensible arrangement between consenting adults. They were both single. She was attracted to him. She needed help, and protection. He was in a good position to offer it. She had her secrets to guard, he had his space to maintain. He would be very clear with her. Honest and respectful.

The idea excited him more deeply than the fuck fantasy had. The water had run cold, so he switched it off, rubbing water out of his eyes, and heard his cell phone ringing. He almost broke the sliding glass door in his haste as he bolted for the bedroom, dove for the phone. "Yes?"

Silence. The hollow kind that indicated that the line was open.

"Hello?" he said, more urgently. "Who is this?"

Click. Whoever it was hung up.

Her phone number had stuck in his mind even after he'd decided that he'd never have reason to use it. He punched it in. It rang, once, twice. The line clicked open. "Margot? You OK?"

Another brief silence. "No," she whispered.

A queasy, crawling feeling squirmed in his belly. "What's wrong?"

"Sorry I hung up on you." Her voice was dull, none of its usual sass. "I lost my nerve."

"Never mind that. What happened?" He waited a few agonizing seconds, and prompted her. "Did Snakey send you another present?"

"I think so. I'm scared to go out and look more closely."

"Shit." He was off the bed like he was on springs, fishing his jeans off the floor. He jerked them over his wet ass, not bothering with underwear. "What did he leave you this time?"

"I . . . I shouldn't have bothered you. I don't know why I . . . I guess I just panicked."

She was chickening out. His instincts screamed to jump

on her, pin her down, quick and fast. "I'll be right there." He shoved wet feet into his boots, struggled with laces. "Fifteen minutes, max."

He hung up, the better to forestall further argument, and dragged on his shirt. His mind flicked across the Glock 9mm in the gun safe.

He decided against it. Bare hands were his preference, with the knife in his boot sheath for backup. He charged out the door and over the dew-soaked lawn. He gripped the wheel to keep his hands steady.

He was an idiot, running into God knew what kind of mess, but he would bet body parts that whatever secrets Margot was hiding were not her fault. And that changed everything.

He knew the difference between reality and fantasy. He'd choked down enough reality when he was ten years old to know exactly how it tasted, but just look at him now. All that meditation and detachment were for shit when that hot button was pushed. Pow, he jumped three feet into the air and charged off, cape fluttering, to save the fair maiden from the gigantic squid. Forever trying to rewrite the sad story's ending.

Not that he was any goddamn superhero. In fact, he was a calculating bastard. Blatantly working the situation to his advantage.

But then again, she was free to tell him to fuck off if she pleased. So Margot Vetter needed help with her mysterious problems? Fine.

Then maybe she could be persuaded to help him with his.

Chapter

6

Blood all over her porch. Spattered over the peeling paint, the windows, the dusty wicker furniture that had been there when she moved in. Her welcome mat was drenched and sticky.

It was a scene straight out of one of those silly horror flicks she used to love, back before she figured out that life had enough horror in it as it was. She stared down at the puddle, remembering how she used to giggle and squeal with her friends at the Braxton theater, screaming insults and admonitions. *Don't split up, you airheads, someone always croaks when the group splits up! Don't go down into the creepy cellar, you brain-dead ditz, can't you hear the freaking music?*

No scary warning music for her. Just birds twittering, tree boughs tossing in the fragrant breeze. Her wind chimes tinkled and clanked. Their hollow, random melody was supposed to be soothing. The lake of blood rendered it grotesque. More horrifying than any splatter flick soundtrack she'd ever heard. No group to split up and pick off, either. Just herself and Mikey, who had called a shaky emergency truce and was huddled behind her ankles, shivering. Mikey would face down ten pit bulls, but he was out of his depth with Snakey, and he knew it.

She was, too. Scared out of her wits. The only thing to do was run, but her emergency stash of money had all been invested in her fake references, still more blown on celebratory crap like the couch, a pretty dress and frivolous shoes when she'd landed the job. What was left had gone for the vet bills and the kennel. The twenty-three bucks in the freezer would barely fill the tank in her dying car.

She had a week to wait for her next piddly paychecks from Joe's Diner and her various gym jobs. She squeezed her eyes shut, and opened them. The blood didn't disappear. Just as well. If she were going bonkers on top of all this, she would be in real trouble.

That thought sent painful laughter jolting through her. Like this trouble wasn't real enough. Framed for murder and on the run from the law. Haunted by a grisly assassin with an unknown agenda. Stalked by a bloodthirsty maniac who might or might not be the same guy. The blood smelled meaty and nauseating. Her stomach bucked and rolled.

Under the circumstances, going bonkers might be a sweet relief.

She had to run. Just like before, a mad dash from nowhere to nowhere, disaster poised over her like the blade of a guillotine. Ouch. A guillotine was most definitely the wrong image to call up right now.

Running was the only option left. So why had she called up McCloud at five in the morning and begged him to come over and hold her hand? She was so lame.

Because he made her feel safe. Because she wanted to see him one last time. Because she wanted to say goodbye.

The answer to her own question came to her like a sharp bonk on the head, startling tears into her eyes. Yeah, that was it. Saying goodbye to a fantasy. Thanking him for . . . for what, she wasn't even sure. For what he might have been to her, if the world had been different.

What a ninny. One sexually charged moment with a guy, and she was mourning the poignant loss of the love of her life. Puh-leeze.

So. The plan. Scrape together every penny she could. Work the shift at the diner for the tips. Try, probably in vain, to get that cheapskate Joe to advance her for the days she'd already worked. Same thing at the health clubs. Pawn that goddamn pendant. And then run.

Jump, and the net will appear, the touchy-feely self-help books said, but she just bet they weren't talking about clueless outlaws.

Davy McCloud's black pickup pulled up at the curb. A funny little sound came out of her throat. She clapped her hand over her mouth to keep any more from sneaking out unawares.

She'd never been so glad to see another human being in her life.

He bounded up the steps, lightfooted and silent. She sniffed back the soggy mess in her nose and leaned out across the gore, steadying herself by clutching the doorjamb. "Go on around to the back door, or you'll track this stuff all over the place. It's still wet."

He stared at her blood-spattered porch for a long moment. "Jesus," he said. His eyes fastened on her face. "You OK?"

She nodded. It was a huge lie, but she so appreciated his asking she almost started sobbing. She wasn't OK. She wanted a hug, this instant, and he was too far away, across a lake of blood. "Go around to the back door," she repeated. "Now. Please. Don't make me wait."

He nodded, and ran back down the steps.

Margot slapped the door shut and scurried towards the back door. She wrenched the warped door open. He pulled her right into his arms. Her face scrunched, her throat quivered, and she buried her face in the soft fabric of his shirt. He was so warm and solid. He smelled so good. She wanted to crawl into his pocket and just huddle there.

He grabbed a napkin left on the counter from last night's Mexican pig-out, cupped her head back and dabbed at her face.

She snatched it away and honked into it. "Sorry. I'm just—"

"Shut up."

She blinked at him. "Huh? Excuse me?"

"Stop apologizing. I'm tired of it." And before she had a chance to get properly pissed at his nerve, he disarmed her by kissing her forehead and folding her back into his arms again. "You call the cops?"

She didn't even bother to answer, and he didn't press the point.

McCloud pushed her into a chair and set about making coffee. She scooped Mikey into her arms, shut her eyes, and let him do it.

"Did you see or hear anything this time?" he asked.

"Like Snakey would make it so easy," she scoffed. "Of course not. I was dozing. The alarm woke me up at four. And I saw . . . the blood dripping down the windowpane." Her teeth started to chatter.

Davy set a steaming mug of coffee before her. "I hope you drink it black. Couldn't find any sugar or milk."

She tried to smile. "Fine. Thanks." She took a gulp of coffee just as he laid his hand on her shoulder. Bracing heat and strength poured right into her body. She choked, sputtering. She could not project her needy fantasies onto this guy. She had to get a grip, right now.

"I know what you're thinking," she snapped. "But it's not true."

"Oh, yeah?" He sounded amused. "Tell me what I'm thinking."

"I'm not running away from my pimp. I haven't ripped anybody off. There's no drug deal gone bad in my past. I don't owe anybody money. I'm a dull person, leading a dull life. All I do is work."

He sat down in the chair across from her and took a swallow of coffee. "It's nice of you to tell me what's not happening. But it would be much more useful to know what actually is happening." He gazed at her over the rim of his cup. Waiting, just as he had last night.

She took a deep breath, opened her mouth, and—

The phone rang. She leaped up, jostled the table and spilled her coffee over herself. "Oh, crap. Sorry. Excuse me while I get that." She scurried into the bedroom, pathetically grateful for the interruption.

Saved by the phone from her own insane folly. She'd been a heartbeat away from telling him everything.

Davy strained to overhear her conversation, but after a moment it rose to a volume he had no trouble following.

". . . I know, but believe me, this *is* an emergency . . . yeah, I know, but if . . . yes, but if I had known beforehand that some sick freak was going to splatter blood all over my porch, I would have arranged for a sub to cover for me, but being as how it was a *surprise* . . . uh-huh, guess what? The last time it happened, I was surprised too, call me silly . . . oh. Gee. Thanks so much for your compassion and understanding, Joe. You're . . . yeah. Whatever. Right back at you."

The phone crashed down. Margot appeared in the kitchen door, cradling her dog. Her face looked pale and pinched.

"Trouble?" he asked.

She grimaced, and cuddled Mikey as she sank back into the chair again. "Nothing I can't handle."

Davy stared at her graceful profile as she stared out the

window, back straight, mouth tight. He wanted to hug her
again, but she looked like she might shatter if he touched
her. "Problems with work?"

She tossed her head, a vain attempt to look casual. "That
was the owner of the diner where I work part-time. I was
supposed to be there by now to prep. I might have just gotten
fired." She dropped her face into her hands. "This, I did not
need. Could things get any worse?"

"Yes," he said.

She looked up, incredulous. "Gee, brighten my morning
a little more, why don't you? That was a rhetorical question,
McCloud!"

"Don't ask questions if you don't want answers," he
replied.

"You're some comfort," she said sourly. "A little ray of
sunshine."

"Comfort won't help you right now." He made his voice
hard. "You need the cops. If you don't want real help, don't
ask for comfort."

She put Mikey down and blew her nose. "I'd rather not. I
rub cops the wrong way. Problems with authority. Daddy issues. You know."

He shook his head. "No, I don't. But if you don't have the
nerve to tell me the truth, at least don't insult me by feeding
me a raft of shit."

She winced, and lifted defiant eyes to his. "Would you
stop that?"

"Stop what?"

"Didn't anybody ever tell you that staring is rude? I can't
deal with that kind of scrutiny today. I don't even have my
makeup on."

He trained his eyes into his coffee cup. "Sorry," he said.
"I can't seem to help looking at you. I find you . . . interesting."

She looked wary, but her lips twitched. "Interesting, huh?
That's one of those sneaky, double-edged words. Interesting

how? Interesting like flesh-eating bacteria? Interesting like something out of *The X-Files*?"

"Let me pick another word," he said smoothly. "Fascinating."

She snorted. "Oh, get out of town. Fascinating, my butt."

"That, too," he said, before he could stop himself.

She muffled a crack of laughter behind her hands. "Look who's trying to be cute. Hang on to your day job, McCloud. You weren't cut out to be a comedian."

He was pleased to have made her laugh, even if it took making an ass of himself. "Please call me Davy."

"Davy." She said the word slowly, like she was tasting it.

He reached across the table and took her cool, slender hand in his. "You want to talk, Margot? I know how to keep my mouth shut."

She hesitated, mouth trembling, and slowly pulled her hand away. "No. Not now. It's a long story, and I'm late for work." Her voice turned brisk. "I dragged you out of bed at an ungodly hour—"

"I get up early anyhow," he assured her.

"I really appreciate the moral support, but if you've got things to do, you don't have to hang around here. I'm past the worst of it. Now I just have to get on with my day somehow."

He could've howled with frustration. She'd been so close to talking. "We could go someplace and get some breakfast," he said.

She flinched at the mention of food. "God, no. I've got to clean that blood up somehow, and get Mikey to the kennel, and see if I can get to work in time to salvage my job, so maybe you should just—"

"I know a good cleaning service that can take care of your porch," he offered. "And I've got a friend at an independent crime lab. I'll take a sample of that blood to be analyzed. You don't know who or what it's from. Don't handle it yourself. Let professionals deal with it."

She looked doubtful. "I don't think I should have to handle it either, but I can't afford the luxury of—"

"They're my friends," he insisted. "They'll cut me a deal."

Her eyes were full of wary confusion. "Don't, Davy," she said softly. "It's sweet of you, but . . . just let it be. I'll take care of it when I get back." She stopped whatever else she was going to say, shook her head and scurried into her bedroom.

He headed out to the porch and stared at the dark, glistening pool. He wasn't great with blood. He could handle it if forced to, but it made him queasy and depressed, stirring memories he really didn't want to unearth. He forced himself to concentrate as he scraped a sticky flake of the blood into a plastic bag with the point of his knife.

When he came back into the kitchen, she was dressed in a dowdy blue waitressing uniform, somehow managing to look sharp and sexy in it. Her hair was twisted up into a spiky fountain of dull brown wisps.

She pulled a set of purple spandex workout gear off the drying rack in the kitchen, shoved them into her gym bag and pulled open the door. She jerked her chin for him to precede her out.

"Will you have dinner with me tonight?" he asked, as she followed him out. "We can do Thai, or sushi. You'll be hungry by then for sure."

A reluctant smile curved her soft mouth. "You're slick, McCloud."

"Call me—"

"Yeah, OK. Davy. But tonight's not good. I've got a lot to deal with. As you well know." She locked the door and marched down the steps, head high, back straight. Her moment of weakness was definitively over.

He tried again as she deposited Mikey in the passenger's seat of her car. "I should drive you to work. Your hands are shaking." He cupped the slender hand that held her car keys. "You want a ride?"

Her hand vibrated in his grip, but she didn't pull it away. "No, thanks. I need to be mobile right after my shift. I've got gym classes to teach afterwards. And, uh . . . Davy? One more thing."

"Yeah?"

She hesitated for a second, then launched herself at him, grabbed him around the waist and hugged him, tightly. Almost angrily.

He practically jerked away, he was so startled. She just hung on harder. He came to his senses and grabbed her back just in time, as her grip was loosening. His heart thundered in his chest, his breath had gone ragged. Every part of him that touched her tingled and burned.

She lifted her face from where it was pressed against his shirt. "Thanks, Davy," she whispered. "For everything."

"For what?" he demanded. "You won't tell me anything. You won't trust me. You won't let me do a goddamn thing to help you."

She shook her head, and rubbed her cheek against his shirt. "You're sweet," she said. "You came when I called you. You gave me a hug when I needed one. You're sweet. A good guy."

"Nah. Not that good." He cut off her reply with his mouth. Her face was wet with tears, her skin exquisitely fine-grained and soft. Her lips were full and sweet and salty, trembling under his.

She opened to him, drinking him in like she was starving. That knocked the lid off, and what he'd thought was just sexual hunger got swept away by something bigger and hotter, something that welled up from deep inside him like a fountain of molten lava.

The kiss went crazy. Her arms went up around his neck. He pushed her back against the car, nudging his thigh between hers as he plundered the tender secrets of her mouth. So sweet and moist and hot.

She pushed at his chest, murmuring soft protest. He finally registered it, and wrestled his trembling muscles back under control.

He stumbled away from her, panting. Didn't even want to imagine the look that must be on his face.

Margot wiped her mouth, her eyes glowing, pupils dilated. Her lips were red, puffy and soft. "That's all." Her voice was wispy and quavering. "That's it. No more. Please don't torture me."

"What do you mean, torture you? Can I call you?" he pleaded.

Her face tightened. She got into her car, started up the engine, and mopped her eyes with her sleeve before giving him a little wave and a tight, fake smile. She pulled away, her car belching black smoke.

He stared after her for several minutes, his brain wiped clean.

Then he walked around to her back porch. The overgrown bushes shielded him from the neighbors' line of sight. His legs shook, his heart still raced. He had a pick gun in his tool stash in the truck, but the flimsy lock on the back door could be negotiated without it. He had to know more before he could help, he told himself as he eased the lock open with his bank card and let himself into the kitchen. He counted the money in her freezer stash, leafed through the envelopes on the counter. Utility bills, past due notices. None in her name, not that he knew her real name. The place must be a sublet.

He scanned every drawer, every scrap of paper, every scribbled grocery list. He sifted carefully through her trash. No clues.

It didn't take long to go through the place. Margot evidently wasn't the type who accumulated stuff. A roll of posters leaning against the wall proved to be Art Nouveau images and classic art photographs. A calendar of flower fairies hung in the hall, incongruously cheerful against the cracked, stained wall. This month was a rose fairy, with a flower petal skirt. Nothing was written on it, no appointments, no phone numbers. The books on the shelf were from the local library. Romance novels, popular bestsellers, inspirational essays, a manual on web site design, books on art history, one on photography. So she was into art.

He tried to justify the intensity of his interest as he sorted through the stuff on her desk, but after years of self-observation, he couldn't fool himself. The first step towards self-control was self-knowledge. Well and good. But when it came to Margot, self-knowledge evaporated. As a consequence, self-control was likewise fucked. He was violating her privacy because he couldn't help himself. A sobering realization. Didn't make him stop, though. The joke was on him.

One sketchbook, with just a few pages used. Doodles, cartoons. Mikey sleeping. Mikey sprawled on his back. Quick, powerful pencil sketches of people. A guy catching a frisbee, a homeless man on a park bench. His eyes lingered over them, fascinated. She had a gift.

The basket on her dresser yielded one item of interest, a heavy gold pendant cast in the shape of a coiled snake. It looked old and valuable, but it was ugly as hell. He couldn't imagine her wearing it, but he'd never claimed to understand women's taste in jewelry.

He turned it over in his hand, wondering how it had escaped the burglary. Maybe she'd been wearing it that day.

Her closet and drawers were closer to empty than any woman's that he'd ever met. A small, discreet vibrator was tucked under a stack of panties in her underwear drawer. He stared at it, his face going hot.

Oh, Christ, later for that. He was still half-hard from that crazy kiss. It would trash his focus completely to picture her using the thing.

He crouched down next to the pallet where she slept. A

quilt folded over three times like a burrito, a sheet folded in half and tucked around it. She'd left it rumpled, the hollow of her head in the pillow.

Anger jarred him, at the thought of her lying on the floor, lonely and scared, while a sadistic stalker lurked outside. She should be in a steel-reinforced concrete fortress. Protected by barbed wire, broken glass, infrared motion detectors, submachine guns.

And himself.

Whoa. Concentrate. He pressed his hand against the pallet. He'd slept in harder places himself, but he'd gotten spoiled in the last few years. If he got lucky with her, he would stage their trysts at his place, in his big, comfortable king-sized bed. Not that it mattered for the sex. A bare floor was fine. Up against the wall, in the shower, in the tub.

Still, he liked the idea of watching her stretch and smile at him, rosy and tousled and relaxed in his bed before he mounted her, sliding his cock slowly into her hot, moist body while she clutched him.

He thought of her flushed cheeks, her fascinated eyes. She liked to be touched. Margot would be red-hot for a man she trusted.

His hyper-trained eye suddenly noticed the crack next to the baseboard. He hooked his fingernails under the floorboard and pried.

Sure enough, it came loose, revealing a shallow cavity. A small spiral notebook was nestled in the space, a felt-tip pen stuck between the pages. He pulled it out and flipped through it, too fast to read.

Her handwriting was small, but bold and graceful. Every instinct in him screamed to read the thing. It was the only source of information he'd found in the place. He wanted to so badly, his hand shook, but he just stared at the diary, paralyzed by a startling realization.

He wanted her to trust him.

He wanted to know all her secrets, but he wanted her trust

even more. She was the type that would never forgive a guy for reading her diary behind her back. He tucked the journal back into the place where he'd found it and dropped the board carefully back into place.

He got up and backed away, feeling cornered and confused. As if he deserved her trust, after picking her lock and prowling through her house. Hypocritical, waffling idiot. He'd gone through her utility bills and rifled her underwear drawer, and he balked at her diary?

Nothing he did today made any sense.

Chapter

7

Faris slowly sipped his second cup of bad coffee at the lunch counter, making it last so he would not be forced to drink a third, and watched Margaret as she charged out of the kitchen with a load of chicken-fried steak and meat loaf. So beautiful, even when her eyes were shadowed, her lovely face pale and drawn. Each day that she worked there, he put on a new disguise and braved the wretched food in order to feast his eyes on her at close range.

"Margot," the beefy man behind the cash register said, as she spun around the end of the lunch counter. "C'mere. Gotta talk to you."

"Hold on, Joe," she said briskly. "Let me just deliver these—"

"I found somebody to replace you," he broke in. "You can work out the next half hour of your shift, and then you're outta here."

Margaret stopped in her tracks. Unfortunately, the tray poised on her shoulder, borne forward by a surge of centrifugal force, did not.

Plates and food flew, crashed, splatted. Glasses, dinner rolls, dripping gravy and green beans fanning out on the floor.

"Changed my mind," Joe Pantani said in the silence that followed. "Don't work out your shift. Clean up that god-damn mess and get out."

"Clean it up yourself, you sadistic jerk." Margaret's voice shook.

Faris wanted to cheer.

"I'm tired of your problems, and it doesn't look like you're getting them under control. I'll cut you a check for the days you worked this week and mail it to you." Joe's voice was heavy with self-righteousness. "Minus the cost of that food and those broken dishes."

"This wasn't my fault," she said fiercely. "None of it was."

"Take responsibility when your life goes down the toilet, hon," Joe said. "Ask yourself, why is this happening to me?"

"Screw you, Pantani. I'm not your hon, and you can spare me the sermon." Margaret whipped off her apron and sponged gravy off her legs with it. Everyone was staring, forks in mid-air, eyes wide with horrified fascination. She spun around, arms flung out. "Step right up, ladies and gents," she an-nounced. "Check out the latest sideshow attraction! Woman Whose Life Is Going Down the Toilet."

Faris hid his appreciative smile behind his coffee cup as many guilty eyes dropped all at once. A murmur started. Forks began to clink.

"Hey, lady, was that our lunch?" A table of elderly men in suspenders and bow ties were staring at her with accusing eyes.

She jerked her chin in Joe's direction. "Take it up with him."

Faris forced himself to finish his coffee after she marched out, despite the feverish excitement bubbling inside him.

The slaughtered dog had been a message, to pique her cu-riosity, so she would start to wonder about him, long for him, dream of him. Last night, he'd tried to show her the difference between McCloud's unclean lust and his own holy adoration with his blood offering. But she hadn't understood. She wasn't ready. He'd been disappointed but not surprised when she had panicked and called McCloud.

No matter, he'd been ready with Plan B; to plunder McCloud's house for the items he needed. Pantani had given him a brilliant idea.

Faris left money on the counter and walked up to the register. He blinked at Joe through the thick, distorting lenses of his glasses. "You should apologize to that waitress." He used the voice that went with his meek public demeanor. "You were unfair to her."

Joe Pantani's eyes went wide. He stopped twirling his gold hoop earring and crossed his meaty arms across his thick chest. "Oh, yeah? No shit. Thanks for sharin' your opinion, pal."

Faris stared into the man's eyes. He saw it already with his acute other vision; the mask of imminent death superimposed upon Joe's fleshy features. The grinning skull beneath coming eerily into focus.

"You just lost a regular customer, as well as your best waitress," Faris said. *To say nothing of your worthless life.*

Joe let out an explosive bray of laughter. "You're breaking my heart. How 'bout you get lost before I bust out cryin'?"

Faris turned his back, and walked out of the restaurant to his car. Margaret was still there, hunched over her purse, her hand pressed against her mouth. Trying not to cry. Brave angel. He ached for her. He wanted to swoop down like a bird of prey, and snatch her away from all this confusion. But the fear and pain was her initiation. The cleansing fire that would burn away her resistance to her new life with him.

He switched on the monitor of the tracking device he had planted in her car as she pulled away, and moved to follow at a discreet distance as he booted up his laptop and wireless modem. He pulled up behind Joe Pantani's red Camaro as he tapped his way deftly into the database of the DMV, using the backdoor that Marcus had bought for him. He plugged in the license plate number, took note of the man's home address. Then he scrolled down to peek at the traffic violations.

Joe had a weakness for speeding. Tsk, tsk. Bad boy. But the temptations of the world were over for him.

Joe Pantani had made his choice. He was just a walking corpse.

It wasn't my fault. None of it was. Whine whine whine.

She wanted to smack herself. Her biggest talent since babyhood was being mouthy, and now even the snappy comeback program no longer ran on her hard drive. Not that it mattered. It was silly to get huffy over a disposable job when she had real problems to worry about.

Big, hairy ones, with long yellow fangs.

She parked on the street outside the house, and Davy's wild, incendiary dawn kiss flooded her mind, filling it so completely there was no room left over for Snakey or Joe or anything. Just Davy McCloud's warm, ardent mouth moving over hers, the rumbling vibration of his deep voice resonating through her. His lithe, strong body insinuating itself against her tender bits, making everything go tingly and soft.

And she had to stop this nonsense. She got out of the car, slammed shut the door, gritted her teeth. Now was not the time.

She stared up the steps, bracing herself to face the blood. She wished she had a personality that could steal and cheat without suffering. She could hotwire a car and speed away, eluding the cops with her super-duper commando skills. A cross between a female Rambo and the new Charlie's Angels. Kicking villains' butts. Rapelling down skyscrapers. Sewing up her own wounds in the wilderness.

But she didn't have those skills. She was a born wuss. She liked hot baths, silk shirts, chocolate truffles. She knew all about design theory, twentieth-century art and architecture, web site tools. She could design and sketch like a pro, she was a pretty good saleswoman and she cooked a mean pasta carbonara. But she'd been playing hooky that day in school when they taught you how to hotwire cars and evade road blocks. If only she'd studied self-defense, but no, she'd gone the vanity route; aerobics, spinning, ballroom dancing. Her tango skills wouldn't help much when it came down to going mano a mano with Snakey.

There was a complex mind-set and science to being an outlaw, and she sucked at it, big-time. She couldn't lie well, for one thing. Running away from unpaid rent and bills made her queasy. She even felt bad about not having time to take back her library books.

But who knew what she might be driven to before the end?

Yikes. Better not get near that thought. She'd start screaming.

She tried to convince herself that Snakey's antics weren't connected with the horror in San Francisco. She'd hoped so hard that her fake identity, the hitchhiking, and her zig-zagging flight had covered her tracks, that it was just bad luck to have drawn the disaster card twice. But the horrific strangeness of what had happened eight months ago had the same spooky quality as slaughtered dogs, buckets of blood.

What baffled her was why Snakey was bothering to play this game of cat and mouse with her at all. She was such a pitifully easy mark. She didn't even exist, officially. He could grab her anytime, chop her up into mincemeat and no one on earth would ever look for her.

Except for Davy. He might spare a thought or two for her.

Yeah, in her dreams. Give it up, already. Maybe Snakey wanted her to run just so he could have the fun of chasing her. Creepy thought. Not helpful. Best to squelch it and keep moving, too fast to let herself be scared. In the moment.

Breathing in, breathing out. A shiver went up her spine. She turned in a slow circle, but didn't see anyone. She shook herself, ran up the porch steps and stopped at the top, stunned.

The porch was resplendent, the peeling walls and floor scrubbed with some strong, pine-smelling solvent. Davy had called the cleaning service after all. That overbearing, adorable sweetheart. Tears sprang to her eyes. And she would never even have a chance to thank him.

She stripped off the gravy-spotted waitress outfit, yanked on some jeans and a tank top, and rummaged in the kitchen for some plastic shopping bags. She raced through the house grabbing silverware, dishes, dog food, pet treats. Dish soap, sponges. Mikey's dishes and basket, a can opener. Toiletries, towels, hair dye, quilt, pillow, clothes. The flower fairy calendar that made her think of Mom. The posters to remind her that there was grace and beauty outside this stinking hellhole. Her sketchbook, her diary. Her one nice dress and shoes, the result of her imprudent celebration purchases, rated their own private bag. The snake pendant she stuck in her pocket, where it made an ugly lump in her snug jeans. She dumped the basket of combs, hairclips and her small stash of makeup into the last bag, and that was it. Her life, reduced to five plastic shopping bags. She was through with this place.

On to the pawnshop. She hurried to the car, looking furtively around. Maybe Snakey was watching right now. She should perform some brilliant evasive maneuver to stymie him.

Yeah. Like . . . what, for instance?

Screw it. She could only do as much as she could do.

Faris peered through the powerful field glasses and watched Margaret leave the Capitol Hill pawnshop ten minutes after she entered it. His eyes followed hungrily as she got back into her car. Her skimpy tank top showed a strip of skin around her midriff. It bothered him. When she was his, he would not allow her to wear trashy clothes.

Margaret pulled away. Faris waited for her car to turn the corner before he walked into the pawnshop. His eyes adjusted to the light that filtered through the cloudy window. A skinny guy in his forties sat behind a glass display case full of watches, jewelry, guns. The man grinned, showing all his gums. "Afternoon. What can I do for you?"

Faris smiled politely as he walked up to the counter. "I was curious to know what the young lady who just left had pawned."

The man guffawed, showing large, yellowed teeth. "Don't blame ya. I told that babe I'd give her an extra twenty if she left me her phone number, but those uppity, high-tit bitches are all the same. Even when they're down on their luck, they look down their nose at a regular working guy." The man registered Faris's frozen expression. His eyes widened. "Shit. You're not, like, her husband or something, are ya?"

Faris forced himself to smile. "Not yet."

The guy's nervous laugh sounded like a dog barking. "Uh, yeah."

Faris waited. "May I see what she pawned?" he repeated patiently.

The man reached behind himself and held up the snake pendant. He laid it on the glass case. "Eight hunnert bucks," he said officiously.

The pawnbroker had probably given Margot little more than fifty.

"I'll give you five hundred," Faris said.

The fellow looked put upon. "No way. This baby's pure gold. Antique, too. It's worth at least—at least—"

"Six, then," Faris said, smiling inside at the feral pleasure that lit up the man's eyes. After all, he could afford to be benevolent. A final pleasure for the man before he died. He'd seen and handled the symbol of the secret Order of the

Snake. There could be no witness to Margaret's sale, or Faris's purchase. Besides, this would be a nice warm-up for the rest of the day's strenuous activities.

"Before you make up the receipt, would you take down . . ." Faris turned, and pointed to a dusty, unstrung guitar that hung high on the wall. "That guitar. I'd like to take a look at it."

The pawnbroker looked puzzled. "Sure, I guess, but I got a whole lot of better ones, if you wanna see some—"

"I'd like to look at that one, please," Faris insisted.

The guy rolled bloodshot eyes, and unfolded himself reluctantly from his chair. His stringy body was lost in his flapping clothing, and his movements released a billowing reek of sweat and stale cigarettes.

He fished a claw-ended grabbing device from under the counter and took it over to the far wall. He reached up, fishing with the grabber for the twine looped around the tuning pegs.

Faris moved silently behind him, the first needle held lightly between his thumb and forefinger. Time and space dilated as his perceptions of the man's body intensified, the flows of blood and lymph and vital energy, muscle fibers, nerve bundles, and the exact . . . perfect spot in the side of his neck, between those two tendons . . . yes.

The needle struck true, snake-quick, accompanied by a shockwave of Faris's vital energy. Then the second needle, slightly lower. Then the third. The man went rigid, and then crumpled to the floor.

Faris knelt next to him, concentrated his qi one last time, and stabbed his two fingers into the trauma point over the man's liver.

He plucked the needles out and tucked them back into his wristband, and peeked beneath the man's eyelids. Perfect. He was the best of the Order of the Snake. None of the other trainees had acquired Faris's intuitive understanding of death strikes, and with each kill, his precision increased. He leaned over the counter and rifled through the receipts until he found the one that documented Margaret's sale. He took it, along with the carbon, tucking them into his pocket, and waited until the man's eyelids fluttered open. "Huh? Whah?" the man said.

"You blacked out." Faris made his voice solicitous. "When you reached up for the guitar. Can I get you something? Or call someone?"

"Nah." The pawnbroker looked dazed. "I'll be OK, I guess. Fuckin' weird."

"It happens," Faris soothed. "Probably it's nothing. You should see your physician, though. You might have low blood pressure. You should have a candy bar, or a cup of coffee, maybe."

The man allowed Faris to help him into a sitting position. "Thanks, man. Sorry if I freaked you out. Man, I feel like shit."

"No problem at all," Faris assured him. "Really, I wouldn't mind running you over to the emergency room."

"Hell, no." The man winced, rubbing the heel of his hand over one of the spots that Faris had struck with the needles. "I stay away from those places. You still want that guitar?"

"Oh, no, thank you. Don't trouble yourself," Faris said. "I'll just take the pendant." He pulled six hundred dollar bills out of his wallet and laid them on the counter, glad that he had thought to paint the transparent layer of liquid latex over his fingertips today.

The man struggled up onto his knees, and then thudded heavily back onto his hind end. "Gotta do up a receipt for you," he muttered.

"Never mind the receipt," Faris said. "I don't need one. Stay where you are for a few minutes. Head down, between your knees."

The man's bleared, confused eyes flickered up to Faris's. He looked lost. "Thanks," he said. "Maybe I will."

"Maybe you should close up shop for a while," Faris suggested. "Go lie down someplace."

"Yeah," the man replied dully. "That might be good."

The pawnbroker did not deserve Faris's respect, but death had claimed him, and Faris found himself lingering by the door, gazing down at the soon-to-be-dead man with a feeling almost like tenderness.

"Goodbye," Faris said gently. "Take care."

He stepped out into the sunshine. The process was irreversible. The man's kidneys and liver would begin to shut down soon. Within twelve hours, he would die. Painfully, bleeding from every orifice.

The door tinkled gently as he closed it behind him. He dropped the pendant into his pocket. All that was left was to eliminate that animal that Margaret kept as a pet, after which it would be time to turn his attention to Joseph Pantini. Ah, the things a man did for love.

The random thought struck him as funny. He sauntered down the sidewalk towards his car, whistling and smiling at everyone he passed.

Chapter

8

"**A**nimal blood? You're sure about that?" Davy said.

"Yeah," Monique said. "I haven't distinguished which animal yet. That'll take more tests, and I was too swamped today."

"Huh. Interesting," Davy said slowly. "How much do I owe—"

"Don't even," Monique scoffed. "It was no biggie. Want to catch me up with what you've been doing lately over dinner?"

Davy hesitated. "Uh, actually . . ."

"Say no more." Monique's voice was regretful, but good-natured. "Can't blame a woman for trying."

"Thanks for rushing this for me," Davy said. "You're really—"

"A pal. I know. Have fun tonight, whatever you're doing. Bye."

Davy clicked the cell phone off and eased into his parking place behind the dojo, thinking about Monique with a combination of affection and regret. She was an ex-client of his, a technician at a crime lab, whose philandering husband had absconded with his mistress and all their assets, leaving her with two little kids, a rented apartment and fifty thousand dollars in debt. Davy had tracked the selfish asshole down and made him pay through the nose. One of the few times that detective work had given him pure, unadulterated satisfaction.

Maybe he should have become a cop, like Connor. Problem was, he was bad at dealing with rules, bureaucracy, politics, power games. Connor had more patience for that crap than he did. Davy had never been much of a team player. A result of his weird upbringing.

Monique was an attractive woman. He'd thought about getting involved with her, and there the matter rested. Thinking. Whereas with Margot, he couldn't string two lucid thoughts together. He was running on mindless impulse. Like driving with his eyes shut, pedal to the floor.

He peered through the door of the dojo. Sean's raucous kickboxing class was in full swing. It sounded more like a street brawl or a wild party than a martial arts class. He kept going, and pushed open the door to the Women's Wellness Center next door.

The place jarred him with its femininity. Pastel colors, plants, the fruit 'n veggie juice bar, perfumes from the aromatherapy shelves wafting over from the New Age boutique.

His tenant, Tilda, who ran the place, sashayed around the bar, a grin flashing in her dusky face. She gave him a smacking kiss. "I'm paid up on my rent, honey, so to what do I owe the honor of this visit?"

Davy eyed Tilda's moist fuchsia lipstick and wondered if she'd left a kiss mark on his jaw. "Just wondering if Margot was around."

Tilda's liquid brown eyes widened in amused speculation. "Yes, actually. Just finishing up Ifs, Abs and Butts."

"No kidding?" He started to grin.

"Great title, eh? Came up with it myself. After that she's

got the evening step class to do, and then she's done. I think she's already doing the cool-down. She'll be out in a minute. Why don't you have a seat at the bar and let me juice you the wheat grass, beet and lemon cocktail? It's a bomb. Keep you going like the Energizer Bunny."

"No, thanks," Davy said hastily. "I'm fine. I'll just wait."

The music faded away moments later, and a stream of damp, exhausted looking women began to trickle out. Margot was the last of them, decked out in her purple outfit that fit her gorgeous body like a second skin. It clashed wildly with green and orange striped tights.

She caught sight of him, and froze in place, eyes wide.

His gut clenched to think that his attentions might be so unwelcome as to seem creepy. He tried a non-threatening smile, and tried not to stare at the sinuous way she walked towards him.

"Hey, there," she said. "What's up?"

"Uh . . ." His mind went embarrassingly blank for a second before he fished the salient item back to the surface. "I got preliminary results back from the lab. It's animal blood."

Her eyebrows shot up. "Huh. Weird. I'm sorry for the animal, but thank God it wasn't . . . well. You know."

"Yeah," he said. "The cleaning service should have been by today, too. They told me they'd take care of it."

"Thanks," she said again. "You shouldn't have done it. I told you not to. But you were a sweetheart. That was really kind of you."

Davy's eyes flicked to Tilda, who was listening avidly to every word. "I was wondering if you would have dinner with me," he said. "I've got steaks marinating at home. Or we could call out for Chinese, or Indian, or anything you felt like. We need to talk about how to proceed."

Her brow lifted. "Oh? Are we proceeding? I didn't know that."

Her cool tone grated on him. "The situation is unacceptable."

Margot's mouth tightened. "You're not the one who has to accept it. Look here, McCloud—I mean, Davy," she corrected. "I appreciate your concern, but I got doused with blood this morning and fired from my restaurant job this afternoon. I'm really on edge, to put it mildly. So don't even think about throwing your weight around with me."

Tilda leaned over the bar. "Don't be an idiot," she hissed. "He offers to help, and you give him attitude? Get a clue, girlfriend!"

Margot did not drop her eyes from Davy's face. "Til, you're a fabulous woman, but this is complicated. So please butt out."

Davy took a deep, calming breath and called on all of his patience. "Would you step outside with me for a minute?"

Her eyes flicked over to Tilda. "I have to teach the—"

"The step class, I know. It'll just take a second. Please, Margot."

She nodded. He followed her out of the gym to the breezeway outside. She bit her lip, clearly nervous. "I don't have a lot of time."

"Let's try this again," he persisted grimly. "Let's get back to the burning issue of steaks, Chinese, Indian, Thai. What's your preference?"

"But you fed me dinner last night," she protested.

"You shouldn't make such a big deal of it," he said. "Especially since it's just a manipulative ploy. I'm softening you up for a favor."

Her eyes widened. Tension suddenly charged the air.

"Don't be so suspicious," he hastened to say. "It's an innocent, G-rated favor."

Her eyes rolled. "There's nothing innocent or G-rated about anything you say or do, Davy McCloud."

"I need a date for my brother's wedding tomorrow," he announced.

Her jaw dropped. She was speechless for several moments. She lifted her hands to cover the flush on her cheeks.

Her lashes swept down to shield her eyes. "You want me? For something like that?"

"I know weddings can be boring, but this one should be relatively entertaining," he hurried on. "Sean alone is a one-man floor show. And Connor wants to have a really wild party. So, uh . . ."

"A family event?" Her voice was soft with disbelief. "Me?"

"It's not that big of a deal," he protested. "It's a nice place. The Endicott Falls Resort. You'd just parade around with me, looking good. We'd mingle, create a buzz of gossip that'll keep my brother's new mother-in-law from trying to fix me up, which I loathe. You may have to dance with me a couple of times. If you like dancing, that is."

"I love dancing," she whispered.

"Great. Excellent news," he said hastily. "So, will you go, then?"

He realized, alarmed, that her eyes were bright with tears. "You're doing this because you want to keep an eye on me, right?" she asked.

"That's just a side benefit," he protested. "I really do need a date. Sean's going to be no help at all. He'll be at the bottom of a writhing heap of bridesmaids as soon as things get going. Please, Margot." He pulled her hand to his face and pressed an impulsive kiss onto her palm. "Don't make me face this alone."

"That's so incredibly sweet." Her voice sounded as if she was talking to herself. "Thank you, Davy."

The sad, faraway note to her voice made him uneasy. "So?" he prodded. "You'll go? Is it a deal?"

She shook her head. "I'm afraid not. I can't—"

"Why not?" he demanded.

She squeezed her eyes shut. "God, you're difficult. I can't leave Mikey, for one thing."

"Bring him," he suggested rashly.

"To a wedding? At a posh resort?" She looked doubtful. "Get out."

"They must have rooms where you can keep pets." He had no clue if such a room was available, but he was up to the kind of hard-core intimidation it might take to make one become available.

Margot shook her head. Another thought occurred to him. "It's a formal afternoon wedding in the rose garden. I'm one of the best men, so I'm stuck wearing a goddamn tux. If you need to buy a dress—"

"Hold it right there, before you say something we'll both regret," Margot's voice was sharp.

He swallowed back the rest of it. "Sorry," he muttered.

"No. I'm the one who's sorry. Thanks for asking me. I would love to go to a big party someplace beautiful where people are celebrating something happy. I really, really wish I could go, Davy, but I can't." She held her hand up and frowned as he opened his mouth. "Don't ask me why. You don't have the right to demand explanations from me."

He wrestled down a red fog of frustrated anger. "Will you at least have dinner with me tonight?" He bit each word out with steely calm.

She threw up her hands. "Davy, please. Let it go. I still have my class to teach, and then I have to pick up Mikey."

"I already bought a dog dish and can of food for him. Mikey's own brand. Mikey's invited to this party. It's a given. No-brainer."

Margot's mouth dangled open for a moment, at a total loss. She gazed at him for a long moment and started to smile, helplessly.

She reached up and rubbed at his cheek with her hand. "You underhanded, manipulative son-of-a-bitch. You know, it's hard to take a guy seriously when he has a big fat lipstick mark on his face."

His face heated up. He scrubbed the spot with his own

knuckles. "Better?" he demanded grimly. "Can you take me seriously now?"

"Yes," she said quietly. "And yes, steaks would be great."

As a favor to Margot, Faris had wanted to dispose of her dog and its remains before he made his move on her tonight. He'd gone so far as to consider letting her keep the dog, to soften the rough transition. Upon more reflection, he had decided that such a feeble compromise was no real favor to her. A radical break with everything familiar would be better, in the long run. He could not be soft.

Softness had no place in the world she would soon inhabit.

Once she'd been properly broken in, he would reward her with a new dog. A quality, purebred animal worthy of her beauty.

He circled the block of the kennel where she boarded the dog and began spiraling out in wider circles. The right person to run this errand would present himself or herself soon. He drove past a sidewalk full of young slackers in black leather sprawled on the sidewalks, and turned the corner to circle around and take another look. He couldn't be seen by the kennel personnel, but one of these disposable persons could.

He knew her the second he saw her. A short girl with stringy, white blond curls, facial piercing, eyes shadowed with makeup. Still pretty, not yet strayed so far from her affluent suburban upbringing as to be useless. He slowed the car and stared at her until she looked up and took notice. She scowled and gave him the finger.

She had the same faint death's-head mask superimposed upon her pale face that he had seen on Joe Pantani. She was the one.

He rolled the window down, and regarded her with his most unthreatening smile. He was lucky in his pleasantly handsome, mild face. He hid his powerful, muscular body under loose clothes so as not to draw attention to himself. Marcus had told him once that from the neck up, he looked like an accountant. He often wore wire-rimmed glasses to underscore the effect, even though his vision was perfect.

"Excuse me, miss?" he called out.

She got up and swaggered towards him. "Whaddaya want?"

"I have a job for you, if you want it."

She shrank back with an expression of loathing. "I don't do that shit for money, man. Stay away from me. Pig."

"Oh no. I don't want sex," he assured her. "I just want you to run a harmless errand for me. It's not dangerous, not difficult, not illegal. It'll take you five minutes at the most."

Her face was twisted with a fierce scowl. "Why should I?"

Faris wondered idly if that row of piercings in her eyebrow was painful when she frowned like that. He fished around in his pocket until he found the baggie full of Ecstasy that Marcus had supplied him with.

He held it up. The girl's eyes dilated. "I'm not sure what your personal preferences are, but these are—"

"These are great." She held out her hand. "Give 'em over. I'll do it."

He pulled the bag back. "Not yet. I need you sharp for this. After."

She stuck her hands in the pockets of her short leather jacket and jerked her chin impatiently. "So? What do I do, then?"

"I need you to go to the kennel on the corner of Hardwick and Sorenson Avenue. You will collect a dog for me there. It's a small black mongrel, part poodle. His name is Mikey. You must say that you are Margot Vetter's niece. Repeat the name to me."

"I'm Margot Vetter's niece," the girl repeated obediently.

"You're picking up her dog early because you're throwing

a surprise birthday party for her," Faris instructed. "Insist on it. Be persuasive and charming."

Anxiety flashed behind the death's-head superimposed upon the girl's face. "What are you gonna do to the dog? Are you gonna hurt it?"

"Don't worry about that," Faris said. "That doesn't concern you. Just think about"——he rattled the contents of the baggie— "these."

He gave her a ride to a point a few blocks from the kennel, repeated the instructions, and drove to their established meeting place, a graveled parking lot behind a new construction site.

Twenty minutes later, the girl appeared from behind the chain link fence. She didn't have the dog. Faris felt his stomach drop. Bad sign. He got out of the car, and asked the question with his eyes.

The girl looked defensive. "They said the lady told 'em under no circumstances could they let anybody but her pick up her stupid old dog. I swear, I tried. I made a big stink. Told 'em they'd totally ruin the party and everything. But it was no use. Shit, man. Fuckin' Nazis."

"It's all right." Faris was surprised that Margaret had second guessed him like this. He should have known.

"So, uh . . ." Her eyes were still hopeful. "It wasn't my fault. I did everything you said."

"I don't blame you," he said gently. He pulled the baggie out and presented it to her. "Go on, take it." He could afford it, after all. Marcus had an endless source of pharmaceutical supplies available to him.

She snatched them from his hand, fished one out and stuck it in her mouth. The desperation of a hollowed-out soul. So young, but inside, she was dead already. His blow would be the touch of mercy, to stop her before she degraded herself further. So sad. For a moment, he actually loved her. He was her salvation now. Her only hope.

The girl flung her head back and stared up into the pale,

late afternoon sky, her eyes wide and glowing bright with anticipation. "This is gonna be awesome," she crooned. "Oh, man. I love you."

"I love you, too," Faris murmured, meaning it with all his heart.

He struck with his fingertip to three points on her spine, whiplike gestures so fast she just gasped and yelped. No need for the needles. Each situation called for its own technique. Each time, his aim was more sure. Death itself guided his hand. It knew its own business.

The blond girl crumpled to her knees. Whump, she fell to her bottom. She flopped onto her side, a black leather comma on the ground, her hair a pale flame against the dark dirt and gravel, eyes frozen wide. The baggie fell to the ground, pills scattered on the dirt.

Faris looked around to ensure their privacy and crouched next to her. He kept a patient, respectful vigil until the convulsions began.

Then he got up and checked his own footprints. Fortunately, the dirt was dry and hard beneath the shifting gravel. He inclined his head in a short bow to the twitching, gasping creature on the ground.

He got into his car and drove away.

Chapter
9

She was insane. Letting herself get steamrolled into a dinner date when she should have been fifty miles down the
road to nowhere by now.

Margot sipped her wine as she wandered around Davy's
house. His lethal combination of charm and subtle coercion got her every time. Even tonight, when she could least
afford it.

Still, she was pathetically glad to get to see him one last
time.

Mikey ran into the living room, tail flapping, to show off
the bone that Davy had given him. Mikey was in a party
mood. He made sure she noticed his good fortune, and trot-
ted back to where the real action was.

Amazing smells wafted out of the kitchen. She might have
known Davy McCloud would be a good cook. A fine caber-
net breathed in a decanter on the table. Mushrooms and garlic in butter sizzled in the pan on the stove. The charcoal grill
was fired up out on his porch, right below which the waters
of Lake Washington were ruffled by a fragrant breeze. Margot

took another sip and reminded herself not to relax. Letting down one's guard was what happened right before getting slammed. Then again, she got slammed whether she let down her guard or not. But stupid or not, she felt safe here.

Davy McCloud's beautiful home was spacious and comfortable. Lakeside property, in Madrona. Wow. The detective business must have treated him really well. She peeked into a big office lined with books, two computers, a laptop and a large array of unfamiliar electronic devices. A big sunken living room boasted soft, textured silver gray couches and armchairs, a pale Berber rug, a heavy, scarred wooden coffee table, a picture window overlooking Lake Washington. It made her nostalgic for her house on Parson's Lake back in San Cataldo. God, how she'd loved that place. Mold, mosquitos and all.

He had a kick-ass audio and video system. The art on the walls consisted mostly of pen and ink drawings, black and white landscape photos, and a couple of delicate, understated paintings, the kind with just a few telling brushstrokes. Comfy, classy, super-masculine, but the place could use a few splashes of color. A fireplace had photos on the mantel over it. She moved closer to study them.

The first was a black and white portrait of a family. A grim-faced, long-haired man with a broad, hard jaw like Davy's hovered protectively behind a light-haired woman who looked much younger than he. Four boys clustered around them. She recognized the nine or ten-year-old Davy instantly, even stringy and thin, with a mop of long hair hanging over his face. His somber, piercing gaze hadn't changed at all. The other boy, next size down, was laughing up into his mother's face, and the other two looked like twins, clowning and mugging for the camera. One of them had to be Sean, but she couldn't tell which one.

Another picture was Davy, Sean and the middle brother, all grown up. Grinning, their arms over each other's shoulders. Yowsa. All three of them had turned out fiendishly good-looking. What were the odds of that? She wondered where the fourth brother was. There was a formal engagement portrait, too, the middle brother with the long hair, gazing adoringly down into the face of a pretty dark-haired girl. How romantic.

Margot took a swallow of her wine and indulged in a sharp pang of envy. She had no brothers or sisters to hang pictures of. Her father had been out of the picture most of her life, and thank God for it. Mom had been great, a tough, funny, salty old bird, but she was long gone. The few precious pictures she had of Mom were lost in the void. She hadn't dared to go back to her place to collect her things after what happened.

What became of the stuff in a rented house if a tenant disappeared without a trace? She had no relatives to claim it. Did the city do something with it? Or did her landlord just shove it all into garbage bags and call the Salvation Army?

Just one more of the many questions that tormented her at night.

Oh, well. Wanting to be part of a family wasn't a weakness of character. Being sick with jealousy over other people's families definitely was, though. She tried to jostle herself out of it. Poor, pitiful Margot. So sad to be all alone in the world. Yeah, yeah. OK, that was enough. The pity party was over. Everybody out of the pool. She had stuff to do.

"Hors d'oeuvres are ready," Davy called.

Her stomach rumbled at the concept, and she headed back into the kitchen to check them out. Mikey was in doggie heaven. He'd already choffed down his dinner, and was getting chunks of raw beef dropped into his mouth for dessert, the little stinker.

"Fresh baguette, olive paste, herbed goat cheese and sundried tomatoes from the Italian deli," Davy said. "Help yourself."

Margot stared down at the colorful spread of tempting

food on the kitchen bar. "Good God. You call this hors d'oeuvres? This is a full meal!"

"Not by a long shot." He dropped another shred of beef fat into Mikey's waiting mouth, provoking a frenzy of wagging and squirming. "The full meal comes after. This will barely warm you up. Besides, you taught Ifs, Abs and Butts today. You can afford to splurge."

Margot's mouth twitched. "Dumb name, huh?"

The deep dimples that bracketed his mouth were so gorgeous when that swift grin flashed out. "Memorable," he said.

Margot rubbed her bottom ruefully. "Believe me, it is. It's a killer."

His eyes traveled the whole length of her body with obvious approval. "If that's how you get that panther woman body, I'm all for it."

She stared at him, startled. "Panther woman?"

His eyes slid away from hers, embarrassed. "Just something about the way you walk. You're so graceful. You know, like a female panther on the prowl. Sinuous and gorgeous. Dangerous."

She felt herself going warm and soft inside, like a whole body blush. "Dangerous? Me?" She tried to laugh. "I wish. Panther woman. Gosh, I like it. You know just how to flatter the socks right off a girl."

"It's not flattery. I wouldn't say it if it weren't true."

She slashed at the air with mock claw hands. "Here comes Panther Woman," she hissed. "She's hungry, too, so watch out. She'll chomp you in one gulp."

The gleam in his eyes turned thoughtful. "I had a dream about your Panther Woman persona last night."

She bit her lip, apprehensive. "Do I want to know what it was about?"

"I don't know," he said calmly. "Do you?"

"Is it sexual in nature?"

"Yes," he admitted.

She weighed caution against curiosity, and caution won. "Then don't tell me."

"Fine. Whatever. Try one of these." He smeared a chunk of crunchy, olive-oiled baguette with goat cheese, laid two gleaming sun dried tomatoes on top, put a napkin under it and presented it to her. "This is for your poor tired butt."

"My butt thanks you," she said demurely. She took a bite, and the intensity of the flavors almost made her moan. She chewed blissfully.

The itch of curiosity got steadily sharper. "Oh, I give up," she snapped. "Tell me your dream. You dirty tease."

His grin was triumphant. "You were a dominatrix. Playing bondage games with me. Ropes, chains, showing me who was boss."

Of all things, that was the last one she expected. She was rooted in place, oil dripping down her arm. Could he have tuned in to the sexual fantasy she'd had last night? She felt transparent and scared.

"Holy cow. How did you . . . is that what you're into?"

He caught the oil drip with a napkin, and sponged it off before it got to her elbow. "No," he said. "I like control. Maybe you've noticed."

"Uh, yeah," she admitted. "It's kind of hard to miss."

"Weird, though." He shrugged. "It worked for me in the dream. I woke up with—oh, well, never mind. Do you like corn on the cob?"

She embraced the change of subject with relief. "Who doesn't? Can I husk it for you?"

"Yeah. The water's boiling. Crisper on the right. Do four for me and as many as you think you can eat. They're really good."

His refrigerator was well stocked, which was no surprise. A body like his had to run on a whole lot of really high-quality fuel. The husks she peeled revealed translucent white kernels set on the cobs like creamy pearls. Water bubbled, mushrooms sizzled, the garlic and shallots in the marinade tickled her nose. Davy McCloud's big, well-appointed kitchen was the most seductive place she'd ever seen.

Probably just because Davy was running it, though.

She dumped the corn into the boiling water and gave the olive paste a try. Fabulous. She mixed it with the goat cheese. Even better. She chewed slowly, savoring the sight of him slicing red onions. Men always looked sexy when they cooked, and Davy was outrageously sexy to begin with. The combined effect was way over the top. He tossed the onion slices into a pan, where they began to sizzle.

"Just look at the guy," she complained. "Give me a break. He chops onions and his eyes don't even water. What are you, anyhow, freaking Superman?"

The grin that lit up his face took her breath away. It was like a ray of light flashing out of him. "Let's throw those steaks on the grill."

They carried platters of gorgeous food to the table on his porch while the steaks grilled, after which they loaded up their plates and set to it. Mikey had relaxed, too. He was sprawled under the table, fast asleep, belly distended, twitching with happy doggie dreams.

She'd almost forgotten what such civilized pleasures felt like. Dining al fresco, sipping fine wine, eating great food, enjoying a soft breeze off the water. To say nothing of the stunning scenery across the table, dressed in jeans and a loose white linen shirt that showed off a tantalizing glimpse of chest muscles. The man was insanely gorgeous.

Delicious, after months of scrimping and scrambling to stay alive.

Dinner was amazing. The steaks were tender, heaped with sweet fried onions and browned mushrooms. The corn exploded in her mouth, sweet and dripping with real butter. The potatoes were aromatic with crushed rosemary. The frilly salad greens gleamed with Tuscan olive oil.

He leaned across the table to refill her wineglass when she finally began to slow down. "We need to talk about—"

"How to proceed, yes," she cut in. "I've been meaning to talk to you about that, Davy. I've told you several times that I can't afford this, and every time you shine me on. I just got fired today, my rent is late, I'm full of bills, and you're out there racking up expenses with wild abandon. Like that cleaning service. And the lab. You've got to stop."

Since you'll never see me again after tonight anyhow. The doleful thought weighed on her more heavily every second that passed.

He took a deliberate sip of his wine, eyeing her over the rim of his glass. "First off, the crime lab is no charge. A friend did the tests for me for free. Second, the cleaning service is my housewarming present to you, welcome to the neighborhood and all that."

"No way." She was already shaking her head. "I can't let you do that. There's a lot you don't know."

"I know about your fake identity, Margot."

That stopped the words right in her throat. "How . . ." She swallowed, licked her lips. "How the hell do you know about that?"

He gave her a no-big-deal shrug. "It's my trade. Did you think I wouldn't check? I've known since the day that Tilda introduced us."

She put her wine down before it could slip out of her numb fingers. "Actually, in the normal world, men don't do background checks on women before they've even exchanged phone numbers."

Davy lazily speared a chunk of crisp golden potato off the serving platter, chewed and swallowed it. "What's normal?" he asked lightly. "Besides, it depends on the man's level of interest."

She folded her arms over herself, regretting the snug tank top she'd worn. It made her feel naked and vulnerable. "I think it depends more on the man's level of paranoia," she said.

"Paranoia and common sense caution look similar, depending on your point of view. In any case, your ID is amateur crap. No depth to it at all. Whoever put it together for you should be put out of business."

She felt almost offended on behalf of her poor crappy ID. "It was all I could afford," she snapped. "Just how far do you feel justified in snooping into my life? What else do you know about me?"

"Not as much as I want to. Let me finish, Margot."

The steely note in his voice punctured the bubble of her nervous anger. Davy stared into his plate, brow furrowed, as if he were choosing his words, one by one. A prickle went up her spine.

Maybe she was about to find out why she shouldn't have relaxed.

"I'm not going to pressure you about your past," Davy said. "What I've done till now, consider a gift. And what I plan from here on out, I'd like to propose . . . an arrangement."

Her nervous prickle intensified, and she wished she'd passed on the wine. "What kind of arrangement are you talking about?"

"First, I want to be real clear with you. I don't want any misunderstandings. I know what I have to offer a woman, and what I don't have. I want to lay it out, all up front. No bullshit of any kind."

"Oh, my God." Margot put her hands up over her cheeks and found them feverishly hot. "Wait, wait. Are we talking about sex? How did we get onto sex without me noticing? I didn't see any road signs."

"Please let me finish."

Her heart pounded. She pressed her hand over her mouth.

"You're a beautiful woman," he said. "I've admired you ever since the day I met you. I'm fascinated by you. I want to go to bed with you."

She looked out at the water, at the salad, at the half-empty wine bottle, anywhere but his eyes. It sounded so . . . bald, put like that.

"Oh," she whispered. "I, uh, see."

"You said last night that you don't have the time or energy for a boyfriend. You also said you don't do no-strings sex. I'm in the same situation. I don't like anonymous sexual encounters, but I'm not interested in commitment or marriage, either. With anyone, so don't take it personally. I value my private time and space and privacy. But I am interested in having an affair with you."

"I see." She couldn't drag in enough breath to fill her lungs.

"You need protection from this stalker," he went on. "You would need it whether you went to the police or not. I would like to help you solve this problem. It would give me a great deal of personal satisfaction to turn this asshole who's bothering you into a grease spot on the road."

"Uh, thank you." She felt like she should say something intelligent at this point, express some opinion, but her mind was completely blank of intelligent opinions. All the available space was occupied by the mind-blowing concept of an affair with Davy McCloud.

"I would be glad to help you out with your financial difficulties," he said. "I'm not rich, but I don't have money problems."

"And in return, I have sex with you?" Margot blurted.

Davy let out a slow breath. She sensed that he was gathering his patience. "In return, we enjoy a mutually satisfying affair," he said carefully. "With no illusions about the future."

She wished she could be cool and detached, like him, but she'd never been able to be nonchalant about sex, no matter how she tried. Confusion and fear churned together inside her. "Why don't you just call a classy escort service? It would be less trouble for you," she said.

The swift flash of anger in his eyes was quickly hidden behind his usual cool self-control. "The idea doesn't turn me on. You do."

"Oh. Thanks, I guess," she whispered.

He picked up his wine and swirled the liquid around the glass. "Just think about my offer. I make it very respectfully."

"Sex without commitment is not respectful," she said.

His eyebrows lifted. "Depends on how one goes about it."

A gust of wind off the lake lifted her hair, and made her shiver. "You're so cool," she whispered. "And I'm so not. I don't know how to be. Not in any sense of the word. I try, but I just can't manage it."

"I know you're not. That's why I want you. I never said I wanted the sex to be cool."

She felt it with an awareness that went beyond her senses; a force blazing out of him that rocked her backwards. A swirl of erotic images went through her mind and her tingling body; naked with Davy McCloud, kissing him, touching him, clutching his big body as he pinned her down, moving inside her. He would be dominant in bed, like he was dominant in everything. He exuded it from every pore.

She didn't go for that, as a rule. She made a point of picking out guys who were unthreatening. Dominant, macho guys weren't her thing, never had been. Too much conflict. Nothing but trouble.

In fact, this was a scenario that would normally have provoked a sense of suffocated panic, swiftly followed by the urge to make a lame excuse and flee like a bunny before things went any further.

The feeling that raced through her now was panic of a very different kind. A flush of heat that swept across her skin, tingling and burning. A clenching, low and tight in her body around a glow of bright awareness, like something waking up inside her, an animal hunger that she didn't even recognize as her own. It pulsed hot and soft in her chest, quivered in her throat, behind her eyes. Tingling in her hands.

Sexual energy pulsed off him in waves, in spite of the cool calculation in his eyes. He was probably imagining the same scene as she; he being the lord of the manor, running the show, taking what he pleased while she writhed and whimpered, in his thrall. Desperate for it.

Her chair flew over backwards and crashed to the porch floor as she sprang to her feet. She avoided meeting his eyes as she picked it up.

She wanted to run, and she wanted him to stop her. He could probably read it in her face, that his twisted offer excited her as much as it shamed her. She turned to lean on the porch railing, lifting her hot face to cool it in the breeze off the lake.

Her classic tendency to get involved with guys who wanted to use her was rearing its ugly head at the worst possible time.

But at least Davy McCloud was honest about wanting to use her, her inner devil slut whispered. No sweet lying promises from him. He just opened his mouth and let the hard truth drop out.

She loved that about him, even when she hated him for it. And he was offering to let her use him, too. No small thing, considering.

Damn him. Damn this whole kinky situation. And damn her for being desperate and screwed up and turned on enough to actually . . .

Consider it.

She felt his warm presence looming behind her. "I didn't mean to upset you." His voice was low and tentative.

"I'm not upset," she lied. "It's just . . . problematic, that's all."

He hesitated. "On the contrary. I'm trying to simplify things."

She shook her head. "You really don't get it, do you? It's simpler for you, but not for me. All the simplicity for you is at my expense."

He leaned on the railing next to her. "I don't follow you. How do you figure?"

She slanted him a quick, impatient look. "Because you're a man! Duh! Because you would have the upper hand from the very start. The power dynamic would be screwy. You might feel entitled to demand sex when I don't feel like it. Or to do things I'm not comfortable with. Or—"

"Not a problem."

She glared at him. "Oh, yeah? And how would you know what is or isn't a problem for me? Are you psychic, or all-knowing?"

"No." He touched the back of her neck, winding a lock of hair around his fingertip. The glancing touch sent pleasure rippling down her back. "It's just that my pleasure has everything to do with yours." He leaned down and pressed his lips against the back of her neck.

She almost sank to her knees, they went so soft. She gripped the porch railing. "Davy. God," she whispered. "Don't do this to me."

His breath fanned across her shoulder. "That's what I'm hungry for, Margot. Your pleasure. I would never do anything to hurt you or make you feel bad. Believe me. It's not my thing."

The words, the images, the rich, dark tone of his voice, all brushed over her like the tender touch of sable, or silk.

"Look at me, Margot," he said quietly.

She did. The controlled hunger in his eyes made her want to grab onto him and cling like a vine, tight enough to cut off his blood supply.

Wow. A shortcut to self-loathing if there ever was one.

She pulled away. It took everything she had.

The devil slut on her shoulder practically howled in frustration. Why she was being so difficult and contrary? For God's sake, a sexy, appealing solution to her problem was presenting itself to her on a silver platter, and she wanted the comfort and distraction of his touch so badly, and he was so freaking gorgeous and yummy, offering to protect her from Snakey, too, and what was she, *nuts*?

Get it while you can, the old song said. Good advice, but the song was talking about love, and Davy McCloud didn't want love. Wasn't in the market for it. Would not welcome it. That gave him the ultimate upper hand, even without his charisma overload, or his killer muscles.

And it gave her diddly squat. She was a mess. Crushed out and dizzy, more than half in love with him already. His strong, silent and mysterious routine made her totally wet. And he was just a guy, after all, which meant that he was capable of messing with her head without even meaning to, and never having a clue as to what he'd done, or how.

Most important, Davy had no idea how deep the trouble she was in actually was. If he found out, as he inevitably would, he wouldn't want to touch her with a ten-foot pole. No man in his right mind would.

She was the kiss of death, and she would hate to see the expression in his eyes change forever when he realized it. The very thought made her want to burst out crying.

She stepped away from him. "No," she said, her voice resolute.

His hand slowly dropped from her hair. He said nothing, but his eyes and the heavy quality of his silence demanded an explanation.

She struggled to put her incoherent reasoning into words, at least the part she could share with him. "I can't afford this," she blurted. "I'm wrecked. A strong wind would blow me away. I can't handle you, too, on top of everything else, Davy. You're too much. You're over the top."

"You're very strong." He did that trick with his voice again, sending delicious shivers over her neck, down her back, right into her lower body. "That's one of the many things that turn me on about you."

She turned away, and leaned her hot face against her folded arms. "You don't know me, Davy. You're just projecting what you want to see. Because believe me, I don't feel strong right now. Not one bit."

"I feel it, even if you don't." His low voice vibrated with intensity. "You have so much power burning inside you. It lights you up. My gorgeous panther woman."

She pressed her face harder against her arms. It had gone hot and red again. "Oh, please," she muttered. "Don't be ridiculous."

The evil, manipulative bastard. There was nothing that he could have said that she more desperately wanted to believe. The whole setup might have been specifically designed to test all her secret weaknesses. Seductive, muscle-bound stud offers to protect her from scary bad guy. In return, he wants only the privilege of driving her wild with erotic pleasure all night long. Whoo-hoo. The guy drove a hard bargain.

She broke into a sweat just thinking about it.

She had to hit the road quick, before she started behaving irresponsibly. "Thanks for dinner," she said. "And thanks for helping me out today. I won't thank you for the indecent proposal, but . . . thanks for not putting the moves on me, at least."

He shrugged. "No is no."

"Hmm. Admirable sentiment. I appreciate your restraint." *Almost as much as I regret it*, her devil slut added in sulky tones.

"It's taking years off my life."

"Oh yeah?" she asked suspiciously. "You're suffering? Really?"

"The torments of hell." His voice was solemn.

She studied his calm profile. "You look as cool as an ice cube."

"It's a clever ruse to mask the seething volcano of my

crazed lust," he said. "To lure you into letting down your guard and reconsidering."

That slow, sexy smile of his made her resolve waver. He was so outrageously cute when his dimples flashed like that. "It's not so smart to give me advance warning about your seething volcano of crazed lust."

"I try to give my victims a sporting chance. It's only fair."

The sexy charm rolling off him was deadly dangerous. "I have to go," she said. "I'm sorry to leave you with all the dinner dishes, but I—"

"Don't." His dimples vanished. "You're not safe there alone."

No arguing with that, but hey, she wasn't safe anywhere. She tried to smile, but the effort was hollow. "I'll be fine."

"Stay here," he said. "Sleep in one of the spare bedrooms. There's plenty of space. I won't come on to you. You'll be safe. I swear to you."

She rolled her eyes. "Yeah. Right."

"What are you implying? That I would force myself on you?"

She laughed at the outrage on his face. "Don't get huffy and self-righteous on me, big guy. You're on shaky ground after your kinky kept-woman proposal. And it's not you I'm worried about anyhow, it's me."

He looked baffled. "What the hell is that supposed to mean?"

"You're not the only one who has to resist temptation," she said. "Some of us poor mortals don't have a lot of iron-clad self-control. Some of us have to use other techniques to make ourselves behave properly. I can't stay in your house. You're way too sexy. My head would explode."

He made a frustrated sound. "That's the most convoluted bullshit I ever heard. For God's sake, if you want me, take me! Here I am!"

She scooped up Mikey, who whimpered in protest at

being woken from his nap. "Sorry. I already explained. Don't make it harder for me."

He slammed his hand hard on the table. The plates and serving dishes jumped and rattled. "Why do women have to be so fucking complicated?" he roared. "Things could be so simple, and women deliberately make them complicated! I do not get it! I will never get it!"

Davy McCloud angry was scarier than she'd bargained for. The controlled volcanic heat seething in his eyes backed her up till she hit the screen door. She fumbled behind her for the latch. "I can't really help you with that one," she babbled. "Have a good night. Try to chill." She grabbed her purse as she scurried through the house, and sniffed back a wave of wistful, nervous tears as she got into her car.

Making Davy lose his temper was by no means as satisfying as she'd thought. Aside from being unnerving, it was a whole lot more fun to make him smile. It would have been fabulous to make him laugh.

Her throat tightened dangerously at the thought.

This wasn't how she'd wanted to say goodbye to him. Not after he'd been so sweet and protective. She'd hoped for a poignant, tender moment that she could take out and mull over for comfort in the tough times to come. Hah. Not. Her life never followed the script.

A farewell kiss would have been nice, too, but the way she was feeling right now, a kiss would've sealed her fate in a heartbeat. She would have ended up sweaty and naked with him in nothing flat.

Her car was finally coughing reluctantly to life when Davy marched out, slamming the front door closed. He strode over and rapped on her window. She rolled it down, stomach fluttering.

"I'm escorting you home to make sure your place is secure."

The stony tone in his voice allowed no room for argument. She gazed at him in blank dismay. Going back to the house was a waste both of her time and her precious gas, and besides, Snakey might be lying in wait for her there. "Davy, please," she began. "You can't—"

"Don't even bother," he growled. "I'm in a shitty mood."

She let out a sigh and waited for him to start up his truck.

She sped through the dark streets, conscious of Davy's headlights behind her. She could feel his anger and frustration pressing against her from behind, like a gale force wind. There was a knock under the hood now, too. Lovely. Car trouble would be the finishing touch.

She had no idea what she was going to do if Davy insisted on coming into her house. If he saw that her stuff was gone, the cat would be out of the bag. She didn't want to have that conversation with him.

She just didn't have the strength.

She forced herself to concentrate on her driving. Mikey stuck his head out the half-open window, tongue flapping in the breeze, not a care in the world. Lucky him. A full belly, a nap, and his cup was full.

What a drag. All the problems of having a bossy, possessive boyfriend, but none of the perks. She almost wished he had put the pressure on her. It would have been the perfect excuse to tumble into his bed—oopsy daisy, he was just so strong and masterful, and she was swept away by his studly mojo, twitter tweet and what's a girl to *do?*

No such luck. He had to be noble and righteous about it. Gah.

She parked on the street, the better for a quick getaway. Davy pulled into her driveway, deep in the pool of shadows formed by the overgrown bushes. He got out and waited in the pool of light from the streetlamp, muscular arms folded pugnaciously over his chest, jaw set in that stubborn way that she was already wary of. Poised to give her a hard time. She left Mikey in the car and got out. Showdown time.

It had started to rain. Her eyes locked with his, and behind the anger and frustration, she saw something indefinable in their depths, something that made her ache with longing. "It's, uh, raining," she said inanely. "I should go inside. You go on home. Good night, Davy."

Light and shadow shifted on the sculpted planes of his face as he nodded. "Just let me come in and check the place out."

"No. I can't let you come in," she said. "I . . . you're too intense."

"I can't help it," he said. "Not when it comes to you."

They stared at each other, neither one willing to let the moment go. It occurred to her that Snakey could be watching the whole tableau, just biding his time. She shivered. "You have to go," she repeated.

"I'll just camp out here," he said. "Stake out your house."

She shook her head frantically. "No. You can't."

"Yeah?" His eyes gleamed with irony. "How do you propose to stop me? Gonna call the cops? Be my guest. Use my cell phone."

"That's not fair!" She shoved at his chest. "Don't jerk me around!"

His body didn't yield an inch. It was as if he were rooted to the ground. "You're the one who's not being fair," he said. "You're putting me in an impossible position, you know that?"

The scant drops of rain got heavier, pattering down on her bare shoulders. "You put yourself into this position with no help from me."

He closed his eyes. The muscles in his jaw were rigid. "Christ, what a mess," he muttered. "Come sit in my truck for a few minutes, Margot. Just talk to me. I hate leaving you alone here with Snakey running around loose. Just fucking *hate* it."

It was a bad idea, in every way, but she couldn't resist an-

other shot at a tender moment with him to suit her fantasy
farewell script.

Just a few more minutes of basking in his warmth, and
she would be ready for her mad, empty dash into the unknown.

"OK," she whispered.

Chapter
10

Davy opened the door for her and boosted her up into the cab of his truck. He'd tried being a charming gentleman, he'd tried humor and reason and gallantry, he'd tried coercion, bullying, intimidation.

It was time to try sex.

He got in the driver's side and folded up the console. She sat there in the dark, tongue-tied and nervous. As well she should be. She wasn't stupid. Stubborn, contrary and irrational, but not stupid.

He wanted to just start up the truck and take her home, but that kind of high-handed move never worked. Fleur had taught him that it was impossible to force a person to accept help, no matter how good one's intentions. Everybody had to go to hell in her own special way. The trick was to detach, not get caught up in the drama.

He couldn't do it this time. Just couldn't swallow it. It wouldn't go down. He reached out across the seat and took her hand. "Go get Mikey and your toothbrush and nightie, and come on home with me. Please."

She tugged her hand, but he refused to release it. "It's not so simple," she murmured.

"It's exactly that simple. I would never hurt you."

"It's not what you do, it's the way you make me feel that's the problem. And besides, you're not thinking this through. Moving a woman into your house is no way to protect your personal space. Particularly not a woman like me. I'm not the meek, quiet mouse type, in case you haven't noticed. I get in the way. I take up space."

"Yes, I have noticed that," he admitted.

"So? If you want to keep your life uncomplicated, this isn't the way to do it."

"That's not important right now," he protested. "You're in danger, Margot. These are emergency measures."

She didn't reply for a long moment. "I don't want to be some guy's emergency measure," she said, her voice full of soft bitterness.

Great. His first fuck-up. Already he had to work his way back up to zero. He reached to touch her cheek. She jerked her face away, but not before he felt hot moisture trickling over her soft skin.

He stifled a groan. "Oh, Christ, no," he muttered. "Margot, please. Comforting crying women is not my specialty."

She yanked her hand out of his grip. "I didn't ask for your goddamn comfort, so get that freaked-out look off your face. Jerk."

"It's pitch dark. How do you know what look is on my face?"

"Just don't get smart with me," she said huffily.

Whatever he said came out wrong. Time to shut his big mouth and use his God-given talents. He reached out for her.

"Huh? Hey! What do you think you're doing?" She struggled frantically as he scooped her up and pulled her onto his lap.

"Holding you." His voice was grim and determined.

"You can't!" She flailed in his arms. "Your motives aren't pure!"

"Fuck my motives." He settled her head under his chin and hung on. "Just shut up for a minute and see if you can remember what it feels like to trust someone. Just try it."

His words startled her into silence. She hid her face against his shoulder. Her hot, damp tears soaked through his thin linen shirt.

He tightened his arms around her and buried his nose in her hair. Flowers and fruit, warmed by the sensual heat of her skin, the salt of her sweat. He slid his hand down her spine. The pressure of her luscious ass against his crotch made his erection tingle and throb. He forced his attention away from it. He was good at delaying gratification.

At least, he'd been good at it until he met Margot.

She pried herself away from his chest and braced her hands against his shoulders, looking down into his face like she was trying to read him in the dark. Something had softened inside her.

She needed comfort. Great. He was ready with it, and ready to plunder all that sexy female sweetness for himself in return. Not just her body, either. The unformed, unfamiliar thought was hard to pin down; just an incoherent longing to get inside her head and wander around the alien landscape of her female world. Full of beauties and mysterious dangers and hidden mysteries. The great unknown.

He wanted to know her. Not just circle around her perimeter, baffled and cautious, using blind guesswork, hoping not to fuck it up. And in the end, always wondering why he'd bothered in the first place.

Being good in bed was one thing. That had never been a problem. Understanding what was in a woman's head was another thing entirely. Women were incomprehensible, for the most part.

He'd never been so intensely motivated to comprehend one before.

Margot put her hands on either side of his face and touched him gently, the bones of his jaw, the lines around his mouth, his forehead, his lips. She rubbed the back of her hand over his beard stubble. He wished he'd thought to shave this afternoon.

"How am I supposed to trust you, Davy?" Her quiet, whispered words sounded almost like she was talking to herself.

He slid his hands into her tangled hair. "Why shouldn't you?"

"You want into my pants," she said simply. "Everything a man says or does under those circumstances is suspect."

He ran his fingertips over her face, trying to feel her expression in the dark. "What does me wanting sex with you have to do with trust?"

She laughed, and leaned her forehead lightly against his. Her hair tickled his cheekbones. "Your world is so simple, Davy. So reductive. Nothing is connected to anything else."

"I don't see why having a hard-on makes me untrustworthy," he protested. "We're talking about an involuntary physical response to a very beautiful woman. That's pretty harsh, if you think about it."

She shook with silent laughter again. "Yeah. Harsh. That's me, Davy. Never say I didn't warn you." She leaned down and touched her lips to his, a featherlight question mark of a kiss.

It made his whole face tingle. He jerked her closer, wound his fingers into her hair and kissed her back, like he'd been burning to do since this morning. Her mouth opened to him, ardent and yielding.

He slid his hand under her tank top, trailing his fingers across her warm, silky belly as he delicately explored her mouth.

She pulled away from his kiss, and yanked her shirt up over her bra. "Oh, go for it. Knock yourself out," she said. "I know you want to."'

He gaped at her. "Huh? I just—"

"Don't even try to be sneaky with me, buddy. You think I'm not going to notice if you try to cop a feel? Hah!"

Her attempt at bravado made him laugh, but the laughter came from a shaky place that made him feel almost as if he were going to cry.

He hadn't done that since Kevin died. Didn't want to do it tonight.

"Would you rather I just pounce?" he asked. "No slick lead-in?"

"This twisted push-me-pull-you seduction routine you've been running on me for the last two days is as much lead-in as I can take."

"OK," he said meekly. "Anything you want." He punctuated his statement by snapping open the front clasp of her bra.

When the garment fell away, her mood shifted. Her prickly, in-your-face attitude sharpened into caution. She wasn't as brash as she tried to appear. He had to be careful. Go slow, and delicately.

He stared down at the gleaming contours of her beautiful breasts, barely visible in the glow of city light that sifted through the bushes, and touched her reverently with his finger-tips. She shivered, but she didn't pull away, despite the tension that made her breath go short and shallow. His fingers stroked, explored, worshipped the full, plump curves, the tight nipples. "It's true," he told her.

"What's true?" Her voice vibrated with tension and uncertainty.

"God exists," he said. "I was withholding judgment. But as of this moment, my doubts have been permanently laid to rest."

She dissolved into nervous giggles. "Oh, please. A pair of bare naked ta-tas is all it takes to convince you? There's three billion women on this planet, so let's call that six billion ta-tas bouncing around, and a lot of them are more memorable than mine. So don't go basing your personal theology on my bra size. It's too much responsibility for my poor boobs. What'll you do when they start to sag? Change religion?"

"Time has no meaning in the face of divine perfection," he said.

She giggled harder. "You're nuts."

Her laughter encouraged him. "But these aren't just any ta-tas," he protested. He slid down and maneuvered her so his face was at her chest level. "I'm talking about Margot Vetter's gorgeous, luscious ta-tas."

"But I—oh . . ." Her words trailed off as he pressed his face to the warm, scented valley between her breasts.

The raw immediacy of every sensation shook him. He had no experience with this kind of feeling, like a filter had been ripped out of his head, and left him naked and trembling at every point of contact with her tender skin. He rubbed her tight, puckered nipples against his hot cheeks, pulled them tenderly into his mouth, grazed them with his teeth. Then swirled in wider circles with his tongue.

Her taste was intoxicating. It drove him out of his mind.

Her arms crept up to circle his neck, cradling him. He was humbled by her trust. He wanted to make up for all the fear she was trying to hide, to lavish her with pleasure.

He wanted to deserve what he would take from her in return.

Every shiver and moan was his reward and his prize. Gone was all his calculating skill, and his bag of sexual tricks. He forgot that they existed and lost himself in her. He wanted more than he'd ever even known there was to want from a woman. Layer after layer of surrender and revelation. A flower unfolding, all her tenderness and trust, all that soft abundance, that power and sinewy strength. His panther woman.

He popped open the buttons of her jeans and slid them down over her ass. Skimpy lace thong panties covered warm, silken flesh.

Her sea and flower-scented female musk made his ears roar. He couldn't tell if the soft sounds she made were approval or protest, and he couldn't stop, in any case. He wanted to make her come. Needed it.

His fingertips circled tenderly over the top of the warm crevice of her labia, and each teasing touch jerked a breathy gasp from her, like shocked surprise. "Davy," she whispered. "This . . . this is crazy."

"Tell me if you want me to stop." He covered her trembling mouth with his own as he said it, drinking in the broken sounds and making sure they didn't have a chance in hell of becoming coherent words. Her jeans were halfway down her thighs, trapping her legs together. He slid his fingers into her panties, teased his way through the warm, humid nest of soft ringlets that hid her soft cleft until his fingers found slick, tender folds. Hot and wet and yielding. She was ready for him.

She squirmed and whimpered at the slow, insistent invasion, grabbing his hand and pushing it harder against herself. "You bastard," she whispered. "You planned this all along, didn't you?"

"You should've known better than to get into the truck with me and my untrustworthy hard-on," he told her.

Reluctant laughter vibrated her body. The muscles in her tight pussy clung to his finger as he thrust it deeper. Her trembling thighs clenched around his hand, and he slid his tongue into her mouth as he circled his thumb around her tight, swollen clit.

He followed every tiny cue she gave him with her jerking hips, her hitching breath, the clutching of her cunt around his hand, and established a slow, tender thrusting rhythm with his hand. With her legs together, he couldn't slide his hand deep enough to catch the hot spot deeper inside. He wanted to spread her wide. Get her on all fours, penetrate her completely. He kissed his way across her face, to her ear. "Will you let me get those jeans off you?"

She tried to respond, but the words broke up, incoherent.

"I want to slide my tongue into you," he whispered. He pulled her earlobe into his mouth, tongued and bit it delicately. "I want to lick up all your sweet juice. Please, Margot. Let me do that."

"No," she gasped out. "Not now. Just . . . harder. Right there. Now, damn it. Yes. Oh God—deeper. Please . . . oh, Davy . . ."

She shoved down on his hand, her fingernails digging into his wrists, her sleek body tightening around him. With every slick thrust of his finger, he imagined how it would feel when it was his cock plunging and sliding inside her. Her legs clenched around him, her nails dug into his back. She was so hot, so responsive. Burning with sexual energy.

She cried out, jerking and throbbing around his hand. The torrential rush that went through her body was so strong, she almost pulled him after her.

Margot lay in his lap, afraid to move. The slightest shift in her weight sent sweet jolts of sensation through her overstimulated body.

He was so good. It was almost scary, like . . . mind control, or something, and all he'd done was pet her. She was in bad trouble.

She didn't want just a poignant goodbye kiss. She wanted goodbye sex. Hot, wild, grinding sex that lasted for hours. No way could she drive off into the dark without knowing how it would be to do the wild thing with Davy McCloud. She would never sleep again.

She clenched around him as he slowly withdrew his hand from between her legs.

"Don't worry, I'll put it back whenever you want. I just had to know how you tasted." He lifted his hand to his face and licked his fingers. "Sweet and juicy," he murmured, his voice husky. "I want to put my head between your legs and never come up for air."

She avoided responding by fishing around awkwardly for the ends of her bra. She struggled to refasten it over her breasts. They seemed bigger, swollen and hot and sensitive, abraded by his beard stubble. She finally managed to yank her tank top down. She took a deep breath and forced herself to say it. "Do you, ah, want to make love to me?"

The quavery, high-pitched sound of her voice embarrassed her, and she hated that she'd used the word "love." She should've asked if he wanted to have sex. Do the nasty. Even fuck. None of these more accurate terms would come out of her mouth. She felt too vulnerable tonight for words with such a harsh edge of reality. She was such a sentimental, girly, romantic wuss. She never learned. Never.

He stroked the tops of her naked thighs. "You'll come back to my place with me?"

She shook her head. "No. I mean here. Now. In your truck. I would do it. If you . . . if you wanted me, I mean."

He laughed. "Of course I want you. Let's at least go into your—"

"No," she said hastily. "I don't like the way I feel in there."

He was silent for a long moment. Bad sign. She started feeling nervous, self-conscious. Ashamed for being so needy and desperate.

"Three things," he said finally. "One, I've got no condoms. You?"

Oh. Yeah. That. She'd lived like a nun for so long, she'd forgotten the ABC's of modern sex. She let out a disgusted sigh. "No."

"Two, Snakey's out there somewhere, and I'd rather have a couple of good locks between us and him, if we let down our guard that much. And three . . ." He brushed her hair off her cheek, a tender gesture that made her breath catch. "You said 'no' earlier this evening. You sounded like you meant it. I didn't mean to pressure you into having sex with me tonight. I just wanted you to know how great we could be together."

"You did. Oh, God, you did," she said fervently. "I'm destroyed."

"You were really pissed at me, for my kinky proposal. If we had sex now, you might get weird about it. Throw it back in my face the next time you get mad at me. Which is liable to be soon. I want to get this right." He paused for a moment, and added, "But I still think you should come home with me. That hasn't changed."

It's now or never, you goddamn tease, she wanted to shriek.

Here she was, a writhing chaos of lust, and he just sat there, holding her bare naked bottom right on top of his huge hard-on, talking about self-control. Trying to impress her. Dolt.

In any other circumstances, she would be impressed. She would be charmed, disarmed, all that good stuff. Just not tonight, poised on the edge of doom. She was losing out on what promised to be the most exciting experience of her life because Davy McCloud just had to be a righteous dude at all costs.

Something had to be done. This was not to be borne.

She scrambled off his lap and onto her own seat, yanking her jeans up over her bottom. He gasped, startled, as she reached out to stroke the length of his erection. Mmm. Long and hard. Very nice.

Good. That was progress. Startling Davy McCloud was no mean feat. By the time she was done with him, he would be more than startled. She wrenched his belt buckle open, attacked his buttons.

By the time she was done with him, he would be dumbfounded.

"Margot." His voice was ragged. "Hey. Wait. You don't have to—"

"Would you please, please just shut up?" She shoved his jeans down. She slid her hand into his briefs until she got a grip on him.

Oh. Wow. He was very hard, hot and throbbing in her hand. Bigger than she'd fantasized, and her fantasies had been extravagant.

It had been a long time, and God knows she'd never dealt with a male member on this order of magnitude. But tonight, she felt inspired.

"Lift up your butt so I can slide your jeans down," she ordered.

He obediently lifted his hips. "Margot—"

"Go on, beg me to stop," she challenged him, jerking his jeans down to mid-thigh. "I dare you."

His burst of ironic laughter broke off into a shuddering groan as she seized his thick, hot shaft and stroked it. Thick and blunt and velvety hot, ridged with veins, she memorized it in the dark with her hands and wished she had more light to see him properly.

"Wow. You're aggressive," he said.

Something went cold inside her. "Does that turn you off?"

He covered her hands with his own, and closed them tightly around his throbbing member. "Do I feel turned off to you?"

"Uh, no," she admitted. "But guys are weird. Delicate creatures. You never know what will freak them out."

"I'm not a delicate creature." He dragged her clutching fists roughly up and down the length of his penis. "But I'm aggressive too, you know. Does that freak you out?"

"It would be awfully unfair of me if it did, wouldn't it?" she retorted. "I guess it just means we'd fight a lot in bed."

"I'm bigger," he said, his voice breathless and rough. He

rotated her hand around the swollen glans, spreading his pre-come until the thick bulb was slippery and wet. "I'd win."

"There are weapons other than brute strength, you over-grown galoot," she informed him loftily. "Big's not every-thing, you know."

"But big is good. You like big. Right?"

She laughed as she leaned over, inhaling the warm scent of him. "Don't be vain," she murmured. "It's unbecoming. Good Lord, Davy. I mean, really. This thing of yours is a lit-tle excessive, don't you think?"

"Sorry." The word strangled off into a sharp gasp as she milked him boldly. "It just . . . uh, grew that way."

She bent lower over his lap. "Oh, I'm not complaining." She gripped the thick root of him firmly in her fist and licked a salty drop of his pre-come off the tip, with a warm, lavish swipe of her tongue. She loved the tremors that racked him, his ragged gasps of pleasure.

She couldn't fit much of him into her mouth, but she wasn't discouraged. She just shimmied around on the seat, search-ing for a more comfortable position, and settled in to drive him out of his head, swirling her lips and tongue around the head of his penis while she stroked its entire length. Slow, deep and hard. She would teach him what aggressive was about. The man would never be the same again.

He gasped, clutching her head. Helpless, just like he had been in her barbarian queen fantasy. It was a wild turn-on to make a man as powerful and self-possessed as Davy McCloud was writhe under her caressing hands, her teasing mouth.

"Stop," he directed her. "Slow down, or I'll come right now. And I want more. I want this to last."

Hmm, not the words or tone of an abject love slave, but whatever. She was so turned on, she wasn't inclined to com-plain, and besides, she liked his self-control. It boded well for when he used that excellent thing of his to please her. If it fit at all, which was anyone's guess.

She was leaving tonight. Don't forget. This is it. No next time.

She shoved that painful thought angrily away. The cab of the truck was too cramped, too small. She wanted to flail around, she wanted to come again, she wanted to be naked with him inside her.

It wasn't fair, that this was all she got. It made her furious.

"Hey. Slow down," he warned her again. "Margot . . . oh, God—"

She ignored him this time, tightened her grip, deepened her strokes. Faster, harder. She ran this show, damn it. She said when.

He convulsed, and spurted his come into her mouth. Hot, pulsing spasms that went on and on. His fists were tangled in her hair, holding her fast against him as his pleasure coursed through him.

He leaned back against the seat, panting. Speechless.

Margot sat up slowly, and swallowed the hot, salty liquid. It burned in her throat, the raw, sharp male taste of sex that she only could bring herself to swallow when she was totally ga-ga in love—and about to get shafted, since the two things were inseparably linked.

She wiped her mouth. Better not to think about that.

Davy slid his pants up over his hips, tucked himself inside, buttoned up, buckled his belt. Little sounds sounded loud in the quiet darkness. He turned to look at her. She couldn't see his face, but she still couldn't bear his scrutiny. She felt as if she were slowly shrinking.

"Uh, Margot? You OK?" His voice was low, nervous and wary.

It was obvious, then. She couldn't hide the feelings crashing down on her. The fear and shame. The sickening anger.

She'd wanted such normal things out of life. Nothing fancy. Work she liked. Career challenges. Good friends, good times. To cuddle on the couch with a guy who thought she was special. And maybe, if she got super lucky, she could have the whole family cliché. Car seats littered with cookie crumbs. A stodgy minivan. Being part of something real and deep and sweet. Not shoved off to the side, forever out of bounds, looking in the window with big, sad, puppy dog eyes.

She'd tried so hard for it. Hoped so hard.

And what did she have? Mikey. A dingy little sublet. Snakey the Sicko Maniac. Grisly memories that wouldn't let her sleep. A crappy fake identity that wouldn't hold up to the most casual scrutiny. Low-paying, mind-numbing jobs that she couldn't even seem to hang on to. A beater car with a knock under the hood, perilously low on gas.

To add insult to injury, when she finally did find a man who rang all her bells, all he wanted was a convenient, undemanding bed partner that he could dismiss when he got bored. And she was so lonely and desperate, she was actually falling for it. She would attack a guy and give him a blow job in his truck because she was afraid to watch him drive away. She was pathetic. As much of a whore as he probably thought she was.

Self-loathing yawned wide inside her like a cold, aching wound. She opened the door, slid out.

"That ought to cover your costs up to now," she said.

She slammed the door shut and ran to the car to retrieve Mikey.

Chapter
11

It took all of three seconds for the top to blast off his fury and break his stunned paralysis.

He slammed out of the truck. Something had broken wide open inside him. He had no idea what he was going to do, nor did he give a shit. He caught up with her as she was jamming her key into the front door, and grabbed her around the waist from behind.

She squawked, and tried to twist away. "Davy, for God's sake—"

"Where the fuck did that come from?"

She tried to elbow him in the ribs, but he immobilized her arms. She flung her head back, her eyes panicked. "Let go of me!"

"No," he snarled. "Explain yourself. I did not deserve that!"

"Oh, no? After suggesting that I exchange sexual favors for goods and services, you get up on your high horse and—"

"Oh, Christ, I thought we were past that. And I never implied that I thought you were a prostitute!"

"OK. You're right, I'm wrong, I apologize. It was a snotty thing to say. I take it back. Now would you please stop squashing my rib cage?"

"You think a snide, half-assed apology like that makes it better? You tear down all my defenses, turn me into fucking mush, and then lob a grenade right in my face. I did not deserve that, Margot!"

She looked down, and her hair fell forward over her flushed face. "I said I was sorry," she said, more quietly. "I meant it."

"And I'm still mad," he said.

She wrestled herself around in the circle of his arms until she was facing him. "What would it take to make you not mad, damn it?"

He stared down at her trembling lips, at the lush press of her breasts against his chest in the low cut tank top. "Oh, I think maybe fucking you hard for about six hours would take the edge off."

She recoiled so violently, she broke his grip and stumbled back. "You pig! I'm not the only one who lobs grenades. Get out. Go!"

She shoved the door open, shooed Mikey in. She tried to slam the door in Davy's face, but he blocked it with his foot. "Wait," he said.

"For what? To get insulted again?" She kicked at his boot with the tip of her high-tops. "Get your enormous foot out of my house and get lost. Permanently. Asshole." Her voice shook with anger.

He leaned on the door and forced it open slowly against her weight. "Margot, don't. I shouldn't have said that."

She made a helpless, frustrated sound as he stepped into her house. He caught her in two steps, pulling her tight against his body, and pressed his lips against her neck. "I shouldn't have said that," he repeated. "I didn't mean to scare you."

"Then stop acting scary!" she yelled. "Let go of me!"

His arms tightened, involuntarily. "Forgive me first."

"Yeah, and what liberties does that entitle you to? Besides, you wouldn't forgive me when I apologized."

"Yours wasn't a real apology. It was bullshit. But I'll forgive you if you forgive me," he offered.

"Oh. So we're back to economic exchanges. I give you this, you give me that. Stop muscling me around, you big . . . stupid . . . *ape!*"

"Margot. Please. I'm bending over backwards here. If you—"

"No, you're bending me over frontwards, you oversexed moron. Stop it this instant." She batted at his arms, still locked around her. "OK, fine! I forgive you! Now let go of me! Now! I mean it, buddy."

He let his arms drop. He was irrationally afraid to let go, as if she would vanish into the dark if he dared to relax his grip. He flipped on the hall overhead light to chase the menacing shadows away.

He felt the change instantly. His photographic memory had stamped every detail of the place into his brain. Something was missing.

The flower fairy calendar. The nail it had hung on stuck out of the scarred wall, empty. He looked into her bedroom. The light spilling in from the hall revealed that her bedding was gone. Nothing was on the floor but her crumpled waitress uniform. He strode into the room and yanked open her closet. Empty. He pulled open her drawer. Nothing.

The rage that had just started to simmer down bubbled back up again. He turned to face her. "Going somewhere?"

Her face tightened miserably. "Davy—"

"Nice of you to say goodbye." The words felt bitter in his mouth.

She hugged her chest. "We've known each other for twenty-four hours," she said. "You're acting like you've got a say in my life."

"I know," he said. "I don't have any say. Believe me, I know that."

It was just like with Fleur, he realized, sickened. He'd fallen into the same fucking trap. Fleur had been dead set on destroying herself. Nothing could stop her from it. Certainly not him.

Fury was giving way to misery, a feeling so huge and dark, it horrified him. He'd built a fortress inside himself to guard against this feeling, and Margot Vetter blew it full of holes without even trying.

It was dragging him down. The awful futility of trying to save someone when there was no saving them. No point. No hope.

Stuck in three feet of snow, tires spinning while Dad roared useless instructions and Mom got paler and paler as the life drained out of her.

Oh, no. Not this. Not now. Please, not now.

His small, white hands clutching the wheel, stretching his foot out desperately to reach the clutch.

Blood all over the seat, the floor, the gearshift. Blood everywhere.

Oh, Christ, make it stop. It had been years, and now was not the time for it to start up again. He pressed his hands against his eyes until they hurt, red and black alternately pulsing in his inner vision, and deliberately replacing the stress flashback with emptiness.

Calm, blank, zero. The blinding white emptiness of the North Pole, the frigid black emptiness of outer space. Codes, numbers, logic.

Slowly, it eased down, and he started breathing again. His heart was still tripping over itself, his face damp and cold.

He let his hands drop, but he couldn't bear to open his eyes for a long moment. He felt exhausted. And ashamed. The woman had enough problems of her own. It wasn't fair to burden her with his demons, too.

"Forget about it," he said dully. "I'm sorry I scared you."

Her eyes were very big. "It's OK," she said cautiously. "I—"

"Don't." The word came out of him with a savage force that made her flinch. He put his hands up. "Please. I don't want to hear it. I'm gone. I won't bother you again. Good luck with . . . with whatever."

She was crying again, and it was his fault, but he had no comfort left to give. He walked past her without looking at her.

He saw it gleaming in the porch light as soon as he jerked the door open. It swung back and forth off the bottom of the clanking wind chimes. The golden snake pendant. Not his business, not his problem, but it was just too unexpectedly weird not to comment upon. He turned back.

"Did you put that snake thing out there on your wind chimes?"

Margot lunged at the door with a gasp. She stopped short, clutching the door frame for support. Her face went dead white.

Faris's blood buzzed with killing euphoria, and a good thing, too, because Pantani's dead weight was hard to handle. It took all Faris's considerable strength to heave, wrestle and fold the corpse into the smallish freezer. It was doable, though. Every bone in the man's body was shattered, which rendered him uniquely flexible, despite his bulk.

The trailing smear of blood that led to the freezer was seeded with hairs and carpet fibers from McCloud's house. The whiskey bottle and shot glasses with McCloud's prints on them were the perfect final touch.

Faris felt much better now. All the pent-up frustrations of the past months had gone into this. The frozen pizzas, ice cream bars, steaks and plastic baggies of various recreational drugs were all melting together into a soggy mess across the bloody kitchen floor.

His cell phone vibrated. Marcus. Faris peeled a hand out of the bloody plastic glove, his heart speeding. If Marcus knew what he was up to, he would be furious. No matter how careful Faris was, Marcus preferred to pilot his brother's kills personally. "Yes?" he responded.

"I have a new job for you," his brother said.

Tears of relief welled into Faris's eyes. Marcus wasn't calling to punish him this time. At least not yet. "I'm ready," he said.

"Driscoll's out of the picture now. Priscilla's got a new lab director. He's arriving in Seattle tonight. Are you paying attention?"

"Yes, yes," Faris assured him. "Tell me. I'll repeat it back to you."

"Good," Marcus murmured. "Very good, Faris."

Marcus explained what he needed. Faris recorded every word, just as he'd learned to do in the memory exercises they'd conducted when he was a little kid. Marcus had taught Faris how to expand his memory capacity. Marcus had used electric shocks when Faris was forgetful back in the old days, but Faris didn't need shocks to remember things now. He repeated every detail back to Marcus when he finished.

"You have to come home immediately," Marcus said afterwards. "We have to step up the pace. Priscilla is leaving this week, and she's anxious to see you back on your choke chain."

"Bitch," Faris muttered. "Why you won't let me just—"

"Because my plan is much more profitable." Marcus's voice was stern. "My plan is to destroy her and make hundreds of millions of dollars in the process. Think bigger, Faris. You're too focused."

Faris looked down at the blood-soaked rubber glove. He giggled. "I suppose. But I would love to make her bleed."

"Have you been making unauthorized kills for your own enjoyment, Faris?" Marcus's voice turned suspicious.

Faris shrank into his bulky plastic raincoat. Marcus always knew. Sometimes Faris lay awake at night wondering if Marcus was a mind reader. All knowing. Like Santa Claus.

Making his list and checking it twice, and Faris was always the naughty one. Always punished.

He dragged in a breath and held it inside himself to keep from whimpering, an old trick from when he was little. "I'm being careful."

"Careful's not good enugh," Marcus said. "I've been putting together this plan for years. Remember all the time and money that has gone into it when you go off on your selfish tangents."

Faris's killing euphoria drained away at the rebuke in Marcus's voice. "I'm sorry," he said, in a tiny little boy voice.

"So you should be. Speaking of sorry, have you made any progress with the Callahan woman?"

"I'm monitoring her," Faris said hastily. "I have a plan."

"You haven't even taken her yet?" Marcus's voice took on that soft tone that made Faris's bowels loosen. "Faris, you idiot. If we don't get that mold before Priscilla leaves, you know what will happen. Failure."

"Failure is unacceptable." Faris's voice was almost robotic.

"Get her tonight, either before or after you take care of Haight. I don't care which, as long as you don't let her wander away like a stray cat the way you did last time. Tonight. And bring her to me. Instantly."

"Tonight," Faris repeated obediently. "I won't fail. I'll get her."

"If I don't hear Callahan's voice on your cell phone tonight, I will conclude that you're not fit for this job. I've already mobilized LeRoy and Karel. They can handle Callahan, if you can't. She's very beautiful, isn't she? They will be enthusiastic to do their part in convincing her to collaborate. Karel in particular, I'm sure. He's a man of appetite, hmm?"

The thought of those filthy, hateful goons putting their hairy paws on his angel made him panic. "But you can't! Karel and LeRoy are—"

"Do not contradict me," Marcus said. "Get to work."

The cell phone clicked shut. Faris gulped back a rush of bile in his throat. He rocked back and forth until he calmed down enough to register the taste in his mouth. Bitter, metallic. Blood and plastic.

His own bloody thumb, still encased in the plastic glove, was stuck into his mouth. He was sucking on it.

Chapter

12

Margot found herself flat on her butt. Her head spun in great, swooping curves like a nightmare amusement park ride. The golden disk swung lazily. Winking. Turning. Twirling in the breeze as the wind chimes clanked their hollow, horror flick theme song.

". . . is it, Margot? Come on, breathe. What is it about the necklace?" Davy's voice penetrated the blanket of roaring in her ears.

She reached out, grabbed his hand. His long, warm fingers closed tightly around hers. "I pawned that thing today." Her voice came out in a wispy croak. "Before my gym classes. Sixty bucks. He robbed me, but I would have practically paid him to take it off me." She tried to swallow. Her throat bumped and scratched. "It's chasing me."

Davy steadied her as she struggled to her feet. She reached out to stop its sickening, hypnotic swing, but Davy stopped her hand.

"It might have prints on it," he said gently. "Let it be."

She let her hand drop. Davy slid his arm around her waist, and she leaned into him gratefully.

"Why do you hate the necklace, Margot?"

"Long story," she whispered.

"Yeah, I bet it is," he said. "The time has come to tell it to me."

Margot scanned the inky darkness that lay beyond the pool of light shed by the porch bulb. "He could be watching us."

Davy pulled her inside and shut the door. "Let me get this straight. You pawned the necklace today. Your secret admirer bought it back, and attached it to your wind chimes. Right?"

She nodded. Her teeth had begun to chatter.

"So we've got a lead," he said. "That's good news. The pawnshop will be closed by now, though. We'll have to go talk to the guy tomorrow."

"I think I have his cell number," Margot said. "He wrote it on the receipt while he was trying to flirt with me." She fished in her jeans pocket and pulled out a crumpled sales slip. *Bart Wilkes* was scrawled on it, a cell phone number written beneath, heavily underlined.

Davy pulled out his own phone and dialed the number. Margot reached out for it. "He's more liable to talk to me than to you."

He handed her the phone without comment. She listened to it ring. Ten, twelve . . . eighteen times. "Not picking up," she said.

"Let's try the phone book. There can't be too many guys named Bart Wilkes in greater Seattle."

He was in the book, but the phone just rang. Margot scribbled down the Central District address listed in the phone book. "I'm going to his house," she said. "I'll hang out until he comes home. I can't wait."

Davy looked for a moment like he was about to argue, and then he nodded. "I'll drive you."

She was so dazed, it didn't occur to her to argue. She

picked up Mikey and headed out the door with a shuffling zombie gait.

Davy followed her a moment later with a plastic freezer bag he'd found in her kitchen. He detached the pendant, careful to touch only the chain, and dropped it into the bag. "Try not to handle this," he said, handing it to her. "I'll see if I can get somebody to run prints on it."

"Don't worry. I won't." She dropped it into her purse with a shudder of disgust and followed him out to the truck.

The flat quality of the silence in the truck inhibited her. She fished around for a loose end, a thread that might lead her into the story, but every thread led to such a complicated tangle. There was no good starting place, no clear middle. And no end in sight.

"I'm waiting," he said.

His tone gave her something to react against. "Don't you give me that what-is-the-meaning-of-this-report-card-young-lady tone—"

"This is now officially my business," he said. "If you don't want me to go to the police, cooperate with me. Right now."

His flinty glance underscored how serious he was. She slid her fingers into Mikey's silky fur for comfort, and grabbed the first random thread that came to her head. "Nine months ago, I was seeing this guy, Craig Caruso," she began. "He was a researcher in a biometrics firm."

"Biometrics. Physical ID? Fingerprints, retina scans, that stuff?"

"Yes," she said. "I was hired to revamp the Krell Biometrics web site, to make it more modern and edgy. That's where I met him."

"So that's what you did for a living," he said. "Web design."

"I never told you that?"

"You never told me anything." His voice was faintly accusing.

Margot stared down into her lap. "Oh. Well, anyhow. Things went relatively well for a while, and then they got strange."

He made a noncommittal sound. "Strange how?"

"He got really tense and paranoid," she said. "Started making noises about quitting his job. Said they were taking advantage of him, spying on him. He decided to break out on his own, rented a space and everything. Then one day I came home early from a conference and found another woman's panties in my bed." She rubbed at her eyes with the backs of her arms. "So off I go, to Craig's new studio, to tell him what a worm he was, and he . . ." She blew out a sharp breath. "I found him hanging from the ceiling, dripping blood. Stuck full of needles."

He glanced at her. "Whoa," he said quietly. "That's severe."

"Mandi, his assistant, was lying on the floor, half naked. Maybe dead already. I took one step towards Craig, and then, pow. Nothing."

He frowned. "What do you mean, nothing?"

She fought down the nausea in her belly. "Meaning that I woke up in a motel room, hours later. Stark naked."

He made a sound like he'd been dashed with ice water.

"My head was pounding. I'd been drugged," she went on dully. "I found my clothes on a chair. My purse was there, minus the gun—"

"What the hell were you doing with a gun?" he demanded.

She winced. "It was so stupid. Craig had given it to me. I hated the thing. I was planning to give it back to him when I dumped him, but . . . well, anyhow. I put my clothes on and stumbled out to ask the front desk who had booked that room. They had no record of anyone checking in. As far as they knew, the room was empty. Nobody had seen this guy. Nobody had written down a name, or given him a key. I was carried up there and stripped naked by a ghost."

"Weird." His voice was thoughtful.

Her laughter had a bitter, crazy edge. "Hah. It gets worse. I called Dougie, my receptionist. He was hysterical. He'd gotten worried after a few hours, so he went to Craig's studio. He found the bodies, poor guy. They'd been shot, many times, at close range. He called the cops."

"And?"

She stared at her hands, twisted into Mikey's fur. "They asked him lots of pointed questions about my relationship with Craig. Asked about Craig's infidelities. If I had a gun. If I was hot-tempered. Dougie's a smart boy. He told me to watch out. That they thought I'd killed them." She covered her face. "Me. As if I were capable of slaughtering two people. God. I cried for a week when I had to put my cat down."

She waited for some kind of cue from him. None was forthcoming.

She took a deep breath and forged on. "So that's it. I panicked. I ran. From the cops, from whoever framed me and took my clothes off me and put me in that room, from everyone. I stopped at a branch of my bank, wrote a check to cash, took out all my money. And that was the end of Mag Callahan. Maybe it was cowardly, but I was so scared."

"I would have been, too," he said.

She shot him a doubtful look. "You? Get out."

"Yeah," he said. "Me."

"The ballistics analysis proved it was my gun that killed them. I should have gone to the police, I guess, but I was convinced that Craig's killer would get me if I poked out my nose. I followed the manhunt on the news. Little old me, the modern day Lizzie Borden." She sighed. "I don't have family living. I decided not to contact my friends. I didn't want them endangered. Bad enough that I compromised poor Dougie."

Davy caressed her bare shoulder. "What about the necklace?"

"Oh, that," she said wearily. "I was wearing it when I

woke up in the hotel room. Like his dog collar, or something. I haven't been able to find anything in the library or the Internet to explain where it's from or what it means. What scares me the most . . ." She shivered.

"Is what?" His voice was gentle.

"I wasn't supposed to wake up before he got back," she said. "Suppose I'd woken up, say, an hour later? Maybe he just stepped out for a burger or to gas up his car. Maybe I got away from that monster by pure chance. It gives me nightmares."

"There is no such thing as chance," he said. "You got away because it's not your destiny to get eaten by a monster."

She braced herself to ask the question. "So you believe me, then?"

He didn't answer for a long time. She tried not to hold her breath.

"Yes," he said.

The simple word rang with sincerity. Her eyes filled.

It had been months since she'd had any point of reference in the world that was not her own shaky, vulnerable self. He'd just given her one, and she loved him for it. She sniffed back the tears and fumbled for something to get her over the awkward moment. "So do you think Craig's killer and Snakey are the same guy?" she asked.

He shot her an eloquent look. "You have doubts?"

"Hopes. Not doubts." She shook her head. "I swear, I did everything I could to cover my tracks. Not that I'm any great shakes as a fugitive, but I did hitchhike all the way to—"

"You *what?*" He sounded outraged. "Do you have any idea how dangerous that is?"

Her laughter had no real amusement in it. "Please. After what I'd been through, hitchhiking doesn't hold much terror for me. Besides, I got lucky. It went fine. I got lots of nice rides. Decent folks. No scary moments, comparatively speaking."

He grunted his wordless disapproval.

"No, really," she insisted. "Not all my luck is bad. I mean, look at Mikey. I defy you to show me a more incredibly special animal."

Upon hearing his name, Mikey leaped up and put his paws on Margot's knees. Davy glanced down at the dog. "I decline the challenge."

"Wise." Margot echoed his cool, remote voice. "Very wise."

"Let's get back to the subject," Davy said. "You've had this stalker problem for what, two weeks? What have you done recently that's different from what you've been doing for the past months?"

"I did buy some fake job references," she faltered. "But not with my old name. I got a job in a graphics firm in Belltown, but the place burned down ten days later. It was right after that when—oh. Oh, my."

"It was your references," he said. "They raised a red flag."

"But I never used my old name," she protested.

He shook his head, started the truck back up and drove on, giving her time to get used to the new ideas jostling in her mind.

"I just don't understand it," she said forlornly. "I didn't step on anybody's toes. I didn't steal anything. I'm not rich, or connected. I don't have a microchip with a code to explode the planet embedded in my teeth. I just design web sites. That's all. Why I should grab somebody's attention to this extent? I swear, I'm just not that special."

"Makes perfect sense to me," Davy said.

Her head whipped around. "How do you figure?"

"I've been thinking about you since the moment I saw you," he said. "You don't need a microchip in your teeth to get noticed."

She licked her dry, swollen lips. "Oh," she whispered. "Wow."

"I can tell you, from direct personal experience, that there doesn't need to be any outside reason for this guy to have fixated on you. You yourself, Margot Vetter, are reason enough."

She couldn't think of a reply at all for over a minute. "Um, I'm not sure whether to say, gee, thanks for what I think was a freaky, twisted sort of compliment, or to just throw up right now."

His mouth twitched. "Please, please do not throw up in my truck."

She started to giggle. "Oh, God. Why am I laughing? This is so not funny. And I just don't get it. Why play me like this? He could nab me or kill me any time he wanted. There's no one to stop him."

"There is now," Davy said.

She looked away. She wasn't ready for this soft, hopeful feeling unfolding in her chest. It was dangerous. Like everything else in her life, it could turn around and chomp her at any time.

"Did you get yourself checked out by a doctor?" he asked, his voice gentle.

"God, yes," she said. "There was no evidence that I was raped, but I still feel raped. I don't know what happened when I was with him. I don't know what I did, or what was done to me. I don't know how I felt about it. I hate it. It makes me feel sick. And helpless."

He pulled the truck over into the shadow of some trees, and reached over to take her hand. "Whatever happened in that hotel room, you did your best," he said quietly. "You were true to yourself. I would bet anything on that."

She could hardly breathe for a moment. She tried to laugh, but the effort petered off to a breathless nothing. "Wow. You're good, Davy. Here I think I'm dealing with Mr. Ice Cube, and out of nowhere, you make me go all gooey inside. It's a diabolical technique to keep women off balance, right? Do they teach you how to do that in man school?"

He massaged her hand. "Nope. I figured it out all on my own."

She stared at her hand, clasped in his. "I haven't been able to even think about being with a guy since then," she whispered. "I got myself tested for HIV and every STD that exists, but they told me I was fine. From a physical point of view, at least."

Her stomach fluttered at the blatant implications of what she'd just said. "Not that it's relevant, or anything," she added.

He nodded. "While we're on the subject, I've been tested since the last time I was involved with someone, too. I have a clean bill of health. Just so you know."

Her hand buzzed, trapped in his delicious warmth.

"Not that it's relevant, or anything," he added awkwardly.

"Of course not," she murmured.

"My timing sucks," Davy said. "But it's hard to find a good opening to make that kind of announcement. You gave me one, so I took it. Didn't mean to make you uncomfortable."

"No biggie," she said. "I'm not uncomfortable. Just surprised."

"At what?"

"I thought . . ." Her voice cracked, and she swallowed to loosen it up. "It's a wild tale, you must admit. I thought you wanted to keep your life simple. I thought that if I told you all this stuff, you would change your mind about wanting to, um, be with me."

He lifted his hand to her face and ran his finger tenderly over her lower lip. It felt like a kiss. "Surprise, surprise," he said. "It hasn't."

His eyes could set fire to an iceberg. She looked down, blushing.

"No pressure," he said. "Really. Relax."

"Relax, my butt," she said. "If you really want me to relax, stop smoldering at me like that."

A slow grin spread over his face. "I don't mean to smolder."

"Oh, get out. You do it on purpose, and you know it," she snapped. "Come on. Let's go talk to this guy before I lose my nerve."

Davy couldn't even explain to himself why he believed her so implicitly. Maybe it was just his dick talking, but he didn't think so. His dick had never played tricks like that before.

By now, he was in the habit of trusting himself. It was the way he worked, the way he reasoned. He fed everything he thought or sensed or felt into the magic machine, and a gut level conclusion churned out the other end. He could either trust it, or not. He didn't know how the process worked. All he knew was that it did. And that the only serious fuck-ups in his life had occurred after not trusting it.

Margot was in truly deep shit, but she deserved some help.

Bart Wilkes lived in a small, nondescript bungalow in the Central district. The lawn was overgrown with weeds and littered with junk, surrounded by a six-foot chain-link fence. A battered, ancient white Chrysler was parked in the driveway. Lights were on inside the house.

Davy maneuvered Margot behind himself as they crossed the lawn to the porch. He knocked on the front door, and waited. No response.

He peered into the windows, which were covered with heavy drapes. "Let's go around the back and see if there's a—"

He cut the words off as Margot marched right on in the door.

"Aw, shit," he muttered. "Wait. Margot. For God's sake."

He stopped to wipe the doorknob, and followed her in. The room was cluttered and stale, with mismatched furniture and dominated by a large screen TV. The coffee table and carpet was littered with overflowing ashtrays, crumpled beer cans and fast food wrappers.

"Bart?" Margot's voice wobbled. She dragged in a deeper breath and tried again, more loudly. "Bart Wilkes? Are you here?"

The depth and heaviness of the silence made Davy's skin crawl. There was a faint, unpleasant smell that went beyond stale cigarettes or spoiled food. Something nastier. Meatier.

"Don't touch anything. Something's not right," he said.

"When is it ever?" She rolled her eyes, her usual brave schtick, but her face was translucent in the sickly light of Wilkes's living room. She squared her shoulders and headed briskly towards the kitchen.

He lunged instinctively to stop her. "Wait. Margot. Don't—"

"Oh, no." She flinched back from whatever she saw in there, bumping off the wall and stumbling into him. "Oh, God," she whispered.

He steadied her, placed her behind himself, and took a look.

It was bad. The man he assumed to be Bart Wilkes lay on the dirty linoleum floor, his long body curled up into the fetal position. Blood was smeared all around him, big swooping streaks, as if he'd struggled and writhed in it. One bloodstained hand was extended in a desperate, pleading gesture. His fingers were drawn into stiff claws.

Eyes wide, face grayish, mouth open in a rictus of agony. Dark blood from his nose and mouth was pooled beneath his head.

"Is that the pawnbroker?" he asked.

"That's him," she whispered. "Oh, that poor, poor guy."

Davy crouched down next to Wilkes and put his fingertip to the man's throat. No pulse, not that he expected one. The man looked very dead, though he wasn't cold yet. He looked around the filthy kitchen. The phone was pulled off the wall. The receiver lay on the floor a few feet from the man, still beeping. He'd tried to call for help. Poor bastard.

He wanted badly to examine the guy's body under the loose, blood-soaked shirt, to see what wounds had caused the bleeding, but he kept his hands to himself. That was for the cops to ascertain. The best way to maintain a smooth working relationship with the local police was to be very careful not to step on their toes.

"Let's get out of here," he said. "This looks like a crime scene."

She followed him out to the truck without protest, her hand pressed hard over her mouth. When he got off the phone with the cops, she tapped his arm. "How do we justify being inside his house?"

"We don't," he said brusquely. "We saw him through the kitchen window when we came to the back door to knock. No way would we just march into a stranger's house uninvited. Oh, no. Not us."

She didn't come back with a smart remark, which was weird. He turned her face towards the streetlight. Her lips were trembling and bluish, her eyes glassy. She was done. Out of gas.

"Get into the truck." He softened his tone. "I'll deal with them."

It took a while, as such things did, but he knew and liked both the cops who came to the scene. He told them he'd dropped by to ask Wilkes if he'd recently moved a certain piece of stolen jewelry, and they had no problem with that story. Nor should they have, since it was literally true. Davy was good at lying when he had to be, with his poker face, but he didn't enjoy it much. Not even half-truths.

He was glad when he finally got Margot home. Mikey trailed alongside, whining anxiously as Davy led her into the house. He wrapped her in a blanket and made a cup of tea, stirring in lots of sugar and milk. He put it into her hands, steadying them with his own as liquid sloshed out on to her lap. "Try to drink some of that."

But her hands weren't steady enough. She gave him an apologetic smile and put the cup on the table. "Do you believe in curses?"

He thought about it. "Depends on how you define a curse," he said. "One thing's sure, though. I don't believe in coincidences."

Mikey snuffled Margot's knee. When she failed to respond, he turned to Davy and propped his paws on the couch, his dark, gleaming eyes full of hopeful speculation. Opportunistic pissant. Davy eyed the dog's long, fine black hair and his own pale gray furniture.

"In your dreams, buddy," he told the dog.

Mikey jumped down, unsurprised, and flung himself over one of Davy's feet with an air of cheerful resignation. He reached down to pet the animal, his fingers tracing the shaved patches where the stitches from Mikey's battle wounds were still visible. Mikey licked his hand in response. A thought slowly took form in his mind. "Margot? You said the dog Snakey left on your porch was a shepherd mix, right?"

Her eyes focused on his. "Could be," she said apprehensively.

"What kind of dog was it that attacked Mikey in the park?"

She stared at him, and her mouth started to shake. "Oh, no. That's so gross and awful. You think that this freak thought he was doing me a favor? That he's . . . he's *courting* me?"

Davy wished he'd kept his mouth shut. Too late now. "It was a message," he said. "Maybe a love note. It would go with the rose petals."

She hid her face against her knees. "Only me," she whispered. "Only I could possibly get a love note like that."

"It's a starting place," he offered.

"It's a terrible starting place," she snapped. "It sucks."

She reached for the tea. He covered her shaking hands with his own as the tea sloshed. "You're going with me tomorrow," he told her. "I can't miss my brother's wedding, and I can't leave you alone. Don't make me be an asshole about it, because I'm more than capable."

A ghost of a smile twitched her pale lips. "I believe it. I couldn't run off tonight if I wanted to. Which I don't." She eyed him. "It's just that . . ." Her voice trailed off, uncertain.

"What?" he asked sharply.

"Are you sure you want a fugitive with a stalker on her tail at your brother's wedding? I'm not a girl you can take home to Mother."

He draped an arm over her shoulders. "You won't be meeting my parents. They're gone now. I wish you could, though. My mom would have liked you. And as for Dad, well . . ." He hesitated. "He would've had a lot more respect for a fugitive on the run from the law than he'd have had for any respectable, so-called normal person."

She frowned, bewildered. "Huh? How so?"

"It was a badge, for him," he explained. "Clear proof that you're fighting the system. You're not a mindless, brain-washed worker bee feeding the evil machine. You're part of the elect outlaw tribe. That really turned him on. Dad was . . . he was unique."

She shook her head. "Wow," she murmured. "Would he have been disappointed to learn that there's nothing I want more than to go back to being a mindless worker bee? That it's my most cherished dream?"

Davy shrugged. "We just wouldn't have told him that part."

"My mom's gone, too," she said wistfully. "I miss her so much."

"And your dad?" he asked.

She hesitated, too long. "Not a player. Gone when I was small, before he could do much damage. I wish I could've met your folks."

"It's just me and my brothers now," he said.

"You're still really lucky, to have your brothers. I wish I had some. Big, mean, scary ones."

"You can use mine," he offered. "They're mean and scary

whenever they need to be. And they'll do anything I ask them to."

Her smile was so tender and unguarded, it pierced right into him. It was an oddly painful sensation, but he liked it. "Thanks, Davy, that's sweet," she said. "Do your poor brothers know that you contract them out behind their backs to strange women in trouble?"

"They'd both go out of their way to help somebody," he told her. "That's just the way they are. Besides, you've got me already. They would just be reinforcements."

She gazed into his eyes, her face bleak. "Have I got you, Davy?"

His breath stuck in his throat. "You've got me bad."

They stared at each other. The air buzzed with tension. Voices in his head told him to back off, chill out. He couldn't hear them over the roaring in his ears. They stood together at a doorway, and he couldn't seem to turn back. The only way he could see was onward. With her.

He scooped Mikey gently off his foot, and slid to his knees to the floor in between the couch and the coffee table. He pushed her knees apart, reaching behind her to cup her bottom and slide her closer to him on the couch. Her legs clasped around him, her arms followed.

He slid his arms around her waist and hid his face against her breasts. Her curves fit the angles of his body perfectly. His chest felt soft and unstable. He didn't dare risk catching a glimpse of his own face in the glass of the stereo cabinet or the reflection of the TV screen.

Margot coiled herself around his body, embracing him so tightly her muscles trembled with the strain. She vibrated in his arms, a frequency too high for tears, and pressed her face against him, pressing soft, tender kisses against the curve of his neck and shoulder.

He loved it. He never wanted her to stop.

Finally she relaxed, her head heavy on his shoulder. He

scooped her into his arms and carried her into his bedroom. He laid her gently on the bed, pulling the coverlet over her body.

He sat down in the chair by the bed. He knew his own chronic insomnia well enough to know he would get no sleep tonight. Every cell in his body was wide awake and zinging with tension.

He might as well just go into the office, boot up the computer and make himself useful, but he couldn't bear to take his eyes off her. There was no place safer than his own bed, but that wasn't saying much. He'd known since he was ten that no safe place existed. Things melted away, things disappeared, things were stolen. No warning, no rules, no laws.

Bart Wilkes's mysterious death chilled him to the bone. That combined with Margot's gothic tale of blood and gore was more than enough to keep his eyes wide open all night long. Speculating, worrying.

Fate had conspired to land her in his bed, and he was by God keeping her there. The world was full of monsters tonight.

He wasn't taking any chances.

Chapter

13

Faris made his way through the upscale Highland Park neighborhood. The address Marcus had given him was of Dr. Nosomi Takeda, a forty-six-year-old Japanese-American cell biologist who researched and taught at the University of Washington.

He was fortunate to have a job to do, because he was so distressed at the thought of Marcus's anger, he could barely control his bodily functions. He'd lost Margaret. Again. The GPS tag on her car had showed her going home, but her house had been dark and empty.

He'd slammed through the empty rooms of Margaret's pathetic little house, almost putting his fists through the thin, water-stained walls, but he knew that he would have much better use for his fists soon. Best not to bruise them now.

His red angel had fallen into McCloud's trap. She was weaker than he'd thought. He was so disappointed. So hurt and disgusted that she was no longer pure for him. Their love had been sullied. That shining perfection that had transformed him could never be regained.

And the hollow screaming place that he thought had been filled with her love was screaming again, and he had to make it stop. Had to.

He only knew one way to do it.

Faris parked a few blocks from Dr. Takeda's house and approached it quietly on foot. The house was secluded, the trees creating pools of convenient shadow. He spiraled in slowly, wary of alarms or dogs. Nothing. Idiots. They deserved anything they got.

He boosted the infrared camera on its mechanized telestick, weaving it delicately through the branches of the pine trees until he got a clear look of the upstairs bedrooms, and hit the master bedroom on the first try. Two lumps in the bed. Good.

The back kitchen door was equipped with an anti-pick, anti-drill Medeco lock as well as a dead bolt and chain, but he hadn't wanted to use the pick gun anyway. It was too loud. It took only a few moments of maneuvering his custom MT device under the door, extending it up to loosen the locks on the door from the inside, and he was in.

He took a moment to orient himself. The remains of a candlelit dinner were on the table. Articles of clothing were strewn in the hall and up the stairs, becoming more intimate in nature as he approached the bedroom. The bedroom door hung half-open, a pair of skimpy woman's panties hanging on the knob. He peered inside, confirmed the presence of the two lumps in the bed, and drifted on like a shadow to check the other rooms. Takeda was a childless divorcée living alone in the house she'd gotten from the divorce settlement, but it paid to double-check.

A shadow in the dark. The shadow of death. He remembered the phrase from when he was a kid in Sunday school. Marcus had used his special memory techniques to help his little brother memorize his Bible verses. Faris had never, ever forgotten them. They were woven into his dreams. The valley of the shadow of death. Inside of him.

He was the shadow of death itself. Silent, invisible. Invincible.

Dr. Haight's lover, Dr. Takeda, was sprawled naked in the sheets on the side closest to him. Faris crept closer, and studied her naked body in the dim light that filtered through from the hallway. She was in excellent shape for a woman of her age, but too thin and narrow-hipped for his tastes, though all women paled in comparison to his red angel.

Takeda's black hair was tangled over the pillows, brow furrowed as if trying to puzzle out the secrets of cell biology in her dreams. Faris uncorked a vial and held it under her nose for a few seconds.

He circled round the bed and looked over the new director of Calix Research Laboratories, Dr. Seymour Haight. Heavily asleep, his mouth open. Mid-fifties, gray-streaked, close-trimmed beard. Thick gray chest hair. Mouth open, distorted against the pillow. Stocky, but muscular.

He looked like Titus, Faris's father. It made Faris nostalgic. He had cried for his father after the heart attack. No one ever suspected what Faris had done with his needles. Invisible. The shadow of death.

Faris uncorked another vial, held it under Haight's nose—and the need for stealth and silence was abruptly over. He could put on heavy metal music to work with if he chose. Now it was grunt work any idiot could do, even LeRoy or Karel.

The thought of them inflamed his anger and jealousy to a fever pitch. How could Marcus pass over Faris, who had tried so hard to please him for all these years, in favor of those grunting pigs? It made him want to kill, to rend and bite. Blood spraying in splattering gouts.

He wrestled himself back under control. Marcus would never forgive him if Faris spoiled his precious plan, though Faris had long ago begun to hate Marcus's plan. Any setbacks, and it was always Faris who was punished. Always poor Faris who paid the price.

He flipped on the light, unloaded the pack strapped to his back, and laid out the three metal cases, each filled with a sheet of soft, fast-setting molding plastic. He picked up Haight's limp, hairy right hand, peeled off the seal and pressed it firmly into the plastic.

The impression was clear. He wiped Haight's hand with a tissue soaked with a cleaning solvent, waited for it to dry and repeated the procedure twice more. Nothing to it.

He packed up the gear, checked to make sure he'd left nothing behind. He was done, but still he stood, staring at the unconscious man and woman in the bed. He still felt a driving need for something more to fill the screaming hole. The feeling was almost sexual, but Takeda's slack-jawed slumber and extreme slenderness did not tempt him. Karel was the sex addict. If Karel had been given this assignment, he would have indulged as a matter of course.

But Faris was different. Base, animal sex repelled him. His appetites vibrated on a higher plane. He couldn't kill Haight, as that would wreck Marcus's precious plan, but Marcus hadn't specified that Haight's lover was off limits. As long as Faris didn't make a mess, he could indulge himself. No one would know. Not even Takeda herself.

Faris sat down next to the sleeping woman, petting her almost affectionately. What lovely smooth skin. She lay on her side, arm flung over her head. So thin, he could count each rib. Her breasts were barely more than creases of extra flesh on her chest, peaked by brown nipples.

Within seconds, inspiration came. He plucked needles from his wristband. One on each side of her throat, to create blocks in one flow of qi, excesses in another. Then a swift, sharp blow with the very tip of his finger, right between the eighth and ninth rib.

Takeda jerked, whimpering, but did not wake.

He'd hardly touched the surface of her skin, and the blow would barely leave a bruise, but the shock wave of traumatic energy he had directed into her body was sufficient to rupture her spleen.

It would take approximately three days for the membranous capsule around that organ to fill with blood. Then the internal hemorrhaging, the sudden drop in blood pressure, and goodbye, Dr. Takeda. So young, to die so mysteriously. How sad.

That was better. Now he could relax, think more clearly. He retrieved his needles, flicked off the light and left, relocking the doors.

Time to turn his attention to Margaret. He was so angry at her weakness of character that even the thought of Marcus questioning her distressed him less than it had before. She deserved to be punished.

He would question her himself, with his needles. She would learn what it meant to betray him. He had tried to be gentle with her, and he had suffered for it, too. It wasn't his fault if she ruined everything.

Stupid slut. She had only herself to blame.

Margot woke up disoriented. She barely remembered who she was, let alone where. All she knew was that she felt wrung out, limp. Floating. She was unusually comfortable, too, sprawled on a soft . . . huh? Wow. It was a bed. A real bed. A very nice bed, in fact.

She rolled over and looked around. The bed was huge. She was lost in it. Moonlight streamed through the big windows of a large, simply furnished room. Outside the moon lit up the shimmering expanse of a lake. Then she saw Davy's long body, sitting in a plain straight-backed chair near the bed. His face was in shadow, but she sensed his tension. He was wide awake, and standing guard.

It all rolled back, a cold, dark tidal wave of memory. The pendant. Bart Wilkes's body. Fear gripped her.

"Rest," Davy said. "Everything's fine. I was just watching over you. Go back to sleep."

Yeah, right. She didn't follow orders, on principle, but Davy just didn't get it yet. She sat up, straining to make out the expression on his face. She tried to think of something to say to him, but the chaotic feelings struggling inside her were too dangerous to put into words.

"I don't expect anything from you," he said. "Not one goddamn thing. So go on. Get some sleep. I'll keep you safe."

His words made her heart go soft. She untangled herself from the bedcovers and slid off the bed. "You know what, Davy? That's the sweetest, sexiest thing a guy has ever said to me, in my whole life."

She saw a flash on his face that might have been a smile. "Yeah?"

"Yeah. Studly, gallant, altruistic. Yum." She grabbed the edge of her skimpy stretch tank top, and peeled it up over her body. "Does that line always work this well?" She pulled the shirt over her head. "Do the girls always start throwing their clothes off when you say that?"

"No. It's very specific. Only you."

"Nice." She nodded her approval, undoing the top button of her jeans. "Very nice. You make me feel special. Women love that."

"I'm not feeding you some bullshit line." His voice was curt. "I couldn't even if I wanted to. Not tonight."

Her hands froze on her buttons. "I was joking, pal," she said tentatively. "Remember the concept? Funny, ha ha, and all that?"

"I'm humor challenged on the best of days, let alone tonight. I'm in a weird space. Too much adrenaline. Maybe it would be better if you got under the covers and closed your eyes. And your mouth."

His hard voice chilled her. Her arms crept up to cover her

bra. "Sorry," she said. "I didn't mean to embarrass you, if you don't want—"

"Like hell I don't want," he snarled. "I want to fuck you so bad, my hands are shaking. But I'm too wound up. I can't take it easy, you get me? I don't want to hurt you or scare you. So don't push me. Please."

Oh, how sweet. Trying to protect her from the power of his lust. How adorably silly of him. The thought of Davy's hands trembling with desire for her . . . wow. It made her lower body tingle and throb. A hot, wild animal feeling. Panther woman. Hear her roar.

An uncontrollable smile spread over her face. She shimmied her tight jeans down over her bottom. "I'll tell you a secret." She tried to keep her tone light and teasing, but the tremor of excitement betrayed her. "I mostly use plain white cotton bikini briefs. But since you started hanging around, I've been using these skimpy lace thingies."

"Is that so," he said.

"Go figure," she said, in mock wonder. "They're uncomfortable as the dickens. Scritchy-scratch, and that damned string always riding up between my cheeks. Sexy panties are an invention of the devil. Along with high heels."

"So take them off," he said.

She unclasped her bra, tossed it away. Hooked her fingers into her panties and swayed her hips. Shimmy, bump and grind. She'd never done a striptease for a guy before. She'd always been too matter-of-fact about sex for silly games. Not anymore.

She pulled the clip out of her hair, arching to take advantage of the boob-optimizing Playboy bunny position. She shook her hair loose. The longest part of the chopped ends tickled the tops of her shoulders.

"I've got adrenaline to unload too, you know." She swung her thigh over his legs and straddled his lap, face to face with him. "But I don't want to hurt you or scare you, either."

He let out a short, harsh laugh, and his hands came up to clasp her waist. She arched and shivered in his hot, possessive grasp. "I told you," he said. "I'm not delicate."

"I noticed. I like that. Sometimes I intimidate guys, you see. I shoot off my big mouth, hurt their tender feelings. You know how I am."

"I'm getting a pretty good idea—" His voice choked off into a gasp as she gripped him, stroking the whole turgid length of his penis through the denim of his jeans.

"But just look at this," she said softly. "This part doesn't feel intimidated. Not one little tiny bit." She leaned forward and touched her lips to his, covering them with moist, lingering kisses. She slid her tongue into his mouth, flicking it against his. "That's one of the things I love about you," she went on. "You're hard to intimidate. I can knock you around all I want, and you just bounce up, begging for more."

He leaned away from her kiss. "What are the other things?"

She was momentarily lost. "Huh?"

"You said that's one of the things you love about me. That implies that there are others. So what are they?"

She was startled into silence for a moment. She started to laugh.

"Just what's so goddamn funny?"

She started unbuttoning his linen shirt. "Like you have to ask," she said. "Tell you what, buddy. I'll show you some of them right now."

"Hey. Are you sure about this?"

She pushed the linen shirt off his shoulders and started fumbling with his cuffs. "Nonverbal communication just doesn't get through to you, does it? What do I have to do to convince you? Tie you down? Ravish you by force? Say the word, pal. I'm in the mood to be wild."

"Just give me a goddamn straight answer." He yanked his cuffs out of her fingers and undid the buttons, flinging the shirt onto the floor. "That's all I ask."

She hesitated. "I really wish you'd lighten up," she said. "My life is awfully grim and serious these days."

"Forget it," he said. "If you want lighthearted, I'm not your man. Not tonight, anyway. Just say it, straight out. Let me hear a formal declaration of intent. Do you want to have sex with me tonight?"

"Do you have condoms?" she asked.

"Drawer in the bedside table."

"Then yes. I'm sure," she said. "Make me feel something good."

"OK," he muttered. "That I can do."

There. She'd done it, she'd thrown herself into the vortex.

His hands circled her waist, just touching the curves of her hips, sliding over her naked skin. Every gentle stroke made her tingle and buzz, every place he touched felt like it should sparkle with light. She cupped his face in her hands and kissed him in her usual bold, take-charge way. He opened his mouth to hers, and their tongues touched.

The astonishing intimacy of the tender contact took her by surprise. Everything went hot and shaky and unstable.

But she didn't want to be shaky, stammering and blushing. She needed all her attitude with a guy like Davy. She wanted to wow him, subdue him, shock him senseless, like the fearless barbarian queen. She wanted some goddamn satisfaction. On her own terms.

But it wasn't going to be that way. It started with just the kiss; one minute she was perched naked on his lap, making love to his warm, sexy mouth, feeling like an invincible siren. The next moment, he was making love to hers, and she'd lost control of the kiss, of him, of herself, of everything. He just took her over, smoothly and completely.

His hand slid down to the cleft of her bottom, delving lower to brush over the curls that shielded her labia. The glancing touch sent a wild jolt of sensation and emotion through her. He pressed the small of her back, pushing her wider as his fingers slid inside her wet folds.

Pleasure uncoiled, unraveling her with every skillful stroke. She was helpless, trembling and soft. He got up, setting her on her feet and pushing her back as he unbuckled his belt. She lost her balance and tumbled onto the bed, scrambling backwards. She'd blatantly provoked him, but the minute he took her at her word, she panicked. This was nuts. She didn't do this, wasn't like this. There was only so far she could go before her back hit the headboard. She huddled against it, knees drawn up to her chest, shivering like a silly, terrified virgin.

Davy stripped off his jeans and advanced across the bed, looming over her in the dark. He put both hands over her knees, and the flush of heat and pleasure that spread down her thighs at the contact made her gasp. He flung himself to the side, his body stretching and flexing as he rummaged in the bedside drawer for a condom. He flipped on the light.

It happened too fast to protest. Margot winced, and covered her face with her hands. "I'd rather you left it off, please."

"No." His blunt refusal startled her. "I've got to see to every detail."

She didn't want him to see to every detail; her reddened eyes, her blurry mouth that couldn't stop trembling. She couldn't do the barbarian queen act with the light on. It wouldn't be convincing.

And she just couldn't get used to how big he was. Extravagantly gorgeous. Those thick, powerful shoulders, that chest that went on forever, dusted with glinting hair, those muscular dips and curves in his hips that she wanted to explore with her fingertips, her lips, her tongue. And his erection—rising bluntly from a thatch of dark blond hair— her gaze skittered away, face crimson, even though she'd already felt it, touched it. Tasted it. She huddled against the headboard, trying to hide from him. As if she were afraid.

But not of him. Apart from his excessive charisma overload problem, he was a good, decent guy. She was sure of that.

It was this feeling she was afraid of. She'd never been moved so deeply. Certainly not by Craig, or his predecessors.

She'd never taken guys too seriously, after her early girlish heartbreaks. Men struck her as comical creatures, for the most part; troublesome when they got silly notions in their heads, sometimes a nice distraction, sometimes a lot of fun, and God knows she'd never given up hopes of finding a keeper someday.

But it was silly to get too worked up about them. The sad, awful truth about men was, the more you wanted them, the less they wanted you. It was a cruel formula, but she'd learned to live with it.

Davy McCloud turned her formulas upside down.

"Why are you scared?" he asked. "I thought you wanted this."

She tried to smile, but her shaking mouth wouldn't cooperate. "You make me feel shy," she whispered. "That's all."

He kissed one knee, then the other. His lips were exquisitely warm and soft. His hands slid down her thighs. A deep, melting sweetness shivered through her legs in their wake.

"Are you trembling because you're scared, or because you're turned on?" he demanded.

"Both," she admitted.

She jerked with startled pleasure as his finger brushed delicately down the damp divide of her labia. "Does being scared turn you on?"

He was doing it again, looking into her head, delving around in secrets she never knew she was keeping. It made her breathless, panicked excitement sharpen to an almost unbearable pitch.

"No!" she snapped. "I've changed my mind. I'm not scared. Not at all. Not of you. Don't think that for one minute."

"OK. I won't think that." His hands stroked the tops of her thighs. "We can stop. If you want."

His voice had a shaky edge. That made her feel better. At least he was struggling, too. She shook her head. "I don't want to stop."

He closed his eyes. "Thank God. You have no idea what it cost me to say that." He pried her hands out of their death grip around her knees, lifted them to his lips and kissed them, front and back. "Relax."

She nodded, but couldn't risk speaking. He slid his arm behind her knees, pulled until she unfolded. Then he pushed her legs open.

She stared up at him, her breath ragged. She'd never felt so naked as she did with Davy kneeling between her thighs, her intimate tender bits spread out for his perusal. Her sex felt hot, tingling. The look in his eyes heated her more than any other man's touch ever had.

"Christ, just look at you," he muttered. "You're perfect."

The woman she used to be would have said something sarcastic about feeding her a line, but his voice was tense. Not a practiced seducer's rap. He sounded sincere. Almost nervous.

Hah. Davy McCloud, nervous. She almost giggled. "Thanks," she ventured. "Hardly perfect, but it's lovely of you to say so."

She pressed her hands against his hot, damp chest as he stroked the swell of her belly, her rib cage. He cupped her breasts, circling her nipples, and she arched and sighed at the ticklish, shivering rush.

He poised his big body over hers, bending to press soft, licking kisses against her belly, her breastbone. His tongue dragged over her breast, sucking with tender, ravenous skill. She dug her nails into his shoulders. Her breasts gleamed where his hungry mouth had been, and his mouth went everywhere, a hot, dizzying swirl of pleasure.

She wrapped her arms around his shoulders and nuzzled

his thick, silky hair. "It feels weird," she whispered. "Being with you."

"Why?" He slid his hand down to her inner thigh.

She put one hand over his to stop its bold path, and laid the other against his cheek. The sensual, sandpapery scrape of fine stubble against her fingertips made her forget what she'd been trying to say. She dragged it forcibly back from the depths. "Because you're so big, I guess," she said. "I'm a tall woman, not skinny, either, but next to you, I feel like a wee dainty slip of a thing. I'm not used to it."

He stretched his body out between her splayed legs, getting comfortable. "You're safe with me," he insisted.

"Hah. Safe? What's safe mean, anyway? There is no safe. You know that. Just like there is no normal."

He slid lower down and answered with hot, sensual kisses against her thigh, then her mound, spiraling slowly and surely in towards the crucial place where she was most sensitive. He took his own sweet time, dragging it out until she was as desperate for his touch as she was afraid of it, and finally slid his tongue between the folds of her labia and flicked it tenderly up, around, over her clit. A tender swirl, the faint drag of teeth, the flick of his tongue, and . . . oh. Oh, God.

Her pent-up, quivering excitement boiled over into a violent orgasm, almost instantly. She went wild, convulsed. She wasn't safe. She was terrified, more naked than she'd ever dreamed of being, crying out at the sweetness of every caress of his lips, his tongue, his hands.

Too much. Unbearable. She fought it, pushing him, writhing frantically away from his touch.

He grabbed her flailing hands, pinned her trembling thighs wide with his elbows. "What the hell?" he demanded. "Am I hurting you?"

"No . . . no." Her voice broke. "I just can't . . . I can't."

"You're scared of feeling good? Why, for Christ's sake?"

"I don't know." She gasped for air, licking her lips, trying to remember how to speak. "Can't help it."

"But it does feel good, right? You came, right? That's how it felt."

"Yes," she admitted, panting. "Oh, God, yes. It's just—too much."

He stared at her for a thoughtful moment, eyes narrowed, and then slid up, covering her shivering form completely with his body.

"If it makes you come, I won't stop doing it," he said.

She tried to think of a coherent response, but she was a shivering mass of electric sensation, uncontrollable reactions. No sense, no logic.

"I think you need to fight," he said slowly. "Right?"

She shoved against his implacable weight. "How the hell would I know?" she flared. "I've never freaked out in bed before. Stop pinning me down. Don't analyze me. Let go of my hands, goddamnit."

"No," he said. "Fight all you want, Margot. I'll win, though." He trapped both her wrists, slid down and put his mouth to her again.

It was true. She could struggle all she wanted, and he just pinned her into place with his powerful body and took her apart.

Time and space swirled into a sensuous blur, hot caramel syrup blending in melting ice cream, and he licked it up with tireless appetite. Each sweet shock of surprise was the most intense she'd ever felt, constantly supplanted by the next that was sweeter; an endless unfolding of shivering bliss. Waves of pleasure rocking and cresting over her, one after the other, even while her muscles trembled with the strain of struggling. She couldn't relax. She would fly to pieces if she let go for a single second. She would disappear.

He slid up over her damp, trembling body and kissed her again as he slipped one long finger inside her, pressing against a spot she'd never known about herself. She jerked and clenched around his hand.

"I don't know what you're fighting so hard to defend," he said. "But the harder you fight, the more I want it."

She shook her head, struggling to comprehend. "Want what?"

"You tell me, babe. Everything, anything you've got. Everything you've never given to a man before. I want it all."

His hand squeezed, probed, and thrust deeper, a rhythmic imitation of sex. Her hips jerked against him, welcoming every stroke, and he shoved her over the brink into another long, shuddering wave.

"I bet no man's ever really gotten through to you." His voice was speculative. "You're a wildcat. Panther woman. Who has the strength to hold you down for that long? Sex with you is a workout, babe."

"Watch it with the delirious power trips, pal," she warned him. "Keep it up, and I'll have to knock you back down to size."

"Sure, babe. Go ahead, keep me on my knees. I know just what to do to you down there." He slid back down.

She struggled up onto her elbows and tangled her hands into his thick hair. "You have got to cool it," she told him breathlessly.

"I do?" He slid his tongue teasingly along her labia, and she gasped and tried to push his face away. "I don't think so. We're not done yet. Not while you've still got the strength to fight me."

"That's kinky," she told him.

"Sure. Whatever you need, sweetheart. I've never done kinky before, but I take my cues from you."

"But you're driving me bananas!"

He grinned. "You say that like it's a bad thing."

"Not bad. Just out of control. I can't stop, ah . . ."

"Coming? I know." His grin widened. "You're incredible. I lost count. I've never been with anyone so responsive. It's great." He fluttered his tongue across her clitoris. "Go on, do it some more."

She writhed, against the delicious sensation. "It's not me," she protested. "I've never been like this with anyone. Not even by myself. It's you. I don't even know what you're doing that's so different—"

"Savoring you." He pressed a hot kiss against her mound, and suckled her intimately. "Taking my time. Treating you right. Is that so strange? Why does it rattle you?"

She had no good answer for that. She just pushed gently at his face. "Please," she whispered. "Really. Back off. I can't take any more."

He wiped his chin. "Now?" His voice was incredulous. "You want to stop now? This is just the beginning."

"No. I mean, yes," she stammered. "I just need a moment to get myself together. I won't leave you high and dry. I'll make you come. I love making you come. But I can't stand crumbling to pieces anymore."

Davy fished around the sheets for the condom, ripped it open with his teeth and spat out the chunk of wrapper. "No fucking way."

His tone alarmed her. "Don't be mad. I just meant—"

"I know exactly what you meant. You think I'm falling for that bullshit? Pull back now, and give you a chance to put all your barriers back up?" He rolled the condom over himself. "Then you'll do your tough chick routine, and pretend you don't need anything or anyone."

Her jaw dropped. "But I never said . . . I only meant . . ."

"I'm onto you, Margot." He shoved her down against the pillows. "I'm not backing off. You had your chance to change your mind. I gave you more than one. So forget it."

"You're overreacting," she protested. "I never said that I wanted you to—" Her words stuttered off as he pressed the thick bulb of his penis against her soft folds, sliding inside. "Oh, Davy."

"I've got you exactly where I want you. I'd be a goddamn

idiot to let you wiggle away from me now. So just deal with me."

She was overwhelmed by his big, hot body poised over hers, his thick shaft pushing against the resistance of her body. She was drenched with her own juices, and even so, she felt invaded.

He paused, holding most of his weight off her. "Go ahead." His voice was taunting. "Fight me. I know you want to."

His tone infuriated her. "You bastard." She shoved his chest, trying to dislodge him, and suddenly understood his strategy. With every writhing wiggle that she made, he slid deeper until he was wedged inside her, and she was panting with a volatile mix of fury and excitement. Her body clenched around him, and he seconded every move she made. Before she knew it, instead of fighting, she was sliding up and down his big phallus, jerking her hips to meet him.

His smile of triumph maddened her. "You love it," he muttered.

"Sneaky, underhanded, dominating jerk," she told him breathlessly. "Get that self-satisfied look off your face right now."

"I can't help but notice that you're not telling me to stop."

She swatted at his chest. He caught her hands in his and pinned them down on either side of her head. "What does it mean when you hit me? Does it mean you want me to fuck you harder? Like . . . this?"

She cried out at the sensation of his penis stroking heavily over that mystery spot inside that flushed and glowed with ever-sharpening pulses of pleasure. "Damn you, Davy," she whispered.

"I just want to get it right," he said huskily. "I can tell it works for you, because I fit perfectly now. All of me. You hug me. So hot and wet."

This was all wrong, all backwards. This wasn't the way she ran her sex life, when she had one. Like being on the bottom. She vastly preferred the top, always had. Feeling squished and breathless made her irritated, and besides which, she had to control the pace and the angle if she wanted a chance in hell of working up a decent climax.

But having orgasms was clearly not a problem with Davy McCloud. The real challenge was to make the orgasms stop for long enough to think a coherent thought. His angle was perfect. His pace was ideal. His big body thrusting heavily into hers was erotic perfection.

She melted softer at every stroke. She didn't even notice the shift when it happened. When she drifted back from the umpteenth rippling shimmer of delight, too limp to move, her terror of disappearing was gone. She wasn't fighting anymore. She didn't remember deciding to stop. He'd won, and she was too exhausted and blissed out to care.

Davy's gaze was fixed on her, an odd expression almost like longing on his face. She reached up, wrapping her arms around his shoulders. "Hey. Don't you ever come yourself?"

"Sure I do." He kissed her, caressing her full lower lip with lingering softness. "Wrap your legs around me."

She obliged him, and sighed with pleasure as they rocked together, clasped tight. "When?" she demanded.

"When you're done," he said simply.

"Oh." She pulled his face closer to kiss him. "Well, then. I'm done. You've proved your point. I'm impressed. You're the man. OK?"

He nodded. She was vaguely surprised when he pulled away from her embrace and sat up on his knees, folding her legs high and wide.

"Davy?" She held out her arms. "Come back to—"

"No," he said curtly.

He thrust himself inside her, his face rigid and far away. The fleeting moment of vulnerability was gone. She'd lost him.

She jerked up onto her elbows and clutched his upper arms, bracing herself against the sensual assault of his body.

The muscles were corded on his neck, his jaw so tight, he looked like he was in pain. His eyes closed as his hips slammed against hers. He didn't want to see her, didn't want to be seen. It made her feel lonely and betrayed. So intimately joined, and yet so far away from him. He let out a choked sound, and flung his head back as his orgasm wrenched him.

She dragged him down against her body, holding him tightly, but he'd already retreated to a place too far away for her to find or reach.

Chapter

14

Reeling back from the brink. That was how it felt, a panicky burst of vertigo, the *what-the-fuck-am-I-doing* feeling exploding in his mind.

He slowly drew his cock out of the tight clasp of her body, and extricated himself from her slender limbs without looking into her eyes.

The feeling was too close to euphoria to be called bad, too similar to terror to be called good. The only way to deal with it was to keep his mouth shut until he got a grip on himself.

He rolled off the bed, his back to her, and pulled the condom off.

Margot sat up behind him. He sensed the question she was too shy to ask, but he had no answer. He'd hurt her by pulling back at the last minute. It hadn't been a conscious choice, but he still felt like shit.

"Davy?" she asked. "Are you—"

"Got to get rid of this thing." He fled to the bathroom before she could ask if he was OK. He would either have to lie and say he was fine, which would be tough in the face of blatant evidence to the contrary, or else explain his behavior. And his feelings. Not his strong point.

He had nothing to say. He'd invested years of his life learning techniques to not feel this way, and all his efforts were for nothing.

Margot was perched on the edge of the bed, lying in ambush when he came out of the bathroom. She was so gorgeous stark naked, with her hair rumpled, a sharp, hectic flush on her high cheekbones. Pissed off. About to give him hell, which he deserved. His wildcat.

His cock rose to full salute instantly.

Her eyes widened. "Wow. That was quick."

He shrugged. His voice was locked in his throat.

It became evident that he wasn't going to reply, and her soft throat bobbed as she swallowed, hard. "Are you coming back to bed?"

He stared at the high, tight points of her full breasts, the curves and hollows of her body, her soft red lips, puffy from being kissed. If he got into bed with her, he would end up on top of her again in seconds. He'd already overdone it. He had to back off, for both their sakes.

"I'm going to go get some work done," he said. "Try to sleep."

"*Sleep?*" Her eyes narrowed to bright slits. "Are you nuts? You're blowing me off? Now?"

"You said you were done, right? No more sex. I'm trying to—"

"Stop trying so hard. Come here. Right now." She held out an imperious hand, and he was drawn to her like a magnet, dragged by his dumb handle. Margot grasped his cock in her hand and cupped her other hand around his ass, pulling him close.

"You're chickening out on me," she accused him. "After all that self-righteous crap about not letting me put up barriers."

"I am not," he growled. "I'm right here."

"Huh-uh. You're a million miles away. Even with a monster hard-on, you do the ice cube act. You pulled me to pieces and then left me all alone when you came. Don't think I didn't notice, buddy."

"I didn't—"

"I consider that a challenge," she announced. "I'm not letting you get away with it." She gripped his cock in both hands and leaned over him, her tongue circling the swollen tip, a hot swirl of blissful sensation.

He almost fell to his knees. "Damn it, Margot. Stop this. I can't—"

"Why not?" Her eyes flicked up at him, bright with mischief, and her mouth went back to working tender magic on the head of his cock.

He steadied himself on her shoulders. Margot pulled him even closer, and cupped her bosom, pushing it high so that his cock slid into the warm velvet cleft between her breasts. The empurpled tip poked its head out the top, gleaming with pre-come.

Stupidly enthusiastic, no matter how the rest of him felt.

"I could make you come like this," she said. "Or you could lie down on the bed and let me do to you exactly what you did to me. How did you put it? Savoring you. Taking my time. Treating you right."

"You've already shown me how good you are at oral sex."

"Oh, that was ages ago. You deserve another five-star blow job by now. You're fabulous, Davy. I've got to scramble to make points."

"This isn't a goddamn game that one of us has to win!"

She drew back, stung. "Wow," she murmured. "You weren't kidding when you said you were humor challenged."

He grabbed a pair of sweatpants from the top of the clean laundry pile and yanked them on. "I never kid."

"Oh. OK. Excuse me. No smiles, no jokes, no laughter

allowed. We're dead serious here. God forbid that I should tease you."

He threw up his hands in furious frustration. "Damn it!"

"Don't tell me this isn't a game," she said hotly. "You tricked me into opening up, and then you cheated and did the disappearing act. Davy McCloud, superstud. Whips the girls into a frenzy and doesn't even work up a sweat."

He looked down at his erection, his shaking hands. "I sweated," he said dourly. "Believe me."

"Gee, thanks for admitting that the experience actually affected you in some way," she snapped.

"You affect me," he said. "You certainly affect my judgment. Otherwise we wouldn't be here."

"Meaning what?" she demanded. "That only crazed volcanic lust would override your judgment to the extent of getting involved with a hard-luck case like me?"

Honesty compelled his answer. "Something like that."

He hated what happened to her face. The red flush faded to icy pale, the bright glitter in her gorgeous eyes was suddenly veiled. It was like a light going out. It made his gut ache, become a cold, hard knot.

Margot pulled the sheet up, looking away from him. "All right." Her voice was muffled. "Work your head off. I'm figuring out the rules. I won't violate the boundaries of your narrow little comfort zone again."

He wanted to hurl a chair through the window. "I'm just trying to keep this under . . ." His voice cut off as he searched for another word.

"Control," she finished for him. "As long as you're running things, everything's fine, but the minute I make a move, you freak out. You—"

"That's enough."

His command voice had no discernible effect on Margot. She charged right on while the tension inside him rose, coiling tighter.

"Maybe you can control your feelings, but you can't control mine. I tried to keep my distance, but you kept following me around, driving me nuts. Luring me with sex. *Want a piece of candy, little girl?* Hah! And when I finally fall for it, you take what you want and it's bye-bye, Margot. Go to sleep. Like I'm a doll with an on-off switch—"

"Shut *up!*" He was on top of her, pinning her to the mattress. Blood pounding loudly in his head. As surprised as she was.

They were both shocked into total stillness.

"Whoa," she whispered. "Chill, Davy."

He lifted himself up off her body. "Shit," he muttered. "Sorry."

"Um, no harm done, I guess." Her voice was small, her eyes wide.

"I'd better get out of here," he said. *Before I fuck up even worse.*

She scrunched down into the bed and pulled the sheet up until only her big, shadowy eyes regarded him over the edge. "McCloud?"

They were back to the surname. Bad sign. "Yeah?"

"Do not ever tell me to shut up again. That's not OK."

"I won't," he said.

He had no idea if he could keep his promise. He couldn't guarantee a thing. He stood there, staring at her stupidly, until she made an impatient gesture with her hand.

"Well? So? Are you going, or are you just going to stand there like a stump?"

He stalked out, slamming the door before he could stop himself.

He didn't understand what was happening to him. This was regression. Retro-evolution. Neanderthal behavior that he'd always despised in other men, like trying to win an argument with a woman using physical intimidation. Classic asshole stuff. The impulse to blunt unwelcome emotions with alcohol, that was another big winner. A pointless short-cut that led exactly nowhere.

Come to think of it, nowhere sounded kind of relaxing tonight.

He headed into the kitchen and rummaged through the cabinet, through the tomato sauce, pickles, oil, spices, beans. The whiskey wasn't there. He never put it anywhere else. Weird. Maybe Sean, for the first and only time in his hap-hazard life, had put it someplace before leaving the other night. Not likely, but he had no other explanation.

He tried the other cupboards, scanned the other rooms, checked the back porch. He even looked in the fridge, just to be thorough.

So much for drowning his discomfort in alcohol. He had beer, but beer wasn't the right vibe for this raw, scary feeling.

He headed into his office, logged on and started his Internet search with the names Margaret Callahan and Craig Caruso. Two hours later, he was still poring through archived news articles, his eyes burning with weariness. It looked bad for her.

Getting his hands on Snakey was Margot's best chance for unraveling that knot. His instincts told him that Snakey wouldn't stay far away for long. The sick creep was in love. It was almost funny. He tried so hard to keep his love life non-problematic, and now he had a crazy assassin as a ro-mantic rival. Time to start packing the Glock.

He heard the cell phone buzz from the other room, and headed into the kitchen to check it out. It was Sean.

He hit "talk." "What the hell are you doing awake at this hour?"

"Wondering why you haven't been answering your house or cell phones for the last five hours," Sean responded. "I was worried."

"I turned the volume down," Davy said. "Margot needed sleep."

"Oh!" Sean cackled with delight. "So that's your excuse for missing the rehearsal dinner! Sleazy bastard. You were the bad brother tonight for once, not me. It's kind of refreshing to take a break."

Davy's jaw sagged in dismay. He sank down into a chair. "Rehearsal—oh, fuck, no. You're kidding me. That was tonight?"

"You knew the wedding is tomorrow, didn't you? Besides, I only knew it was tonight because you told me." Sean was enjoying himself hugely. "You even wrote it on my girlie calendar the last time you were at my place. You knew. At least you did before sex hormones wiped your brain clean. Bye-bye, Mr. Perfect. Nice knowin' ya."

Davy rubbed his face and groaned. "I can't believe it."

"Yeah, neither could anyone else. Nobody was fussed about it except Erin's mom, though, so don't sweat it," Sean said, relenting. "I told Barbara that any guy capable of coordinating army intel in Middle Eastern hot spots was up to handling a wedding ceremony on the fly. She was real unimpressed, though. I hope I didn't make things worse for you. Prepare for some freezing glances."

Davy groaned softly. "I'll live. We'll be there before two. You can fill me in on the choreography before the ceremony."

There was a delicate pause. "We?"

"Yeah, yeah, I'm bringing her along," Davy said tersely. "But don't get gooey on me. Things are just too strange to leave her alone here."

"Yeah? Strange how? Tell me!"

Davy paused. "You alone? Or is your bed full?"

"She's asleep," Sean assured him. "No problem."

"Like hell. Get your clothes on and go outside," Davy said. "I don't want to discuss this in front of one of your bridesmaids."

Sean's voice made soothing, explanatory murmurs. A

drowsy feminine voice in the background responded to them.

"OK," Sean said, after a few moments. "Goodbye warm sheets and smooth, silky female limbs. I'm shivering half naked and barefoot on the cold, wet grass of the lawn to suit your paranoid whims, so out with it."

"How is the bridesmaid situation shaping up, anyhow?"

Sean made a growling sound. "Succulent. It's the bridesmaid buffet. A nibble of this, a nibble of that. There's Marika, the blonde waif with the big gray eyes who's wearing lapis blue. I'm escorting Belle, this cute, chubby redhead with yards of cleavage who's wearing amethyst purple. I just want to put 'em in my pocket and take 'em all home."

Davy grinned to himself. "Which one are you in bed with now?"

"Oh, that is Cleo. She's wearing topaz. She's hot. They're all hot. But get to the point. It's friggin' cold out here in the middle of the night. What is it with Margot? Is it just the stalker, or is there more?"

"Do you have a gun with you up there?" Davy asked.

"Uh . . . yeah, sure," Sean said slowly. "I've got the Sig. Why?"

"Wear it under your tux tomorrow," Davy said.

Sean whistled. "Spill it."

Davy outlined Margot's story and Snakey's exploits. He felt uneasy doing so without discussing it with Margot, but he needed backup. Besides, Sean was such a spaz, he would only treat the situation with proper gravity if Davy told him what was really happening.

"Whoa," Sean breathed, at the end of Davy's terse monologue. "You make me jealous."

Davy snorted. "Yeah? How so?"

"Here I am, messing around with bouncing bridesmaids while you've got a mysterious, gorgeous desperado in your bed. Damn. That should be me. I'm the one who likes to play with fire. You're the one who likes to keep things under control. Right?"

Davy winced at his brother's choice of words. "It just happened."

"Want to trade?"

"Don't even go there with your mind. Smart-mouthed punk."

Sean's laughter had a triumphant ring. "God, I love to see you get worked up about something."

"I'd rather it didn't involve murder," was Davy's dour observation.

"Me too. You should have brought her here tonight," Sean fretted. "I don't like you in town all alone with a pissed-off psycho on your case."

"We'll come up tomorrow. Oh, yeah. Ask Miles if he would look after Margot's dog for us during the reception, if he's not still pissed at me. Tell him I'll pay him. Free coachings, whatever he wants. And don't tell Connor about this. He's had enough trouble. He deserves a break."

Sean made a derisive sound. "Like I could if I wanted to. He disappeared with Erin right after the rehearsal. They're off combining their DNA in a locked room someplace, I expect."

"Good," Davy said. "Keep it that way. Tell Seth and Nick about the stalker part. I want some other suspicious, paranoid sons of bitches prowling around being vigilant tomorrow. Especially since you'll be gorging yourself at the bridesmaid buffet."

"Piss on you for your lack of faith in me," Sean said mildly. "I'm a born multitasker. I could flirt with ten cute girls while defusing a bomb. What you think of as scatterbrained is actually concentration in a higher form than you could possibly comprehend."

"Yeah, yeah." Davy rolled his eyes.

"You think concentration means staring at something

until you burn little eye-shaped holes in it. That's just obsession, bonehead."

"How about we debate this later?"

"Yeah, run back to make sure that the covers are tucked in tight around your sexy fugitive nymph," Sean said. "Give her a long, wet kiss from me. Oh, and Davy? About the fugitive thing . . . I don't suppose you told her that the wedding is going to be crawling with FBI agents?"

"Considering that she's being stalked by a homicidal maniac, I consider that an advantage, rather than a disadvantage."

Sean grunted. "She might disagree. Chicks are contrary. It would be smart to prepare yourself. Like, with a bulletproof vest, maybe?"

"Yeah, thanks for the tip. Oh, and hey. Sean. One last thing. Did you do anything with my bottle of Scotch?"

"Nope." Sean's voice was puzzled. "Why would I? I loathe that stuff. Makes my tongue shrivel."

"Just wondering. I can't seem to find it. Weird, that's all."

"Maybe your good twin poured it down the toilet while you were sleeping," his ever helpful brother suggested.

Davy sighed. "Take it easy, Sean."

He clicked the phone shut and wandered into the living room.

The missing bottle of whiskey was ominous. He wished he'd given into his buddy Seth's urging to install a home security system. He'd scoffed at the idea at the time. His locks were excellent, his hands and feet should be registered as lethal weapons, and everybody in the neighborhood knew he was a martial arts expert as well as a detective. God help the intruder stupid enough to bother him. That had been his reasoning thus far, but looking around at his quiet, well-ordered house, he got a creepy sense that his barriers had been breached.

Yeah, right. By a malevolent entity who went for a half-empty bottle of whiskey, and left tens of thousands of dollars worth of cutting-edge computer, audio and video equipment alone.

He brushed the thought away, angry at himself for giving in to stupid paranoia, even for a moment. Paranoia was a family weakness, to be guarded against at all times. Even so, he would swallow his pride tomorrow and tell Seth he'd changed his mind about the alarms. The place needed another line of defense if Margot was going to be here.

The implications of that thought hit him, and he went hot and cold all over. God. What was he thinking. He seldom let women into his house. He preferred going to theirs, so he could gracefully control the timing of his amorous encounters. He liked to leave when he was done.

And he really, really liked having the option of removing himself quickly from tense, uncomfortable situations. Like the one he'd just gone through in the bedroom with Margot.

The more he thought about it, the more agitated he got. Brain racing, breathing choppy and short, muscles knotted.

He needed to practice kung fu. Moving meditation was his only hope of chilling out. When nightmares and insomnia gripped him, a few hours of kung fu practice rested him more than twice as many hours of sleep ever could. A brain wave phenomenon. Whatever worked.

He headed into the practice room, formerly a back terrace. He'd glassed it in and turned it into his personal martial arts studio. Paneled with fragrant red cedar, tatami covering the floor, a bank of windows streaming moonlight. He positioned himself in the middle of the room.

Crane flies into the sky . . . crane stretches left claw . . . crane cools his wings . . . his body knew the form so well, he didn't have to think about the movements. He tried to keep his mind empty, but thoughts kept springing up. He brushed them gently away, one after the other.

An instant later, another would bounce up to take its place.

Lazy tiger stretches his back leg . . . and even when he'd been involved with Fleur, it hadn't felt like this. Fleur had been so fragile and damaged. She'd aroused all his protective instincts. As emotionally immature as he'd been at the time, it had felt like love to him. *Crane guards the cave* . . . *crane leaps up and kicks behind* . . . *crane guards his nest* . . . she'd been beautiful, too, in a wispy sort of way. He remembered having sex with her so carefully. Holding her like she was made out of blown glass.

Wild tiger looks back . . .

Nothing like what had just happened in the bedroom with Margot. Wildcat. Panther woman. He'd barely gotten out of there in one piece.

Back to *wild tiger raises his head* . . . and he had a hard-on again. This was a challenge. *Golden dragon stretches out his left claw* . . .

The door opened to the living room. Margot was silhouetted against the light, wrapped in his huge terrycloth bathrobe.

"Oh," she said. "There you are."

"Here I am," he repeated, for lack of anything better to say.

She walked in and closed the door behind them so they were alone in the moonlight, and watched as he finished *watersnake swims to the surface*. He stopped, and waited.

"Do you always work out in the middle of the night?" she asked.

"Often," he said. "I don't sleep real well. This is a good substitute."

"Me, neither. Maybe I should try it." She stared at him, her eyes haunted looking pools of shadow in the moonlight. "I'm sorry I shot off my mouth," she said. "I didn't want to make you mad."

"I wasn't mad," he said.

"Were too," she said. "Madder 'n hell. You big fibber."

"I'm not going to argue with you again, so don't start with me."

Margot looked down. "I'm doing it again already," she murmured. "I can't seem to get out of your face. I'm just compelled to bug you."

"Wow, what an honor," he muttered.

She let out a cute snort of laughter, and an awkward silence fell.

He bore it for as long as he could stand. "Do you want something from me?"

He immediately regretted the words. They were an invitation to intimacy. The last thing he was equipped to deal with right now.

Margot stepped closer. "Last night, when I came to your gym, and saw you doing your kung fu . . ."

"What?" he prodded, after several maddening seconds.

"You were so gorgeous," she whispered. "Like something out of my wildest fantasies. You hardly seemed real."

He had no idea what to do with that. His face was hot. Hard to believe that much blood had actually managed to divert itself from his throbbing groin. He was grateful for the concealing shadows.

"Uh, thanks," he mumbled.

She wrapped her arms around herself. "You were so sexy, I forgot all the stuff I was worrying about and started to picture, um . . ."

"Yeah?" His heart was thudding again, at a hard gallop. "Stop torturing me, for God's sake. Just tell me."

"That I was a martial arts expert, like that girl in *The Matrix*. Trinity. Dressed up in tight black leather." Her voice was dreamy and hypnotic. "I would jump on you and wrestle you to the ground. Have my wicked way with you, right there on the mat."

"Uh . . . wow."

She let out a self-deprecating laugh. "But I'm not a kung fu expert. So much for that fantasy."

"You've got secret weapons of your own," he said.

"Do I?" She moved closer, and reached up, petting his

bare chest. Her hand slid down his belly and stopped, uncertain of her welcome.

He grabbed her hand and dragged it lower, tugging down his sweatpants so that he could wrap her cool fingers around his cock. "When you say stuff like that, you could knock me over with a feather."

"Really?" Her voice was soft with wonder.

"Try me," he said rashly. "Go on. Attack. See how you do."

Her smile in the moonlight was mysteriously beautiful. "OK," she whispered. "Imagine that my finger is a feather."

Her strong, slim hand gripped his cock, caressing him with bold, sensual strokes that jolted agonized pleasure through his body. She reached out with her other hand and traced a delicate, lacy pattern on his chest with the very tip of her forefinger. Her touch was so light, it barely brushed his chest hair, as ticklish as a puff of air, but his nipples tightened and his breath roughened to audible gasps.

"Just the tip of a feather," she whispered, tracing the forefinger over his shoulder, his throat, his face. Her other hand gripped and swirled, milking him tenderly.

He couldn't handle the feather torture for another second. He pulled her hand away from his cock and dropped backwards onto the tatami, pulling her after him so that she tumbled over his body with a startled gasp. "Uh, Davy? What are you—"

"You knocked me down," he explained. "With your feather. I'm helpless." He arranged her so she was straddling him. "You go for that, right? Being in control, running everything? That's your comfort zone."

She stiffened. "You should talk! It's your comfort zone too, buddy, except that you've got eight inches and a hundred or so pounds on me. I'm not the only one around here who's afraid to—"

"Don't be mad," he pleaded. "It's not my fault that I'm bigger. Besides, I'm trying so hard. You've won. I'm flat on my back, at your mercy. Pinned. What the hell more do you want from me?"

Margot trailed her fingertips over his chest. "I'm not sure," she murmured. "At the very least you should promise that we take turns running things. That way nobody gets a swelled head."

"OK," he agreed readily. "Anything you say. You're the boss."

"Oh, don't overdo it, or you'll ruin it."

"God, no." He made his voice meek. "Never that."

She scowled in mock fury as she reached into the pocket of her robe and pulled out a condom. She shrugged the bathrobe off her shoulders, letting it drop down onto his thighs behind her.

He couldn't believe how beautiful she was, no matter how many times he feasted his eyes on her naked body. Curvy and sinuous and lush, all at the same time. She ripped the condom open with a dramatic flourish, rose up onto her knees and proceeded to make the sheathing of his cock into its own slow, sensual ritual.

"You're beautiful in the moonlight, Davy," she said softly.

He was startled and embarrassed. "Uh . . . you're beautiful all the time," he offered, feeling awkward.

Her sweet, unguarded smile flashed again. She pulled his cock into position and nudged it between her slick, tender folds, arching back as she sank down onto his cock.

A groan rasped out of him. "God, you're tight. It's amazing."

"I think you're the amazing part of this particular equation," she murmured, laughter in her voice.

She rode him, first slow and deep, massaging his shaft with all the tight, greedy little muscles inside her, and slowly picking up speed. She incited him with her hands and her eyes and her desperate, jerking hips. He bucked and surged beneath her, giving her everything she needed. Her conquest, her pleasure, her victory, whatever. Anything.

He surrendered to the moonlight, to Margot's passionate ardor. She had him stretched out helpless and writhing on the floor. At her service, and content to be there. A sweating, whimpering sex slave.

She danced over him, her body contoured with moonlight and shadows as it rose and fell over him. Only by sheer luck did he manage to wait for her. He felt her climax building, and pulled her down on top of him as his own floodgates opened.

He flung his head back, crying out in a ragged voice he could barely hear inside the storm in his head. He was torn open. Light poured into his body. Violent pleasure wrenched through him

Annihilating him.

When he opened his eyes, Margot's soft hair was tickling his face. She kissed his cheeks, his eyes. That was when he felt it. The hot moisture. Oh, Jesus. Not him. This was not him. He stiffened, almost panicked, holding very still as she kissed all his tears away.

She pressed her damp, salty lips to his. Kissed him, over and over with a sweet tenderness that threatened to unravel him all over again.

"Thank you," she whispered.

He shook his head, swallowed hard. "I've got to get rid of this—"

"I'll do it," she whispered. "You stay right there. You just stay mellow." She slid the condom off him, and got up. Her naked silhouette appeared briefly in the door against the living room light.

He lay there, immobile, too weak and astonished to move. He had no words for what had just happened, no precedents. She came back quickly, and lay down next to him, cuddling herself into the crook of his shoulder. She pulled the bathrobe up, tucking it around his chest.

"Sleep now," she crooned, as if he were a baby.

He stared down at her slender hand on his chest, her soft

lips against his shoulder. He wanted to tell her that he didn't need to be soothed like a scared little kid, that he was perfectly fine, but the words wouldn't form. Her hands, her lips, her soft voice, were a balm for an ancient ache he was unwilling even to name.

He loved it. Couldn't get enough of it.

He stared up mutely at the moon and gave into her tenderness, letting the moon swim and swirl into a shapeless, watery blaze of light.

Chapter
15

*S*he was galloping across a grassy mesa on a wild stallion, *flying through the air, too exhilarated to be afraid. The mesa was broken by vast rocky canyons that fell abruptly away from jewel-green grass—chasms of untold depths, full of rolling banks of mist. The huge sky was full of brilliant white and ominous gray thunderheads, glimpses of electric blue sky showing between them. Bolts of sunlight slanted through ragged glory holes, so bright they made her eyes water and swim . . .*

She blinked, squinted. Sunlight was streaming in the windows, pressing against her eyelids. She was hot, everywhere. Sweating.

And there was a big, solid male body beneath her own, his heart beat slow and strong against her ear. She was sprawled on top of Davy. His eyes were somber and thoughtful as he gazed into her face.

"Good morning," he said.

She smiled at him, blushing as the memories of last night's intense intimacy flooded into her mind, in vivid detail.

"Hi," she whispered. "How long have you been awake?"

"A few hours," he said. "I've been watching you sleep."

She jolted up off his body. "What? You've been lying there with me on top of you for hours? You're nuts!"

"You needed to rest," he said quietly. "You were tired."

"What time is it?"

"Late, I imagine," he said. "Noon, maybe. The sun is pretty high."

She rubbed her eyes and pressed her thighs tightly around the ache that came from having scads of fabulous, unaccustomed sex. She'd pulled the bathrobe off his body when she slid off him, and his erection stood high and thick and flushed against his belly.

His eyes followed her gaze, and a grin lit up his face."Did you put two condoms in the pocket of that robe last night?" he asked.

"No," she admitted. "Only one. I was thinking in the moment."

"Huh. I guess we don't have time, anyhow." His voice was businesslike. "Have a shower while I put some breakfast on."

He rolled to his feet with sinuous grace. It dazzled her. Davy's naked, aroused body lit up by sunlight was too much stimulation for her poor nerves. She was going to short out. Emit smoke from her ears.

She flung the bathrobe at him. "Cover yourself, for God's sake."

He yanked on his sweatpants, grinning. "Can't handle it, huh?"

He disappeared into the living room, leaving her alone and bemused in the middle of the beautiful, empty room.

Huh. So he was in a playful mood. Sex had smoothed out all his jagged edges. She wished she could say the same for herself. She felt so fuddled and soft. The glitter of sunlight on the surface of the lake outside was so beautiful, it brought tears to her eyes.

She wandered out of the bathroom twenty minutes later, hair still dripping, and stared at the table in awe. The man went all out, every meal he ate. No cornflakes, pop tarts, bagels or shortcuts of any kind. It was a starving lumberjack's breakfast of pancakes dripping with maple syrup, scrambled eggs, grilled bacon, sliced strawberries, orange juice, toast, strong French roast coffee with cream. Outrageous.

She didn't slow down until she was halfway through the second fluffy stack of hotcakes. "Don't we have a wedding to go to? Shouldn't we be saving our appetites? Is this a sit down lunch, or a buffet?"

"Both, I think. Don't worry," he said. "That's the thing about an appetite. It never goes away for very long."

Margot's eyes lingered over Davy's torso. "With your muscle mass and metabolism, you can reason like that. If I ate like this all the time, I'd be the size of a humpbacked whale."

His eyes slid appreciatively over her body, swathed in one of his big towels. "We've come up with some great ways to burn calories."

She coughed on her coffee. "Um . . . speaking of which."

His fork stopped halfway to his mouth. "Yeah?"

"Maybe we should talk about, uh, what happened."

"Let's not, and say we did," he replied. "We just crash and burn whenever we talk about us. Let's just relax and go with it."

"You mean, stick with the wild monkey sex, and conveniently not think about anything else?"

He shrugged. "Sounds like a great plan to me."

She almost laughed at his simplistic male reasoning, but she didn't want to start out the day by making him mad. It was too stressful in her current vulnerable state. "I wish it were so easy," she said.

"Why can't it be?" His eyes challenged her over the rim of his cup.

"I told you," she said. "I can't take ambiguity."

He set down his cup. "I haven't been ambiguous with

you," he said. "I've gone to great lengths to be honest with you. Every time, I've gotten punished for it. I don't feel like getting punished this morning. I don't feel like trying to say whatever you want to hear, either."

"I never said I wanted you to—"

"What I want is to have breakfast with a gorgeous, fascinating woman who drove me crazy all night long. That's all I'm aiming for. No more, no less. Let's keep things simple. Please."

She covered her face with her hands, unsure whether she wanted to laugh or cry. "I'm trying. Really. The truth is, with a guy like you, an arrangement like what you proposed to me yesterday isn't really—"

"What kind of a guy am I?" he demanded suddenly.

She floundered. "Uh, gee. Let's see. Gorgeous? Smart? Financially solvent? Fabulous in bed? Is that enough for you, or shall I go on?"

He looked bemused. "Thanks."

"I'm not flattering you. Don't be vain. I'm trying to make a point, but if you keep fishing for compliments—"

"Sorry," he said meekly. "Make your point."

"As I was saying," she grumbled. "Even without commitment and flowers and love and yada yada, just plain old straight sex for the sake of sex with a guy like you is not a bad bargain. Considering."

"Considering what?" He looked suspicious.

"That is, it wouldn't be if I could separate sex from emotion," she pressed on. "I truly wish I could. I would have a lot more fun. But I can't. Particularly not . . . sex like that."

"Sex like what?" he nudged.

She scowled at him. "You're fishing again. It's bugging me."

His slow grin began to spread. "So it was good for you, too, then?"

She rolled her eyes. "Oh, please. Don't even start. You know exactly how good it was for me. I may never recover."

"I've barely even started," he said softly. "You have no idea."

Heat raced over the surface of her skin.

Davy shoved a strawberry around on his plate with his knife. "Try not to think about it so hard," he suggested. "I can't leave you alone when you're in danger. The sex is a separate issue. I told you last night. I don't expect anything from you. If you want sex from me, you've got it. If not, no problem. I'm not going to bully you into being my love slave."

She pressed her thighs together over the shivery rush that went through her at the very thought. Davy McCloud's love slave. Ooh, lordy.

"What if I bully you into being my love slave?" she demanded.

"Bully away. I'm ready to serve," he said promptly. "Anytime."

Her eyes slid down to the sweatpants that showed off the length and urgency of his erection. "Wow. Are you always at the ready?"

"Only one way to find out," Davy said. "Consider it a challenge, Margot. Wear me out. Blow my mind. Let's see who crumbles first."

She knew it was a bad idea even before she said it, but she couldn't stop herself. "What if all this hot sex turns my brains to mush and I fall madly in love with you? What'll you do then?"

His smile vanished. The teasing warmth in his eyes transformed itself to glacial ice. "I really, really wish you wouldn't," he said finally.

It was what she deserved, for asking such a dumb question. So last night's sweet, lovely meltdown in the kung fu room hadn't made a dent in his armor. There was zero possibility of something deeper between them. It was a silly, wishful fantasy, fueled by moonlight.

Gah. What an idiot she was.

"You know how it is." She tried to make her tone light. "You play with fire, you're gonna get burned."

He took a final swallow of his coffee. "We're late," he said coolly. "We should leave in fifteen minutes. Get yourself ready, please."

So much for the wild, crazy strawberry and maple syrup sex on the breakfast table. The L word trashed his mood. Predictable, but it still made her feel sad. Stupid, too, for setting herself up for rejection.

"We have to drop by my place to get my dressy clothes," she said. "And then we have to take Mikey to the pet hotel."

He frowned. "I thought we were bringing him along."

She shook her head. "I'll feel conspicuous enough at a fancy wedding without being that girl with the dog. I hate to leave him there overnight, and he'll hate it too, but he'll live."

A curt nod was her reply. Davy stalked off in the direction of the bedroom. Margot got dressed and was just finishing up the dishes when Davy came into the kitchen in jeans and a black T-shirt, smelling of soap and aftershave, looking gorgeous. A garment bag hung over his arm. He scowled at her. "You didn't have to do dishes."

She shrugged. "Breakfast was fabulous. It's only fair."

The stop at her place was just a brief moment of rummaging through plastic shopping bags in the trunk of the car, gathering up her makeup, hairpins, underpants, toiletries, and her one pretty outfit. Thank goodness she had one. She was compromised enough already without letting Davy McCloud buy her clothes.

Next stop, the pet hotel. Davy followed her in, glowering to the right and left as if someone might jump her in the parking lot. Mikey carried on with his usual histrionics, trembling and whimpering.

"Stop torturing me, you little twerp," she hissed at him as she smiled at the chubby girl behind the front desk. "This isn't my fault, and I'll fix it as soon as I can. Hi, Amy, how's it going?"

Amy grinned back. "Oh, hey, there. Happy late birthday, by the way. Did you have a good time at the party?"

Margot blinked. "Party? What party?"

"Your niece said . . . uh . . ." Amy backpedaled, confused. "Wait a sec." She stared at Mikey, then at Margot. "You're Mikey's person?"

"Yeah. Of course. Why? What's this about a party?"

Amy looked nervous. "Well, your niece came by yesterday to pick up Mikey for your surprise party, and we told her we couldn't—"

"I don't have a niece," Margot said. "I have no family here. And my birthday's in December."

"Oh. I'm sorry. Maybe I got it mixed up," the girl said miserably. "I don't know. She said she was your niece, I swear. I would have said something last night, but I didn't want to spoil the surprise."

Margot's stomach had tightened to a queasy, heaving mass.

Davy stepped forward. "Would you describe this girl for me?"

"She was about my age," Amy said. "Platinum blond dye job. Dressed in Goth stuff, lots of piercing. Black leather. She had a tattoo on the side of her neck. A scorpion, I think. We didn't let her take Mikey, of course, 'cause you'd marked your preference against it on the form."

"Thank God." Margot cuddled the dog closer. "I've changed my mind. Mikey's staying with me today after all."

Davy dialed Raul Gomez as they walked out to the truck. Gomez was a homicide detective in the SPD, an army buddy dating back to the days of Desert Storm. They'd worked together over the years on several successfully resolved cases. Gomez also owed him for having unmasked a predator who had targeted Gomez's vulnerable widowed sister some years back. Between Davy and Gomez, the guy had ended up with good cause to regret his choice of prey.

"Gomez here," came Raul's deep voice over the phone.

"It's McCloud," Davy said.

"Hey. I was about to call you. About the dead guy you called in?"

"What about him?" Davy felt his neck begin to prickle.

"The autopsy's still pending, but I just heard a weird fun fact from the morgue. The guy doesn't have a mark on him. Not a cut, not a bruise. And yet he bled to death internally. From both ends."

"Poor bastard," Davy said. "It looked bad."

Gomez grunted. "Maybe he was sick and didn't know it, but we contacted his sister, and she said as far as she knew, he'd been fine."

Davy waited, patient with Raul Gomez's meandering way of getting to the real point. "What are you thinking, Raul?"

"Weird, creepy stuff. Remember that night in Baghdad years ago when you told me all those legends about Dim Mak?"

Dim Mak. Death touch. Thoughts of that had run through Davy's head all night after seeing Wilkes's contorted body; ancient tales of the Chinese warrior monks who could cause delayed death with a single well-placed blow, hours, days, even months later.

"It crossed my mind, too," Davy said. "Let me know what they find. But I've got a question for you, too. Have you guys recently seen or heard of a platinum blond Goth girl with facial piercings, black leather, a scorpion tattoo on her neck?"

Gomez was quiet for a long moment. "What do you know about her?"

"Nothing," Davy said. "Why do you think I'm asking you?"

Gomez grunted. "Hicks was talking about a girl who fits that description this morning. Lila Simons. Seventeen years old, from Tacoma. A runaway. She'd been on the streets since March. We've had her in here a couple of times for dealing Ecstasy."

"I need to talk to her," Davy said. "Have you got her in custody?"

Gomez hesitated. "Not exactly," he said. "She's in the morgue. Some kids playing in a construction site found her body this morning. Looks like an OD. It's not my case, I just happened to overhear Hicks talking about her this morning. He's the one who had to call her folks."

"Oh." The chill in Davy's guts got sharper. "I see."

"You got any leads for Hicks?" Gomez prodded. "It sounds like you might."

"Not yet," Davy hedged. "I'll let you know as soon as I know more."

"Huh," Gomez sounded dubious. "Been keeping busy, huh?"

"Busy enough," Davy said.

"I think maybe we should get together, talk about what you've been up to. I'm starting to get real curious about your recent activities."

"I will," Davy promised. "Just not today. I'm heading up to Endicott Falls this morning. Connor's getting married."

"No shit. Tell him congratulations from me." Gomez's voice warmed. "Call me as soon as you get back."

"Will do," Davy said. He hung up the phone, and stared out the windshield for a long moment before he looked at Margot. "The Goth girl's dead," he said reluctantly. "Looks like an OD to the cops."

Margot's freckles stood out in sharp relief against her pallor.

"Maybe it's not the same girl," he offered. "Or just a coincidence."

She petted Mikey as she stared blindly out the windshield. "You said you don't believe in coincidences. I don't, either. Not anymore."

Caught in his own trap. Damn. "Whatever," he said. "I'm just glad we're leaving town."

"Um, Davy?" Margot's voice was tentative "Are you sure you still want to take me to this wedding? If you want to bail . . . I mean, bodies are starting to pile up in my wake."

"Don't even start."

She flinched at his tone.

Minutes of deadly silence went by. He was ashamed of himself for snarling at her when she was scared. "This is not your fault," he said.

Margot hid her face with her hair. "Why do you believe me, Davy?"

"Believe what?"

She shot him an incredulous glance. "Duh! That I didn't kill Craig and Mandi. What do you think I meant?"

"Oh. That." He had to realign his thoughts, he'd been so busy speculating about the pawnbroker and the Goth girl. "That's easy."

"Yeah? Hah. Do tell."

"For one thing, Snakey himself and all the weird shit he's doing backs up your story to a certain degree," he began. "For another, I have a lot of experience in interrogation. I've talked to guilty people. I know what guilt looks and feels and smells like, even when I'm dealing with a pro. You're not a pro. And you're not guilty."

She shot him a nervous smile. "Just guilty about dragging you into my mess, that's all."

"I jumped," he said. "Feet first. I was not dragged." *Except for maybe by his dick.* But he kept that crass observation to himself. "I checked the newspaper articles about you last night on the Internet," he told her.

She looked up at him, wide-eyed. "Yeah? And?"

"I would have smelled something off with that story even if I'd never met you," he said, with complete honesty. "And furthermore . . ."

"Yes?" Her eyes filled with trepidation.

"You're cute as a redhead," he told her.

He felt obscurely better when she started giggling. Tearfully, but still giggling. It was better than nothing.

* * *

It was a long drive. The thickness of the silence in the truck was driving Margot nuts. She'd never been good at silence. Particularly not now. It gave her too much time to think about the rising body count in her life. How Bart Wilkes had looked on the floor last night. How painful and frightening it must have been, to die that way. Alone and desperate.

It was so scary and sad, it was sending her straight into the hole.

She had to distract herself, quick. Davy had smothered previous attempts at conversation with monosyllabic answers, but if this went on, she'd be hysterical and babbling by the time they got to the resort.

"Can I ask you a question?" she demanded.

Davy looked dubious. "Depends. Try it. See if I answer."

"Smart-ass," she grumbled. "How is it that you have all this time to follow me around? Don't you have to work, like normal people?"

He gave her a funny look. "I'm perfectly normal."

She rolled her eyes. "Right. Sure you are."

"I'm not working any other cases. I teach at the dojo, but we just went on our summer break. And I'm phasing out the P.I. business."

"So that wasn't just a line to get rid of me?"

He shook his head. "I'm starting up a security consulting business with Sean and another friend, Seth Mackey. You'll meet him at the wedding. I'm burned out on private investigating. And I never want to deal with people looking for proof of their spouses' infidelity, ever again. Big depressing bore."

"I see," she said.

"Nailing that son-of-a-bitch Snakey, though," he went on. "That would be fun. I could really sink my teeth into a project like that."

"But being as how that's not a paying proposition, how do you make your living?" She winced, embarrassed. "Oops.

Sorry. Call it a rhetorical question. None of my damn business."

"It's OK," he said. "I don't mind. I got into trading a few years ago, when the market was good. Did pretty well. Got lucky a few times, reinvested my profits, bought a few rental properties."

"Like Tilda's gym?"

"Among other things. The detective business went pretty well, too, from a financial point of view. I'm in a good place for a career change."

"Lucky you," she said. "So you don't do trading anymore?"

"Nah. I—"

"Don't tell me. Let me guess. You conquered it, consumed it, and got bored with it. Right?"

He shrugged. "Once I'd figured out how it worked, why continue? I was doing fine, money wise. Money's not a good enough reason to run around in circles. It was time to move on to something new."

"And you're like that with your lovers, too?"

His smile disappeared.

"Oh, crap. Sorry," she said hastily. "That was unfair. I never said it, OK?" There was an awkward pause. Margot rushed to fill the hole.

"Really, I admire that. The money thing, I mean. Working the system, never letting it work you. I wish to God I could do that."

"You will," he said. "You'll find your groove again."

"I thought I'd found it, back in my old life," Margot said wistfully. "My business was going so well. I was so proud for making it all happen. And then all of a sudden, poof, it's gone, and I'm as desperate as I was years ago, after Mom died." She studied his profile. "I bet you don't even know what desperate feels like. You act like you were born knowing exactly what you're doing."

His smile was ironic. "I was eighteen when my father died," he said. "No income, no marketable job skills, and three little brothers to support. I know what desperate feels like."

Something twisted in her chest; the thought of a teenage Davy McCloud feeling desperate. "Sorry. That was a silly thing to say."

"No problem. I don't mind."

The coolness in his voice bugged her. "Of course not. You make like nothing ever bothers you. It's an act, though. I see right through it."

He whistled. "Uh-oh. I think I'm about to find out what Margot really wants to talk about. Nowhere to run, nowhere to hide."

"That's better," she said. "I actually prefer it when you're mad, or sarcastic. At least then, I feel like you're with me. What I hate is when you get all remote and detached, like you could give a rat's ass."

He scowled out at the road. "Detachment gives you the space to choose your response rather than reacting blindly. It's a good thing."

"That's not what you're doing," she told him. "You're afraid to throw yourself into the middle of anything messy. You'd rather float above it. Detachment the way you do it is a cop-out."

Davy flicked the turn signal on, pulling abruptly off the highway. He drove without speaking until he found an unpaved road. They rattled and bounced into the shade of the tall conifers, out of sight of the road. He braked and killed the engine.

"We're talking about last night, right?" he demanded. "You're still mad at me. About the sex, about my proposition. Right?"

Margot looked away from him, swallowing nervously.

"You're pissing me off on purpose, Margot. Why?"

It was true. She didn't know why. And she couldn't seem to stop.

Davy got out of the truck and circled around to her side. He yanked her door open, grabbed her around the waist and jerked her down into his arms. Margot stared up into his face.

"I'm throwing myself into the middle of this thing with you," he said. "Stalkers, murder, mysterious women on the run from the law, is that not messy enough? Does that not get me points?"

"Yeah, but that's not what I—"

She forgot what she was going to say when he kissed her.

It was consuming, incendiary. She grabbed him and realized all at once exactly why she goaded him the way she did. She craved him like this; fully engaged with her, involved and connected. Fierce, hungry, almost scary. Not holding her at arm's length, doing his cool routine. Anger and sex was the quickest way to it.

He was all hers—if she was woman enough to handle him.

He dragged her jeans down, and slid his hand down to tangle in the silky puff of gingery ringlets at her crotch. He wrenched her panties down. The fabric ripped and gave. His fingers slid between her legs, stoking the yearning ache his kiss had already kindled.

"Is that red the real color of your hair?" he demanded.

"Sort of copper colored," she told him shakily.

"I can't wait to see it like that." His other hand slid into the mass of brown hair rumpled around her face. "I've been wondering about your real hair color since the first day I saw you."

She was dismayed. "Is it so obvious that it's a dye job?"

"Only to me. I was staring at you obsessively every chance I got," he admitted. "Studying you. Speculating about you." He turned her around and pulled her hips back so that her bare bottom was bent over, provocative and invit-ing. "I've been fantasizing about seeing your ass like this since the beginning. God, it's gorgeous."

She tensed. "No, Davy. Wait. I don't like—"

"Trust me." His voice was husky and soft. She heard the sound of his belt being unbuckled. "I've got condoms. I'll make this good for you."

"No," she said, more forcefully. "Wait, Davy. I don't like this position. It makes me feel like a piece of meat. Stop it. Please."

He froze, his hands digging into her hips for a long mo-ment, and then spun her around to face him. His face was hard with anger.

"You've got a talent for making me feel like an asshole, Margot. You push, and push, and I follow your cues, and then you chicken out on me, and I get to be the bad guy. Piece of meat? Who the hell do you think you're dealing with?"

"I don't think you're an asshole," she mumbled. "Or a bad guy."

She pulled her pants up, but he grabbed her arms and backed her up against the truck before she could zip them. "But you don't trust me."

"What's to trust?" she snapped back. "Look, Davy. Chill! It's just a sexual position that doesn't work for me! Don't take it so personally. Am I not allowed to have some prefer-ences? And don't muscle me around, either. I hate that. This is why I don't get involved with big guys. I must have been nuts, to take up with a hulking tank like you."

"You can trust me," he said simply.

The tension drained out of her muscles, leaving her limp and trembling. Her chin began to shake. Damn him. Here she was, pinned against his truck, and he had the gall to say that.

"Trust you for what?" she spat out.

"In general."

She shoved at him, furious. "That's so lame. In general? You know me. I need specifics. Black and white. Spell it out."

His brows came together. "You can trust me to tell you the truth."

"Oh. Gee, thanks," she shouted. "Even if it hurts like hell!"

His heavy silence was affirmative.

The truth. Huh. It was better than nothing. More than any other guy had ever offered her. She wished he'd gone further with it, though. It would be great if she could trust him to be on her side, to be there for her, to root for her. To trust her back. Even to . . . love her. And she was bananas, even letting such a thought cross her foolish, mushy mind.

"Let go of me, please," she whispered.

"Why do you say you don't like being with big guys? Did somebody hit you?"

She flushed. "Davy, I don't want to—"

"Just tell me."

She concluded that he wasn't going to back down any time this century. "My dad hit my mom, when I was little," she said.

His eyes narrowed with concentration. He waited.

"She finally got up the nerve to leave him when he started in on me," she continued. "I was eight or so at the time. We ran away. Never saw him again. And that's all there is to say about that. OK? Satisfied?"

He leaned forward until his forehead barely touched hers. He brushed her cheek with his knuckles. "I'm sorry that happened to you."

"I don't want to dwell on it," she snapped. "Let's move on."

He lifted her clenched fists up to his face and dropped a tiny kiss on each of them in turn. "You can trust me never to hit you."

"Oh." A spasm of hysterical laughter shook her. "That's nice."

He shrugged. "I know it sounds stupid, to say such an obvious thing out loud, but I think it ought to be said."

Feeling embarrassed and emotional always prodded her into full-out smarty-pants mode. "OK, cool. I promise never to hit you, either."

He grinned. "Thank you. That eases my mind."

"Smart-ass," she muttered.

He shook his head. "No, really. I don't like getting hit any more than the next guy. Why do you think I studied martial arts all my life?"

"Is that the reason you're so good at, ah . . . you know?"

"I'm not sure what you're referring to," he said cautiously.

She shoved at him again. "Don't be coy. You know. In bed. You know things. About my body. Things I didn't know myself. It's wild."

"Oh! That." He looked pleased, and slid his hand into her unzipped pants. "It's your body that tells me what it wants. I've never clicked with anyone like that before. And you do the exact same thing to me."

"Oh. I, uh, see," she whispered.

He kissed her, nipping tenderly at her lower lip. "Are you calmed down yet?"

"Calm isn't how I would describe this feeling. You yanked my pants down, you dirty dog. Who could be calm in those circumstances?"

"I'll pull mine down too, if it'll make you feel better," he offered.

She choked on a crack of nervous laughter. "I thought we were late for this wedding. Aren't you the best man?"

Davy glanced down at the bulge in his jeans. He looked at his watch, and sighed heavily. "Damn. All this time wasted on a pointless argument when we could've been having hot sex."

He stepped away from her with obvious reluctance. Margot rearranged her clothes, as disappointed as she was relieved. Sex with him was wildly exciting, but it reduced her to a trembling heap, to say nothing of being badly in need of a shower. Not the condition in which she wished to face a big formal gathering of Davy's family and friends.

It was just as well they were late.

Chapter

16

When Davy's truck pulled up, Sean loped out to the turnaround, raffishly handsome in his black tuxedo. A diamond glinted in his ear. He opened Margot's door, pulled her out and gave her a big bear hug.

"About time you two lazybones got here. I reserved you one of the posh suites. In-suite bar, hot tub on the private veranda, the works. It took me an hour of hard core flirting with the ladies on the management staff to pull it off, but I managed it. You owe me, dude."

Mikey leaped out of the back, sniffed Sean's gleaming dress shoes, and propped his paws on Sean's knees, yipping a shrill, excited greeting. Her dog seemed to like McCloud men.

"Is it a room where you can keep pets?" Margot asked.

Sean bent to pet Mikey's head, his brow furrowed. "Shoot. I forgot about the dog, but my personal motto is, better to ask forgiveness than permission. Leave the little guy with me while you check in. But get your ass into that tux, bro. I have to brief you on the choreography."

Margot was intensely self-conscious in the luxurious lobby in her faded jeans and skimpy tank top, carrying a plastic shopping bag that bulged with clothes and toiletries. She didn't have time to dwell on it, though, because a beautiful woman with long, rippling blond hair and silvery eyes came up to her, smiling, and touched her shyly on the arm. She was dressed to kill in an long ice-blue taffeta skirt and a corset top.

"Are you Margot? I'm Raine. Sean's been telling us all about you."

Margot tensed, but she couldn't help but smile back into Raine's lovely face. "I didn't know Sean knew that much about me to tell."

Raine laughed. "Oh, you know Sean. He doesn't need to know much about a thing to have a lot to say about it. It's enough for us that you're Davy's mysterious new girlfriend. We're so curious. Davy is a big enigma, you see, so any woman he gets involved with is sure to be an object of intense scrutiny. Prepare yourself."

Margot was horrified. "Oh, no. I forgot to take my intense scrutiny endurance pills this morning. I am so screwed."

Raine laughed. "A few glasses of champagne will do the trick."

"But Sean got it wrong," Margot said desperately. "I'm not Davy's girlfriend. We've only just met. It's not like I'm a real date, or anything."

Raine reached out and poked Margot's shoulder. "You feel pretty real to me," she said. "Sounds like Davy's technique is slipping. Guys, phooey. Sometimes they surprise you. Sometimes they just don't."

"Oh, no. Davy's been great," Margot assured her. "He's just real clear about not creating false hopes. Which is fine, since I don't have hopes anyhow, false or otherwise. I just came along for the party. And he only brought me along because I have this stalker problem."

Raine hid a smile. "False hopes, my butt. That clod. I

have to pop him one. Sean told us about the stalker. That's one thing you won't have to worry about, with all the FBI agents running around. So kick back and have a good time." She pressed an impulsive kiss on Margot's cheek. "I'm so glad you came. We'll talk more at the reception."

Margot had turned into a pillar of ice. She was unable to respond to the sweet gesture. "FBI?" she whispered.

"Hey, Raine." Davy kissed the blonde woman on the cheek and slid his arm possessively around Margot's waist. He felt her tension, and frowned down into her face. "What's up?"

She stared up into his eyes. "FBI?"

"Davy, didn't you tell Margot that Connor was a fed?" Raine slapped his arm. "The bride's father was, too. This place is crawling with them. Your stupid old stalker doesn't stand a chance. You guys hurry up and get ready. I'll tell Erin to take her time draping the veil."

She cast an angelic smile over her shoulder and swept away, trailing her long, triangular ice-blue train behind her.

Margot was still frozen in place. "FBI?" she repeated stupidly.

Davy's eyes flicked uncomfortably away. "Later for that. I'll explain. The ceremony's about to begin, and we have to get—"

"Have you gone completely insane?" she hissed.

"Davy, you big handsome devil," said a languid, accented female voice. "Pissing off your lady friend already? And the day is so young."

Davy swung around. A stunning woman in black taffeta smiled at them. Her black hair was twisted into a knot, with blunt cut bangs across her forehead and a gleaming tail dangling over her shoulder.

"Oh. Hi, Tamara." His voice distinctly lacked enthusiasm. "Didn't recognize your new look. You look like Cruella DeVil."

"Gallant as ever, I see," Tamara said. "By the way, today I

am Justine Theron, an interpreter from Brussels, if anyone asks. Erin and I met on her studies abroad. I just wanted you to know that you'll be my escort up the aisle. Lucky you. That executive decision was made before anyone knew about your mysterious companion." She studied Margot, her red lips curving with sly amusement. "So don't be jealous."

"Oh, I won't be," Margot assured her.

"You? A bridesmaid?" Davy looked horrified. "I thought the bridesmaids wore jewel tones. And what's with the fake accent?"

Tamara smoothed her elegant gown. Margot noted that the black skirt and corset bodice were the same cut as Raine's ice-blue dress.

"Black's a jewel tone," she said, her voice faintly hurt. "Onyx? Obsidian? Black opal? And how do you know my accent is fake? Maybe the American accent is the fake one. Make no assumptions, Davy."

"I don't have time for this. We've got to get ready. Later, Tam. Come on." He grabbed Margot by the hand and pulled her out into the corridor that led to the elevator. "I can't believe Connor let Erin invite that woman to the wedding," he fumed. "His brain is completely fried."

"Who is she? And why were you so rude to her?" Margot demanded. "Is she an ex-lover of yours, or something?"

Davy winced. "Christ, no. Perish the thought."

"How come? She's gorgeous. What's wrong with her?"

Davy dragged her out of the elevator and down the hall to the end of the corridor, fitting the key card into the lock.

The luxurious room was dominated by a huge bed. Davy flung his garment bag onto it and peeled off his T-shirt. "What's wrong with her? She's a career criminal, to start with. Wanted in twelve countries, maybe more. I don't know what for, and I don't want to know. The real problem, though, is that she's a grandstanding diva capable of stirring up trouble just for the fun of it. She makes me nervous."

"Wow," Margot murmured, impressed. "So why is she here?"

Davy shook his head, a short, angry gesture. "She saved my brother Connor's life a few months ago. He saved hers, too, but that's beside the point. Long, complicated story. I'll tell it to you sometime."

"You most certainly will," Margot said fervently. "I'm so curious."

"Anyhow, like it or not, she's in the club." Davy pulled a gun out of the back of his jeans, laid it on the bed and wrenched the jeans off. "You know us McClouds. That old outlaw tribe. When you're in, you're in, right or wrong. It's stressful."

Margot stared at the gun, chilled. "Wow. What a wacky family."

"Tell me about it." Davy unzipped the garment bag. "I urged Erin not to invite her," he grumbled. "I begged Connor to put his foot down. And what happens? They make her a bridesmaid, and put her on my arm. This is my punishment for blowing off the rehearsal dinner. I'm pounding that lovesick geek of my brother into hamburger as soon as he gets back from his honeymoon."

Margot blinked. "Uh, I don't know quite how to break it to you, Davy, but considering the legal status of your current date, you hardly have the right to criticize."

"That is completely different!" Davy yanked the tux pants off the hanger and frowned at her as he sat down to put them on.

"Oh yes? And how is that?"

"Because you're innocent! Plus, you're in danger. And besides which, you're my date. Nobody will mess with you, Margot. Relax."

She was amused by his conviction. "You're overestimating your sphere of influence, Davy. I appreciate your faith in me, but it's not going to help much if somebody recognizes me from the papers."

Davy groped for the tux shirt. "I saw those newspaper photos. You look completely different now, with your hair dark and grown out." His eyes raked over her, assessing every detail. "You're thinner. More muscle tone. Your jaw is sharper, your cheekbones more pronounced. Your eyes are memorable, but the pictures I saw didn't do them justice. Try not to look nervous, and you'll be fine. Every man in the room will be looking at you, but not for the reasons you're worried about."

Margot dragged her eyes away from the sight of him buttoning the crisp white tux shirt over his sinewy chest. His body looked just as fine in a tux as it did buck naked. "This wedding is bizarre. Like one of those TV shows that are on cable because they're too weird for prime time."

Davy's chest shook with derisive laughter as he shrugged on a shoulder holster for his gun. "Uh, Margot? For the love of God, get ready. Please. The ceremony is supposed to start"—he glanced at his watch—"in four and a half minutes."

"OK, OK." Margot fled into the bathroom with her plastic shopping bag and shut the door. Here went nothing.

She stared at her pale, scared face in the mirror. Her choppy hair was tousled into a snarled halo, the grown-out remnants of what had once been a two hundred dollar salon haircut. Those were the days.

She wrenched off her clothes, and stared with dismay at the ripped thong, destroyed by Davy's hand. It dangled off her hips in pitiful shreds. Damn. The dress was clingy, and the cotton panties she had in the bag were briefs that would show panty lines egregiously under her skirt. To say nothing of having no stockings, no jewelry, and limited makeup. She was fashion challenged.

Ah, well. At least she had a decent dress. It was crinkly, stretchy stuff, completely unwrinklable, worn over a black slip with spaghetti straps. It was the color of smoke, deepening gradually in color toward the fluted frill where charcoal turned to black right below the knee. A boat neck showed off her cleavage. Cap sleeves showcased her arms, which were looking very nice, she had to concede. Her reward for all those sweaty exercise classes. Too bad her butt hadn't followed suit. It was as prominent as ever. Her butt had an agenda all its own.

Her hair she twisted into a sorta-kinda French roll, which it was barely long enough to hold with the help of a few thousand hairpins and generous globs of gel on the sides for wisp control. She tugged a few locks loose to dangle around her face for that wind-whipped fugitive look. For makeup, she had eyeliner, mascara, and one single tube of deep red lipstick. No blush, no eyeshadow, no foundation, no concealer.

No more tricks in her bag. That was it. Best she could do.

She grabbed some tissues, stuffed them in her purse and marched out of the bathroom with all the attitude she could muster.

Davy stared at her, his eyes moving over her body.

"Jesus," he said quietly. "Just look at you. You're gorgeous."

A blush was coming on, and she whipped up some instant crabbiness to head it off at the pass. "I've got panty lines, and it's all your fault," she said. "You wrecked my thong, you panty-killer."

Davy walked over to her, and placed his big, warm hands on her waist, sliding them slowly over her hips, as if he'd forgotten that they were in a hurry. "I'm sorry about your thong."

She sniffed. "I just bet you are."

"I've got a solution for you, though."

"Oh, yeah? Postpone the wedding so I can run out to a mall and buy underwear? That'll make a great first impression on your family."

He sank to his knees, caressing every curve. "Take them off."

"Oh, please. And go to your brother's wedding bare-assed? Every draft that blows under my skirt tickling my un-mentionables? Dream on, you sex-crazed—"

"It'll drive me out of my mind." Davy slid his hands up under her skirt. "To know that there's nothing under there but silky beautiful legs, fuck-me shoes, and up here . . . that tender, naked—"

"Stop that!" She struggled and swayed in his grip, clutch-ing his thick, short hair for balance. "Behave!"

He hooked his fingers into her panties. "You can't go down there with panty lines," he said earnestly. "It would be wrong."

"Oh, shut up." She was breathless with giggles. "If you make me laugh any harder, my eyes will water and my mas-cara will run."

He yanked the cotton panties down to her ankles and lifted her skirt. She flung her head back with a sigh that was almost a whimper when he pressed his face to her mound, his breath a moist, tickling caress that weakened her knees. "Oh, God," she whispered. "Please, Davy. Don't take me to pieces. I'm so scared already."

He rubbed his cheek against her thigh, cupping her naked bottom in his big hands. "Don't be scared," he insisted. "You're safe here."

"Right." She wiped her watery eyes.

"I'll be right there with you, every minute," he insisted. "Anybody bugs you, anybody at all, I'll rip off both his arms. You got me?"

She tried to smile. "That's sweet, Davy. Bloodthirsty, but sweet."

A shrill whistle sounded outside the door; a long tweet swooping upwards and three short sharp ones coming down. Davy sprang to his feet so quickly, he almost knocked Margot off balance. He yanked the door open. "What the *fuck* do you think you're doing with that signal?"

Sean blinked at him. "Lighting a fire under your lazy ass, bozo."

"Never joke with that shit! Dad would've kicked your ass up the mountain and back down if he heard you playing with his signals!"

Sean's eyebrow took on an ironic tilt. "That's nothing compared to what the bride's mama's gonna do to you if you hold up her baby girl's wedding. You've seen that woman on the rampage. Look sharp."

Davy grabbed Margot's hand and pulled her out the door. She stumbled after him. "What does the signal mean?" she asked.

Davy and Sean exchanged narrow glances, and Sean shrugged. "Our dad was a combat veteran," he explained. "He taught us some of his tricks when we were kids. That one means 'get your ass out of there because I'm throwing in a hand grenade in X number of seconds.' Depending on how the signal's modified. There are variations."

Margot tripped and caught herself against Davy's broad back. "You mean, you guys played with hand grenades when you were kids?"

"Aw, hand grenades are kid stuff," Sean scoffed. "Big bombs are a lot more fun."

"Shut up, Sean," Davy growled.

There was no more time to follow this fascinating avenue of research. In the rose garden, Margot soon found herself in the midst of a quiet flurry of whispered instructions. She was led to a folding seat on the lawn by a hulking young man in a tux with unfortunate glasses and lank dark hair. He had been introduced to her as Miles. Mikey was cradled contentedly in Miles's elbow. Someone had decked out Mikey's curly fur with a cheerful tangle of colored silk ribbons.

The grassy space was flanked with banks of blooming roses. A fountain blew mist into the breeze. Miles deposited Mikey at her feet, flushed crimson and loped away like a startled gazelle when Margot smiled and thanked him. A string quartet struck up shortly afterwards.

Davy was first up the aisle, Tamara smiling mysteriously on his arm. They looked disgustingly gorgeous together, but Margot tried not to loathe her for it. It wasn't fair, for one thing. For another, a fellow outlaw deserved a smidge of solidarity, no matter how hot she looked.

Sean was next, grinning down at the chubby redheaded girl on his arm. Miles reverently escorted a slender brunette dressed in red. Raine followed, accompanied by a grimly handsome black-haired man who clutched her arm in a possessive grip. His suspicious eyes swept the assembled crowd as if searching for masked gunmen. They were followed by pairs of girls, their multihued gowns as bright as a bouquet of flowers. Then came the bride and groom, hand in hand. They looked so radiantly happy, Margot groped instantly for a tissue.

It was a beautiful ceremony; tender and simple and full of heart. The love and trust in the faces of the bride and groom made her dab at runnels of dissolving mascara throughout the whole thing, and Davy shot her a funny look as he strode down the aisle at the end.

Moments later, he was looming over her chair. "What's wrong now? What happened? You OK?"

She snuffled into her tissue and dabbed beneath her eyes. "Don't give me that terrified look," she said in a soggy voice. "You're the one who brought me here. I didn't beg to come. So cope, already."

He looked bemused. "I'm coping. Just as long as you're not—"

"I'm emotional, OK?" she yelled. "Get used to it! I get weepy at weddings, funerals, puppy chow commercials! Try not to make me more self-conscious than I already am, OK? I promise, it's not catching."

He leaned down behind her and pressed a soft kiss

against the back of her neck. "Whatever. It's time for the photos."

"So off you go." She shooed him away. "Get far away from me. Scat. Begone. I don't want cameras anywhere near me. Go!"

She sneaked a look in her compact. The remnants of wet mascara gave her a vaguely slutty look, but any more rubbing would make her eyes red and irritated. Drat. She would never achieve the Ice Queen look. She looked around at the chattering crowd of guests, wondering what it would feel like to be part of the normal world again.

If she were even capable of such a thing anymore. What had happened to her had changed her so completely, she felt marked. Almost as if she'd been infected with an incurable disease.

Her gloom deepened as she thought about it. Even if she did manage to pass for a normal citizen of the universe, it would always feel like a disguise. Her world was a nightmare of uncertainty.

In light of that, fountains and roses and all the happy festivity felt like a cruel mockery. And whoopsy daisy, check her out. Sending out embossed invitations for another pity party. Bad idea, since she was almost out of tissues. Mikey leaped up with his paws on her knees and licked her hand, and his big, worried dark eyes under his floppy bangs made her smile through her tears. Sweet old Mikey. What a life saver. She stroked his silky ears and told him so until his whole body wagged.

The grass behind Mikey was suddenly covered with a swathe of opalescent black taffeta. Margot's eyes traveled up the skirt until they reached Tamara's curved lips and impenetrable dark eyes.

Tamara stared at the mascara-stained tissue in Margot's hand. "Touching ceremony, hmm? Almost shed a sentimental tear myself."

The soft mockery in her voice stung. Margot mopped at her nose one last time, and shoved the tissue into her purse. Tamara's beaded black evening bag made her abruptly conscious of the fact that her brown leather purse clashed tragically with her dress.

Oh, how she missed her stash of accessories.

"Yes, it was. Very beautiful." Margot stared at the other woman's face, curiosity battling with good manners. She wondered how Tamara would react if Margot asked her how to hotwire a car.

Tamara's eyes flicked towards the fountain. "They're doing photos over there, but I don't do photos."

"Me, neither," Margot admitted, after a nervous pause.

Tamara's eyebrows shot up. "Oh, no? Why not?"

Margot blew out a shaky breath. "Same reason as you, I expect."

"Ah! So Davy told you about me, then?" Tamara's smile widened. "I knew it. No wonder you're jittery. On the run from the law? And you let Davy drag you into a hornets' nest of feds? Not too smart, but he's a forceful guy. I have a weakness for forceful guys myself, being as how I totally destroy any other kind I get involved with. Ain't love grand?"

"You're a fine one to talk about it being smart to be here."

"It turns me on to play with fire." Tamara flicked at a lock of Margot's hair with her finger. "That hair color doesn't work for you, by the way. You're a redhead, right? You'd be better off going ash blond. Some honey-toned highlights, maybe. And for God's sake, get it done by someone who knows what he's doing. Don't do it yourself."

"Thanks for the tip," Margot said, between set teeth. Lovely. So her dye job sucked. Yet another thing to feel self-conscious about.

"I thought I'd seize the opportunity to talk to you while Davy was hung up with the photos. He violently disapproves of me, so he probably won't let me near you for the rest of the evening," Tamara said.

Margot's spine straightened. "I decide who I talk to. Not him."

"Good, good," Tamara clapped her hands. "Keep that feisty attitude. You'll need it. Those Master of the Universe types are tricky to handle." Her face grew thoughtful. "Davy's got that hero streak, just like his brother. I expect he wants to rescue you. How adorable. It'll probably get him killed, but it's still endearing."

"Oh, no. It's not like that at all. I'm just using him for sex."

Tamara's laughter rang out, clear as a bell. "Tough chick, huh?"

Margot crossed her arms. "I try."

Mikey flung himself onto his back on Tamara's taffeta train and writhed, inviting her to pat his belly. *Good boy*, Margot told him telepathically. *Go on. Shed. Drool. Be doggish.*

Tamara tugged her skirt loose and obliged Mikey with the bottom of her elegant shoe. Mikey wiggled in ecstasy. "It's not a matter of trying, no matter how hard. Either you are . . . or you aren't."

Margot's discomfort intensified. "What's that supposed to mean?"

Tamara's eyes were bleak once the humor faded. "You're not like me," she said. "You want to be, but you're still hoping that it's not true."

Margot shifted nervously on her chair. "What's not true?"

"That the world really is just a corrupt wasteland of cruelty and greed." Tamara's voice had hardened. "You suspect it, but you're still hoping that someone'll come charging along in shining armor—probably a handsome blond someone—to prove you wrong."

Margot shook her head. "I don't think that at all. I know better." Her voice sounded colorless and small to her own ears.

Tamara jerked her chin towards the flock of bridesmaids

posing in front of the fountain with the bride in their midst. Their feminine laughter drifted over on the breeze. "You're more like those girls than you are like me. So hopeful, and so fearful. Hope and fear are two sides of the same coin, you know? You'd be better off without either one."

"Oh, for the love of God, Tam." Davy's deep voice cut through Tamara's soft monologue. "Cut out the bleak existential alienation."

Tamara's mysterious smile switched back on at full force as she spun around to face him. "Hello, Davy. I've been chatting up your lovely fugitive friend. She intrigues me."

"I was afraid of that," he said sourly. "This is my brother's wedding, Tam. If you would at least make an effort not to deliberately ruin anybody's day, I would count it as a personal favor."

"I'm only trying to help." Tamara brushed Margot's cheek with a cool fingertip. "I like her. Naïve, but game. Be nice to her. Or else."

Davy made an impatient sound. "Go put the fear of God into somebody else. Look around. There's plenty of fresh meat for you."

Tamara gave him a cool, narrow look, and smiled at Margot. "Ta, you two. Stay sharp."

"Tamara?" Margot called.

The other woman turned back, eyebrow raised inquisitively.

"Do you know how to hotwire a car?" Margot asked.

Tamara's smile widened. "Honey, I know how to hotwire the global economy. Would you like some lessons? You look sharp enough to catch on. And you probably need a new career, am I right?"

"No," Davy said. "We're not going there."

Tamara's silky laughter bubbled up. "Let her decide for herself," she teased. "You McCloud boys just refuse to think big. All that brain power and seething testosterone, crippled by misplaced morality. Such a tragic waste of potential. It's just criminal."

"No. On the contrary," Davy said. "Thank God."

"Tamara?" Margot called. "One more thing."

Tamara's brow tilted higher, her red mouth a twist of irony. "Yes?"

"You don't fool me," Margot said. "You're still hoping to be proven wrong, too. And you're just as afraid as I am that no one ever will."

Tamara's face froze into a smiling mask. She made a dismissive gesture with her hand as she spun around. Her long, shining tail of hair swished back and forth over her bare shoulders as she marched away.

Davy stared after her. "I've never seen anybody get under that woman's skin before," he said slowly. "I thought she was armor plated."

"Everybody's got her soft spot," Margot said. "I'm onto her. Roses in bloom, your brother and his bride all blissed out and madly in love. It's hard to take. I just figured she felt . . . kind of like I do."

Davy looked like he was bracing himself. "And how is that?"

Margot shrugged. "Left out," she said quietly. "Jealous. Sad."

He looked baffled and helpless. "I can't fathom the concept of Tamara having those kinds of emotions."

Margot just looked at him until his eyes dropped.

He scooped Mikey into his arms. "This stuff is too heavy for me," he muttered sourly. "Let's find Miles to look after Mikey, and get you some champagne. Quick."

Chapter

17

Hotwire a car, for Christ's sake. Over his dead body. He could teach her to do that, if she really wanted to know. He could teach her to build and detonate a bomb, or defuse one. How to organize an ambush, how to rig a deadfall, how to slit someone's throat in the dark and then hide the body. How to use any kind of weapon.

All the tricks his father, Crazy Eamon, had taught him and his brothers to survive against all odds in a hostile environment after the fall of civilization and the total anarchy that was sure to follow. The fall hadn't happened, but every one of Eamon's tricks had proved useful to him and his brothers at one time or another in their eventful lives.

It wasn't what he wanted for Margot. She should be busy with her career. Shopping, working, having lunch with her girlfriends, doing whatever carefree young women did with their time. Not that he had any clue what that was, but it wasn't hotwiring cars, or running for her life from psycho stalkers. It wasn't hotwiring the global economy, either. He didn't want her to end up like Tamara. Hard as nails, cold as ice.

Fuck that. Not his Margot. It made him so angry, he wanted to knock over tables and smash all the glittering crystal glassware.

He hated it that she felt left out and jealous and sad. Somebody was going to pay for what had been taken from her. He would see to it.

Margot stumbled along, her spike heels tangling in the grass as she struggled to keep up with his long strides. He wasn't behaving well. He could tell from her quick, nervous glances. One would think that a night of incredible sex would chill him out. On the contrary, it had blown the lid off his self-control and revealed it for the cheap smoke and mirrors illusion that it had always been.

Raine and Seth were seated at the table. Seth was fiddling with the neckline of Raine's dress, and Raine was swatting his hand down, saying something stern, trying not to smile. Business as usual.

Seth didn't bother with self-control. He was a wild animal most of the time. Only Raine could cow him. Still, Davy couldn't help liking the guy. Seth was rude and crude and out of his gourd, yeah, but he was smart, cunning and loyal, and a good man to have on one's side in a fight. Those were far more important qualities, in Davy's opinion.

"Raine, you've met Margot," he said. "Margot, this is her husband, Seth Mackey, one of my future business partners."

Seth took his hand away from his wife's cleavage and held it out to Margot, a wolfish grin animating his lean, dark face. "My pleasure."

Davy pulled out the chair next to Raine's and seated Margot in it without ceremony. "Have you guys seen Nick?"

Seth jerked his chin towards the opposite corner of the room. "He's over at the bridesmaids' table, picking out his flavor."

Davy tilted Margot's face up and gave her a hard, possessive kiss. "You still have that snake thing in your purse?"

"Yes," she said. "Do you—"

"Give it over," he said. "I have to talk to Nick about running prints on it. Wait here. Don't move."

His brother Connor's FBI colleague Nick was pouring champagne for a table full of simpering, jewel-toned girls. His sensual dark good looks, full lips and long dark hair were having their usual effect.

"Yo, Nick," Davy said. "A word."

Nick cut off whatever flirtatious bullshit he was spouting and looked up into Davy's eyes. He rose to his feet. "Excuse me, ladies." He dimpled at them all indiscriminately. "This won't take long."

They moved to a space in the middle of the dance floor near the bandstand. The band was tuning up, providing a sound screen.

"I need a favor," Davy said, without preamble.

Nick's expression was grimly resigned. "Name it."

"I want you to run prints on a necklace for me, and run a search in the IAFIS database. I need it done as quickly as possible. Like, right now. And I don't want anybody to know about it."

Nick's face tightened. "Jesus, Davy. What's the big secret?"

Davy just looked at him. "If you can't do it, just say so."

Nick looked away, cursing under his breath. He was stuck, and he knew it. A few months ago, Connor had been struggling for his life against the psychotic zillionaire, Kurt Novak. Nick hadn't believed him, in the face of the contradictory evidence. He'd cut Connor loose.

That error in judgment had almost cost Connor his life.

Nick felt like ten different kinds of shit about it, as he damn well should. Connor had forgiven him, since that was just the kind of guy he was. His brother couldn't hold a grudge to save his life, particularly not when he was in love. He wanted to forgive the whole freaking world.

Even Sean found it in his heart to be relatively cordial to Nick. Sean's attention span wasn't long enough to hold a good grudge.

But Davy had no problem at all with long-term anger. He saw no reason to forgive Nick, and no reason not to milk the situation to its fullest extent, either, since Connor wasn't going to.

What he was asking of Nick was risky and illegal. Too fucking bad. The further Nick's ass dangled out in the wind, the better Davy liked it. "Just say so," he said mercilessly. "Yes or no. Real simple."

Nick sighed. "Give it to me. I'll try to take care of it to-morrow."

Davy opened up Margot's purse and fished out the plastic bag. "Don't mention this to Connor. I don't want him bothered about anything right before he leaves for his honeymoon."

Nick held up the bag and peered at the thing through the plastic. "There's only one smooth surface on this," he said. "If it's been bounced around in a girl's purse for a while, there's not going to be much left on it that's identifiable, even if your mystery entity did leave prints. And keep in mind that the latent print examiner at Quantico is going to know about it. Nothing I can do about that."

Davy stared straight into Nick's eyes. "So beg," he said coolly. "Grovel. Offer sexual favors. Be creative. Do what you have to do."

Unspoken anger hummed between the two men.

Nick nodded curtly and stalked out of the ballroom.

The band was striking up a slow, sexy number as he wandered back across the room. Erin and Connor were moving into the middle of the dance floor, gazing into each other's eyes. In la-la land.

Davy's jaw tightened, his gut along with it. He didn't understand his reaction. He should be happy for his little brother. All he'd ever wanted was to see that look on Connor's face. He loved the guy.

He was being a cynical son of a bitch, and it was getting worse every minute that passed. If this went on, he was going to end up challenging Tamara for the Black Hole of Negativity title.

There was Cindy, Erin's little sister, dancing with some guy he recognized as another of Connor's colleagues from his undercover FBI unit. Miles watched from the sidelines, clutching a panting Mikey in his arms. His shoulders were slumped, misery written clearly on his face.

Davy gritted his teeth and walked on past. Miles had to work through the love thing on his own, but Cindy's manipulative, selfish obliviousness still pissed Davy off. Everything was pissing him off.

His old habit of self-observation was a big pain in the ass in cases like these, when he didn't particularly want to analyze himself, but by now it was a machine that functioned on autopilot. No stopping it.

It occurred to him that being angry was easier than being scared. And much easier than feeling sad. About how it had felt to lose Kevin twelve years ago, for instance. Or scared at how incredibly close he'd come to losing another brother to the grinding jaws of death just a few months ago. Scared at how close death and tragedy always were.

This was a piss-poor train of thought to have climbed onto, but it was too late to bail, it had already picked up too much momentum.

It infuriated him that Kevin wasn't there to dance at Connor's wedding, or his parents, either. It made him sick that love and family and all that assorted warm fuzzy stuff was forever teetering on the fucking brink of disaster. Always with a goddamn knife to its throat.

Like the one that was at Margot's.

Margot watched Davy stride away, feeling abandoned.

"What bug crawled up his ass tonight?" Seth asked.

He and Raine turned to look at her, and Margot was startled to realize that it was up to her to answer the question.

She was the current resident expert on Davy McCloud. Wow. What a responsibility.

"I think what set him off was Tamara offering to give me lessons on how to hotwire the global economy," she offered. "I thought it was an intriguing offer, but it seemed to make him really tense."

Seth's face lit up with comprehension. "Ah! Yeah, Davy doesn't have much of a sense of humor about that stuff. Myself, I'd jump three feet in the air to have that woman teach me some of her—"

"No, you most certainly would not," Raine broke in. "Not if you know what's good for you."

Seth lifted his wife's hand to his lips and began to smooch his way up the length of her bare arm. "I know exactly what's good for me, angel baby," he crooned.

Raine wrestled her arm away, giggling. "Stop it! You're being a pain in the butt today! What do I have to do, sedate you?"

"It's the dress, babe," he protested. "How do you expect me to control myself when you show all that creamy skin?"

Raine slanted Margot an embarrassed look. "Excuses, excuses."

Seth tilted his chair back and gave Margot a thoughtful once-over. "Sean told us about this sick fuck who's been stalking you—"

"Seth!" Raine broke in. "Please!"

"It's OK," Margot said hastily. "That's an excellent description."

"That reminds me. I have a present for you. Sean told us about you worrying about your dog, and I just happened to have a prototype on hand of this thing I've been fiddling with in my spare time. A new product. You still got that thing in your purse, babe?"

Raine rummaged in her ice-blue satin evening bag, pulling out a plastic-wrapped object. She handed it to Margot with a smile.

Margot turned it over in her hand. A circle of heavy black leather, with a silver medallion hanging off it. "What's this?"

"It's a dog collar," Seth explained. "A Colbit GPS petfinder. If you lose your dog, you call me, I look him up on my system and tell you where he is. Or you can buy the software and the equipment if you want to look for him yourself. The battery's good for a month. I have to make you a recharger. The prototype I had wouldn't fit in Raine's purse."

"Uh . . . wow," Margot said helplessly. "I'm just . . . thanks."

"Nobody told me your dog was so shrimpy," Seth grumbled. "That collar's big enough for a rottweiler. I'll find you something smaller."

She stared at the silvery medallion, and the thick leather collar, adorned with wicked-looking silver studs. "That's . . . that's so sweet."

"Soon as we get back to town, I'll rig you some of my vidcams at your place," Seth said. "We get your stalker on film, then we catch him and we squish him like a grape. Splat."

Margot was touched by the grim purpose in Seth's voice. "That sounds really great," she said hesitantly. "But the truth is, I don't have the budget for a complicated, high-tech—"

"Davy's family," Seth cut her off.

"But I'm not," Margot pointed out. "You guys don't even know me."

"We can't wait to know you," Raine said. "I asked Erin's mom to seat you with us on purpose. So fill us in, tell us everything. Where are you from? What do you do? How did you and Davy meet?"

Thank God, at least the last question was innocuous enough. "I teach exercise classes in the gym next door to his dojo," Margot said. "A couple of days ago, I dropped by to ask him what he thought of my stalker problem. We've barely met, really. I was hoping to pump you guys for details about him. He's so mysterious, you know."

That was a pretty slick job in deflecting questions, or so she hoped, but Seth and Raine exchanged dubious glances, and Margot shoved on with the first thing that popped into her mind. "For instance, I saw four brothers in the pictures on Davy's mantelpiece, but here there are only three. What happened to the fourth McCloud brother?"

Raine's smile faded. Seth's jaw tightened. Margot had a sudden sinking feeling that she'd stuck her foot in it. Way deep.

"Dead," Seth said heavily. "Twelve years ago. His truck went off a cliff. His name was Kevin. He was Sean's twin. He was only twenty-one."

Margot swallowed over a hard, dry bump in her throat. "Oh dear," she whispered. "Oh, ouch."

"Davy was overseas at the time," Seth added. "Intelligence work, in the Army. He never told you how he and his brothers grew up?"

Margot shook her head. "Just that his parents are both gone, and that his father had some, ah, unorthodox political ideas."

"Hah," Seth grunted. "I guess that's one way of putting it."

An odd, tense silence fell. "So? You guys are killing me," she said nervously. "For God's sake, clue me in. Don't leave me hanging."

"Their dad was nuts," was Seth's blunt reply. "He was a wacko, survivalist type. An ex-commando Vietnam vet. Raised his kids way out in the hills. Taught them to hunt and trap and fish and fight like fucking demons. He wanted to prepare them for the fall of civilization. Then their mom died, and he really lost it. Went certifiably bonkers."

Margot forced her mouth to close. Wow. Her thoughtless comment about how Davy didn't even know what it felt like to be desperate floated into her mind. How stupid she must have sounded.

She cleared her throat. "I didn't mean to get into the scary private stuff," she said, her voice unsteady.

"With the McClouds, it's all scary private stuff," Seth drawled. "They've got a weird talent for attracting intense drama into their lives."

"You're a fine one to talk," Raine said tartly.

"So are you, my darling pet." Seth leered at her and did something under the table that provoked Raine into kicking him. The table shook. Champagne flutes wobbled dangerously.

"Stop that!" Raine turned to Margot, her face apologetic. "He's not usually quite this bad. He acts out like crazy whenever there are new people around to shock and impress."

Margot hid her smile. She sensed that Seth was playing the clown on purpose to divert her, but she wasn't ready to be diverted yet.

"How old was he when his mother died?" she asked.

"Erin told me Connor was eight," Raine said. "So that would have made Sean and Kevin four, and Davy, let's see . . . ten."

"Uh, babe?" Seth's voice was cautious. "Davy's not gonna be thrilled with you for telling a bunch of unauthorized gut-wrenching stories about him behind his back. Guys hate that shit."

Raine tossed her head. "Well, I'm not particularly thrilled with Davy at the moment. I think he's being self-absorbed, bad-tempered and rude. So I'll tell all the gut-wrenching stories I want on him."

"OK, fine. Just don't get mad at me about it," Seth said hastily.

"You mean there's more?" Margot whispered, appalled.

"Just how his mom died," Raine said. "Erin told me. They lived way out in the hills behind Endicott Bluff. It was the middle of the winter. Three feet of snow. She had a tubal pregnancy and bled to death while they were trying to get to the hospital. Davy was the one driving the truck. Connor said he didn't even speak for months afterwards."

Margot's stomach dropped into a bottomless, icy nowhere.

She got to her feet, clutching the edge of the table. "Excuse me."

"Are you OK?" Seth and Raine's anxious faces receded, expanded.

"I just need to, ah, run to the ladies' room." She turned, and found herself blocked by a solid wall of scowling, tuxedo clad males. "Oh. You."

"Where the hell do you think you're going?" Davy growled. "Oh, Christ. You're crying again. What did you guys say to her?"

Raine lifted her slim shoulders in an innocent shrug.

Davy dropped her purse on her chair and slid his arm around her waist, dragging her out onto the dance floor. "Come on. Let's dance."

Several couples already swayed on the dance floor to the slow, sexy number, including the bride and groom. They looked up from their blissful, dreamy togetherness to give Margot a curious once-over.

"Congratulations," Margot called out to them.

"Thanks," they said in unison, and that was the end of that interchange as Davy swept her quickly out of range.

"What the hell did Seth and Raine say to you?" he demanded.

"We were talking about you. Raine told me how your mom died."

Margot stumbled over his feet as he abruptly stopped moving. He caught her gracefully. "Fuck," he muttered. "This is all I needed."

"It's terribly sad, but nothing to be embarrassed about," she said quietly. "You don't have to be mad at Raine. I was curious. I asked."

"That's not the point!" he snarled.

"Point? Is there ever a point?"

He twirled her away from him, then yanked her aggressively back into his arms. "Why get churned up about ancient history?" he demanded. "I have never understood that impulse! There are plenty of fresh new problems to worry about without digging up old stuff."

True enough, but Davy's thunderous expression bothered her. "What is with you, anyway?" she demanded. "You're mad at Seth, at Raine, at Tamara, at everybody. Lighten up, for God's sake."

"I can't," he said, from between gritted teeth. "Everybody is bugging me. And I didn't like the way Tamara messed with your head."

"I don't think she meant any harm by it," Margot argued. "I just don't think she knows any other way to interact with people. To tell the truth, I kind of like her, in a perverse way. And my head's tough. If it can handle being messed with by you, it can certainly handle Tamara."

Davy's jaw tightened. He dipped her very low and held her there, helpless and suspended. "Don't you start bugging me too."

He yanked her back up. She blinked, dizzy. "You're being awfully sour for this joyful occasion." She gazed into his stormy eyes as an intuition took hold in her mind. "You're scared for your brother because he's so happy, right? You're afraid he's setting himself up for a fall."

Davy's hand tightened on her waist. "Do we have to analyze it?"

"Or is it just jealousy? Do you want what he's got? Love, romance, happily ever after? Everybody does, whether they admit it or not."

Davy's face went blank. "Fuck, no."

"Hmm," Margot murmured. "That was a violent response to my innocuous question. Overcompensating, are we?"

"I was clear about where I stand on marriage and commitment," he said. "Nothing's changed. Nothing's going to. Don't get any ideas."

She bristled. "Don't flatter yourself. You insensitive lout."

"Stop teasing me, or I'll make you dance with the new Assistant Special Agent in charge of the Seattle FBI Field

Office," he whispered into her ear. "He's right behind us, staring at your ass."

She lunged up to pull his earlobe between her teeth and give it a nip. "You sick, evil bastard," she hissed back. "That's not funny."

"Then why are you laughing? I feel it when you laugh, even when you don't make noise. Your whole body vibrates. It's sexy."

"Oh, you think everything's sexy." She gasped as he suddenly dipped her low over his strong arm. "Davy! Are you drunk?"

"Nope. I never get drunk. I'm just in a weird mood."

"You've been in a weird mood since the day you met me."

"Guilty as charged," he agreed. "Go ahead, goad me. Torment me, insult me, scold me. I want to fuck you so bad, all I hear over the roaring in my ears is blah, blah, blah."

She was speechless for a moment while her mind changed gears.

"Oh. I see," she said. "So we're reducing it all to cheap, mindless sex. Your one single, solitary safety valve. You're so predictable, Davy."

"Blah, blah, blah," he taunted. "Ever since we left the hotel room, I've been thinking about your bare naked ass underneath that cock-teasing dress." He dragged her closer to his body. She could feel the heat of his erection against her belly. "See what it does to me?"

Her legs quivered at the raw sex in his voice. "You're going to have to control yourself, Davy. It's going to be a while before we can—hey!"

He grabbed her hand and yanked her behind a bank of potted Norwegian pines and into a corridor. They sped into it, Davy trying doors right and left until one of them opened.

He pulled her in, slammed the door and locked it.

He flicked on the light. They were in a small internal conference room, just big enough for a long, gleaming table of rosy colored wood.

"I want to put my hands under your skirt," he told her. "Pet the hair between your legs." He advanced on her. "Till you're all wet and soft, and you're giving me that panther woman look, like you want to eat me alive. It drives me . . . fucking . . . crazy."

She backed up till her bottom hit the table. "Davy, you're perverse," she said shakily. "Totally schizo. I thought you were pissed off at me, and all of a sudden, you morph into a raging sex fiend."

"You provoked me." He grasped her waist and hoisted her onto the table, leaning forward until she was forced to lean back. "Because you like me like this. Out of my mind. Right?"

She arched back, propped on her elbows inside the cage of his arms, trapped by the animal heat in his eyes. "Yes," she admitted.

"I knew it. Otherwise I'd keep my raunchy fuck fantasies to myself. I'm discovering a whole new world of bad behavior, babe."

She pushed his chest, but that unbalanced her so that she fell onto the table, flat on her back. "You're making me nervous."

"Yeah. You like that, too. It makes you come like crazy." He swooped down to nuzzle her throat.

She licked her lips and shivered at the tender nip of his lips against the sensitive tendons of her neck. "I never felt that way before."

"Good. That makes it all mine, then." His hand slid under her skirt, stroking up the length of her thigh and dragging her skirt up with it. He tugged it up until the fabric was bunched in a crumpled wad over her belly. She was naked from the waist down.

"Davy," she whispered. "Oh, God."

"Ever since you walked out in that dress, I've wanted to drag you off into a dark corner and slide my hand up between your legs," he said. "Open up for me, sweetheart. I want to see you just like that."

Her eyes fluttered open, blinking. "Like what?"

He kissed her jaw, drew her trembling lower lip between his teeth and tugged on it. "Your face glowing, your eyes dilated. Your body shaking because you're so excited. All your secrets, wide open to me."

Her shaky laughter made the trembling worse. "That's not a panther-womanish scenario, Davy."

"Sure it is. If I'm the only one panther woman trusts enough to sheathe her razor claws and let me into her sweet tender places."

She squeezed her eyes shut against the rush of tears. "Stop it."

"Stop what? It's working. Just look at you."

Stop making me fall in love with you, you cruel bastard. "Stop torturing me," she pleaded.

"No," he said. "Open up, Margot. Let me see you. All of you."

She opened her thighs for him. Her body had a will of its own.

"You're so soft and wet already." He breathed the words out as he touched her labia delicately, sliding his finger up and down the slick folds. "You suck me right in," he murmured. He kissed her, his tender lips coaxing her mouth open. He caught her cry against his mouth when he angled his hand to caress her clitoris. He fumbled at his crotch, freeing the jut of his erection from the tailored trousers.

Margot dragged her face away from his kiss, and stared down at his penis bobbing heavily between her legs. Her face was on fire. She couldn't get enough air. "You don't have any condoms," she said.

He shook his head slowly.

"You're nuts." She tried to sharpen her voice, but it shook too hard. "I've never let a guy . . . not without latex. Never. It's not smart."

"No," he agreed. "Definitely not." He pushed her legs wider and pressed the head of his penis against the inner lips of her labia. The hot kiss of contact made her flinch and gasp. "None of this is very smart."

"You're too much." Her chest heaved for breath.

"I won't come inside you," he murmured. "I just have to feel it. My cock, sliding into you. Feeling you clutch me, so tight and delicious. Just let me feel it. Just a few slow strokes. I'll be good. I promise."

She wiggled, but not to get away. "This is way over the line."

He slid his penis tenderly around her clit and then down to lodge in her slick, flushed opening, pulsing against her. "Is that a no?"

She closed her eyes and licked her lips and prayed for strength, common sense, basic brains. There was none within reach.

She shook her head. "No. I mean no, that's not a no."

His slow, beautiful grin did something devastating to her insides.

"So that's a yes?" he said. "Two no's cancel each other out and make a yes, right? Don't make me guess. This is too important."

"Please." It was all she could force out. She swallowed, licked her lips and tried again. "Just do it."

His laughter cut off into a grinding moan as he pushed himself slowly inside her. He dragged himself almost completely out of her body, so just the tip of his thick penis was clasped between the lips of her sex.

"Put your arms around my shoulders." His voice was rough and breathless. "I want you to watch, when my cock disappears inside you . . ."—he thrust, deep and slow—". . . and comes out all slick and shiny from your sweet lube."

She clutched at his shoulders, digging her nails into the smooth fabric of his tux jacket. He slid a supporting arm around her back.

They huddled together, forehead to forehead, silent but

for their labored breathing, the wet, tender sounds of their bodies' contact.

She abandoned herself to his hypnotic pleasure spell, seduced by sensation, the sensual, relentless rhythm of his tender thrusting. Her body was incandescent, so alive to feeling it almost scared her. Every muscle quivered with strain. She held herself upright and gazed down into the shadowy space between them, eager to catch every detail; the hot scent of sex, the sight of his thick, ridged shaft stroking her.

Bursts of pleasure rocked her, each one blooming sweetly out of the last. Finally she gripped his upper arms, inciting him with her body to give her more than that maddening slow pulse. "Davy. Harder."

"No," he said. "Can't risk it. Not without a condom. This is as fast as I can go, until we're back in the room. Then I'll give you anything you want. God, it's hard to stop." He withdrew himself from her body, and tucked himself into his pants with a grimace of discomfort.

"You're going to leave me in this condition?" She was outraged.

"Yeah," he said. "You're gorgeous in this condition. Your eyes glowing like that. Every man in the room will know you're taken."

She closed her legs, smoothed the skirt over her throbbing nether parts and slid off the table, unsure if she could even stand. "That's an awfully primal sentiment for a detached guy like you," she told him.

"I know."

He offered no further explanation, just pulled her into his arms and held her tightly until they were ready to face the world again.

The rest of the afternoon and evening swam by, in a colorful blur of images. Dancing, conversations she couldn't remember as soon as she'd had them, bites of delicious food that she had no appetite for, icy champagne that went straight to her head. The bridesmaids' dresses were colored so brightly, they hurt her eyes. Every sappy song the band played wrung her overstimulated emotions.

She sneaked peeks at Davy, wondering how he could look so calm when she felt torn wide open. Her skin was so sensitized, every brush of fabric a caress. The condensation on the champagne flute was a cold, wet kiss. Her body ached for the moment they got back to the bedroom.

She was in love with him. Against all odds, she'd succeeded in making her life even more complicated and dangerous than it already was. She got the grand prize for total idiocy.

Hope and fear. Two sides of the same coin, Tamara had said.

Too bad. She didn't want to give up hope, so she was just going to have to live with the fear. God knew, she should be an expert by now.

An affluent upbringing had its advantages, Faris reflected, as he wandered through the wedding crowd. One tended to look at home in a suit, champagne flute in hand. He smiled and nodded at everyone he saw in such a way that they would all assume he'd met them, and that they were the socially inept clods who didn't remember where or how.

Marcus had once commented that both of them had just the kind of bland, unremarkable good looks that gave the vague impression of having been seen before. It was a very useful quality.

Surveillance of his angel was momentarily obscured by a white blur. He focused in on it. It was the bride. She unfastened her filmy veil from her upswept dark hair, revealing a soft, slender neck adorned by waving wisps of dark hair. He gazed at her neck hungrily. Twenty seconds alone with her, a couple of well placed needles, and she would die on her honeymoon of an unexpected coronary embolism. Hmm.

He didn't need a reason. Musicians loved to play, painters loved to paint, hunters loved to shoot, tax lawyers loved to crunch numbers. He loved to kill. If there was a God, he must operate like Faris. Reaching out at random, the touch of a fingertip, and *pow*—a car accident, an armed intruder, a fulminating infection. Faris embodied that same power of random chaos. He was God's agent, the shadow of death.

He was debating ways and means of getting a private moment with the bride when the girl in the ruby red bridesmaid's gown bounced up, burbling some female inanity. Sisters, he concluded, noting the similarities. The ruby red girl took the veil from her sister as the groom walked up, beaming like an idiot. The man was oblivious to everything around him but his bride. He pulled her back out onto the dance floor, whispering something into her ear that made her giggle.

Faris heaved a private sigh of regret. There went that opportunity.

He turned his attention to the ruby red girl, noting all the vital Dim Mak points that her strapless bustier displayed. Ruby Red was an easier target. Less observed, sillier, not distracted by a new husband.

And already shooting curious glances at him.

Faris put on his most charming smile. Ruby Red took the bait and sidled closer. "Romantic, isn't it?" She gestured towards the newlyweds.

"Terribly. I keep looking for Disney birds and butterflies."

Her smiled widened. This was going to be almost too easy.

"Are you one of Connor's friends?" she asked.

Faris let his eyes drop to the girl's hiked-up cleavage for a telling instant as he pretended to sip champagne. "Oh, yeah. We go way back," he said easily. "And you must be the bride's sister?"

She simpered. "I'm Cindy."

Faris took her hand and lifted it to his lips. "Cindy. I'm

Cliff. You are stunning in red. Would you do me the honor of dancing with me?"

Her smiling lips opened to reply when a tall, pale young man with lank black hair and hideous glasses lurched towards them. Margaret's crippled pet was draped over his arm. Its pink tongue hung out as it panted gusts of fetid dog breath. Faris's heart began to pound.

"Oh, Miles. Hi. This is Cliff, one of Connor's friends," Cindy said. "Would you hold Erin's veil for me while I dance with him?"

Cindy draped the veil over Miles's arm. He gazed down at it, dismayed. "But—"

"You're right, the dog might get it dirty," Cindy said. "Take it over to Marika and let her look after it."

"But . . . but I asked the band to play your favorite Eric Clapton song next. You said you'd dance with me for that one," Miles said, his voice forlorn. "Don't you remember?"

Cindy sighed. "That was before I knew you'd be dogsitting for the entire evening. I don't know what you were thinking when you agreed to that, but it certainly wasn't about dancing with me."

"I'll watch the dog for you while you dance," Faris offered. "Really. I'd be more than happy to. He looks like a friendly little guy."

Cindy's mouth set itself in sullen lines. "It doesn't make sense for both of you to ruin your clothes with drool and dog hair."

Miles shoved the veil back at her and backed away, blinking rapidly. "OK, Cin. I get a clue. Fine. Whatever. I don't give a shit."

Faris watched the dog's panting pink mouth retreat, draped over Miles's arm. The filthy little animal almost seemed to be taunting him.

It took effort for Faris to suppress the blaze of venomous anger that burned inside him as he turned back to Cindy. Self-absorbed bitch. A cerebral aneurysm would be just right for her. He forced himself to smile as the band struck up a slow, lazy version of "Layla."

"Well?" he said. "Shall we?"

Cindy tossed the length of tulle onto a table full of half-empty champagne glasses. He swept her out onto the dance floor.

"Are you an FBI agent, too?" Cindy asked.

He couldn't help but smile at that. "I work in the private sector."

"Oh," Cindy breathed, as he slid his hand over her slender hip.

"Your friend seemed jealous of our dance," he commented.

"Oh, Miles." Cindy tossed her head. "He's being ridiculous. He's a great guy, and I like him a lot, but we're just friends. That's all we'll ever be, but it hasn't quite sunk into his head yet. And then he ends up bodyguarding Margot's stupid little dog. I was, like, excuse me?"

"Who's Margot?" Faris asked. "What's the matter with her dog?"

"Connor's brother Davy's new girlfriend," Cindy explained. "Nobody knows much about her except that Davy's crazy about her, and she's got some weirdo stalking her. It's creepy, but the dog bodyguard thing is over-the-top paranoid. But the McClouds are just like that. You know how Connor is. His brothers are just as bad."

"Of course," he murmured.

"I mean, please," Cindy nattered on. "Like anything bad would happen to it if she left it in the hotel room. Silly, if you ask me."

Oh, but I didn't, you empty-headed little whore, Faris thought, as he maneuvered her towards the corridor at the edge of the ballroom.

Chapter

18

The dessert fork full of moist, goopy wedding cake covered with raspberries and crème Chantilly made its way slowly into Margot's mouth. Davy watched every second of that pornographic event from across the table. He wondered if he would ever have the nerve to stand up again. His relentless boner was starting to worry him.

He should have had Margot make him come before leaving that room. She would have obliged him. Skillfully, eagerly, any way he wanted it. But he'd been too attached to the idea of saving every last drop for the privacy of the bedroom. He wanted it to last for hours.

She was licking crème Chantilly off her fingers, opening another Pandora's box of erotic fantasies. He shifted uncomfortably on his chair.

". . . do you think, Davy?"

He yanked his attention back to Seth, who was staring at him with a wicked gleam in his black eyes. "Huh? Think about what?"

"You didn't hear a word I said, did you?"

Davy grunted something unintelligible and stuck a wedge of melon into his mouth. Seth followed his gaze. Margot was dipping a raspberry into cream as Raine whispered into her ear. She laughed and popped the berry into her mouth, sucking her creamy fingers again.

Seth laughed at him. "You're fried, man. Some advice? Just give in. The harder you fight, the more stupid you look in the end."

"I'll skip the love advice. What were you asking before?"

"It can wait," Seth said. "No point in talking business to you until after you get laid a few more times—"

"Watch it."

Seth lifted meek hands. "I'm as respectful as a virgin choirboy. Just thinking about your health, that's all."

Davy shook his head and stared down at the piece of wedding cake on his plate. Connor and Erin were safely off to the airport for their night flight to Paris. Any minute now, he would quietly excuse himself, grab Margot by the arm and drag her off to his cave. As soon as he dared to stand up, that is. The hard-on was all that inhibited him.

"Hey, Davy!" Miles skidded to a stop next to the table. "Do you know a sleazeball called Cliff who says he's a friend of Connor's?"

Davy's instincts snapped into high alert at the strain in Miles's voice. "I don't know anyone named Cliff." He looked at Seth. "Do you?"

Seth shook his head and put down his glass.

"If Connor knew a guy well enough to invite him to his wedding, we would recognize the name," Davy said. "Where is he?"

"It's that asshole who's dancing with Cindy," Miles said. "Looks like some kind of stuck-up lawyer type. He's over by the—hey. They're gone. They were dancing right over by the potted plants!"

Davy followed Miles's pointing hand towards the Norwegian pines shielding the door through which he'd pulled Margot some hours before.

He was on his feet and running before he knew he'd gotten up. The image of Bart Wilkes, curled up on the blood-smeared linoleum jarred his mind's eye. He flung open the doors in the corridor. Seth and Miles caught up with him as he flung open the last one.

It was a library. The light streaming in from the corridor revealed Cindy sprawled on the carpet. The French doors that led out to the rose garden hung wide open, the night wind blowing in. The crumpled folds of Cindy's crimson dress gleamed like a pool of blood.

Miles flung himself down next to her. "Cin? Are you OK?"

Cindy stirred, and pushed herself up onto her elbows. "Um, yeah, I guess." Her voice was squeaky and high. "I just—he just started kissing me, and then we heard a noise in the hall, and he just . . . pushed me down onto the ground and ran out the door."

Seth bolted out into the garden. Davy itched to follow, but he knelt down next to Cindy. "Did he hit you, Cin?"

Her big brown eyes blinked and welled full of tears. "No," she whimpered. "He just . . . he just . . . oh, God. Oh my God."

And that was the end of that. Getting a coherent story out of Cindy would have been no small task even if she'd been her normal bubbly self, let alone freaked out and buzzed on champagne. Eventually she started to sob, which he took as his cue to leave her to Miles and head out into the gardens after Seth and Snakey.

He scanned the shadows, his stomach a knot of misery and guilt. Too busy thinking with his dick to see the signs, even after what had happened to Bart Wilkes and the Goth girl. Dragging Margot up here for his own sexual convenience, telling himself it was to keep her safe.

He'd fucked up worse than he'd ever dreamed. Under-estimated his opponent. Endangered everyone in the world that he cared about.

Seth emerged cursing from a thicket of bushes, plucking thorns and rose petals off his tux jacket. "Not a goddamn trace. Is Cindy OK?"

"She appears to be fine," Davy said. "The guy just kissed her. He could be just another resort guest, cruising for free booze."

Seth's eyes narrowed. "You don't think that, do you?"

Davy rubbed his face. "No," he said wearily. "I don't think that."

"This thing is bigger than Sean said, right? This isn't just your garden variety stalker thing."

"It's a long story," Davy admitted.

"Thanks for keeping me in the loop." Seth's voice was hard. "Next time you guys invite me and my wife to a party, do me the favor of letting me know if you've got dangerous scumbags on the guest list."

Davy lifted his hands. "I barely found out myself what's—"

"How about you cut out the part where you grovel pathet-ically, and make it right with me by telling me everything now?" Seth suggested. "Come on, let's go in. I don't want Raine out of my sight."

Davy quietly told him what had happened over the last two days, and Seth listened, impressed. "I might have known you'd get embroiled in that magic hoodoo shit. Touch of death, my ass. Only you, Davy."

"You know as well as I do that it's not magic hoodoo," Davy said testily. "Just energy manipulation."

Seth's grunt sounded unconvinced. "It's that funky gray area that makes me nervous. I prefer techno-toys. They do as they're told."

"If Cindy's guy was Margot's stalker, she was about ten seconds away from dying young," Davy said. "And it would have been my fault."

Seth's face tightened. His steps quickened. They rejoined the table, where Miles was depositing a pale, swaying Cindy into a chair.

Margot held Mikey on her lap. Her shadowy, haunted eyes met Davy's eyes, full of silent inquiry.

He shook his head and gave her a who-knows shrug.

"That asshole offered to hold Mikey while we danced," Miles said. "Lucky for Mikey you have shitty taste in dance partners, Cin."

Cindy barely reacted to the venom in Miles's voice. "He seemed so normal," she said faintly. "Good-looking, funny. He seemed so nice."

Miles's laugh had a bitter edge. "Yeah, all the guys you pick seem nice. Until they turn out to be dickheads, or pimps, or drug dealers or pathological liars. Next time we might not be around to bail you out."

Cindy's face crumpled. She jerked out of Miles's grip. Raine scooted her chair closer and put her arm around the younger girl.

"Cool it, Miles," Sean said gently.

Miles shot up out of his chair, sending it spinning across the floor. "How am I supposed to cool it? She picks out the scum of the earth. They treat her like crap. I keep rescuing her, and she cries all over me, boo-hoo. But if a guy is dumb enough to actually care about her, forget it. She could give a flying fu—"

"Miles." Davy used his command voice. "Chill. Now."

Miles choked off his words and turned away, fists clenched.

"You can't make her feel the way you want her to feel." Davy made his voice calm and steely. "You've got to let it go. Now is not the time."

Miles shook his head, yanked off his glasses and rubbed his eyes.

"Oh, fuck it." The words exploded out of him. "Fuck all of this." He took off across the dance floor, bumping into dancing couples on his unsteady path. Everyone at the table exchanged uncomfortable glances.

Mikey leaped off Margot's lap and scampered after Miles, yipping anxiously. Miles scooped the dog up over his arm and stalked on.

"Unrequited love," Seth offered dourly. "It's a bitch."

Sean gave Margot a long, assessing glance and looked at Davy. "You taking her up home to the mountains tonight?"

Davy nodded "Would you two guys run security? I want someone looking out for the wedding party until every last one of them leaves."

Seth's eyes lingered regretfully on Raine. "I had other plans for the night, after staring at that dress all day. But I guess they'll keep."

"I'm sorry, man," Davy said. "This is my fault, and I'd do it myself if I could, but I want to put some distance between Margot and—"

"Don't bother trying to justify why you get to drag the hot babe off to the mountain hideaway while Sean and I get to prowl hotel corridors all night." Seth winked at Margot. "Get out of here. Scram."

"Sean, stay with Margot at the entrance while I bring the truck around," Davy said.

"I'll do it." Tamara rose to her feet, smiling. "I have some final pearls of wisdom for your lady friend."

Sean hesitated. "Are you armed?" His eyes slid over her revealing gown, lingering appreciatively over her bosom.

"Are you kidding?" Tamara's teeth flashed against red lip-stick.

Margot smiled at everyone at the table. "It was wonderful meeting you all. This has been the most interesting wedding I've ever attended."

Davy's laugh was bitter with irony. "Too interesting."

* * *

Margot tottered in the fragile heels of her sandals as the three of them made their way to the front entrance, thinking with longing of her high-top sneakers. "Aren't we going back to the room to get our stuff?"

Davy shook his head. "I'll have Sean bring it to you later."

They stopped in the luxurious lobby just inside the glass double doors. "But what about Mikey? I can't just—"

"Miles will look after him tonight. I arranged it already. He has the dog dish, the food, the works. Stay here with Tam while I get the truck."

His commanding tone made her back snap up, ramrod straight. She suppressed the sarcastic urge to click her heels together with great difficulty. Davy was in no mood to be goaded. Things were too grim.

"My, my," Tamara murmured, as Davy strode purposefully out into the parking lot. "Masterful, hmm? He's really intense about you."

"He's intense, period," Margot said.

"I thought Connor was the intense one. Sean is the clown, or at least he pretends to be," Tamara said. "It's the ultra-controlled ones that make you wonder. But he's not cold now. He's wired to blow. You're going to have an interesting evening, once you get wherever it is that you're going."

The amused speculation in Tamara's eyes made Margot blush. "Let's not even start with that," she mumbled.

"Oh, you're no fun," Tamara scoffed. "One last thing. I've got a little present for you." She pulled a silver hair ornament out of her bun, shaking loose a gleaming mass of black hair over her shoulders and held it out. The thing was beautiful, a starkly elegant, angular design. "Pay attention," she said. "Press on this knob, and look what happens."

A spring snapped. A piece came loose. Tamara showed her a tiny retractable nozzle. "Point this into someone's face and press on it. The spray will knock them out. It's not lethal, but it's a strong soporific. The effect lasts about ten minutes, depending on the strength of the dose."

Margot shook her head, backing away. "I can't."

"Your outfit needs something extra," Tamara said briskly. "Here. Let me." She snapped the piece back into place and fastened the pin through Margot's wispy French roll. "There," she said, with satisfaction.

Margot reached up and fingered it. "But—"

"It's not much," Tamara said. "Just a silly little novelty item. Another card to play. You need some more cards to play, Margot."

Margot's protests faded away as she looked into Tamara's somber face. "Thank you," she said quietly.

Davy's neck started prickling from the moment he stepped into the parking lot. He drew his gun out of the shoulder holster and held it ready in his hand. The slots for the vehicles were covered by wooden shelters to keep off the weather and the pitch that dripped down from the towering trees. He peered into the shadows of the shelter when he reached his truck. He saw no one, but he hadn't lived to be thirty-eight years old by ignoring a prickling neck.

He'd almost decided to backtrack and ask Seth and Sean for reinforcements, but he pulled out the penlight attached to his keys first, shone it behind the truck, and below it. Nothing and no one, unless Snakey had glued himself to the tailgate.

He let out a long breath and headed into the shelter.

A cat-light shadow falling behind him brushed across his consciousness. He spun around just in time to face the attack. The sneaky bastard must have hidden himself in the pine boughs brushing the shelter roof, but the moment for self-reproach was gone; a whip-swift kick slammed Davy's gun hand into the side of the truck.

His gun clattered to the asphalt while he jerked back, blocking the finger stab that would have gone right through his eyeball and into his brain. He grab-twisted the fingers, yanked the guy off his feet with his own weight, and flung himself backwards, hurling Snakey over his own supine body and into the back wall of the shelter.

A thud, a grunt, a rustle in the dark, and Davy rolled up onto his feet just in time to block the next attack. Jesus, the guy was fast.

A flurry of parried kicks and jabs followed. It had been a while since he'd fought for survival. Too long. He'd lost his edge. He almost fell for a feint to the gut, but last-minute instinct whipped his guard up to ward off a fatal jab to his neck. The guy wore a suit, but he had on a hood like an executioner's mask. It gleamed, like silk or synthetic.

Davy stumbled back to duck a kick to his face, whipping to the right and left to evade jabbing blows. Couldn't spare a split second to look for the gun. Formal menswear was not made for fighting, neither were these stiff, slippery shoes, but the anxious chatter in his mind was easing down into the coiled, silent stillness of combat zone.

He darted back, out into the open, parrying a snake-quick jab to his throat. He hooked the attacking arm down, swept his leg behind, swung his arm down to slam his elbow into the asshole's collarbone. A sharp gasp was his reward, a split second respite as Snakey danced back. With any luck, he'd driven a broken bone into the guy's lung.

No such luck. Snakey came back at him with a hiss of rage.

Davy danced back, assessing his opponent. Professional. Favored the snake style. Pressure points. Sting of death in his fingertips. Very high pain threshold. All bad news.

Snakey lunged. Davy blocked an uppercut strike to his armpit and snatched the guy's wrist. Yank and pull with a dragon's claw, and wham, he got in a rotating blow to the solar plexus. Snakey stumbled back again. This time his grunt had a note of angry surprise.

Anger was good, in one's opponent. He couldn't indulge in it himself. Snakey was panting now, his eyes glinting in the orange glow of the streetlight as if he really were a reptile. Davy blocked high, and whipped in a backhand knuckle blow to the guy's temple.

Snakey stumbled away, and let fly with a spinning kick. Davy lurched back to evade the blow to his ribs, and his shoes slipped on the asphalt. He went down backwards and rolled up to his feet in time to see Snakey disappear into the thicket of pines below the parking lot.

He gave chase, heart thudding, but he didn't get far before he realized that the dark was impenetrable, and so were the trees. He blundered through the dense darkness, branches scratching his face. He forced himself to stop and listen. Far ahead, to the right, he heard a rustling snapping noise. The sound faded to nothing as he listened.

No way to find the guy now, not without searchlights and helicopters, and by the time he got help, Snakey would be long gone. He wanted to kill that bastard so badly, it burned in him like acid.

He slogged up over slippery pine needles toward the parking lot, assessing the damage. Scratched face, his cheek wet with blood. Sore shoulder from that clumsy fall, hand starting to throb from being kicked into the truck. Could've been worse. He could've been killed. Easily.

So this was the asshole that was stalking Margot. Her problem was deeper even than he'd thought.

Margot lunged through the double glass doors towards him when he got out of the truck, her eyes horrified. "Good God. Are you—"

"Fine," he said, flinching back as she reached for his face. "I made Snakey's acquaintance in the parking lot, that's all. Get in, Margot."

"That's all?" Her voice rose. "What do you mean, that's all?"

"Meaning I lost the bastard." His voice was a rasp of frustration. "Tam, tell the others. The guy was tall, well built, a little shorter than me. Wearing a hood, so I didn't see his face. He wore a suit. If you meet him, watch for eye and neck jabs. He likes those. I pounded him some, but he could still do plenty of damage if he felt like it. He's dangerous. I can't stress that enough."

"I'll tell them." A gun had appeared in Tamara's hand. All mockery was gone from her beautiful face. "Take care."

He pulled out of the resort parking lot and onto the winding mountain highway, conscious of Margot's anxious eyes on his face.

"We should stop at the emergency room. Your face is bleeding."

"I just got scratched by the trees. It's no big deal."

"Where are we going?" she asked.

"My brothers and I have a place up here in the mountains. The house where we grew up."

His cell phone rang. He pulled the thing out of his tux jacket. The display showed an unknown number. Strange. Nobody unknown had this number. The list of people who had it was short enough to be numbered on one hand. He punched "talk." "Who's this?"

"It's Gomez." His friend's voice was low and tense.

His own tension rose to meet it. "Hey, Gomez. What's up?"

"I have to meet with you. Right now. It's important."

"It'll have to wait till tomorrow," Davy said. "I told you this morning, I'm up in Endicott Falls for Connor's—"

"I'm up here now, in Endicott Falls. I just drove up from the city. I'm calling you from a pay phone."

That silenced him for a moment. "Uh . . . OK. Where are you?"

"Convenience store at the junction of Moffat and Taylor Highway."

"I'll be there in ten," Davy said. He hung up the phone and dropped it back into his jacket.

"So? Who was that?" Margot asked.

"My cop buddy, Gomez. He drove up from Seattle because he has to talk to me. In person. Right now."

"Oh," she whispered. "That doesn't sound too good."

"Sure doesn't," he agreed grimly.

Minutes later, they pulled into the parking lot. A handsome dark-haired man got out of a battered gray SUV and leaned on his car, waiting. Davy slid out of the truck and slammed the door.

Margot hesitated for a moment, and followed him.

Gomez's sharp dark eyes took in every detail; the dirt on his tux, the blood on his face, his swollen hand. They flicked to Margot.

"You didn't say you weren't alone," he said.

"You didn't ask," Davy said.

Gomez folded his arms. "Wild party, huh?"

Davy shrugged. "Eventful."

Gomez waited for more. The seconds ticked by, and his face hardened. "Get into the car with me. I need to talk to you. Privately."

Davy glanced back to Margot's bright, haunted eyes. Her arms were wrapped around her chest, the night air making goose bumps on her bare arms. "You can say anything you want in front of her."

Gomez shook his head. "Shit," he muttered. "OK, here goes my career. You know a guy named Joe Pantani?"

Davy shook his head, as they both heard Margot's sharp intake of breath. They turned to her. "You know the name?" Nick asked sharply.

"I waitressed at his diner off and on for the past few weeks," she faltered. "Until . . . until yesterday, around lunchtime, that is."

Gomez's face darkened. "Shit. Tell me you're not Margot Vetter."

"Uh . . . why shouldn't I tell you that?"

"You're the waitress who got fired yesterday?" He waited for her nod. "You're wanted for questioning in the murder of Joe Pantani."

Her hand flew up to her mouth. "Joe? Somebody killed Joe?"

Gomez's eyes turned back to Davy. "Yeah. Very thoroughly. Beat him to death. Every bone in his body pounded to splinters."

"I don't know why you're giving me that look, Raul," Davy said. "I don't know the guy."

"And you were never in his house? For any reason?"

Davy shook his head. Raul cursed viciously in Spanish. "You've got problems, then," he said. "A whiskey bottle and two shot glasses in Pantani's house. Good quality latent prints all over them. They ran them through the local and state AFIS and found nothing, so the latent print examiner forwarded them to a friend of hers in the Feds. He ran it through IAFIS—and hit on a potential match. Guess whose military ID number popped up on their screen, buddy?"

Davy felt a chilly, strange sensation, as if jaws of iron were creaking closed around him. "A bottle of my Scotch disappeared from my house yesterday," he said. "I was looking for it last night."

"Did it, now. Do you have a nasty new enemy these days?"

Davy touched the dried blood on his face with his swollen hand. "Actually, I do," he said grimly. "Now that you mention it."

"Three dead bodies in the space of twenty-four hours," Gomez said. "And your name comes up in connection with every single one of them. It looks bad, man. I didn't tell anyone else about your interest in Lila Simons. Not yet, anyway. Give me a good reason not to, Davy."

"You know me, Raul," Davy said. "I'm not a killer."

Gomez looked haunted. "Yeah. At least I thought I did.

Well, that's it. That's all I have to say to you. The report hasn't been signed off yet. The FBI latent examiner still has to pull the hard copy of your prints from your military records and do the visual exam to make the ident, but he thought it was a match just from eyeballing it. You haven't got much time before that happens. They'll rush this one. Count on it."

"Jesus," Davy muttered.

"They're going to want to test your DNA. The way my life is going, I bet they'll find a match," Gomez said. "If your mysterious new enemy stole your prints, he should be bright enough to steal your comb."

"When was he killed?" Davy asked. "Last night?"

"Yeah, based on when he was last seen alive." Gomez's voice was hoarse with weariness. "He was found at four A.M., when his girlfriend came home from her bartending shift. Exact time of death is hard to determine. The killer folded him up and stuffed him into the freezer."

Davy winced. "Ouch."

Raul turned his gaze on Margot. "This is all about her, right?" he demanded. "You're doing it again. Just like you did back in the Army. What was that dancer chick's name? Fran? Fern?"

"Fleur. And this is nothing like what happened with her."

"No. This is way worse. This time you might wind up in prison, instead of just getting the living shit kicked out of you."

"Goddamnit, Gomez—"

"Hey. You're the one who wanted to have this conversation in front of your girlfriend. And I'm sticking my neck out for you so far, it's about to snap. So don't give me any of your fucking attitude."

Davy swallowed back his angry words. "Yeah. I know. Thanks."

"Keep your goddamn thanks. If you're innocent, why aren't we working together on this?"

Davy hesitated. "This thing just exploded in my face,

Raul. Stopping to fill out all the forms would slow us down just long enough to get her killed." He jerked his chin in Margot's direction.

"Oh. Thanks for your faith in me," Gomez said bitterly.

"It's not you," Davy said. "Don't take it personally. I know what it means for you to have told me this."

"Yeah, it means I should turn in my badge right now and save everyone the trouble. My life will be worth shit until you get your problems under control, so get on it. And if I find out that you're lying to me . . . God help you, Davy. I swear. I will destroy you."

"I'm not," Davy said. "And I wouldn't. You have my word. You know me well enough so I shouldn't have to even say it."

Gomez just shook his head. "Where were you last night?"

Davy gestured towards Margot. "With her. At home."

"Oh." Gomez laughed scornfully. "That's just great. Real helpful. Two worthless, piece of shit alibis for the price of one." He wrenched open the door of his SUV and got in. The engine started up with a roar.

The car jerked to a stop, and the window rolled down. "Don't get killed." He spat the words out with vicious force. "Dumb-ass."

The window went back up. Gravel spat behind the wheels as the SUV accelerated out into the night.

Chapter

19

They stared after the red eyes of Gomez's retreating tail-lights. Margot's eyes swam and burned. The wind gusted her skirt, making it flutter around her thighs. She shivered as if it were January. She'd been so angry at poor Joe. Her anger seemed so silly and shallow now.

Guilt twisted painfully inside her at the bleak, cold look on Davy's face. She'd infected him with the Margot curse somehow, like she did to everyone who came in contact with her. The Goth girl, the pawnbroker, Cindy, Davy. Joe. Poor pigheaded, cheapskate Joe. He hadn't deserved to die like that. And now Davy had been set up for murder.

"He must have been in the diner yesterday," she whispered.

"Who?" Davy jerked, as if waking from an unpleasant dream.

"Snakey," she said. "He must've been in the diner when Joe fired me. God. That's so creepy. I probably served the guy lunch."

"Don't think about it. Get in the truck." Davy's voice had

the whipcrack of command, but she was glad of an outside impulse to break the paralysis of her body. She tried to stop shaking as she climbed into the truck, but the shudders were deep, unrelated to cold.

The truck roared to life, and Davy pulled out onto the highway.

She knew this feeling. She was slipping into the vortex. She didn't want to go where it was taking her. She had to distract herself.

"Davy," she began timidly. "I'm so sorry."

"Don't even start."

She didn't blame him for being short with her. She felt so helpless and stupid. What could she say? *Gee, I'm sorry that hanging out with me has put your life and liberty at risk and endangered your whole family. What a bummer. Don't you just hate it when that happens?*

Yeah. Right. She took a deep breath and tried again. "That guy, Gomez. He's an old friend of yours?"

"We served in the Army together. First Gulf war."

No further details were forthcoming. She tried to think of another angle to start from. "Davy, what are you going to do about the—"

"I don't know, Margot. I have to think."

That terse answer, too, dissolved into empty silence. The light of the headlights swerved around the dark curves of the unknown road.

This was unbearable. She preferred to piss him off, even goad him into a fight rather than endure this deathly false calm.

She gathered up her nerve and went for it. "So who's Fleur?"

The truck speeded up. He glanced over at her and shook his head.

A manic recklessness was coming over her. Her shivers had begun to feel like tremors of hysterical laughter. "Oh, come on. If you don't tell me, the stories I'll make up for myself will be a million times more lurid and compromising than the dull truth."

"Don't jerk me around, Margot. It's not a good time."

True, but what did she have to lose? "You asked for it," she told him. "Let's see ... Fleur was a beautiful foreign spy, right? A pistol strapped to her perfect gartered thigh. She seduced you and betrayed you, abandoning you to certain death after painting your naked body with honey and staking you out over an anthill—"

"I'm not falling for this," Davy said.

"Am I close? Am I warm?"

"North Pole," he said. "Outer space."

She was undaunted. "OK, let's try this again. Fleur was the rebellious daughter of an evil international arms dealer. She met you over the blackjack table in a sleazy nightclub in Tunisia, and—"

"Fleur was my ex-wife."

Her mouth flapped helplessly. "You were married?" she squeaked. "Why didn't you tell me?"

"Why should I? It's irrelevant. Not a happy subject, either. It lasted about three months. It happened over fourteen years ago."

"What happened?"

He made a frustrated sound. "You never let up, do you?"

"It's a terrible character defect," she admitted. "Gomez said she was a dancer?"

"Yeah. In a strip joint near the Army base where I was stationed."

She was startled. "Wow," she said. "Was she, um, very beautiful?"

He shrugged. "Sure, she was pretty. She had a problem with pills that I found out about later. An even bigger problem with a violent ex-boyfriend. She left him because he beat on her. Glommed onto me for protection, and like a twenty-four-year-old brain-dead asshole, I fell for it. I doubt I would have married her otherwise. I wanted to save her, see."

"Oh." The ironic edge in his voice made her stomach tighten painfully. Tamara's words floated into her mind. *I expect he wants to rescue you. How adorable. It'll probably get him killed . . .*

"I figured once she felt safe and protected, the pill thing would resolve itself." His short laugh was harsh and telling. "Uh-uh."

"Is that why you guys broke up?" Margot asked.

"One day her ex paid me a visit, with six of his friends. I wound up in the hospital with tubes stuck up various orifices in my body."

She dragged in a sharp breath. The thought of him being hurt so badly made her body recoil. "That's awful. What did Fleur do?"

It took a long time for him to answer, as if he were searching for the right words. "She went back to him," he said finally. "She filed for a divorce. She came to see me while I was in the hospital. She had bruises on her face and neck already. Begged me not to press charges against him for assault. Told me that he would hurt her if I did."

She winced. "Oh, ouch," she murmured. "And you let it go?"

"I was in traction, zonked on drugs. Yeah, I let it go. She'd already moved back to Florida with him by the time I got out of the hospital. I heard she died of an overdose a couple years later. I wasn't surprised."

She blew out a long, shaky breath. "Oh, Davy, I'm so sorry."

Davy's profile looked graven in stone as he stared out the windshield into the night. "So there it is, Margot. My terrible secret. I tried to save her, but I failed. You satisfied now?"

She sputtered in angry confusion. "You did not fail!" she

burst out. "That weak, stupid cow! She should've conked the bastard over the head with a skillet for hurting you! The minute his back was turned!"

He looked perplexed. "That wasn't her style. Fleur was—"

"I don't give a damn what her style was!" she yelled. "It was her duty to protect you!"

He contemplated that. "Nah," he said finally. "She was broken already. She didn't have the strength. I don't blame her."

"Well, isn't that admirable of you," she said hotly. "I'm not as evolved as you, I guess. I say she was a big loser. She let you down."

A painful thought struck her. Her face heated up. "Not that I've got much right to judge," she added. "Gomez was right. I've already gotten you into way more trouble than Fleur ever—"

"Stop it." His voice made her flinch. "You didn't do this to me. Snakey did. Get it through your head. If you take it onto your conscience, you won't think straight enough to solve the problem."

"I shouldn't have involved you." Her voice was stubborn.

He grunted. "You tried to run." He turned off the road, which had been a narrow, rutted, unpaved track for miles now, and plunged into a tight dark canyon of trees. "I stopped you, remember? Got my feelings hurt, laid a big guilt trip on you, carried on like a jerk."

"True, but I—"

"I got myself into this by my own stupidity. And horniness."

"Great. Gee, thanks, Davy. That's real comforting," she muttered.

The road twisted, switching back higher and higher as they climbed the hill until it opened into a clearing. The headlights revealed a forbidding, ramshackle house. Davy parked the truck, killed the lights.

The moon was very bright. Davy flung open his door. "Let's go in," he said. "I'll feel better once we're barricaded inside."

She wobbled uncertainly in the gravel in her spike heels until Davy seized her arm and led her towards the house. He flicked on a penlight and went through a complicated series of locks, bolts and codes on the door before pushing it open. He preceded her inside.

She waited in pitch darkness until a match sputtered and flared.

Davy was lighting a kerosene lamp, the wavering flame casting a warm light over his face. They were in a big, roughly finished kitchen, paneled with raw planks. A trestle table and a large wood stove dominated the room. Davy left the lamp on the table and locked the door, keying a code into a blinking device on the wall.

"An electric alarm, but kerosene lamps?" she asked. "Strange."

"None of us wanted electric light in the kitchen," he said. "We've got electric lights and heat up in the bedrooms because we're soft, lazy bastards, but it just didn't feel right down here. Dad would spin in his grave if he saw us sucking on the electric tit of the evil establishment, so we left the kitchen pure in his memory. Except for the motion detector alarm. Even Dad would've gotten off on that little toy."

"You McClouds are a very strange bunch," she murmured.

A grim smile flashed across his face. "Yeah, we know. You want something from the kitchen, Margot? Water, coffee, a beer?"

"Nothing, thanks."

"Let's go upstairs, then," he said. "I want out of this monkey suit."

A loaded silence followed his words. Davy's jaw tightened. "There's plenty of beds, if you want to be alone," he said. "You don't have to to—"

"I don't want to be alone. That's the last thing I want. I want you."

He closed his eyes for a brief moment. "Good."

He took her hand, and pulled her towards the staircase. She followed him without hesitation. She didn't care how much this was going to hurt later. All that mattered was this hot ache of longing.

She wanted as much as she could get of him. She could face harsh reality another time. No need to chase after it right now.

Combat adrenaline always left him dangerously horny, and he'd been bad off to begin with, even before the fight. The combination was explosive. Davy ripped open the buttons on his shirt and wrenched the bow tie loose on his way up the stairs. Raul's revelation blew his mind. Christ, the irony of it. A fugitive, after an entire adult lifetime of playing the tightass, keeping his nose clean, being respectful of law and order.

One thing was for sure. If he was ending up an outlaw, he was going to be pure burning hell as an outlaw. He would make the whole fucking world sorry for having shoved his back against the wall.

And he had to mellow out. Margot was already shy and quiet as she tiptoed up the stairs behind him. She was tough, but he didn't want to scare her. Fuck her brains out all night long, yeah, but not scare her.

Margot lingered in the hall while he stopped in the bathroom to rinse the blood and dirt from his face and hands.

He grabbed her hand and led her to his bedroom, which was pretty much as he'd left it when he joined the Army at age twenty-one. He'd replaced the severe, military cot his father had mandated with a decent double bed, but the coverlet was still an olive drab woolen army blanket, tattered around the hem. The concept of bedspreads had never occurred to him or his brothers, at least not until Connor had started bringing Erin up here. Now Connor's bed boasted sheets with flowers embroidered around the borders, a pansy-assed colored quilt and a pile of superfluous pillows on top. Women.

He tossed the ruined jacket on the floor, kicked off his shoes and unfastened the shoulder holster, laying the gun on the bedside table. Shirt, cummerbund, bow tie, pants, all soon followed. In seconds he was naked, and standing at attention, as hard as steel, and Margot was still poised by the door as if contemplating escape.

His eyes dragged over every sexy curve. No escape for her tonight.

"That was bullshit, about letting you sleep alone," he said. "You'd have to chain me to a tree to keep me away from you tonight."

The seductive glow in her eyes deepened. "If I had you chained to a tree, Davy McCloud, I'd do more interesting things than sleep alone."

"Oh, yeah? Like what?"

"Let's see," she murmured. "I'd start with a slow striptease. Right in front of you. Just out of reach of your chained hands."

The heavy throb of blood in his groin deepened. "So far, so good."

"Then . . . then I'd suck on your nipples," she offered. "Run my fingertips over the surface of your skin with my magic feather. Half tickling, half petting. And when you're struggling and pleading, I'd get down on my knees—and lick the tip of your, um—"

"My cock?" he supplied helpfully.

"Just barely," she warned. "We're talking torture here. Just a tender swirling lick, like I'm tasting a new flavor of ice cream." Her voice shook slightly. "I'd tease that sensitive spot underneath the, um, head . . . and lick away the shiny drop that's forming right in the slit at the—"

"Margot," he said. "Get the dress off. Now."

She backed away as he moved in on her. "Hey! Watch it. Don't you dare hurt this dress, Davy McCloud. Not only is it the one nice dress I own, it's also the only thing I have to put on my body."

"Take it off." He couldn't control the rasp of menace in his voice.

She grabbed handfuls of the skirt and stared at him, wide-eyed. Every time he got too aggressive, she drew back and tightened up. He didn't have the patience to coax her back, or the self-control to let her lead. But he didn't dare screw this up. It would kill him to stop now.

He backed up until he felt the rough planking of the wall scrape his bare back. "Don't worry," he coaxed. "I'm chained to a tree, remember?" He held out his arms and splayed them against the planks. "Can't move a muscle. Go on, have at me. Be cruel. Make me suffer."

A nervous nod, and she shimmied the dress up. Wisps of hair clung to her face as she pulled the garment over her head. The slip hugged every swell and hollow of her body.

"Take it off," he urged, his voice rough. "All of it."

She licked her lips, tugged the straps down till they cleared the satin demi bra that propped up the cleavage that had taunted him all day. She unclasped it, baring those lush, soft tits that never failed to steal his breath. She worked the slip down over the swell of her hips, let it drop around her feet, kicked off the fragile high-heeled sandals.

She plucked out hairpins, undid the silver pin that was stuck through her hair, and shook out the thick, wild mass. It twirled every which way, all the crazier for having been confined all day. She moved closer, so he could smell the scent of her skin and hair, the hot, rich scent of her arousal. Her eyes dazzled him, fever bright with excitement.

"That first night, at my house, when you took off your shirt, I wanted to touch you like this so badly," she said. "I ached for it."

"Do it now," he urged. "You're killing me. Do it. Do anything."

She pressed her warm, soft lips to the hollow at the base of his throat, cuddling closer so that his cock brushed against her belly. She shimmied closer, lodging the tip of his cock between her strong thighs, squeezing until he gasped. The skin of her thighs was so fine and soft, the puff of pubic hair between them barely tickling his cock.

Her fingers caressed him, murmuring her approval. She tilted her head lower and suckled his nipple as she pulsed her thighs around him. He flung back his head and sucked in a deep breath to keep the pleasure from spilling over into ejaculation.

Energy shot up his spine, exploding in his head like fireworks.

When he opened his eyes, she was gazing at him, puzzled.

"It felt like you just came." She slid her hand down to investigate, tenderly caressing his cock. "Except that you didn't. Apparently."

"I sort of did," he admitted. "I stopped right at the edge. I could do that all night, and never get tired. It's just a trick of concentration."

The wondering look in her eyes turned into a catlike, approving smile. "All night? Very cool. I like your sex tricks, Davy. Let's see you do it again." She knelt, sliding her hands down over his hips. "Can you control yourself like that if you're in my mouth?"

He cupped her face in his hands. "Is that a challenge?"

She licked him from base to tip, and slid her hand between her legs as she drew the head of his cock into her hot mouth and sucked it.

She held up fingers that glistened. "See what you do to me?"

He sank down to his knees, seized her hand and brought it to his mouth, sucking the salty sweet lube off her fingers.

"I need you now. I don't want to play around." He pulled her to her feet and groped in the dresser drawer for the condom stash.

"Hey, buddy. I thought you were chained to a tree!"

"So I cheated. Call me Houdini." He fumbled the thing on with desperate haste, and tumbled her onto the bed.

She glowed against the dingy blanket, luminous. He wished there were something softer on the bed for her. Scratchy wool that smelled like mothballs and dust was fine for him, but not good enough for her.

Not that he could even hold a thought for very long. The shadowy beauty of her body made him distracted. Dazzled and stupid.

He stayed on his feet, stroking the tender cleft between her thighs with his fingers, spreading the wet pink folds. He thrust himself deep.

She braced her hands against his chest as she stared into his eyes. "Are you OK?" she asked, her voice tremulous.

"Never better," he said. "That's my line, anyhow. Are you?"

The giggles made her pussy contract deliciously around his cock. "Yes, I'm great," she said. "You just looked kind of scared, that's all."

"It's been a scary day. But this makes up for a lot."

She nodded and began to move, inviting him with her body to indulge himself. No fighting, just sweet eagerness. She had surrendered to pleasure. The more open she was to him, the wider open he was to her. It was a feeling that grew, expanded into a blast of raw energy. His body surged into hers, out of control, but she was with him all the way, cluching him with her arms and legs and pulling him down on top of her. His lifeline. They shot together over the edge, lost in a pleasure so huge, it blotted out all coherent thought.

He opened his eyes when he felt the soft vibration. Her face was wet, eyes squeezed shut. "Hey. Margot. Are you—"

"No. I'm not OK. I'm a train wreck." She mopped her eyes with her fingers. "Of all times in my life to feel like this about a guy. I knew it. I knew you'd be too much for me, and I just went ahead and jumped."

He felt bewildered and helpless. "Margot, I didn't mean to—"

"Don't." She covered his mouth with her hand. "My stupid feelings are not your fault. You're doing your best, so don't even say it. Just . . . let me get up, please. I need to run into the bathroom for a sec."

This isn't my best, he wanted to say, but he didn't know what the words meant, or where they came from. He slid out of her body. She got up and scurried out of the room.

His best? He didn't know what his best was. He was changing, mutating before his own horrified eyes. It was tying him in knots.

He disposed of the condom and got between the threadbare sheets, fingering the limp weight of the coarse wool blanket. When he brought Margot here again, he'd bring some new bedclothes with him.

When she ventured back into the room, she looked shy, her eyes damp and pink. He scooted over to the cool side and lifted the covers for her. She slid into the bed beside him. Every inch of his skin rejoiced at the contact. He wanted to tell her that, but he couldn't think of a way to express it that wouldn't make her start crying again. God forbid.

He smoothed her hair away from her face. "I love your hair."

She twirled a lock of her hair and smiled at him. "You should have seen it back in the good old days, when I was a redhead and could afford expensive haircuts. I looked pretty fine, if I do say so myself."

"I saw pictures of your haircut. You looked great, but I like it better long and soft and loose around your face. It's sexier."

"Oh. Thanks." She vibrated against him, that suppressed emotion he'd begun to recognize as neither laughter nor tears, just an overflow of whatever she was trying to hold inside herself. It made his chest ache with tenderness. He wanted to see that coppery color framing her beautiful face. He tightened his arms around her. "Grow it out for me."

She gulped. "Um . . . OK. If you like."

It occurred to him that hair grew out slowly. It took months. Years, even. The thought, far from alarming him, was oddly comforting.

Margot was too wired to sleep. She was unwilling to miss a single second of the delicious heat of Davy's naked body behind hers. He held her tightly, spooned up back to front to get as much skin contact as possible. She'd assumed that he was sleeping until he started petting her, his hand stroking her belly, sliding lower until it teased the tangle of hair between her legs. A questioning stroke as light as a kiss.

It was ridiculous, but she couldn't deny him anything. Not the way she felt tonight. She loosened her thighs and pressed his hand deeper, moving around his fingers to seek out more of that sweet, desperate unraveling that only he could wring from her.

Then he slid his other hand under the curve of her bottom, seeking the same soft well of silken liquid heat from behind.

Her eyes flew open. She tried to wiggle away, but he'd already slid his finger inside her. Cold alarm fluttered in her belly. She'd never liked being touched from behind. It made her feel helpless and ashamed.

But then again, this was Davy. He circled her clitoris from the front while his long finger thrust tenderly inside her. She squirmed against him, caught on a merciless prong of sensation.

Suddenly, shockingly, it boiled over into spasms of pleasure.

Whoa. She trembled in his arms. That was . . . new.

She didn't even have time to comment on it before she

felt him fumbling behind her to smooth a condom over himself, and suddenly he'd replaced his fingers with his penis. He pushed himself into her slick opening, gaining entry one little, surging thrust at a time.

She wiggled against him, but his arm held her fast. "That was sneaky," she said. "I told you. I don't like it from behind."

He did not stop his slow, rocking thrusts. "Why not?"

"It makes me feel cheap," she whispered. "Like someone's helping himself to a piece of me without even looking at me."

He stopped moving, his arms tightening. "I'm looking at you," he said. "I'll stop if you hate it. But it doesn't feel like you hate it, Margot. It feels like you're about to explode all over again, if I rub you—right here, while I push my cock against this spot inside you . . . like that. See?"

She cried out as the deep, sensual push against her sensitive inner hot spot that nudged her into another long wave of sensation.

He kissed the side of her neck. "I want deeper inside," he said. "Let me in. Roll over onto your stomach and open your legs."

The words were spoken with the command that was as habitual to him as breathing. As if he had not the faintest doubt that he would be obeyed. Part of her resisted, but a deeper, quieter part understood the language of his body, the pleading caresses of his hands, his lips.

He was a big, powerful man. He could push her into any position he liked, but he didn't. He just waited, petting and nuzzling her nape.

She did as he asked, and rolled over. Not obeying, but consenting. The wordless wisdom of her own body could tell the difference.

He rolled with her, still joined, and made a low satisfied sound in his throat as her thighs loosened. He gripped her hips, pulling her bottom back towards him. She pressed her face against the pillow, grateful for the privacy. She was melting from the inside out. Emotions shaking her, softening her throat, making her face quiver and vibrate.

The erotic pose had a strange effect on her. She saw it so clearly, the pride and fear inside her that objected to the incredible vulnerability of sex, but with Davy, there was no escape from vulnerability, in any sexual position. Her heart had no shields from him. It never would.

He moved inside her, a deep, sliding stroke right against the place where she so desperately needed it. She swayed back to meet him. The sounds were loud in the quiet room; their labored breathing, the wet, slapping sounds, the whimpers that she couldn't control. She had already yielded more than she ever wanted to, but it was too late now. He was inside the fortress, laying claim to anything he pleased.

His sensual, relentless rhythm drove her to the edge, and over.

She lay with her face hidden, struggling for breath. She'd never been with a man so skillful, so seductive. Let alone fallen madly in love with one. There was probably nothing he couldn't convince her to do.

Davy lifted his weight off her with a sigh, and rolled to the side. He shoved her hair off her face, and tried to pry it up from the pillow and make her look at him. "Margot?"

She shook her head and burrowed deeper.

"Oh, shit," he muttered. "Don't tell me you're mad at me again. Damn it, Margot. Talk to me. What have I done now?"

She tried three times before she could make her voice work. As she started speaking, she realized she hadn't thought of anything to say.

"You always win," was what came out, even though it wasn't exactly what she meant.

He flopped over onto his back with a sharp sigh, and covered his eyes with his hand. "We both won," he said, his voice tight. "I cannot win this game unless you win it too. Why the fuck do you not get that?"

Because I'm in love with you, and you're not with me, she wanted to scream, but that was a bomb that would explode in her face too.

Davy sat up on the bed, his broad, rigid back to her, radiating anger as he disposed of the condom.

She curled up onto her side. "Don't be mad," she said. "I wasn't going to say anything. You dragged it out of me."

"Everything I do makes you feel attacked," he burst out. "Even when it makes you come. You drag all your past stuff into bed, and the bed's too goddamn crowded. It's no longer relevant. It's gone. Let it go."

His self-righteous tone irritated her. "Don't you act superior with me, Davy. I'm not the only one who has past stuff to deal with. Mine is small enough to fit inside a double bed. But yours, whoa. It's huge."

"You lost me, Margot. What the hell are you talking about?"

Your mom's death, maybe? Your father's illness? Your ex-wife's betrayal? She didn't have the nerve to throw the big bombs, so she just shoved on with the next thing that came into her mind. "Remember when you proposed that kept woman arrangement to me—"

"You're never going to stop throwing that in my face, are you?"

"Not until you get my point, and God knows when that will be. Nothing can challenge this fantasy you've got about controlling yourself and your world. But you can't control my feelings, Davy. I can't even control my feelings, and believe me, I really, really want to."

"Margot, I just wanted to—"

"You wanted to have sex with me, but you didn't want to be responsible for how I might feel about it," she pushed on. "So here's your perfect plan. Draw up a contract in which I promise not to feel any inappropriate, inconvenient emotions. In return, you'll protect me from Snakey so I'll be all fluttery and grateful. Hah. It's not working."

He shook his head. "You'll twist anything I say out of recognition."

"On the contrary, I think it's a pretty accurate analysis," she said.

"Yeah? I'm still waiting for the point of this accurate analysis."

She glared at him. "You can cut out the snotty tone any time."

Davy sighed, and stretched out next to her, folding his arms over his chest with an air of patient martyrdom. "So? Lay it on me, Margot. Rip me to shreds. It's just that kind of a day."

"You turned yourself into an ice cube to deal with all the things that scare you," she told him. "You don't need anyone, except for maybe your precious brothers. You zoom above it all. Whoosh, there goes SuperDavy, faster than a speeding bullet. Never needing anything."

He propped his head up onto his hand. "If I didn't have needs, we wouldn't be having this conversation."

"Yeah, sure. Sex." She snorted. "You'll admit to needing that, but you probably wish you didn't, right?"

"That sounds like a trick question." His eyes slid over her body. "Before I met you, I wished I didn't need it. I don't feel that way anymore."

She struggled to decode that statement. "Just sex," she repeated, just to be sure he didn't mean . . . no. No way.

"No. You." He emphasized each word. "Sex is general. You can have it with anyone. What I want is specific. Sex . . . with *you*."

"Just sex," she repeated. It was like pressing on a painful ache. Waiting, hoping for him to take it just one tiny little step further.

She could soon see from his face that he wasn't going to. "Jesus, Margot," he said curtly. "What do you want from me?"

"Something I can't have, evidently." She looked down,

plucking at a hole in the ragged wool blanket. "Tell me something. Would you have felt differently about me if I weren't a fugitive with a fake ID and a ninja stalker and a trail of bodies, and all my funky extra baggage?"

"No. I never judged you. That stuff isn't your fault."

"So if you'd met me when I was Ms. Pillar-of-the-Community with a job and a slick car and a salon haircut, it wouldn't have made a—"

"Not one damn bit of difference. I've had plenty of girl-friends like that. I didn't marry any of them. I've worked hard to get my life to this point. I like choosing how to spend my time. I like controlling my space. I like my freedom. I don't want to compromise that for a woman."

"Oh. Well, according to your friend Gomez . . ." She hes-itated, as his face darkened. "You, uh, just did compromise it. In a big way."

"Let's keep the issues separate." He bit the words out, sharp and hard as stones. "That's a different problem, with a different solution."

"I'm not real great at keeping things separate," she said quietly.

"Yeah, I've noticed. I was straight with you from the be-ginning, Margot. If you choose to get your feelings hurt, that's your own—"

"Oh, shut up. Don't you dare use a stale, stupid line you've used before on your other women when they started to cling. I can tell right off if you're using stock phrases. With me, you better be original."

Davy cursed softly. He fumbled in the drawer in the bed-side table, until he found a silver flask. He opened it and took a swig.

"What, am I driving you to drink?" she demanded. "Am I going to have that on my conscience, too?"

He grunted and tossed back another swallow. "If anyone could, it would be you."

"I've never seen you do more than nurse a beer or sip champagne," she said. "It's strange to see you guzzle hard liquor."

"I'm not guzzling," he said, irritated. "It's a sip, for Christ's sake. I don't get drunk. But I like a shot of good single malt sometimes."

"I'll remember that on your birthday." Oops, she was babbling. Like she was going to be in his life on his birthday. "When is your birthday, anyhow?"

His mouth twitched. "November third."

"Of course. A Scorpio. I might have guessed." She covered her discomfort with more chatter. "I'm a Sagittarius myself. December tenth. Don't worry, though. I won't expect you to remember my birthday, being as how you're so wild and free and uncommitted."

"I've got something original to say," he said.

That cut off her babbling abruptly. "Oh, yeah?" She braced herself. "If it's original, then let's hear it."

"Usually, this kind of conversation with a woman makes my dick retract into my body. But take a look at this. Weird."

Margot glanced down at his enormous hard-on, and up into the hypnotic brilliance of his eyes. "It's true," she said. "You never get tired."

"Not of sex. Not when you're around," he said.

The man was a master at confusing mixed messages, but she didn't want to call him on it or pick another fight. Not now.

She jerked the whiskey flask out of his hand, and scrambled out of the bed. "Let me try some of that stuff," she mumbled. "I need help."

She sniffed at the complex fumes, took a sip, and grimaced. "Ay-yi-yi. Not for me. I like sweet things. Pina coladas, frozen margaritas."

"Good Scotch is a different thing." He slid out of bed and moved behind her, putting his arms around her. He lifted the flask to her nose. "Smell it again. Sweet things are for the tongue. This is for the nose, and the mind." His hand curled over the nape of her neck.

She sniffed again. "It burns my nose."

"It's a complicated flavor." His voice was a low, husky murmur. "Earth flavors. Wood, smoke, peat, ash, fire. Green hills. Cold fog rising off the rocky coast of Scotland. Gray and black pebble beaches, rattling every time a wave of dark Atlantic water washes over them. Smell it?"

Under the spell of his soft, hypnotic voice, she actually did. She tried to make light of it. "You're so poetic, Davy. Who'd have thought?"

"Shh," he brushed her words away. "Taste it again. Let the vapor rise up into your nose and expand. Like a bubble with a picture in it."

She sipped it again, and the images he had invoked bloomed in her mind while the burn of liquid fire trickled down her throat. She swallowed it, a shudder through her as its power warmed her.

It was like sex. The taste of desire. The earth, the elements. Just a sip of whiskey with Davy McCloud was foreplay. His lips covered hers, flavored with whiskey while his hand slid between her legs, caressing her. He raised his fingers and sucked them into his mouth. "I love your taste. Better than Scotch. Rich and subtle. Sweet and salt. Delicious."

She seized his erect penis and caressed it, running her hand tenderly over the swollen head. She licked her fingers just as he had, savoring his taste. A silent ritual, charged with unvoiced longings.

He cupped her cheek, and rubbed his face against hers. The faint rasp of his beard stubble made her want to purr with pleasure.

"I wish you would trust me more," he said.

She pressed his hand harder against her face, trapping him there. "I wish the exact same thing," she told him.

They stared at each other as Davy slid his hand down the

curve of her back. "We'll just have to keep doing the best we can."

She nodded, wrapping her arms around his waist.

Davy grabbed a condom from the gaping dresser drawer. He rolled it on and looked down at her, waiting. For what, she wasn't sure.

She blew out a long sigh, and moved another step closer towards the abyss. "Do you want me, ah, from behind? I know you like that."

"Yeah, I do like that. I love the way your beautiful ass looks in that position. The curve of your back, your perfect skin. The shape of you, opening up like a ripe peach. I love watching myself slide into you."

Her legs shook. His soft, husky words cast a sensual spell. She could have come then and there, just from clenching her thighs together.

"But if it makes you feel bad, I won't pressure you again," he went on. "I want to make you feel good, Margot. I don't want to hurt you, ever. In any way. Do you get that? Do you believe me?"

She nodded.

"You call it," he said. "Any way you want. From here on out, you pick. I don't care. I love it all. I'm not fussy."

She turned her back, and crawled onto the bed, leaning forward onto her arms until she was on all fours. The blanket was scratchy beneath her hands and knees. She arched her back, offering him everything she had to give. She waited, her body trembling.

"Hey." His deep voice was soft with caution. "What's this about?"

"This is about me, trusting you," she whispered.

His warm hands grasped her hips, caressed her. "You sure about this? You're not going to give me a hard time afterwards?"

She nodded, shook her head, and laughed at herself. "Yes, I'm sure, and no, I won't give you a hard time, but I wish you

would get the hell on with it already, because I'm ready to—
oh, God—"

"You're so beautiful." And he was kissing her there, his
mouth so sweet and tender. She'd never known how sensitive
the skin of her bottom was, forgot everything except his
stroking hands, his lashing, probing tongue. She was primed
when he finally slid inside her, giving her all of his passion
and strength with each stroke.

He made it last, until she collapsed onto the bed, exhausted. He followed her down, covering her with his warm
weight. She hid her face against the pillow, but he tugged her
hair. "Stay with me," he said. "Don't go off into your own
head. We do better when we stay together."

She tried to speak, but couldn't. She nodded.

"Come now. With me," he demanded, surging deeper.
Harder.

I can't do it on command, she wanted to say, just as she
realized that it wasn't true. He unlocked her with his words.
Emotion and desire rushed out, hopelessly mixed. It churned
them into blinding froth.

She was drifting to sleep when he spoke again. "December
tenth."

"Huh?" Her eyes fluttered open. "What?"

"Your birthday. Sagittarius." He dropped a soft kiss on
her shoulder. "I won't forget."

He slid into sleep, leaving her wide awake once again, her
heart aching with a painful mix of fear and hope.

Chapter

20

She woke as morning lightened the curtain over the window. Davy was cuddled up to her back, holding her tight against his body.

She studied the room for clues about Davy's childhood. It was as spare and austere as a monk's cell, which she guessed said it all. There was a straight-backed chair, a rough, simple wooden dresser, hooks on the walls for clothes. A packed bookcase. A battered old steamer trunk.

No closet, no pictures, no mirror, no photos or ornaments or memorabilia. She thought of what Raine had told her. The thought of a ten-year-old boy losing his mother like that made her flinch. She was too raw inside herself to contemplate anything so painful and sad.

Not that there was much left in her life to contemplate that wasn't painful and sad these days, she reflected.

Just Davy. She could contemplate him. He was problematic, but he made her mind and body fizz like champagne. He was probably destined to break her heart into bits, but oh, would it ever be one wild ride while it lasted. That was something. She could hang onto that.

She rolled over carefully, so as not to wake him, and was startled to find his eyes open and clear, not a shadow of sleep in them. The scratches on his face had scabbed over. She hated that he'd been hurt. She reached down to inspect his injured hand. It didn't seem swollen.

"It's OK," he told her. "I'm fine."

She dropped a kiss on his hand. He turned his fingers to stroke her face. A pale beam of sunlight found its way between the curtains. It lit up his eyes till they glowed like glacial water. His fingertips on her face were so gentle. Memorizing every detail.

There were so many things she wanted to say. How sorry she was for every scratch and bruise. How she regretted dragging him into this awful tarpit of hers. And how incredibly grateful she was not to be all alone there, guilty though that made her feel.

And underneath it, an emotion she couldn't admit to him, but could no longer deny to herself. She trembled like water shaken by deep currents, aching with longing deeper than anything she'd ever known.

She was in love with him. She had to be so careful. Stay sharp, keep things light, while her heart quaked and her world fell apart.

"We have to decide what to do," he said. "We can't stay here."

She was unprepared to think about such immediate practical problems as staying alive. "What do you want to do?"

He twirled a lock of her hair between thumb and forefinger into a loose ringlet. "I've been thinking about it all morning. I don't want to be a fugitive. I had other plans for my life. I like being Davy McCloud. I've invested a lot of energy in that persona, and I don't want to be cut off from my brothers, either. But if you want to run, I won't leave you."

He took her breath away. She gazed at him, wet-eyed, and

swallowed. "I can't run anymore," she said. "I'm run into the ground."

"OK, then. I'm going back to where it all started. To San Cataldo." He stroked her cheekbone with his fingertip. "I'll start digging. Shake trees, turn over rocks, try to figure out who did this to you and what the hell they want. When somebody gets nervous and reacts, I'll have a place to start. That's my hope."

"What do you mean, I?" she said. "It's we, Davy, not I."

He shook his head. "You'll stay with Seth and Raine up at Stone Island. It's only accessible by boat. Bristling with Seth's spywear. You'll be safer there than anywhere else."

She laughed in his face. "Right. Like I want to sit around in some island fortress while you're out mucking around with killers."

"I can kill, too, if I have to," he said. "I'm not an easy target."

"Ouch, Davy." She shuddered. "That's not comforting."

"You know me. Comfort's not my strong point." He studied her face. "Does it freak you out? That I can kill?"

She shook her head. "It's just that I've always lived in a different world, where that kind of danger and violence wasn't real," she said. "And you've always lived in a world where it is. It's discombobulating."

"There's only one world," he said. "It's violent and dangerous. Always has been. Anyone who thinks it isn't is just fooling himself."

"My, aren't we cheerful and positive this morning," she murmured. "I'm sorry if it makes you nervous, but I'm coming, too."

He shook his head. "Bad idea."

"It's not your decision," she told him.

His face went hard with anger, and she braced herself against the elemental force of it. "The hell it's not. You'd complicate everything, if I have to constantly worry about you."

"You're under no obligation to do anything of the kind."

"That is such a crock of self-serving, manipulative bull-shit—"

"I'm not going to cower on an island worrying about you while you're out there investigating my problems!"

"Didn't you hear what Gomez said last night?" His voice had taken on a vicious edge. "They're my problems too, babe."

"Yeah, well, they were my problems first. Nyah-nyah-nyah. Do whatever you have to do, but I'm going back to San Cataldo."

Davy rolled over on top of her. "Margot. It's not going to happen. Get it through your head."

"Do not bark orders at me in that tone of voice, Davy McCloud."

"What tone of voice?" he snarled.

"The military sounding one," she said. "I will not say 'sir, yes sir,' after everything you say. So don't even try it."

He rolled his eyes. "Tone of voice is subjective. Another way for women to whip themselves into a frenzy over insignificant issues."

She shoved him until he rolled off. "Welcome to Planet Female," she said sweetly. "Enjoy your stay. The first stop on our tour will be Insignificant Issues. Please open your guidebooks to page 317."

He clapped his hand over his eyes. "Oh, God, why me?"

"Are you wondering if having wild crazy sex all night long is worth this kind of abuse?"

A dimple glimmered in his cheek. "How'd you know that?"

"I know how men's minds work," she said. "Men are predictable."

He glared at her. "I am not predictable."

"You are insofar as you are a man," she said. "Women study men a lot more than men study women. Sad, but true."

"I'm not going to debate that with you. That stinks of a

trap." He pounced, pinning her down, and this time there was no dislodging him. His erection pressed hard against her belly. "Now, if we were to have wild crazy morning sex, I'd be convinced that it's worth the abuse."

"You think you're so slick," she said. "You think you can distract me? You think it's that easy to persuade me to let you go off alone—"

"We will discuss that later." Davy's voice was steely, but his skilful mouth licked and nibbled the tendons of her neck until she quivered.

"You're doing it again," she warned. "That military tone. I won't have it." She started tickling him.

He clamped her arms closed, trapping her in a breathlessly tight embrace. "And you're challenging me. You get off on that, don't you? Provoking me, making me lose it. You love that." He rolled a condom deftly onto himself that he'd pulled out of nowhere, trapped her wrists and pinned them over her head. "I've studied you, too, Margot. I know what you want in bed. And I can give it to you."

"Macho, arrogant . . ." Her voice trailed into a choked gasp as he slid his penis tenderly up and down her labia. "I'll make you pay."

"Yeah, you do that, sweetheart. Have at me. I can't wait."

He took himself in hand and slid inside her. After all their passionate love play the night before, she was ultrasensitive, but soft enough so that he entered in one long, slick delicious glide that made them both sigh with delight. It started out playfully rough, her arms pinned, his teeth set against her throat while his hips surged.

She writhed and tossed in mock struggle, but they couldn't keep that up for long. The pleasure was too sweet, the feelings between them too strong. Clear and bright, lit up from inside, like his beautiful eyes.

Soon they were clinging to each other as they rocked together. Davy angled himself against her expertly, pressing his surging hips against the yearning ache of her clitoris, slow and steady and relentless, until the warmth crested, and overflowed. She dissolved around him.

When she opened her eyes, he was still rocking tenderly inside her, pushing damp hair off her face. "You're going to Stone Island."

She gazed up at him. "No," she said. "You can't control me with sex. I'm not putting my fate in someone else's hands. Not anymore."

His face tightened. "Goddamnit, Margot—"

"Please, Davy. Not now," she pleaded. She reached up to caress his face. "It's so sweet. So perfect. Let's have this fight later."

He pulled out of her body and rolled her onto her stomach, winding his fingers into her hair. He pressed his face against her neck, and drove into her from behind. She whimpered with pleasure at each savage, passionate lunge. He exploded with a cry almost like a snarl.

He lifted himself off her trembling body. She reached out to touch him, but he pulled away from her and slid off the bed, taking off the condom. The magical tenderness had vanished behind a cold mask.

"Davy. Please. Don't be—"

"We'll talk about it after we eat," he said. "Get yourself ready."

Cooking while angry was a messy, dangerous business. He was so distracted, he almost burned the ham that was browning in the skillet while the pancakes rose on the griddle. He was too busy contemplating strategies for convincing her to go to Stone Island to keep it all together.

Or failing that, coercing her. Whatever the fuck it took.

She ventured down the stairs, damp and sweet smelling from her bath, and stared at the table. "Wow. You never cut corners, do you?"

"Blackberry jam or raspberry for your pancakes?"

"Um . . . raspberry, I guess."

They ate in almost complete silence, washing the food down with coffee sweetened with a can of condensed milk he'd found in the cupboard. She kept shooting him nervous glances, like she wanted to talk, but he refused to meet her eyes. He didn't trust his own temper.

Adrenaline shot through him at the sound of a car. He leaped to his feet, gun in hand, and twitched the curtain aside. A black Chevy Avalanche, and a white Taurus. He was so relieved, his knees wobbled.

"Who is it?" Margot asked.

"Seth," he said. "And another car. That's Miles driving."

He tucked his gun into the back of his jeans and walked out the kitchen door. Margot followed him out, barefoot.

He knew she had nothing else to wear, but her clingy slip bothered him. She looked like a woman who'd been passionately fucked all night long. Flushed lips, wild hair, lush cleavage, nipples poking through the clingy fabric. Jesus. He would have wrapped her in his shirt, if Seth hadn't already been getting out of his truck.

Seth's dark gaze raked over Davy's body, lingering on his scratched face. "Everything mellow up here last night?"

Davy grunted. "More or less. I found out last night that I'm a murder suspect. Our stalker buddy beat a guy to death and planted a whiskey bottle with my prints on it at the scene a couple days ago."

"Fuck." Seth's jaw tightened. "That's bad."

"Yeah," Davy agreed dourly. "Big bummer. How was last night?"

"Long and boring. Sean and I could both have had a lot more fun in our respective hotel rooms, but whatever. We love you, man." He held out a plastic bag to Margot. "Here's your stuff. Sean collected it this morning. He's babysitting the lingering bridesmaids, but I don't think they're gonna leave until he does. He's keeping an eye on Mikey."

She took the bag. "Thank you. I really needed my clothes."

Davy turned to greet Miles, who was crunching morosely through the gravel, head down. "Hey, Miles. I didn't know you had new wheels."

"He doesn't. Those are your new wheels," Seth said. "Or to be more precise, those are Michael Evan's new wheels. Remember when I told you I'd grown you an alternate identity? And you gave me a lot of high and mighty moralistic attitude about working inside the system?"

"Those weren't my exact words, but I do remember the incident."

"I was figuring you might have changed your mind," Seth said. "Snakey might have tagged your car. I would have, if I were him. And if the police are after you . . ." He dug into his pocket, pulled out a wallet, and tossed. Davy caught it one-handed. "License, credit cards, video clubs, library card, Social Security number. Solid credit history. Michael Evan is a mellow, crunchy kind of guy. Votes Democrat. Member of the Sierra Club. Donates to UNICEF. You'll like him. The rental car info is under the visor. Knock yourself out, dude."

Davy flipped through the wallet. "Thanks," he said. "I think you just saved my ass. Come in and have some coffee. You want breakfast?"

"Nah," Seth said, as they trooped into the kitchen. "I stuffed myself at the resort buffet, and Miles is on the love diet."

Miles flung the rental car keys onto the table. "Am not," he mumbled. "I just don't feel like eating, that's all."

"You should've kept Miles out of this," Davy said to Seth. "It's getting dangerous."

"I am a goddamn adult, and can goddamn well decide for myself what I get involved in."

Davy was startled at the savage edge in Miles's voice. "Uh . . . OK."

"I have a favor to ask of you, Miles," Margot said. "About Mikey. I have to do some traveling, and I can't take—"

"You're not going with me to San Cataldo," Davy cut in.

Margot's chin went up. She continued without looking at him.

". . . and I wonder if you could dogsit for me. Mikey likes you."

Miles folded his arms over his chest. He shot a cool glance at Davy. "Free kung fu and karate lessons for one year," he said. "Use of the dojo for practice and weight training whenever I feel like it."

"Jesus, Miles," Davy muttered.

"Private coaching in kung fu forms. Once a week. For one year."

Seth whistled. "Whoa. Did you take a cynical pill? Or are you just hanging out too much with the likes of us?"

"I'm through being the chump asshole who gets walked on by everybody." Miles's voice was very hard. "I'm getting a clue. Finally."

"Is this about Cindy?" Davy asked warily.

Miles shook his head. "No way. This is about me having better things to do than obsess over a brainless piece of fluff."

Davy and Seth exchanged telling glances. "About time he woke up," Seth murmured. "About your road trip. Want reinforcements?"

Davy hesitated. "I don't want you guys implicated. And besides, I was going to ask you if Margot could stay up at—"

"Thanks, but Margot has other plans," Margot broke in.

"We're working out the details," Davy said, through clenched teeth. "And a man and a woman attract less attention than a group."

Seth eyed Margot's clingy slip with approval. "Depends on the woman. If you want to fly under the radar, I recommend a baggy T-shirt and some uglifying glasses for your girlfriend."

Davy's jaw began to ache. "You can stop ogling her anytime now."

Seth's teeth flashed white against his dark skin. "Whoa! Mr. Cool is getting jealous and territorial. It must be love."

Davy's savage irritation edged higher. He turned to Margot. "How about you take that bag upstairs and make yourself decent?"

Margot's cheeks flared crimson. She snatched up the bag and stalked towards the stairs, head very high.

Davy would have felt like an asshole even without the uncomfortable glances Miles and Seth gave each other.

"Uh . . . wow," Seth said. "I've never seen you like this."

Davy had nothing to say for himself. He was suffocating in here. He tossed back the rest of his coffee and stomped out the back door.

The phone started ringing while Margot was in the bedroom, lacing up her high-tops. It rang and rang. She hesitated, and ran to the window. Davy was out in the meadow, talking to Miles and Seth, far enough away that even if she called him to the phone, he would never make it in time. She was being silly. Now was not a time to miss an important call. The worst that might happen was an uncomfortable conversation with one of Davy's ex-girlfriends. She could survive that.

She ran down the stairs and grabbed the phone. "Hello?"

"Hey, is this Margot? It's Sean. Where's Davy?"

She sighed in relief. "He's outside with Seth and Miles. He didn't hear the phone. Want me to call him in for you?"

"No, I can tell you. Nick called, Connor's FBI buddy. He's been trying Davy's cell all morning but the mountain house never gets cell phone reception, so he called me. He found someone to do prints on your snake thingie."

"And?" she said eagerly. "Did he find a match?"

"Sure, but not a helpful one. There was only one good latent print, and the print examiner said that the only potential hit she found was Davy."

Her hand tightened on the phone. "Davy's?" she said, bewildered.

"Yep. All us poor schmucks crazy enough to join our glorious armed forces have been printed. Keeps us honest, I guess. Sorry I don't have more useful news for you. I'm gonna give Davy a hard time for putting his oily paws all over the evidence like some geek amateur."

Margot didn't know what she said to end the conversation. She might have hung up in Sean's face for all she knew. She stood there, paralyzed, unwilling to follow this thread of reasoning all the way down to the dark place where it led. It didn't matter. It was dragging her.

Davy had never touched that necklace. She ran through every moment she'd spent with him. She'd never taken the thing from the place where it lay buried among her hairpins, clips and scrunchies.

He had been in her house three times. Always with her. The first time he'd ever even seen the snake necklace was when he'd seen it hanging from her wind chimes, and he'd made a big point of not touching it then. Which meant that— no. He couldn't be. Not Davy.

But why go to the trouble of getting someone to run prints on the necklace if he knew that his own were on it?

Because he had fully expected to field this call himself, a cool voice in her head said. Nick had tried Davy's cell phone. This call had slipped by him by chance. No one was perfect. Not even Davy McCloud.

A cold, dense feeling solidified in her gut, weighing her down until she doubled over, almost crouched on the ground. Panting around the cramp of pain. And fear. How incredibly stupid. A little tenderness and attention from a man, and she fell. Plop. Like an overripe fruit.

It wasn't possible. She wasn't going there. Anywhere else. Not there. The recent events of her life cataloged themselves mercilessly in chronological order. She'd started teaching at Women's Wellness three weeks ago. The rose petals started two weeks ago. The burglary was a week ago. The dead dog six days ago.

She thought of that first visit to his gym. How he'd blocked her exit, grabbed her, scared her out of her wits. And then come to her house that night, after she'd specifically uninvited him.

In fairness, she reminded herself, she'd let him in. He'd stood on the porch and waited for her permission. If she'd been bowled over by his charisma and sex appeal, that was not necessarily his fault.

She couldn't face it. She'd let down her guard with Davy more than with any other man in her entire life. She'd felt his inner self. Felt the world change course. Her judgment couldn't be that wacked.

She was in love with him. Had been almost since she met him. He was everything she longed for in her deepest, most secret fantasies. But since a person's deepest fantasies were formed by their more or less screwed-up childhoods, it made sense that anything based on them would end up a betrayal. After all, look at what had formed Davy's.

Watching his mother bleed to death. Watching his father go nuts.

Not fair, something screamed inside her. Nobody was responsible for the bullshit that happened to them when they were kids. Nobody.

Her hands were clamped over her mouth. A high, keening sound was coming out of her mouth that didn't drown out the cold voice in her head. She'd suspected from the moment she laid eyes on the man that he was too good to be true. Too sexy and gorgeous, too smart, too good in bed. Too passionate and protective.Too damn perfect.

There was always a catch. Always.

Uglier doubts began to squirm. Joe Pantani, beaten to death with bare hands. Bart Wilkes, who would never tell who had redeemed the snake necklace. The Goth girl, who would never identify who had used her to try and collect Mikey. The blood, the dead dog, it all started after she started working at Women's Wellness . . . and met Davy McCloud.

She'd been so desperate and vulnerable. The perfect state in which to be swept away by someone forceful and strong.

God knows, her luck with men was grim and spotty, from the luckless Craig all the way back to her own father, Greg Callahan. Handsome, charming, violent. The clearest memory she had of the guy was the smell of liquor on his breath. No wonder she was a basket case. Her wires were crossed from the get-go.

But she had no business cowering. She had to think for herself, to be strong and cold. She couldn't wait for Davy to explain everything, to take matters back into his big, capable hands and make it all OK.

Maybe there was a logical explanation for his fingerprints being on her necklace. She wanted to believe that so badly, she was more than willing to be stupid and credulous. She had to guard against her own blind spots and weaknesses, no matter how painful and difficult.

On your feet, girl, she told herself. Davy was still outside. The keys to the rental car were on the table. At least she didn't have to hotwire the thing. She would have laughed, but it was so unfunny.

She darted up the stairs to the bedroom, stuffed her slip, dress and sandals into her plastic bag. She couldn't think about this, or she would lose her nerve. Down the stairs, stumbling in her haste. She grabbed the keys, tiptoed out the door and down the drive, doubled over behind the file of vehicles. Barely out of the men's line of sight.

She slid into the unlocked car, grateful that it was parked at an uphill slant. All she had to do was release the emergency brake and roll slowly down the driveway until she disappeared into the trees. The crunch of gravel under the wheels sounded deafening to her ears.

No alarm was sounded. The hairpin turns were tricky to negotiate rolling backwards, but she managed. She was concentrating so hard, the tears rolling down her face surprised her when she got to the road.

She fired up the engine, wiped her eyes with her arm and took off. The rental sedan jolted around the curves of the mountain road.

She could not afford to get pulled over for speeding once she got onto the highway. She was a car thief now, too. The situation was degenerating fast. But even the prospect of facing a state trooper in a stolen car with a fake ID paled in comparison to facing Davy's angry green eyes.

Faris could not believe his eyes. He pulled the car out of the concealing foliage where he'd huddled all night, festering with rage as he imagined McCloud soiling his angel with his filthy body. He had even gone so far as to wish he'd brought a gun. He'd always thought himself to be far too talented to deal death with such a crude weapon.

But he would do anything to eliminate McCloud.

And Margaret had run away. His blood sang with triumph. She was pure at heart. McCloud had forced himself on her, but she had wanted desperately to escape all along. To stay pure . . . for Faris.

She was so brave. So valiant and strong. His joy almost balanced out his humiliation at what had happened the night before. He had never been defeated in combat, since very early on in his training with the secret Order of the Snake. He'd been the strongest of all of the trainees. The very best. Marcus had arranged it all for him, had organized and paid for everything. Marcus had been so proud of how accomplished his brother had become. How useful his skills were.

Faris had wanted so badly to be useful to Marcus.

There is no such thing as defeat, Faris. Defeat is unacceptable. You know what happens to losers, Faris. Do I have to show you again?

He could not go back to Marcus, battered and bruised, and tell him that McCloud had beaten him and kept the girl. Unthinkable.

There is no such thing as defeat, Faris.

He could see her white car below him, the next switchback down. It was pure luck that he'd jolted out of his doze at the sound of her car, or he would've continued to follow the GPS signal in McCloud's truck.

If he could extract the information Marcus needed from her, Marcus would have no reason to damage her. Prying information was easy, with his needles, but Faris had never done it to someone that he did not want to damage. Oh, well. He had to be strong, and practical. He would love her and pet her and caress her until pleasure made her forget what she had suffered. The way Marcus had always done to him.

And Faris did love Marcus, in spite of the pain and the fear. Love and pain and fear were all mixed together. That was how the world was.

Afterwards, she would bond with him in isolation from the world. They all had, in the end, but the others had degenerated, broken and babbling. He'd been forced to dispose of them all, eventually.

He wouldn't have to dispose of Margaret, though. She was strong.

Chapter

21

Davy left Seth and Miles in the kitchen and went looking for Margot. He had the vague notion of telling her he was sorry for being such a dick, and besides, he wanted her under his eye. Not that she was in danger up here, but still, his neck was crawling weirdly.

The phone lay off the hook, beeping. He picked it up, stared at it, and hung it up. He punched in the code that redialed the last caller.

Sean picked up. "Oh, hey, it's you. Did Margot tell you what I—"

"What did you say to her?" Davy demanded.

"Didn't she tell you?" Sean sounded puzzled. "Nick called me. He's been trying to reach your cell. The only print on the necklace that was decipherable was yours. Did you touch the thing before you bagged it?"

"Oh, *shit*." Davy's stomach sank. "You told her that?"

"Why shouldn't I tell her? And since when did you get so careless, anyway? Since you started getting laid?"

"Christ, Sean, you should have talked to me before you

shot off your big mouth! She didn't know I'd ever handled the thing!"

"What do you think I am, psychic? How am I supposed to know about your communication problems with your girlfriend?"

"Later. I have to fix this now." Davy slammed the phone down. "Margot?" He ran up, checked the bedroom. Her clothes were gone.

Seth was slouched in one of the kitchen chairs, swilling coffee. He saw the look on Davy's face and stiffened. "Problems?"

"I can't find Margot," Davy said. "I handled her necklace, the one I told Nick to run prints on. Sean just called and told her that my prints are on it. That jaw-flapping *idiot*."

Seth blinked over his coffee cup. "And this a problem . . . why?"

"Because she never saw me touch the goddamn thing!" Davy yelled. "She probably thinks I'm the stalker now!"

Miles's eyes widened in alarm. Seth hissed through his teeth.

"Yikes," he said. "How about Miles and I hit the road? This is one conversation I would really rather not overhear."

Davy was already out the door, scanning the driveway. There were only two vehicles, not three. "You won't overhear anything," he said. "The rental car's gone. She's split already."

Seth and Miles followed him out the door. The three of them stared at the driveway. There was a long, dismayed silence.

"That, uh, sucks," Miles faltered. "Got any idea where she went?"

Davy's hands clenched. "She thinks it was me," he muttered. "Un-fucking believable. There's a killer out there gunning for her, and she thinks I'm wasting my time playing dirty tricks on her."

"Uh . . . shit." Seth floundered. "Women get weird ideas,"

he offered tentatively. "You've only known her for what, two days? And she's been living on the edge. It screws with your judgment. Believe me, I know. Don't take it personally, man. I can tell she really likes you."

Davy spun around. "Likes me? Are you out of your fucking mind? This guy's a trained assassin, and she's running straight into his arms!"

He lunged away from them, picked up a wheelbarrow that leaned against the woodshed, and hurled it right through the weathered siding. A rending crunch, and they all stared into a splintered dark hole in the wall. Seth's mouth gaped. Miles backed slowly away.

Davy stumbled back in the long grass, the sick certainty coming on. The blood-tinged darkness. Not now, please not this, not now . . .

Cold, small hands clenched on the steering wheel, snow falling thick and fast and silent, tires spinning uselessly. Spinning and spinning.

"Davy? Hey! What's going on? What are you . . . Davy?"

His foot, stretching desperately to reach the clutch. Dad yelling hoarsely, Mom as pale and transparent as a wax doll.

Blood, spreading. Everywhere. So much of it.

"Yo! Davy! Snap out of it, man. You're giving me the creeps!"

The images faded from his vision. He was doubled over, his forehead slick with sweat. Breakfast seriously threatening to come up.

He straightened up carefully, trying to make his breath go deeper than the panicked, hitching gasps that shook his chest.

He looked into Seth's angry face. Miles had skittered back to a safe distance, face pasty white, eyes huge behind his round glasses.

"Jesus, man. You scared us to death! What the hell was that?"

Davy willed his stuttering heart to slow down. He ignored Seth's question, replacing the images with blank, neutral ones; his proven favorites; ice fields, sand dunes, the pock-marked face of the moon.

They didn't work. Not with Margot's face superimposed over every one of them. "Everybody's got their crap to deal with," he muttered.

"Ain't that the truth," Seth said. He patted Davy gently on the back, as if afraid that he would break. "You, uh, gonna be—"

"I'm fine," Davy said sharply. He turned to Miles, glared at him too. "Perfectly fine."

Miles nodded rapidly, still speechless. His Adam's apple bobbed.

Seth looked unconvinced. "You going after her, then?"

Davy stared bleakly down the road. "I know that Snakey's not me. She doesn't. I can't sit around on my ass while she gets slaughtered." He turned back to the house. "Got to haul ass. Now."

"You can't travel in your own vehicle," Seth said. "If they're not watching for it now, they will be soon."

"I don't have time to find something else."

"Take mine," Seth offered. "I'll dump yours in town somewhere."

"You mean the Batmobile?" Davy spun around, startled. Seth was fiercely territorial about his super-customized vehicle.

"It'll save you time," Seth announced, with stoic martyr-dom.

"Thanks," Davy said. "Yes. I accept. Give me the keys. Now."

"Maybe Miles and I should go with you," Seth said cautiously. "You shouldn't be driving in your, uh, condition."

"I do not have a fucking *condition*," Davy spat out.

"So you've never gotten one of those spells while driving? This is my beloved car, man."

"I don't have time for this." Davy strode to the kitchen.

"I'm out of here. Not that I've got the faintest clue which way she went."

"Sure you do," Seth called after him. "Just follow the beacon."

Davy whirled again. "Come again? What do you mean, beacon?"

Seth had a self-satisfied gleam in his eyes as he sauntered into the kitchen. "I gave her a petfinder. She didn't tell you? Her dog wasn't wearing it when Miles and I took off this morning, so it's probably still in her purse, right? Bingo, man. You got her cold."

Davy stuck his gun into his jeans and grabbed a jacket off the wall. He plucked the keys to his own truck off the wall hook and tossed them to Seth. "I owe you a drink."

"You owe me a six course meal, you cheap bastard." Seth dug his keys out, and passed them to Davy. "I've got X-Ray Specs loaded onto the computer on the dash. Just enter the code, which I have . . . in my wallet." He passed it over. "You've run that program before, right?"

"Yeah, sure." Davy stuck the printed card into his pocket.

"And there's a briefcase in back. My emergency kit. It's got a laptop, and some of my spyware techno-toys, if you feel the need. Not that you deserve to profit from my genius, since you took my beacon out of your cell phone. That hurt my feelings, you humorless dickwad."

Davy entered the alarm code into the door. "Being tagged by a beacon is an unacceptable infringement of my privacy and my personal freedom," he repeated, for what had to be the thousandth time.

"Spare me the dogma. You love it when I conveniently infringe upon your lady's privacy and personal freedom, right? Hypocrite."

"She's got a murderer on her tail," he pointed out.

Seth rolled his eyes. "Yeah, sure. Don't they always."

"Seth, get real! I am up to my neck in shit!" Davy yelled. "How can you joke about this right now?"

Seth and Miles exchanged worried looks. "Because it helps," Seth said bluntly. "I laugh so that I do not weep. Try it sometimes."

"Today is not the day for me to develop a fucking sense of humor." Davy got into the Chevy, fired up the engine. He slewed the truck around, wallowing in gravel, and floored the bastard.

Theoretically, her body needed food. She'd been driving like a demon for twelve hours straight, stopping only to re-fuel the car and pee.

She should be ravenous. Maybe some strange chemical was released by the brain when a person ceased to care what was going to happen. She felt cut loose, floating. The tears she'd shed this morning had run their course and left her empty as a shell. Better that way.

At least she had a destination. San Cataldo was the only place with a magnetic pull strong enough to make her move through space.

She didn't care enough to keep running from whoever had killed Craig and Mandi. She didn't have the energy to start over. Even Mikey was gone, and he'd been the only thing that kept her feet on the ground.

Enough. She was done with running, hiding, lying to sur-vive. She would do for herself what Davy had proposed to do for her. Turning over rocks, shaking trees until someone got upset. The thought of being put in jail or killed no longer elicited any emotional reaction.

She wondered if this was what Tamara meant when she talked about giving up fear and hope. Was this what freedom felt like? Numb, no need for food or drink, company or com-fort. Careening through space with no past, no future. Taking each second as it came.

She'd stuck to the smaller roads. The line on the accelera-tor trembled over eighty-nine mph. It was a miracle that she hadn't gotten stopped. When she was too broke to buy more gas, she would ditch the car and start hitchhiking. Minute would keep following minute, until the minutes stopped. For whatever reason.

Hours slid by. Bizarre waking dreams ran through her mind, more vivid than the dashed strip dividing the blacktop. Twice she wavered onto the shoulder and jerked back onto the road with a faraway jolt of alarm. Next time she might flip over the guardrail, or plow into an oncoming car. Not that death held much terror, but she could still whip up enough juice to feel reluctant to hurt somebody else.

She got off the highway and started looking for a cheap motel. The dilapidated Six Oaks Hotel fit the bill. The vacancy sign missed the first three letters, so the sign flashed ". . . *ancy* . . . *ancy*," over and over.

She pulled up outside reception. The glass door was locked, but she kept pounding until a heavily jowled man in his undershirt stumbled out of a nook behind the lobby. He wore two large hearing aids. He unlocked the door and glowered. "It's after midnight, lady."

"I'm so sorry to have disturbed you," she said. "I just couldn't drive any further. I promise, I'll never do it again. Could you give me a room that faces away from the road? Please?"

He grumbled as he fished for a form and shoved it across the counter. "$29.79 with tax. Gimme your card."

She scribbled a fake license number and pushed it back at him along with two of her precious twenties. "Can I pay in cash? My purse got stolen, and the credit card people haven't mailed me my new—"

"Don't tell me your problems after midnight. I ain't a bartender. Gimme a hundred bucks for a room deposit."

She counted what was left in her wallet, and reluctantly pulled out the last three twenties. Nothing left in there but a five and a few ones. "Uh . . . will sixty be enough?" she asked. "I don't have—"

"Give it over." The guy scooped up the twenties, shoved a key back at her. He turned away and shuffled back toward his dark den, where the eerie blue light of a TV flickered fitfully.

She drove the length of the long, L-shaped building. Her room overlooked a Dumpster and what appeared to be a gravel pit. Dismal, blighted, perfect for her mood. The interior wasn't much better, dusty and reeking of cigarettes, but she wasn't disposed to criticize.

She almost collapsed onto the bed, but she wanted to shower the burning grit out of her eyes. Then she would lie down and close her eyes. And that was as far into the future as she was willing to project.

She stayed under the pounding water until she was squeaky clean, her fingers wrinkled and pruney. She never wanted it to end. Neither the past nor the future could intrude upon a good hot shower.

She turned it off regretfully, dried off, and wrapped the clammy, skimpy towel around her body, hoping that the bed didn't sag or lump. She exited in a billowing cloud of steam, all ready to fall right into the—

"Hello, Margaret."

She screamed and stumbled back into the bathroom.

She had never seen the guy who sat on the bed facing her. He was a hideous apparition, dressed in a suit that was ripped and torn, his shirt bloodstained. Short dark hair. His gray eyes were wide, full of broken capillaries which made him look as if he were weeping blood. His lips were swollen and scabbed, his skin clammy. Dotted with sweat.

She clutched the door frame. "Who are you?" she whispered.

His distorted mouth stretched wide. "You know me. You're my red angel. Marcus told me to kill you with Caruso and Whitlow. It was supposed to be a murder-suicide, but when I saw you, I knew you were mine. You were too special to waste. I didn't kill you. I couldn't."

She could think of nothing to say. What was there to say? *Gee, thanks?* The one frantic thought rattling around in her mind was how naive she'd been to think she'd burned out fear. Hah. She was vibrating with it, her backside pressed painfully against the sink.

Her eyes swept the bathroom. One tiny louvred window high on the wall. Nothing in the bathroom that would serve as a weapon. Thin hand towels. Cheap soap. *Oh, Davy. What in God's name had she done?*

"It was you who left me in that hotel room?" she asked cautiously.

A muscle began to twitch in his cheek. "You should have waited, Margaret." His voice quivered with tension. "You shouldn't have run away. You caused a lot of problems for me. You hurt me."

A self-control she had never known she possessed quenched the sharp replies that flashed through her mind. She forced the meek, soft words out. "I'm sorry. I . . . I didn't know."

It was the right response. His expression softened. "I know you didn't," he crooned. "You didn't mean to betray me. And we'll fix it now."

Tenderness on this man's face was almost more frightening than anger. "How could I betray you?" The words burst out, propelled by months of desperate confusion. "I don't even know who you are!"

His mouth stretched into a ghastly smile. His teeth were bloody, one of his eyeeteeth missing. "You know me," he said. "I knew it when I found this." He reached into his jacket and pulled out a folded scrap of paper. He unfolded it. It was a drawing from one of her own stolen sketchbooks. A coiled snake, rising up out of the darkness. An image from her recurring nightmares. One morning in a fit of self-help zeal, she'd tried to exorcise it by drawing it. Acknowledging her feelings, yada yada, etc. It hadn't helped the nightmares one bit.

Looking into Snakey's pale, mad eyes, she could see why.

Her subconscious mind had known how scarily deep the shit she was in actually was, even if the rest of her had not. "I drew that," she said.

"It's me." His voice was hideously gentle. "I am the snake. It's my Order. My symbol. I knew when I saw this that you can feel me, Margaret. You're the only woman who could truly understand me."

Her gorge rose. She swallowed it down. The last thing she wanted to do was to hurt the guy's feelings by urping all over his declaration of love. "This is, um, kind of a lot to take in all at once," she said. "So it was you who killed the dog who attacked Mikey?"

"I am your champion," he said, in soulful tones. "Forever."

"And . . ." She swallowed again. "Joe Pantani?"

"That worm." His face twisted, muscles spasming. "You should have heard him. I made him scream like a pig for what he did to you."

Margot held her breath, and blew it out slowly as she tried to keep her face calm and placid. Oh, poor, poor Joe.

"He learned what happens to anyone who hurts my angel," Snakey said hoarsely. "I'll show McCloud, too. I'll show them all."

"No!" she burst out.

Snakey's smile faded, replaced by that mad, twitching tension.

Margot backpedaled, her stomach fluttering. "All I meant was that McCloud never hurt me. He's so insignificant. Don't waste your time on him. He's nothing to us, really. Less than nothing."

Snakey folded the snake picture up and tucked it back in his pocket. "You're very brave, Margaret. But I know the truth. I saw you escape. He kidnapped you. He violated you."

"But he—"

"Never think about him again." Snakey's voice cracked with strain. "You're mine, now. I'll protect you. And I'll take care of him."

Margot had no idea what might set him off. She tried to keep her shaking voice gentle and soft. "What do you want from me?"

"Now we fix what you wrecked eight months ago." Snakey rose to his feet and grabbed her hands. He lifted them to his lips.

The hot, moist contact almost made her retch. Her towel began to slip. She tried to catch it with her armpits, but Snakey pried her arms up high. The towel dropped, leaving her stark naked and shivering.

"I've seen you before," he said. "Don't be shy. You're beautiful."

She tried to pull her hands away, cowering into the space between the sink and toilet. A sick wave of faintness was rolling over her, but she could not faint. Not an option. "Please," she whispered.

"Oh, no. It's too soon to make love," he crooned. "That will be your reward when you tell me where you hid the mold. If I bring Marcus the mold, he won't have to torture you. You don't want Marcus to torture you. He doesn't love you like I do. He wouldn't be careful, like me."

The word "torture" had the effect of scrambling her stressed brain so completely, she barely understood the rest of what he'd said.

"The—the mold? I've never heard of any—"

"Don't." His face twitched. "Don't make me hurt you. I love you. I don't want to hurt you. But I will if I have to. I will, Margaret."

"How?" she asked desperately. "Why should you hurt me? Do you mean mold like on bread, or mold like a cake pan? I don't—"

"I didn't want to." His voice broke, almost as if he were in tears. "I love you. Remember that afterwards. Promise me you'll remember."

He reached up to her throat, and pinched her with his thumb and forefinger, quick as a snake. The pain was huge. She shrieked.

* * *

Davy scanned the lot of the Six Oaks Hotel for the white rental car. The beacon said she'd been here for twenty minutes, but Davy's skin crawled like a nest of ants had invaded his clothes. Snakey had caught up with her. He could feel the guy. That, or he was going nuts.

Neither possibility would surprise him much today.

He would have arrived with her, if not for the cop who'd ticketed him for going 98 in a 60 mile an hour zone. He would have paid ten times the sum to get those lost twenty minutes back.

His heart leaped when he turned the corner. White Taurus, Washington plates, and his instincts screaming louder every fraction of a second that passed. He jerked to a stop, killed the engine and hit the pavement running, gun in hand. The lock was engaged, but the flimsy door yielded to the battering ram of his shoulder with one blow.

Margot was naked on the bed, arms stretched up high, plastic cuffs fastening her wrists to the wooden knobs on the cheap headboard. She was gagged with a strip of white cloth, eyes wide with terror, but she was alive. Snakey spun around, sinking into guard. A case lay open on the bed, full of things that glinted evilly in the overhead light.

Davy took aim and shot at the sick son of a bitch, but Snakey was quick, whirling in an acrobatic blur over Margot's body. He took cover on the other side of the bed, snatching up the bedside table to shield him from Davy's next shot. An explosion of splinters, and Snakey hurled the thing across the bed. Davy ducked, and the heavy thing bounced across the same shoulder that had knocked the door open.

Pain blossomed, the gun dropped to the floor from his numb fingers, and Snakey hurtled like a cannonball across the bed, fingers poised to stab and gouge.

Davy parried the blows, but Snakey's momentum drove him back against the wall with a force that knocked his wind out. The next split second of timeless, airless infinity was a flurry of blocks, blows and gasping for breath. His reflexes were slowed by twelve hours of driving with his heart in his mouth. Snakey should have been in the same boat, but the sick fuck didn't show it. Davy's back to the wall left him barely enough space to block a jab that should have driven his facial bones into his brain. Blood squirted. He was too busy to care.

Snakey wiped blood from his face from a wound Davy didn't remember inflicting. He screamed something incomprehensible as he knocked the TV stand over towards Davy, toppling it off its perch.

Davy danced back to avoid the explosion of broken glass. A pale swirl of movement caught the corner of his eye, and Snakey stumbled forward with a grunt of surprise. Margot had swung both legs up and kicked him in the back of the head. Yay, panther woman. He used that precious fraction of a second to dive for the fallen gun.

Snakey came at him again with a bellow of rage, reeling to the side with a furious hiss as Davy took aim. He bolted out the open door.

Davy lurched to his feet and gave chase. He got off two more shots as Snakey sprinted across the parking lot. He slowed down his mad dash to squeeze off another shot, hoping anyone listening to this fight had the good sense to stay huddled in bed. Snakey jerked, but recovered and kept running, disappearing around the side of an SUV.

The motor roared to life. Davy sprinted faster, peering for the license number. Snakey reversed and speeded back towards him, forcing Davy to fling himself to the side, tuck and roll. Same fucking shoulder. He bounded to his feet and aimed for the tires.

No luck. The vehicle screeched away. Davy stared after it, panting. Dark liquid gleamed on the asphalt. He'd wounded the guy, who knew how badly. If he ran for the Chevy and floored it, he might catch up—or he might not. In any case, a car chase lasted as long as it lasted, and Margot was bound and gagged in a shot-up hotel room in the middle of nowhere with the door hanging open to the night.

He couldn't leave her like that. Hell, he couldn't leave her at all, even when she took him for a crazy murderer.

And now that Snakey was gone, anger was roaring back into the raw, inflamed place where terror had so recently been.

It was a really bad combination.

Chapter

22

The door creaked open.

It was Davy who walked in. She sagged, every muscle in her body slack with the intensity of her relief. Tears spilled onto her cheeks and into her nose. She was already struggling hard to breathe with the wad of torn sheet in her mouth.

Davy stood in front of her. His nose was bleeding, and he was holding his left side, breathing heavily. She expected him to take out her gag, but he stumbled into the bathroom, turned on the faucet.

He came out, sponging his face with a damp hand towel. He held it to his nose as his eyes traveled the length of her naked body.

"I didn't get him this time, either," he said. "I just wounded him. I don't know how badly. But I lost him again. I don't know how long he'll be gone. He could come back any time."

She pleaded with her eyes for him to take out the gag.

"Of course, this could all just be an elaborate trick. I could have hired that guy to play out a charade just for your benefit. What do you think, Margot? A guy who's capable of scratching his face to fool you into thinking he'd been fighting? He'd be capable of anything, right?"

She shook her head desperately.

"Like murder, for instance. Beating innocent people to death? Slaughtering animals to freak you out? Is that what you think of me?"

She shook her head, made a high-pitched mewling sound. He leaned forward and plucked the gag out of her mouth, letting it dangle under her chin. She spat the rest of the cloth out and gasped hoarsely for breath, coughing. "Untie my hands," she begged.

He didn't respond. It was as if he didn't hear her words at all. "Davy," she said, more sharply. "Untie me. This minute."

He shook his head. "No. I'll leave you just like that for now. It's the only way I can be sure you'll stay in one place long enough for me to say every last thing I want to say to you."

"Davy—"

"Shut up and listen for once in your life, or I'll gag you again."

She tried to swallow, but her throat was scratchy. "I'm listening."

"Truth is, I like the scenery, just like this. It suits my mood to have you tied up naked. It underscores the point I want to make."

A chill went through her as she stared into his eyes. She looked down. He had an erection. Her legs clenched around a shiver of primitive fear. He followed her eyes, and let out a bitter laugh.

"So I'm capable of rape, too, right? Wow. The sky's the limit."

"Davy, don't do this," she pleaded.

"I wouldn't have thought that seeing you tied up would make me hard," he said. "But then again, I've never been this angry before."

"Stop it right now. You're deliberately trying to intimidate me."

"Yeah, I am. Check me out, Margot. You bring out the absolute worst in me. I've been more of a dickhead with you over the past three days than I've been to the rest of the world in the past thirty-eight years combined. What does this tell you?"

"That you should stop it right now and untie me." Her voice was too broken and hoarse to sound authoritative.

His eyes had a feral glow. "Weird, that I never fantasized about this. It would be fun to go down on you when you're tied up. I always have to hold you down, but if you were restrained, I could fingerfuck you at the same time. Make you come until you fainted."

She struggled to swallow again, but her voice was strangely steady when she spoke. "You wouldn't do anything to me that I didn't want," she said. "So go ahead. Let it all hang out. Talk as nasty as you like. You don't scare me, Davy. You might as well skip this part."

His shoulders slumped. He looked exhausted.

"Untie me," she said again, more quietly.

Calm seemed to work, where anger and pleading had failed. Davy knelt down and pulled a long, black-bladed knife out of an ankle sheath on his boot. He hesitated. "You trust me?"

"Yes," she said.

"Then don't flinch. This thing is sharp."

Two sharp snicks and the cuffs gave way. Margot sagged onto the bed and rolled onto her side, rubbing life into her numbed hands.

"Why did you run from me?" Davy asked her.

"Why were your fingerprints on the snake?" Margot countered.

Davy crouched to replace the knife in his boot. "I picked your lock," he said. "I went into your house after you went to work, the morning that Snakey dumped blood on you."

"You sneaked into my house? And went through my stuff?" She sat up on the bed, open-mouthed.

He nodded.

She waited for an explanation. He just looked grim and obdurate.

"Why?" she demanded.

"Because I was frustrated," he said. "I was curious, and you wouldn't tell me anything. I wanted to help and you wouldn't let me."

"You shouldn't have done that," she said.

"Yeah. I knew it was wrong when I did it, but the rules just fall apart when it comes to you."

Margot's dry, scornful laugh turned into a cough. "Oh, great. The story of my life. The whole world has that attitude towards me."

His shrug was angry and defensive. "So? I snooped through your stuff. It was dumb, it was wrong, and I'm sorry. Can we leave it?"

"That's stalker behavior, Davy," she said.

His face tightened. "Yeah, sure. Slap my hand and put me in the corner. I would never hurt you. I didn't kill anybody, human or animal."

"What do you want now, a medal for comparative good behavior?"

He turned away, sponging at his face with the towel.

Margot slid off the bed and picked her way through the devastated room towards the plastic bag on the floor that held all her current worldly possessions. She pulled out the slip and yanked it onto herself. When she turned back, Davy was staring into the case that lay open on the bed. His face looked grim. She picked her way through the bits of broken TV and peered at it.

"What is that stuff? It looks like . . . what are those, needles?"

"I think you were about to learn more than you ever wanted to know about the dark side of acupuncture," Davy said.

It made her think of Craig. She turned away and forced herself to breathe. "I'm glad you came for me," she said. "Thank you."

Davy's eyes were bleak. "I'm glad I did, too," he said. "No matter what you think of me."

She shook her head. "Davy, I don't think you're—"

"You judged and convicted me without even giving me a chance."

She searched for a way to explain the tangle of feelings to him, but words fell terribly short. "You don't get it," she said softly. "I don't have the luxury of giving people chances. What would I have done if I'd bet on you, and lost? How could I have dealt with you?"

"You would have bet on me and won," he said. "You really think that I'd be capable of hurting you? How could you think that?"

The hurt in his eyes twisted in her chest like a knife. "I didn't want it to be true," she said. "But if I ran, I could always leave open the chance that it wasn't you. My fantasies could stay intact."

"You'd rather just wonder for the rest of your life than know for sure?" He shook his head, wondering. "That's fucked, Margot."

"So's the rest of my life." She pressed her fist against her mouth and breathed down the urge to cry. "In case it means anything to you, I'm not wondering anymore. I know everything I need to know."

"Yeah, me too," he said wearily. "More than I ever wanted to." He pulled out his wallet, and peeled out a wad of bills, flinging them so that they fanned out across the rumpled bedspread. "Take it."

"Put that money away," she said.

"Shut up and take it. Pride makes you stupid, and stupid will get you dead. I only followed you because I didn't want you to deal with Snakey alone. And I wanted you to know that it wasn't me who tried to hurt you. It was real important to me that you know that. That's it, that's why, that's all. OK?"

"OK," she whispered.

"Don't worry, I got the hint," he added. "I won't bug you again. But I suggest you get your ass in gear. Snakey strikes me as real focused." He stopped. His chest jerked in a mirthless bark of laughter. "If you believe that he's real, that is. It could all be theater, of course." He lifted the wet towel from his nose and stared at the gory stain against the white cloth. "Could be fake blood, I suppose."

She couldn't stand the look on his face. "Stop it, Davy."

"Why should I? I might as well take this last chance to get all my dumb-ass hurt feelings off my chest before I leave. It's not every day a guy's girlfriend accuses him of being a psycho maniac. It kind of takes your breath away." He wiped his face one last time with the towel, and flung it into the bathroom, where it splatted on the floor. "You are a huge pain in the ass, Margot Vetter. But I still wish you luck. Try not to get killed. If you can possibly manage it." He walked out the door.

Margot followed him out into the parking lot on her bare feet and watched his slow, measured strides towards the truck. She ached to call him back, but her voice was stuck behind a burning lump.

She'd waived the right. He was through with her, and rightly so. She'd screwed things up beyond repair.

He stopped by the cab of the truck, and just stood there, immobile. Seconds ticked by.

Wild hope flared inside her. Maybe this move was hers to make after all. Her feet moved before she even knew they were moving, first timid steps, then a wild dash across the asphalt to reach him before the moment was lost. Before he changed his mind and disappeared.

She grabbed him from behind and wrapped her arms around his waist, pressing her face against his back.

His body shook in her embrace. He spun around to face her. They came together, in a furious, consuming kiss.

He demanded her surrender and she demanded his, but somehow the wild clash fused magically into something perfect and wild and exquisitely right. She wrapped her arms around his neck, her emotion so heightened by her own desperation that his could not frighten her.

He wrenched her slip down, snapping the fragile shoulder straps.

"I want to fuck you," he said.

"Do it," she replied.

He lifted her up, his hands under her bottom. She wrapped her legs around his waist. He carried her back to the room, glass crunching beneath his boots as he made to lay her down on the rumpled bed.

She pulled away from his kiss. "Not on the bed. I just can't."

He looked at the mess of broken glass on the ground, and carried her back to the door. He slammed it shut, pulled his gun from the back of his jeans. He laid it on the table and flipped off the light.

"Forget this room exists," he said. "Forget that guy exists."

"Make me," she flung back at him.

He wrenched the slip down. Her deadening apathy was gone, swept away by a blaze of feeling. Pinned in the dark between the door and the man she wanted more than anything else in the world.

They weren't gentle with each other. She dug her nails into him as he wrenched his jeans open. He probed his way inside her, driving against the resistance of her body in one hard, relentless shove.

She let her head drop back with a gasp. He arranged her legs so they draped over his arms, and pulsed against her, sliding deeper. She softened for him, a hot liquid rush, and she could move, clenching and undulating around him. The power and energy of his body flooded into her. She was strong enough to take it all and give it back to him transformed. He was so beautiful when he gave himself to her, nothing held back. The vulnerability beneath his mask broke her heart.

The door rattled and thudded with the force of his thrusts. They cried out as they hurtled straight into the heart of the explosion.

He held her there for a long time. She could have stayed in his powerful embrace forever, but he finally straightened up, withdrawing from the clasp of her body. "Time to face reality," he said.

She shivered. "I'd rather stay where we were."

"Too bad. Brace yourself. I'm turning the light on."

She flinched as he did. It was so harsh to her tear-blinded eyes.

Davy's face was closed again. The magical fusion and understanding they had during sex had vanished. It wasn't the first time, but still, it hurt. "Davy?" she started timidly. "Do you—"

"We don't have time to talk about our feelings. We've indulged ourselves way too long already. The cops could be here any minute, if anyone called in about those shots I fired. Which is probable."

She hadn't even thought of that. "Ah . . . what are we—"

"We're getting that rental car out of this lot and dumping it somewhere. I don't want this identity compromised. Did you put the license plate number down when you registered here?"

"I scribbled down a bogus one."

"Good. Get dressed. Now."

"But I—"

"In case you're wondering, you just lost your chance to get rid of me. It's too late to ditch me now."

"I don't want to ditch you," she said.

Subtle tension eased around his eyes. He made an impatient gesture. "Then move your ass."

Something else intruded upon her consciousness as she picked through the rubble for her scattered things. The hot trickle of fluid between her legs. Oh, Lord. She hadn't given so much as a fleeting thought to latex. "Davy," she said. "We didn't use anything."

He waited by the door, gun in hand. "Yeah," he said. "So? What do you want me to say? That I'm sorry? I'm not, particularly."

She tugged the slip up over her breasts. "You're still furious."

"It's been a tough day," he said. "It's going to take more than one amazing fuck up against the wall to iron this one out."

It was always this way. The more completely he let down his guard during sex, the more impenetrable his barriers were afterwards.

She tied the broken straps together across one shoulder to keep the slip on, pulled on her high-tops and crunched through broken glass to the bathroom. "A second in here, and I'll be ready," she promised.

"Hurry," he growled.

She frantically calculated the days of her cycle as she dampened a washcloth and sponged herself off. Problem was, she'd been so stressed out and eating so little, her period had been irregular for months.

A sharp knock on the bathroom door interrupted her frantic reflections. "Margot." His voice had a harsh warning tone.

"I'm ready, I'm ready," she muttered.

No point in worrying about it now. What would be, would be.

* * *

They left the rental car in a mall parking lot a couple of towns further down the highway. Davy watched as she locked the car and walked towards him, the faraway streetlights outlining every curve of her body with swathes of light and shadow. Amazing, that he could still think about sex, the way his body ached.

He was still wonky and stupid from the fight and the sex, shaking with a combination of fear and anger and lust. He hadn't been this far off the deep end in years. No, not ever. The goatfuck with Fleur had been kid stuff in comparison.

He started in on her as soon as she climbed into the Chevy. "You were heading to San Cataldo, then?"

"I couldn't think of a better plan," she said.

"Staying on Stone Island was a *much* better plan," he snarled.

"Let's let it go, OK? It's old news."

He took a slow breath. "Learn anything useful from Snakey?"

She rubbed her eyes. "He thinks that I'm his soul mate. And he answers to a guy named Marcus. It was Marcus who arranged to have Craig killed. Snakey and his boss Marcus are convinced that I have this . . . this mold, he called it. Oh, and Craig's murder was supposed to look like a murder-suicide, but Snakey decided he wanted me for himself." She shuddered. "So that's why he didn't kill me. Brrr."

"You don't know anybody named Marcus?" he asked.

She shook her head. "At least I know that it's a physical object that they want. If I knew what the hell it was, I'd just give it to them."

"Did you keep any of Craig's stuff?"

"He was practically living in my house on the lake. A lot of his stuff was there. But I got rid of it all that morning after I came back early from the conference and found . . . you know. The panties. God. It seems so silly and insignificant, now."

"Got rid of it how?"

She winced. "The usual pissed-off girlfriend way," she said uncomfortably. "I admit, I behaved childishly. I shoved all his stuff into a big garbage bag and dumped it off my dock into the lake. I meant to say, you want your junk, buddy? Go fish for it." She went on in a smaller voice. "But I never got the chance."

"Do you remember what was in the bag?"

Her brow furrowed. "The usual stuff. Clothes, shoes, toiletries, computer equipment. His mail. There was at least one box that day, I think. He had lots of packages sent to my address. He was working on patenting some of his engineering designs."

They looked at each other. "Looks like we're going swimming, huh?" Margot said slowly.

"Looks that way," he replied.

"But whatever it is, if it's there . . . it'll be ruined, after eight months under water."

"We'll see. All this happened on a single day? First the panties, then you dumped his stuff, and then you found him strung up?"

"Right," Margot said.

"Snakey said it was supposed to be a murder-suicide," he mused. "How did they know you'd show up?"

"I had a lunch date with Craig that day," she said. "I was going to stand him up, but he called my office, and Dougie said he sounded flipped out and desperate. A matter of life and death, he said. So I went to his studio. My big plan was to fling the panties in his face."

"So Snakey coerced Craig into calling you. It was all planned."

Margot stared out the windshield, eyes frozen wide with ugly memories. "But how could he have known I had a gun in my—"

"Maybe Craig told him. Or maybe the killer had another plan ready, and your gun was just a happy accident for him."

Margot pulled her legs up tight to her chest, pressing her face against her knees. "Could we not talk about this for a while?"

"Do you want to solve this problem, or don't you?"

She didn't respond, or even make a sound, but he knew that vibration in her shoulders all too well. Time to shut the hell up before he made her cry. God forbid. He was dangerously close to it himself.

They got to her ex-house on Parson's Lake right before dawn. The air was damp and chill. Davy wished she had a jacket when they got out of the truck. He was buying her clothes today. It was distracting, the way her tits bounced all over the place in that raggedy thing.

She looked sad and lost as she wandered up the walkway to her former house. The lawn was forlorn and overgrown. She peered into the uncurtained windows. The interior was dusty and bare. "Come on," she said quietly. "There's nothing left for me here. Let's go around back."

He followed her around the house, gun in hand. He would have followed her anywhere. This crazy feeling was getting steadily worse. She looked like something out of her flower fairy calendar in that brief, tattered slip, the wet weeds and flowers clinging to her beautiful legs. More erotic and dangerous than the flower fairies, though. More like a hot, feverish dream of wild sex with a silkie or a forest nymph. He could have forgotten his anger, forgotten the danger. Just shoved her down onto the long wet grass and taken her again, right there.

In back, a deck overlooked a length of pebbly beach. Neighbors' lots were fenced off on either side. A narrow wooden walkway led out from the beach to a floating dock that rocked softly on the waves. Margot walked out onto it and knelt to undo the laces of her sneakers.

"Hey. What the hell do you think you're doing?" he demanded.

She yanked both shoes off and gave him a bright, challenging smile. "I put that bag there, and I'll be the one to retrieve it."

"I'll do it," he said. "Put your shoes back on."

"Davy. Be reasonable. Snakey could be expecting us here. You've got more clothes on, you've got a gun, and you know how to use it. I would much rather you cover me than have clueless, clumsy me trying to defend you from evil bad guys while you're underwater. OK?"

She had a point, but it still took his breath away when she peeled off her slip and stood poised on the edge of the deck stark naked.

"Jesus, Margot! What the fuck are you doing?"

"Plus, I've had that not-so-fresh feeling ever since our wild crazy sex last night." She winked impishly. "I could use a bit of a wash."

"This is a residential neighborhood!" he hissed.

"Oh dear. Have I scandalized you?" She grinned. "You big ol' prude. Panther woman can't be bothered with society's silly rules."

She leaped, in a clean, shallow dive off the end of the dock.

He knelt down and peered through the water for her pale, wavering form. Seconds ticked by. He started unlacing his boots.

She burst up suddenly in a shower of drops, gasping for breath.

"You got it?" he asked.

"I found it," she said, gasping. "Oh, this water is freaking cold! I had to kick off a lot of slime, but it's there. Now I just have to get it."

A flash of her pale, round ass and down she went, for another interminable wait. She burst up, clutching the dock, and pulled a handful of plastic to the surface. "It's full of water. It'll be super heavy."

It was. He hauled the thing up onto the deck, and leaned down to grab Margot's arms. He yanked her up onto her feet.

God, she was so gorgeous dripping wet, grinning triumphantly. She wrung out her hair, sticking her tits out just for his benefit.

"Cover yourself, for God's sake," he begged.

Her eyes sparkled. Big mistake, to let her know she'd gotten under his skin. "Don't you like me this way?" She spun around, lifting her arms over her head, flinging her head back in sensuous abandon.

He grabbed the slip off the deck and dragged it over her, tugging it down until her head emerged, locks of hair clinging to her face.

Before he knew it, he was kissing her cool wet face like a starving man. He dragged himself away. "We don't have time for this."

"Hey, buddy. Take responsibility. You're the one who kissed me!"

This was a dead end argument if ever there was one. He abandoned it, and crouched down to open the bag. Margot knelt beside him, and together they picked through silt, disintegrated fabric, paper that had turned to slime, toothbrushes, razors, shoes and belts.

They found the box at the bottom. The waxed carton had somehow retained its shape, though it fell to pieces under Margot's touch. Inside were two objects sealed in heavy plastic, coated with pale brown mud. He brushed away the silt, prodding at them gently.

The first was a metal box, the shape and size of a large book. The second was pale, irregularly shaped, yielding to the touch like rubber. It was difficult to figure out what those things protruding from the—oh.

Fingers. The thing was a human hand.

Chapter

23

Margot jerked back with a cry. She would have fallen into the water if Davy hadn't grabbed her. If there had been anything in her stomach, it would have come up. As it was, she doubled over, retching.

"Hey. Margot." Davy's voice was gentle. "It's not real."

"Huh?" She looked up at him, wild-eyed.

He put a warm arm over her shoulder. "The hand. It's fake. It's made out of some kind of gummy rubber stuff. Relax."

"Oh." Her butt thudded hard onto the dock. "Marcus's mold."

How silly. After all the grisly stuff she'd seen, a rubber hand threw her into a tizzy. Next she would start screaming at plastic dog poo.

Davy rinsed the silt off the bags with a few handfuls of lakewater, and pulled her to her feet. "Let's get the hell out of here. I'm getting nervous. And I want to find a place where you can get warm and dry."

That, as it turned out, was easier said than done. It took a tediously long time to find a hotel. Every place they stopped had some fatal security flaw, according to Davy. Finally they pulled into Bob's Motel and RV Park, where he promptly made it clear that her job would be to huddle in a heavily curtained room like an animal in a cave.

"I can't have you running into ex-boyfriends in hotel lobbies," he said, in response to her protests.

"So I have to hide under the bed?" she said crabbily. "Just let me get some makeup and a pair of glasses, and I—hey!"

He shoved her head down as a car drove into the lot next to them, leaned over her, and tangled his fingers into her hair, painfully tight.

"Do not whine, and do not fuck with me." His voice was soft with menace. "You would have been safer, more comfortable and less of a liability to me if you'd trusted me and gone to Stone Island. Remember the state you were in last night when I found you."

That effectively cut off all protests. He waited for a cowed nod from her, got out and locked the doors as he headed off to check in.

She huddled against the fragrant leather of the seat, her insides churning with anger. Davy hadn't calmed down in the least. His fury flared up to singe her every time she let down her guard.

Once inside their suite, he dumped the contents of a paper bag across the table. Crackers, smoked oysters, a small loaf of cheese, sausage, sardines, and a six pack of fruit juices in a box. "Breakfast."

Margot was too wound up and jittery to get any food down, a problem which Davy did not share. He got to work as soon as he'd finished, opening the grimy plastic bag and removing the case, which proved to have a negative impression of a hand set in a plastic claylike substance inside. Then he extracted the ghastly rubber hand.

She knew it was fake, and it still made her shudder.

Davy peered at it. "Craig specialized in biometric security?"

She nodded. "Fingerprint technology, in particular."

"He must've been developing techniques to beat his own machines," he said. "And then he tried to double-cross whoever paid him to do it. This Marcus, maybe."

Margaret pressed her hands to her eyes. "That idiot," she whispered. "All this violence, just for money. How empty and stupid."

"It usually is." Davy slung a metal briefcase up onto the table and started rummaging through the contents.

"What are you doing?" she asked.

He pulled out something that looked like a button, and compared it to the one on his jacket. "I want to talk to the people at Craig's old job. This is one of Seth's recording devices. Digital, undetectable, voice-activated." He pulled out a sewing kit, and ripped a button off his jacket. He threaded a needle and deftly sewed on the new button.

"I would never have thought you were the type that could sew," she said. "You are a continual surprise."

His mouth twitched. "I had three little brothers and no mom. If I wanted their clothes to stay on their bodies, I had to make it happen."

He held the jacket up, inspected the result and tossed it aside, apparently satisfied. Then he pulled a laptop out of the case, hooking it up to the room phone and dialing up an Internet connection. "Who did Craig work most closely with at Krell?"

She thought about it for a moment. "You should start with Mike Wainwright," she said. "He's the CEO. And Bob Kraus, too, the head of marketing. Oh, wow. That's Krell," she said. "I designed that web site."

He nodded, clicking through the pages. He grabbed his cell phone and dialed the number on the home page. "Yes, may I speak to Mr. Wainwright? My name is Michael Evan."

He listened for a moment. "How about Mr. Kraus . . . certainly. I'm a security consultant at BioGen Laboratories in Salt Lake City. We're upgrading our security system, and I've been researching the best the market has to offer in terms of biometric technologies. Krell is on my short list. I just happen to be passing through town today, so I thought . . . yes, sure, I'll wait." He clicked slowly through web pages as he waited.

Memorizing everything he saw, no doubt.

It was strange, to see work she'd done a lifetime ago glowing brightly on the screen. A relic of a time when her world was so different. Safer, better behaved, more predictable.

Smaller, too. She looked at Davy. His face was faraway, lost in a trance of fierce concentration. His brush of dark blond hair stuck straight up in spikes when it was neglected. She loved every detail. The bruises purpling beneath his eyes just emphasized their brilliant color.

He fascinated her. Opened up the horizons of her world until they felt limitless. That feeling would have terrified her once. Not anymore.

"Yes? Excellent. That would be great." Davy's voice jerked her out of her reverie. He snapped the computer shut. "Yes, I can be there at two. The address . . . ? OK. Thank you. I'll see you then."

He snapped the phone closed and turned to her, frowning. "I'm going to talk to Kraus. I don't like leaving you alone. I'll leave my gun."

"No!" She winced. "Bad idea. Look what happened the last time I had a gun. Guns are nothing but trouble for me."

"I'll teach you to use—"

"You will do no such thing," she said hastily. "Keep it. I promise, I'll lay low. I'll be so good. I won't move a muscle."

"I'm going to call Seth and Sean to come down," he said. "Once they get here, there's going to be somebody with you at all times."

"Gee, thanks," she murmured. "That's sweet of you."

His brows drew together. "No, it isn't. I just don't want to come back and find you filleted. That would seriously bum me out."

Margot's stomach rolled at the image his words invoked. They both needed to get off this uncomfortable line of thought, and the quickest, surest way to change the subject was always near to hand.

"May I use that sewing kit to fix my slip?" she asked.

"Be my guest," he said.

She threaded the needle from the spool of black thread, then pulled her slip off over her head. She was naked, but for her high-tops.

"Oh, Christ," he muttered. "Margot. Don't."

She gave him an innocent, fluttering-lashes glance as she struggled to undo the knots she'd made in the straps. "Something wrong?"

"I'm in the wrong mind-set for this. If you want me to fuck you, say so. Don't play games."

"What manners," she said. "You do know how to sweet-talk a girl."

"I keep telling you, I'm not sweet. Particularly not today."

"That's for sure," she said. "You're in a foul, horrendous mood, and you're not making the slightest effort to control your behavior. So why should I control mine?" She finally worked the knots loose, and carefully sewed the frayed strap back onto the stretchy fabric.

Davy got up and jerked the drapes closed with a violent tug that threatened to snap the curtain rod right off the wall. "This exhibitionist routine of yours is starting to seriously bug me."

She knotted the thread and snapped it with her teeth. "Just what doesn't bug you about me, Davy? You started the no-panties trend in my life. If I'm turning into an exhibitionist nymphomaniac, it's your fault. And it's time you got over your mad, because I am sick of it."

He sat back down. "You got some strategy in mind for that?"

A beam of sun that made its way through the slit in the drapes fell across his face, lighting up his eyes. He was so gorgeous, it made her breath squeeze in her lungs. "I'm open to suggestion," she said. "Go ahead, Davy. Inspire me."

He leaned back in the chair, lacing his fingers together behind his head so that his golden, muscular torso rippled and flexed. His body was so long and beautiful stretched out like that, his erection pressing against his jeans. "I love the way you suck my cock," he said.

His cool, taunting eyes challenged her.

He knew exactly what made her angry, what scared her, what excited her, and how to mix them up. She resisted being dominated, but couldn't seem to stop goading him into doing exactly that. It turned them both on, the constant push and pull.

The only problem was the anger that simmered in his eyes.

Davy unbuckled his belt, his gaze locked onto hers. He undid the buttons, and slid them down over his hips. His erection sprang out, flushed and heavy. He stroked it slowly, dragging his big fist up and down the thick shaft. "Suck me, Margot," he said. "Go on, make all this crazy, overwrought bullshit worth my time."

"You're trying to make me mad," she told him.

"Sure. You love when I push you into the danger zone. The farther I push, the wilder you get. It's hard to stop."

Margot sank onto her knees. "I've been in the danger zone ever since I met you." She pried his hands away and stroked him, delighting in his velvet soft skin sliding over the solid heat of his erection. "I'm getting used to the danger zone. It's starting to feel like home." She licked him, savoring the salty taste. "I've felt that way ever since you made me fall in love with you."

He stiffened. His hands clenched into fists on the arms of the chair. "What?"

"I said, ever since you made me fall in love—"

"I heard that part."

She swirled her tongue around him. "Good," she murmured. "A little reality in our fun and games is a good thing."

He pushed her head away. "Are you punishing me?"

"Just telling you the truth," she said. "Don't worry, I don't have any pathetic fantasies about my love melting your icy cold heart or anything like that. All I'm saying is, if you didn't want me to fall in love with you, you shouldn't have seduced me. You shouldn't try to save me like an avenging angel. You shouldn't tantalize me like you do."

He passed his hand through his rumpled hair, and yanked his jeans up, tucking his hard, flushed erection back inside them as best he could. "I don't know how to give you what you want," he muttered.

It was all there, blazing out of his tormented eyes, shimmering hot and vital and real in the air between them. Everything she could ever need or want, whole and complete. Her wildest dreams. But he was so damn stubborn, he couldn't give in to it.

She touched his face. "Yes, you do. Why are you so set on protecting me? Why did you sneak into my house? Why did you follow me when I ran off? Why won't you admit you feel something for me?"

He shook his head.

"You don't have to keep such a tight lid on yourself," she said. "If you could just let yourself go—"

"What the *fuck* do you know about letting go?"

She lost her balance and tumbled back onto the carpet, she was so startled. "Davy?" she faltered. "I—"

"When you let go, things get broken." His voice was like a whip cracking. "Shit blows up. People you care about get hurt. People can die. I have spent my entire life making sure that does not happen."

"Oh, Davy," she murmured. "I didn't mean—"

"My dad went crazy, did you know that? Completely whacked by the time I was fourteen. I raised three brothers on my own while protecting them from him. I have *never* had the luxury of letting go."

She shook her head frantically. "I didn't mean—"

"And now, when we're both murder suspects and you've got a maniac assassin stalking you, you decide that *this* is the opportune moment to dismantle my entire fucking personality structure?"

"Davy—"

"No. I will not rip myself into pieces to suit your whim, Margot."

"I'm sorry," she whispered. "I didn't want to rip you into pieces. Never mind. I just love you. I can't help it."

"Shut up. I don't want to hear it." He got up, stalked across the room to look out the window, his back to her. He sank down into the kitchen chair, and hunched over, hiding his face in his hands.

She stood there, in an agony of doubt. He might hate her for touching him when he felt like that.

Hell with it. She couldn't tiptoe around the man forever.

She walked over to him, and draped herself over his broad back. She clasped her arms around his heaving chest, pressed her face to the velvety curve between his chest and shoulder. He could shake her off if he wanted to, but she damn well wasn't going to make it easy for him.

He didn't shake her off. After a few minutes, she felt like she'd melted right into his body.

He finally lifted his head. "You can relax," he said dully. "I'm not going to lose it."

She kissed his neck. "I am relaxed. And it wouldn't be the end of the world if you did."

"Let's not discuss that, OK? It's a dead end topic."

"Whatever." She rubbed her cheek against his shoulder,

savoring the raw force of this feeling that vibrated inside her. Like the low, sweet hum of some deep musical instrument, throbbing with delicate pathos.

Davy twisted his head around, and rubbed his face against hers. Their lips met, and the fire flared up, hot and sudden. He grabbed her hand and pulled it down, pressing it against his bulging crotch.

But it was a gesture of silent pleading, not macho arrogance. She stepped around in front of him and sank to her knees again, craving the raw, hot male taste of him. Making love to him was the sweetest, most exquisitely perfect thing that would ever happen to her. Something to set in the scales against the bad stuff that had come before, the bad stuff that might possibly come later. Nothing would take it from her.

He pulled her to her feet before she could take him in her mouth, and slapped open the door that led to the connecting bedroom.

She landed, bouncing, on the bed in the dim room. Davy bent to unlace his boots, never taking his eyes off her. He'd drawn all the curtains when they arrived, but a narrow beam of sunlight sliced through the divide. Dust motes thrown up by landing on the bed glittered and danced in it wildly.

He climbed on top of her, pushing her legs wide. Last night's thoughtless insanity blazed through her mind. They still didn't have any condoms. She couldn't possibly compound her idiocy.

She jerked up onto her elbows. "Hey. Davy. We don't have—"

"Shh." He shoved her back down, covering her with his big, hot naked body, and all that came out of her mouth was a shaky moan as he entered her—and low sobs, at each slow, heavy sliding stroke.

"Davy," she said, breathless. "This is insane. You have to stop."

"I don't want to," he said. "You make me crazy. You melt my brain." He stroked her cheekbone with his thumb. The wild fey glow in his eyes almost frightened her. "Do you want a baby from me?"

Her mouth flapped, open and closed. "What?" she squeaked.

He kissed her lazily as he pulsed his hips in a slow, sensual grind against hers. "You heard me."

"I . . . I . . ."

"It's a yes or no question." He cupped her bottom in his hands, lifting her higher to meet his thrusts.

"That's not true." She tried to control her shaking throat. "It's not a yes or no question. It's a have-you-lost-your-freaking-mind question."

"Oh. Well, the answer to that is definitely yes," he said. "I have now officially lost my mind. I'm completely out of control. I thought that was what you wanted. Well? Here I am, babe. Happy now?"

"Don't you dare twist what I say against me! That's mean!"

He cradled her bottom tenderly, angling her closer towards him so that he pressed deeply against her most sensitive points. "You told me if I lost it, that it wouldn't be the end of the world," he murmured, kissing her jaw. "I've lost it, Margot. Is the world ending?"

Her arms circled him, clinging to his neck. "Yes."

There was no stopping them. She was too far gone. There was nothing she loved better than going to that wild place with him, writhing and yelling as he churned her into a frenzy of emotion, of sensation. They exploded together, crying out in unison.

Only after many long, panting minutes did it unfurl again in her mind. What she had allowed to happen. Again.

He was still inside her, enjoying the last residual clutches of her orgasm milking him. They were glued together, sticky and wet with his semen. Her eyes fluttered open. He gazed straight back.

He knew exactly what he'd done. It had been deliberate.

She licked her dry lips. "Why did you do that?"

"Because I wanted to." His gaze was unblinking.

"That's not a good enough reason."

He shrugged. "It's the only one I've got." He pulled away, got up and disappeared into the connecting bathroom without looking at her.

Again. Unreal. That sadistic bastard. She stared at the closed door, her fury building while the shower hissed.

She was on her feet and ready for him the minute the door opened. "Goddamnit, Davy. Stop doing this to me. Stop it right now."

"Doing what?" He toweled off his hair, his face impassive.

"You say these crazy, manipulative things, and get me all worked up, and then bam, you shut me out! I can't stand it anymore!"

"Yeah?" His eyes narrowed to slits. "And what do you call what you did yesterday? Deciding I was your stalker, stealing the car?"

She swallowed back a hot lump of tears. "You are such a prick," she whispered. "You want to punish me *now?* After what you just did?"

He let the towel dangle from his hand. "I don't do it on purpose," he said, in a hesitant voice. He fished his jeans off the floor and pulled them on. "It just happens. It's like an automatic door. It opens and shuts whenever the fuck it wants, and I don't have the remote."

It wasn't what she wanted to hear, but at least he was telling her the truth. She could feel it.

"I have to go to this interview now," he said, in a tight, measured voice. He sat down on the edge of the bed, began to tug on his boots. "It's work time. I need to be cool. Concentrated. Now is not the time for all this crazy emotional stuff."

"It's not crazy stuff! It's basic stuff! Davy, I just want you to—"

"Let me finish," he said. "I can't open up on command, and say and feel whatever it is that you want me to say and feel—"

"Then you'd better buy some goddamn condoms!"

He nodded. "Fair enough."

She covered her shaking face with her hands. After a moment, she felt his hand against her hair, stroking her. "I promise I'll come back, though." His voice was delicately cautious. "You can bounce me around and scream and yell and make all the unreasonable emotional demands you want. I don't know what I'll do, or how I'll cope, but I'll be here. I won't disappear on you."

"Oh, stop it," she muttered sourly. "Don't do me any favors."

He slid his fingers around the nape of her neck and squeezed gently with his warm hand. "I'm sorry I hurt you. I don't want to."

She nodded. For Davy, that was as close to a declaration of love as he was willing or able to go.

"I need to stop at a mall before I go to Krell." His voice took on a businesslike tone. "My pants are filthy and bloodstained. I'll pick up some clothes for you, too. What are you, size ten?"

"Eight, lately. Except for my unreasonable size twelve ass."

"Let me see that unreasonable ass." He turned her gently around, sliding his hands down the curve of her back. They fastened onto her hips, a warm, strong grip. He kissed the back of her neck.

"No more skin-tight jeans for you, babe," he murmured. "Nobody but me needs to know how good your ass looks naked."

"That's just the kind of confusing, irresponsible remark that's driving me nuts," she snapped. "Get going, Davy. Stop torturing me."

He lifted his hand off her body, and silently left the room.

She held her breath until she heard the cabin door shut behind him, and then dissolved into tears, shaking with terror and guilty hope.

Hope and fear, her two big bullies. Meanwhile, a gazillion tiny McCloud sperm were racing madly towards the finish line. God help her. The man literally threw a fit when she'd told him she loved him.

She could just imagine how he would react if she told him she was pregnant.

Chapter

24

"Do you realize what you've done, Faris?" Marcus struck his brother in the face. "You've failed me. We're out of time now, and the plan is ruined. You should have brought her to me immediately."

Faris was tied to a chair, hands bound, eyes blindfolded. Having his eyes covered made his little brother more docile and amenable. Marcus had discovered that helpful fact when Faris was barely more than a toddler. He'd developed a wide array of management techniques for his brother over the years, both physical and psychological.

"I was going to! I was just questioning her!" Faris's voice was whining and babyish. "I wanted to get the mold and bring it to you, but McCloud burst in and startled me!"

Marcus was relieved to hear the childish tremor in his brother's voice. Faris was finally breaking out of the dangerously rebellious state of mind he'd been in since he'd fixated on the Callahan woman.

"But you didn't do it, Faris. You failed." Marcus back-handed him again. Faris whimpered like a kicked puppy.

He was relieved to have Faris back under his physical control. He'd invested a great deal in his brother's unorthodox training. It was a lifetime's work, begun almost by accident after their mother left.

Faris had been a needy, clinging four-year-old, left entirely to his teenaged brother Marcus's tender mercies. Most sixteen-year-old boys would have found a whining brat of a little brother cramping their style, but Marcus had always been unusual. Quick to exploit the potential of any given situation. The helpless little Faris was a blank slate. It was an experiment in mind control. Their father was busy with Calix and his succession of subsequent wives. Worthington House had an unobtrusive domestic staff that didn't dare to interfere. No one was watching. No one had cared. It had been fascinating.

Stimulating, too.

"My instructions were to bring her to me immediately," Marcus scolded. "You suited your own whims. You went on a killing spree, too, didn't you? I hope you were discreet, because I'm not covering for you."

Faris's mouth turned down in a childish pout. "I'm not stupid."

"No," Marcus agreed. "But you are crazy. I'm the only one who knows what you really did to Constance. And to Titus, too. You know what would happen if I told. It would be back to the hospital for you, and given your talents, they would probably physically restrain you at all times. Or drug you into a drooling vegetable. Is that what you want?"

Mention of their father's third wife, Constance, had its predictable result. Faris began to sob. Marcus circled his brother's chair.

"You made me do it," Faris whimpered, hiccupping.

"But you're the one who actually did the deed," Marcus crooned. "And you liked it. That's what counts when the white coats come to take you away. Were you so impressed with Margaret Callahan because of her red hair? It never occurred to me till now, but she looks quite a bit like Constance. Did you have impure feelings for Constance, Faris?"

"She was a bitch." Faris's voice was thick. "She was mean."

His father's third wife Constance, younger than Marcus himself, had tried to exercise power over her stepsons. She had thus become the fourteen-year-old Faris's very first, improvised assignment.

The operation had gone with a smoothness beyond Marcus's wildest hopes. No one had suspected Faris. It was then that Marcus had begun to realize the potential of the situation. The power of a man who had mind control over a killer. It was dizzying. So it was that he'd begun to invest heavily in Faris's specialized training.

Faris had been in and out of institutions for much of his troubled adolescence, but no doctors or drugs had ever broken the invisible bonds his brother had instilled. Faris had never betrayed him.

Until now. For that problematic bitch, Margaret Callahan.

Perhaps he should have become a psychiatrist. Manipulating his brother's mind and psyche had been the most absorbing project of his life, more compelling by far than his spotty professional career. He would have been brilliant in that field, but he would also have been hampered by a tedious code of ethics.

For Marcus, private freedom was sweeter than public acclaim.

"If you'd obeyed me, I would have left Margaret undamaged," Marcus said. "As it is, we'll just have to see. In any case, your women wear out fast, Faris. You're very hard on them, I've noticed."

"Margaret will be different." Faris's voice was unexpectely clear. "The others were weak. They broke. Margaret won't break."

"Yes, she does strike me as resilient," Marcus murmured.

So Faris was still rebellious, despite the bullet wound.

Marcus circled the chair considering how best to quench this rebel spark.

His cell phone rang. The number on the display made his heart thud. He hit the talk button. "Yes?"

"Mr. Worthington?"

"Yes," Marcus said. "How are things at Krell today? Do you have something for me, Miriam?"

"Um, maybe." Miriam's voice was a whispered squeak. "I'm in the ladies' room. Calling on the cell LeRoy delivered the other day."

"Of course," Marcus said impatiently. "You would never have reached me otherwise. So? What have you heard?"

"This guy came in just now to talk to Kraus. He's just exactly like what LeRoy said to look out for. Real tall, dark blond, kind of military looking. Super good-looking. Scratches and bruises on his face."

"What name did he give?"

"Michael Evan," Miriam whispered.

"Hold the line, Miriam." He hit the intercom. "Karel?"

"Yes, Mr. Worthington?"

"A man answering Davy McCloud's description is at Krell right now. Bring him here immediately. Prepare to drug him if necessary. He's very dangerous."

"We're on it," Karel replied.

Marcus put the cell phone back to his ear. "Thank you, my dear. You've done very well."

"Um . . . does that mean that I—that you won't—"

"As always, it depends on you. You know what will happen if I am forced to tell your part in what happened to Craig Caruso and Mandi Whitlow. You were very helpful, keeping us abreast of all his social appointments. Such a talented little secretary."

"But you never told me you were going to hurt them!"

"Don't whine," Marcus said. "It's doubtful that the police would look favorably on you if the truth came out. Not after they monitor the electronic deposits into your bank account."

"I can't stand this," she whimpered.

"Continue as you have been, and everything will be fine. You'll find a nice gift in your checking account tomorrow. I'm sure that will brighten your mood. It always has before." He broke the connection and punched in a code that would render the number Miriam had dialed obsolete.

He cupped Faris's face in his hands. "You're in luck, Faris. We may have found McCloud. Which means Margaret isn't far behind. Perhaps we can salvage the plan—if I get my hands on her today."

"Don't hurt her," Faris pleaded. "If you have to torture her, at least let me do it. I'm good. Better than you. I can use the needles."

Marcus backhanded him. A thread of blood trickled out of his brother's nose. "Do not tell me what to do. You've failed me."

"Let me kill him," Faris whispered brokenly. "I can do it. I swear."

"He beat you before," Marcus pointed out mercilessly. "Twice."

"It was a fluke," Faris protested. "The first time I didn't expect him to be so accomplished. And the second time—"

"Excuses make me angry," Marcus said. "Failure is unacceptable. I taught you that a long time ago. Don't you remember the lesson?"

"I remember." Faris's mouth trembled. "Please. Let me kill him."

"We'll see." Marcus wiped away the bloody mucus rolling out of Faris's nose with his handkerchief. "You're too agitated, Faris." He kissed the top of Faris's head, and caressed his face tenderly. "Try to relax."

* * *

Davy was very smooth at social engineering after years as an investigator. In fact, his formidable skills at manipulating people into giving him information were one of the reasons he'd decided to get out of the business. He'd decided to develop more ethical talents.

Still, the skill was handy in a pinch. A few minutes of studying Krell's web site, a handful of memorized jargon, a dose of bullshit, and it wasn't hard to pose as a potential client for a massive, costly biometric security installation. Besides, Kraus talked so much, Davy hardly had a chance to inadvertently reveal his ignorance. The real challenge was in keeping an interested look on his face for the droning sales pitch.

Kraus paused at one point, focusing on Davy's face. "Excuse me for asking a personal question, but where'd you get those bruises?"

"Free-climbing up on Mt. Ranier," Davy lied easily. "I got caught in a rock slide."

"Free-climbing?" Kraus's eyes widened. "Daredevil type, huh?"

Davy lifted his shoulders in a noncommittal shrug. "Now and then. I've got a personal question for you, too, Mr. Kraus." Davy drummed his fingers on Kraus's big, gleaming desk, and looked grave. "My employer has expressed some doubts about, uh . . . what happened last fall."

Kraus's face darkened. "I wondered when you were going to get around to that. Look, the first thing I want to emphasize is that what happened to Caruso had nothing to do with Krell. It was a direct result of the sloppy way the guy ran his personal life."

Davy gave him an encouraging nod, and waited.

"You have no idea the trouble we had because of him," Kraus complained. "Our stocks fell. The press hinted at links with organized crime. His secretary Miriam, the girl out front on the phones, had a breakdown. All because the guy just couldn't keep his pants zipped."

"Ah. So Caruso was a womanizer?"

Kraus snorted. "An alley cat. Don't get me wrong. I believe that a guy's gotta do what a guy's gotta do, but he should be discreet about it. And he should have known better than to mess with Mag Callahan."

"And Mag Callahan would be . . . ?"

"The woman who murdered him. We hired her to do web design. The first time I laid eyes on her, I knew she was trouble. She was gorgeous, but I believe in staying clear of women who would rather die than give a guy a break, you know? Craig should have known better."

"Hmm." Davy kept his face carefully neutral. "I see."

Kraus was warming to his topic. "I mean, I can understand the impulse. The body on that woman, whew. But I also understand him wanting to kick back with someone like Mandi. Mandi was less, I don't know. Challenging, you know?"

Kraus gave him a man-to-man smile. Davy couldn't bring himself to smile back, but fortunately, Kraus was too self-involved to notice.

"Turns out Mandi was more challenging than we knew. They found the guy strung up from the ceiling, naked. Mag walked in on them, and I guess she figured she had to one-up Mandi, so she emptied out her clip." Kraus shook his head. "Women. You never know."

"Hmm," Davy murmured. "So the police didn't have any doubts?"

Kraus shrugged. "Who else? It was her gun. She's on the video going into the building. No one's seen her since. You do the math."

Davy nodded. "What exactly did Caruso do for you?"

"Research and development. Mike Wainwright knew the guy from Stanford. Caruso was a hell of an innovator, I'll say that much. A lot of the features that make Krell so competitive for a small company are his ideas." Kraus blew out a sigh. "But that's how it goes. So? What else can I do for you, Mr. Evan?"

Davy sighed inwardly. If someone at Krell was responsible for what happened to Caruso and Margot, Kraus didn't
know shit about it, and the other guy Margot had mentioned
was out of town. He would have to come back the following
week.

Davy shook hands, promised to be in touch and headed
out to reception. Caruso's ex-secretary Miriam was on the
phone. He watched her discreetly. Young, blond, plump.
Blandly pretty. Her eyes flicked up to Davy's as she talked
into the headset. They froze wide open.

His neck crawled at the wave of fear he sensed from her.

"I'll have him call you, Mr. Tripp," she said. "Yes, and
you have a great day now, too. Bye-bye." She looked up at
him. "Can I help you?"

He put on his most charming smile. Her eyes slid away.
No answering smile. "Mr. Kraus told me you used to work for
Craig Caruso," he said. "I wanted to ask you a few quick
questions."

The pink in her cheeks abruptly faded. "I worked for him,
but I didn't exactly know him," she said. "It was so awful,
what happened."

"Did you know Mandi Whitlow?" he asked.

"A little, but it's not like we were friends. She was a tech,
and I reported to the office manager. So I can't tell you much
of anything about them. Anything at all." She blinked
rapidly.

"Ah. OK," he said gently. "Sorry to have bothered you."

"No bother." Her bright smile was like a plastic mask.

He walked out into the hot sun, puzzled and thoughtful.
Miriam was acting guilty. Bob Kraus had not. He should
have brought Sean along. Sean was brilliant at prying info
out of females; a skill which baffled his brothers. Davy had
never had the stomach to flirt with any woman he wasn't
genuinely interested in. It made him feel like a user.

Sean, on the other hand, overcame this obstacle by being
genuinely, sincerely, intensely interested in all of them. Plain

ones, shy ones, fat ones, thin ones, even the weird ones, Sean found them all fascinating. It was his secret weapon. They melted into goo for it.

He headed towards the car. An engine revved, and he turned to see a gray van with tinted windows pulling up behind him. The side door slid open. Two men jumped out and pointed silenced pistols at him. They had the businesslike air of seasoned professionals.

His stomach dropped. He'd been a pussywhipped asshole for bringing Margot here. He should have kept driving until they were in Mexico. He should have gone to ground, gotten her a new ID, taken her to Europe. There were a million other things he should have done, but here he was staring down the barrels of two guns, and Margot was all alone. Seth and his brothers were too far away to help her.

And behind it, pain twisted like a knife in his gut, keen and sharp. *He hadn't even had the balls to tell her that he loved her.*

One of them circled behind him. The barrel of a pistol pressed against the nape of his neck. The other stabbed a syringe into his arm.

Aw, shit was the last coherent thought he managed to think before icy darkness spread, and everything went away.

Chapter
25

Davy was stuck in a stifling nightmare about blood and snakes and pain. Pounding head, aching body. Someone was shaking him. A sharp blow cracked against his face. He dragged his eyes open to investigate. A face stared into his. He struggled to focus.

A lean, handsome guy in his late thirties, dark hair trimmed short. Smiling. His white teeth and white shirt hurt Davy's eyes. He squeezed them shut against the pain. The man slapped him again.

He opened his eyes. "Who the fuck are you?" he mumbled.

The source of the pain focalized. His arms were wrenched back, bound behind him at his elbows and wrists. His hands were numb.

"Where is Margaret Callahan?" the man asked.

His drugged brain struggled to connect the dots. Callahan. Margot's real name. "I don't know anybody named Margaret Callahan."

The man slapped him again. "Wrong answer, Mr. McCloud."

Davy took stock. He was seated, bound to a heavy wooden chair. The guy in front of him was not Snakey, though he was similar in looks. He was older, somewhat slimmer. "Where's Snakey?" Davy asked.

The man looked politely puzzled. "Excuse me?"

"The ninja asshole who's been killing people right and left."

The man looked amused. "Oh. My younger brother, Faris. So he went on a killing spree after all, did he? You'll be meeting him again later. He's resting up. His last encounter with you left him somewhat the worse for wear."

"Who are you guys?" Davy demanded.

"You can call me Marcus," the guy said. "Let's talk about the whereabouts of Margaret Callahan. Or Margot Vetter, if you prefer."

No point in playing dumb. "What do you want with her?"

"I want what she took from me," Marcus said flatly.

"She doesn't have a goddamn thing."

Marcus let out a bark of laughter. "I'm not surprised if she opted not to tell you. Hundreds of millions of dollars are at stake."

Davy looked around at the sumptuous library, decorated with costly Persian carpets and fine art. "Everything she owns is in five plastic shopping bags in the trunk of her car," he said. "There's nothing worth hundreds of millions of dollars in those bags."

"I don't know where she's hidden it," Marcus said patiently. "That is exactly what I want to discuss with her. As soon as possible."

"I don't know where she is," Davy said.

Marcus pulled Davy's cell phone out of his pocket, and dangled it from his fingertips. "We'll discuss that. But I doubt her whereabouts will be a mystery for long, no matter what you say or don't say. I just have to wait for her to get anxious and call you. And then we'll see how much you are worth to her. Are you worth hundreds of millions?"

Davy stared at the guy. So this simpering piece of dogshit was the guy who had ruined Margot's life. God, she deserved so much better.

He braced himself. "Go fuck yourself," he said quietly.

She paced, chewed her nails, tore at her hair. It couldn't take long to talk to those self-important blowhards at Krell. A half hour to shop at the mall, fifteen to get to Krell, an hour to talk to the blowhards, fifteen to come back, and that was being generous.

He'd been gone for over three hours.

The queasy, crawling feeling was driving her nuts. Of course, she'd had that feeling more often than not for eight months, but it was measurably worse than usual. Verging on the screaming, writhing level.

She had been grabbing and hanging up the phone for the past hour. As the minutes passed, she clutched the receiver for longer and longer, finger floating over the number pad.

Why not? Worst case scenario, he would be irritated with her for being hysterical and needy. Could she live with that? Hell, yes. If she could handle him being furious, she could handle him being irritated.

What she could not handle for one second longer was this yawning vortex of fear, big enough to suck up the entire known universe. And since her entire known universe at this moment was Davy, well, that clinched it. There were limits to a girl's self-control.

She grabbed the phone and dialed his cell number, praying for him to be in range. It rang, praise God. The line clicked open.

"Davy? Is that you?" she asked. "Can you hear me? Hello?"

There was a brief pause. "Margaret Callahan, I presume?"

Next thing she knew, she was sprawled on the floor, her legs having folded up and dumped her ignominiously onto her butt.

It was hard to force out words when there was no breath behind them. "Who am I speaking with?"

"With someone who has been wanting to meet you very badly for eight months now," said the silky voice. "You've been very elusive. It's been driving us mad."

"Why do you have Davy's phone? Where's Davy?"

"He's here, with me. We were just discussing your location. He's been unhelpful so far. I was about to take the gloves off, so to speak, and voilà, the phone rings. Ms. Callahan, you have a sixth sense."

"Let me talk to him," she said.

"Certainly. Mr. McCloud? Your lady friend wants to speak to you."

"Margot?" It was Davy's voice, hoarse and ragged.

"Oh, God, Davy, what has that bastard done to—"

"Listen to me. Run. Hang up the phone and run like hell."

"But I—but you—"

"Don't waste time. Hang up the phone and run. Don't even talk to this asshole. He's not worth it."

"Davy, I can't—"

"It's me again, Ms. Callahan," said the soft voice. "I'm touched by your lover's devotion, but I don't recommend taking his advice. Not if it is of any interest to you how many pieces I cut him into."

She'd thought she'd known what fear was, but she'd never seen it until this moment. Never even imagined it. "Are you Snakey?"

"Snakey?" The voice rumbled, a low, fruity chuckle. "I love his new pet name. It suits him so well. No, but Snakey is here, and eager to see you again. You made such an impression, Margaret."

She barely kept her voice steady. "What do you want from me?"

"Very good, Ms. Callahan. Short, to the point, no histrionics. I like a practical woman. But you know what I want."

"No. I don't. I swear to God—"

"The part where you insist on your ignorance bores me. Let's skip it. It would be unlucky for Mr. McCloud if I got annoyed."

She could have screamed, she was so frustrated. She must be under a curse, condemned to blindly grope for a key to the blank prison wall in front of her face. "Humor me," she pleaded. "Be specific. I want to cooperate. This is too important to risk any misunderstandings."

The mystery voice let out a theatrical sigh. "This is an unsecured line, Ms. Callahan. Don't be obtuse. I want back what's mine. You were the last one to have it. Does that ring a bell?"

"But I—"

"I will give you some instructions. I don't recommend contacting the police. They are unlikely to believe you, and even if they did, I would know, and McCloud would pay. Understand?"

"Yes."

"Listen carefully, then. The number 313 city bus leaves the central station downtown at twenty minute intervals. You will take the one that leaves at 6:05. It runs down Wyatt Avenue for four miles, then turns south at Trevitt. Are you following me?"

"Yes," she said. "6:05. Bus 313. Wyatt, Trevitt."

"The second stop after the bus turns onto Trevitt is at Rosewell. Get off, and walk ten blocks south. There will be a freeway overpass. On your left is a small grocery and an auto parts store. There is a pay phone between them. You will receive further instructions there. If we are convinced that you are alone and haven't been followed."

"Wait," she said. "If I can't—"

"There is no can't, Ms. Callahan. If you don't arrive on schedule with my property, McCloud will die. Badly."

"But how do I—"

"Good luck. I look forward to meeting you."

The connection broke, leaving her adrift. That cold, sick

feeling was rising up again, as if she were going to black out or barf. She flopped onto her back, propped up her knees, forced herself to breathe.

She did not have the luxury of freaking out.

It had to be the mold and that ghastly rubbery hand the guy wanted. Why, she could not begin to imagine. It was hard to think with her brain squeezed by a fist of fear, but beneath the fear was something new. Sharp, burning anger. It steadied her.

That evil son of a bitch was hurting her Davy. She was going to do everything in her power to make him stop. And make him pay.

Davy had told her to run. Very noble and heroic of him, and she adored him for the gesture, but her life would be worth nothing if she ran off and left the man she loved to die. There was just no point. She might as well just throw herself under a bus and be done with it.

The only card she had left to play in this game was herself. She would stick that icky thing into her shopping bag, put on Tamara's hair clip, and follow the guy's instructions.

And hope like hell, if nothing else, for a chance to kill him.

She dialed the number Davy had left her for Sean. He picked up instantly. "Yeah? Who's this?"

"We're in trouble," Margot said flatly.

"That was quick." His voice without laughter was unrecognizable.

Margot recounted Marcus's phone call and instructions. "I'm going to the rendezvous," she concluded. "There's nothing else I can do. Nothing you can do either, but I thought at least you should know."

"We're on our way," Sean said. "Me and Seth. We took off just a few hours after you guys did. Just the time it took to throw our arsenal together and hit the road. We've still another hour and a half or so to San Cataldo, but we'll get there as soon as we can."

She was dumbfounded. "How did you guys know where we—"

"How do you think Davy found you?" Sean's voice was impatient. "Do you still have Mikey's dog collar on you?"

"Uh, yes," she said, startled. "Should I—"

"Fuck, yes. Keep it on you. Better yet, just wait for us. Stay clear of that scumbag. That's what Davy would want."

"Staying clear wasn't one of the options the scumbag gave me," she told him. "They've got Davy. They'll hurt him if I don't go."

"Shit," Sean muttered. "You have a weapon, at least?"

"Who, me? Hah!" Margot said. "Gotta run, Sean. Good luck."

She hung up on him and called the operator. "Give me the San Cataldo Police Department, please."

She waited forever. "Dispatch," a woman's voice finally said.

"Hi. I urgently need to speak with whoever was in charge of the Craig Caruso and Mandi Whitlow murder investigation."

"Hold the line, please."

She stared at herself in the mirror as she waited, noting dispassionately how awful she looked. Face bone white, eyes hollow, jeans and tank top dingy and wilted. A voice snapped her attention back to the phone. "Detective Sam Garrett here," said a deep male voice. "You have information regarding the Caruso case?"

"I'm Mag Callahan," she said.

There was an astonished pause. "Where are you, Ms. Callahan?"

"I'm sorry, but I can't tell you that right now," she said. "I've been trying to figure out who framed me for the last eight months. I think I've found the bastard, or he's found me, I should say. I also doubt that I'm going to survive the encounter, so I wanted to go on record first as saying that I'm not a murderer. OK? Write it down. Tell everyone."

"Uh . . ."

"And neither is Davy McCloud," she added, for good measure.

"Who?" Garrett sounded baffled.

"My boyfriend," she explained. "He's been framed for murder, too. And if that wasn't bad enough, now he's been kidnapped, to control me. By the same filthy scumbag who killed Craig and Mandi."

"Hold on. I'm confused. You say that your boyfriend has been kidnapped, and that you are—"

"You're not the only one who's confused, Detective," she said. "I've been confused for months. I'm sorry I can't explain better. I'm on a real tight schedule, and I'm afraid they're hurting Davy. I just wanted to give you guys a heads-up. If you find me in a Dumpster somewhere, the guy who killed me is the same one who killed Craig and Mandi. And he's not working alone. He's got a sicko ninja-type assassin working for him. OK? Got that straight?"

"Who is this man, Ms. Callahan?" Garrett's tone was that of a man trying to reason with a demented person. "Help me out here."

She laughed out loud. "Do you think that if I knew who he was that I'd be in this kind of trouble? I would've turned this nightmare over to you guys months ago if I could have, believe me. All I know right now is that he calls himself Marcus. If I live through the night, I promise I'll contact you and tell you the whole story."

"But we—"

"And that's all I can say right now. Thanks for your time."

She slammed the phone down. Good. That was done, and it felt right. Futile maybe, but symbolically appropriate. She'd reached the end of the line. She checked the clock, calculating how long it would take to cab it to the station, and concluded that she could have five minutes to spiff herself up for the end of the world. She'd be damned if she'd go out to confront her ultimate mortal end looking like a schlump.

The only thing she had to wear besides the jeans and tank top was the dress she'd worn to the wedding. It was too sexy for the occasion, but it would have to do. She wrenched off her clothes and yanked the thing on. Panty lines be damned.

She looked at the spike-heeled sandals, and decided there were lengths to which she would not go, even to avoid edge-of-doom fashion don'ts. It was doubtful Fate would give her a chance to run like a rabbit from Snakey and his buddies, but that was no reason to hobble herself.

The battered red high-tops it would be, then. At least they packed a visual punch, in their own spunky, scruffy way.

Hair. She gelled her already crazed nest-crest until it stood out in snarled tufts. Then she twisted everything she could catch of it into a tight roll, crunchy enough to hold Tamara's hair clip. No need to fuss with the rest of it. It was perfect as it was, sticking out every which way in the nutsoid, probably-on-drugs look of a high-fashion runway model.

She rummaged through her plastic bag for her makeup stash and applied liquid eyeliner and mascara with slutty abandon. With her eyes as hollow as they were, she should go for the deliberately smudged look.

She painted on the lipstick with a bold hand, studied herself critically in the mirror, and dabbed more lipstick onto her pale cheeks, rubbing it in hard to give herself a smidgen of color.

She rummaged in her purse for Mikey's studded dog collar and buckled it around her neck. It barely fit. She slid the medallion around to the back, tucking it inside the band, and pulled some hair loose over her neck to cover it. She checked out the final effect in the full-length mirror, and blinked with her heavy, crusty eyelashes, startled.

Gosh. Well. It was a look. Not one she'd ever dreamed of putting on before, but somehow appropriate for running into the face of doom. The garish spots of lipstick on her pallid cheeks gave her the dramatic look of a tubercular nineteenth-century prostitute, and the studded dog collar was a kinky final touch. She wasn't sure what message she was sending with it, but hey, what the hell. Keep 'em all guessing.

She reached into her bra to fluff up her boobs and tugged the dress down a couple inches. Retro-tech-punk collides with the Addams Family. She decided she liked it. It was a fuck-you outfit. A tiny extra charge of power to put in the balance against this huge fear.

And her five minutes had stretched into seven. No more stalling.

She emptied out the plastic shopping bag. Tucked the mold and the rubbery hand into it, grabbed her purse, and ran out the door.

At first she was afraid her outfit would give her problems hailing a cab, but one screeched to a halt as soon as she held up her arm. The cabbie kept shooting her fascinated looks, but she was too occupied trying not to imagine Davy in pain to be bothered with him. She fished in her purse for the fare. Amazing how her feelings about money had changed since she'd stopped hoping to live through the night. She just needed the price of a bus ticket. After that, her cash had no more relevance than Monopoly money. Once she paid the cabbie, she could throw the rest out the window. Not that there was much left to throw.

Dressed as she was, Rosewell Avenue wasn't the best part of town to get out of the bus and walk ten blocks. Margot realized this as soon as the bus pulled away, revealing the adult book and video store, the men's weight-lifting gym, the dingy massage parlor. To say nothing of the scantily clad ladies who X-rayed her with hostile eyes from their various places on street corners and in doorways. She spun in a circle, clutching the shopping bag to her chest, trying to spot whoever must be monitoring her. No luck. She straightened her shoulders and got her feet moving, counting blocks as she passed them, careful not to return the stares that came her way.

Amazing, how different Davy's penetrating gaze was to these jerks' clumsy attempts to intimidate her. The difference between real power and feigned power. Davy was for real. Heroic and brave. Telling her to run away while they were hurting him. Oops, none of that. Sobbing uncontrollably was not the plan, not with three blocks between her and an unspeakable fate. One foot in front of the other. Cracked sidewalk beneath her feet. Broken glass, syringes, used condoms, cigarette butts. The roar of the freeway overpass got louder. Sweat trickled down her back. The colors burned her eyes, the odors tickled her nose. Exhaust, pot smoke, pee, rotting garbage. There it was, just as Marcus had said. The auto parts store, the grocery. The phone between them rang as she stared at it. She walked towards it, and reached for the receiver with all the enthusiasm one might have for handling a poisonous snake. "Yes?"

"Margaret Callahan?"

"That would be me."

"A gray van will pull up behind you in thirty seconds. Get into it."

"But I—"

The phone went dead. She dropped it. It swung back and forth on its metal-wrapped cord like a black plastic pendulum. Marking the time to the end of the world. Thirty seconds passed. An engine hummed. She turned. The door slid open in a gray van. A man with a black ponytail was crouched in the door. He grinned at her. "Margaret Callahan?"

She nodded. He held out his hand for the bag. She handed it over.

The man peered inside it, and passed it to someone in the front seat. He turned back, his eyes dragging over her body. "Get in."

She stared at him, paralyzed with dread.

"If you ever want to see your boyfriend again," he added. She got in.

grabbed it, and swiftly controlled her-
miss it," she went on dreamily. "Feeling a
me while I dance naked. If you want, I could
al command performance, just for you, Karel."
lungs burned with the need for air, his muscles
from straining against the bonds. He hoped to God
had a plan.

Karel looked doubtful. "I don't need any help getting hard."

She rubbed her bottom against him. "That's obvious," she purred. "I just wanted to give you something . . . special."

Karel reached back, pulled out his gun, cocked it. "I think you're fucking with me, Margaret," he said. "Don't try to be smart."

Margot's bright red lips curved in an inviting smile. "If I didn't like playing with fire, do you think I'd be where I am right now?"

"You have a point." Karel spun her around to face him and kissed her, his tongue thrusting into her mouth. "You like it like this?" He pressed the pistol between her breasts, and slid it up to her throat.

She didn't flinch, so Davy flinched for her. She just kept smiling, as a pistol dug up in the soft spot beneath her chin. The guy kissed her again, and bit her lip, hard enough to make her gasp.

"Just remember," he said. "The boss has what he needs. You're expendable now. And after trouble you've caused, I think you're chances of getting expended are real high."

Margot pouted her soft, red lips at him. "You're no fun. I

Chapter
26

Marcus had been holding himself back.
Davy was plenty dazed and battered from the blows to his face, but he knew damn well how much worse it could have been. Marcus was saving him for later. Maybe for Snakey. Or maybe he was waiting to have Margot for an audience. Best not to think about that.

The library was empty now, but for himself. There was a flurry of activity elsewhere in the place, barely audible. The house must be huge.

Marcus had gagged him before he left the room, and with the nosebleed he was having, that was a torture in itself, strug-gling through bubbling liquid for each labored breath.

The door burst open. Margot was shoved into the room, blindfolded, arms fastened behind her. She stumbled to her knees and fell forward onto her face. One of the goons who had nabbed him at Krell crouched on top of her, straddling her, and pulled out a knife.

He looked up and gave Davy a big, shit-eating grin as he dragged the tip of his knife slowly down Margot's spine, to the plasticuffs that bound her hands. Snick, and the knife snapped through them.

Davy started at least trying to breathe again.

The goon wrenched Margot to her feet and tugged the blindfold off. Holy shit. That crazy makeup of hers was surreal.

Margot blinked and dragged in a sharp breath as she saw him. She lunged towards him. "Oh, my God, what have they—"

The goon yanked her back. "Huh-uh." His thick arms snaked around her from behind and cupped her breasts, pinching and squeezing. "Oh, nice," he crooned. "The boss said I could have all the fun I wanted with you, as long as we do it in front of him." He jerked his chin towards Davy. "Fine with me. I've never minded an audience. Kinky is fun. We'll have a fine old time."

Davy finally understood the torture Marcus had in mind. So this was the main event. Marcus had wanted him sharp and alert for it.

Margot's eyes locked with Davy's for a moment that was both timeless and horribly brief. Suddenly she changed, as if a switch had flipped inside her. The naked emotion in her eyes that had pierced through him transformed into a brilliant, strangely unfocused smile.

His Margot disappeared. In her place was a smiling, sexy doll.

She twisted, pressing her breasts against the guy's hands to accentuate her cleavage, and flung her head back against his shoulder. Her eyes glittered as if she had been drugged. He prayed to God for a chance to rip these sadistic sons of bitches into tiny, bloody pieces. The anger built inside him until the pressure hurt more than any physical pain he'd ever felt.

"You know, if we're going to get to know each other so quickly, you should tell me your name," Margot said huskily. "Karel," the guy said huskily. He pinched her nipples.

don't want to th
This might be my
fun. Let's make it cou
"You bet," Karel croo
"Let me dance for you,
that, for old times' sake. I'll be
seen."

Karel grabbed a chair and sat d
her. "OK. Go on. Impress me. Just do
Or I'll hurt you."

She started to move. Davy watched her,
fear and fascination. She was terrifying, with th
in her eyes. She shimmied and swayed, humming
tune low in her throat. She moved closer to Karel, b
dance behind his chair.

The pistol went up. She stopped in her tracks.

"Right back in front of me, bitch," Karel said. "Right where I can see you. And get the dress off."

"Sorry," she whispered. She began again, slowly, sensuously tugging and wriggling her overdress up over the slip, over her hips, her belly, her breasts, her neck. The dress covered her head. She seemed to struggle with it for a moment, and when she finally pulled it off, her hair had shaken loose, a wild, shaggy halo.

She swung her leg over Karel's lap, straddling him. The slip rode up high on her thigh. Karel pushed it higher, stroking her hip with his gun. Margot's hand flashed up, towards Karel's face. Suddenly the guy's eyes went wide. His gun hand went slack, flopping to his side.

What the fuck? Davy watched, astonished, as the weapon thudded to the carpet. Karel's head lolled back, mouth open. Margot scrambled off him, backing away. She ran to Davy, prying out his gag. "Oh, my poor baby. Did they hurt you bad? Are you OK?"

He coughed, tried to swallow. "Goddammit, I told you to run!"

"I don't follow orders well, in case you haven't noticed," she said crisply. "Great to see you again, too. Did you miss me?"

"What the hell did you do to him?" he demanded.

"Later," she snapped. "I have to find a knife and cut you loose."

"They took mine. Fuckhead had one, though. Check his pockets."

She sprinted over to Karel and rummaged through the pockets of his cargo pants. Seconds later she was kneeling behind Davy's chair, sawing away at the tough plastic.

"Did you really lapdance back in college?" he demanded.

She choked on her nervous laughter. "You are such a dog. You just lost fifty points for asking such a stupid, irrelevant question."

A disembodied voice came from a loudspeaker on the wall. "Step back and drop the knife, Margaret."

The doors burst open, on both sides of the room, and several armed men spilled in. A handsome dark-haired man sauntered in after them. "That was even more entertaining than I expected," he said. "I said to step back. Put the knife down, get up, and walk towards me. Or I will have McCloud shot immediately."

Margot looked around at the guns, laid the knife down and did as she was told. She might have known it couldn't be so simple. Now she'd played the last card she had to play. Oh, well. She'd expected this.

Time for Tamara's chilly, calming mantra. No hope, no fear. Her knees trembled under her, but she tried hard to keep her back straight.

The man raked her with critical eyes. "Your style has changed."

"Have we met?" Margot kept her voice cool. "How on earth could you know my style before?"

"I saw pictures of you. I studied you, before the Caruso event. I admired you then. So elegant. You look like a crack whore now."

Margot shrugged. "Being on the run from both sides of the law is hell on a wardrobe," she said. "I take it you're Marcus? The sick son of a bitch who murdered poor Craig and Mandi?"

"Oh, harsh words!" Marcus chuckled. "Actually, Faris did the physical deed, the fellow you call Snakey. He's my younger brother. He's the warrior of the family. I'm just a mild-mannered scientist myself."

Margot's gaze swept the battery of guns trained on her, and Davy's battered face. "Yeah, I'm so sure," she muttered. "Meek as a lamb."

"You cut quite a swath with men," Marcus said in a teasing tone. "Poor Faris, and Karel, too." He nudged Karel's shoulder. The unconscious man slid sideways off the chair and flopped heavily to the floor. "And McCloud under your spell. You're a real femme fatale."

"Hardly," Margot muttered.

"You don't need her anymore," Davy said. "Let her go."

Marcus motioned to his men. "Gag him again. He bores me." He turned back to Margot and shook his head ruefully. "I meant to teach McCloud and Faris both a lesson by having them watch you with Karel. They're such primal, possessive types. But as usual, you swept the rug from beneath my feet." Marcus bent down to pick up the tiny spray pin she'd let fall to the carpet while looking for Karel's knife. He turned it over in his hands and slipped it into his pocket. "Clever little thing."

"You have what you want," she said. "Let us go."

"You know I can't do that," Marcus chided. "I'm sure you knew that even before you came. You're not stupid."

Stony fatalism propped her up in place of hope. She might as well die with her curiosity satisfied. "So Craig was working with you, then?" she asked. "You guys were running some kind of a scam?"

"No. He did not work with me. He worked *for* me," Marcus said sharply. "That little distinction is exactly what got him killed."

"I see," she murmured. "He found a way to fool Krell's sensors?"

"The perfect technique," Marcus said. "Graceful, stream-lined, and it took everything into account, the optical scan-ner, the ECG, the thermal and pressure sensor, pulse oximetry, electric resistance, the ultrasound, all of it. He truly was a genius."

"Using a fake hand?" she asked. "Like the one I brought to you?"

"Oh, no. Better. We made a double-layered gelatin glove. The gummy hand is just to quality test the reproduction of the minutia. The BioLock Identipad rejects everything but a warm, live hand with blood pulsing through it. Craig found a way to give it one. He was so gifted. And not just with his brain." Marcus chuckled. "He even sacrificed his virtue to get the last piece of the puzzle. That bad boy."

"What puzzle?" Margot struggled to follow him.

"Priscilla Worthington," Marcus said impatiently. "My esteemed stepmother, the Bitch of Buchenwald. The mold you just provided."

Realization dawned. "Oh. Wait. Does this Priscilla have long black hair and black lace thong panties?"

"Black hair, yes. As for her panties . . ." Marcus shud-dered delicately. "I don't want to know. My tissues recoil at the very thought."

Margot's feminine instincts told her he was itching to brag. Surrounded with meatheads like Karel and psychos like Snakey, there was probably no one to appreciate what Marcus saw as his genius.

She should use his vanity and solitude to play for time. She tried to look fascinated. "So what will you do with the mold now?"

His gratified smile indicated that she'd read him right.

"I've been planning this for years," he said. "Tonight, the video surveillance at Calix Research Laboratories will mysteriously fail. To access the top secret laboratory, the two people with the highest security clearance must present their handprints at the same time. Tonight, according to the Krell BioLock Identipad, they will both do so. They will then remove ten vials of R-8424." He noticed Margot's clouded, doubtful gaze. "It's a flu virus," he said helpfully. "Very virulent. Quite nasty."

Margot's blood would have run cold if it had not already been the consistency of icy sludge. "Dear God," she whispered. "You're kidding."

"Oh, no. Not at all." Marcus giggled at her reaction. "I've seen to it that neither of them will have an alibi tonight. Who knows who they will sell the virus to? No one will be able to answer that question. It's like a game of Russian roulette, but no one will know who is holding the gun."

"You're risking a world epidemic . . . for *money*?" Her voice cracked with horror. "What the hell is in it for you?"

The more shocked and horrified she was, the more Marcus liked it. "Revenge, untold wealth and world domination, of course," he said, his voice jolly. "Years ago, I started devising my plan. I invested in a pharmaceuticals firm that developed a vaccine for R-8424. When the news hits the press, two things will happen. Priscilla will become the most despised, vilified woman in the world—and I will become the richest man." He beamed. "I'm already immune to R-8424, of course."

She was too horrified to look admiring.

"I've been waiting for months for you to contact me to start negotiations," he said petulantly. "My contact for the virus was completely out of patience. What on earth were you waiting for?"

I didn't know you existed. She stifled the words. Foolishly proud, maybe, but she was embarrassed to reveal the extent of her ignorance to this crazy freak. "I didn't approve of your plans," she said frostily.

True enough, as far as it went.

"Oh, no?" He grabbed her hand and inspected it. "Small, delicate hands, just like Priscilla's. Good. You'll wear Priscilla's glove tonight. This is all rather hastily improvised, you see. I had no idea when I would finally get my hands on the mold. You showed up just in time."

"I will not help you do this sick, evil thing," she said.

"Sure you will. We'll see how many of McCloud's body parts I need to remove before you change your mind. I'll start with his hands, hmm? What do you think? Since hands are the theme of the evening?"

Margot swallowed. He had her, and he knew it.

Marcus clapped his hands briskly. "While my people put final details into place, I propose an entertainment. A duel between your two suitors. I promised poor Faris a last whack at him. If Faris wins, he gets to keep you as a toy, though I suspect he will choke on you. He would have to keep you constantly confined, and probably medicated, too. You don't strike me as either docile or trustworthy."

The thought of a vague, horrific captivity stretching into forever made her queasy and faint. "No," she said. "Not particularly."

"For Christ's sake, would you floor the fucking thing? You're crawling!"

Seth held steady at 86 as he flipped on the turn signal for the San Cataldo exit. "We'll lose more time getting stopped for speeding that we'd gain by flying off the handle like a couple of jerk-offs."

"Since when did you become the voice of goddamn reason?" Sean fumed. "I thought I could count on you at least not to be a pussy."

"It's your brother out there, and that's the only reason I won't slam your sorry ass for saying that. Chill out, or you'll get us killed."

Sean dropped his head back and blew out an explosive breath. "Connor should be here. If I fuck this up—"

"It's not your fault he's not here," Seth cut him off. "Connor took off for Paris before you or I or even Davy knew what we were dealing with. Even if he'd turned right around and gotten on the next plane home, he still wouldn't be back yet. Shit just happens. Calm down."

Sean stared out the windshield. "I can't go through it again."

Seth shot him a worried glance. Seth had lost his own brother less than two years ago. Sean had lost his twin twelve years ago. There was nothing he could say to make the fear any easier to bear.

"Don't think about it," Seth said. "You're just a soldier with a job of work to do. We go in there shooting, we mow those fuckers down, and you'll feel a whole lot better right away. Got the plan straight?"

Sean's eyes flicked down to the case at his feet that held the fully automated Mac 10 machine pistols they'd picked out for this adventure, along with several 30-round clips of extra ammo. The Uzis were in the trunk, just for backup. He slanted Seth a derisive look. "Such as it is."

"Hey, we're good at improvisation," Seth encouraged. "We can see through walls with the thermal imaging goggles. And we're almost there, so make yourself useful and get your eyes back on that monitor. Are you sure Davy's going to remember those signals your dad taught you?"

"Davy's never forgotten anything in his life," Sean growled.

"Except for the rehearsal dinner," Seth pointed out.

Sean grinned, in spite of himself. "Only because he was finally getting laid by a gorgeous babe after months of abstinence."

Seth cackled appreciatively. "Brain melt."

"Yeah. And to think that I was the one who pushed him into hooking up with her. God."

"Who knew?" Seth said wryly. "She's hot. Who could resist?"

Sean shook his head. "This is the last time I try matchmaking," he muttered. "That shit can get you killed."

The goons dragged Davy down through several long, dim corridors. Too bad they'd left his legs tied. He was in the mood to kill someone, or better yet, several someones. He wanted to eviscerate Marcus for what he had done to Margot. Or would have done, if Margot hadn't been such a magnificent avenging warrior goddess.

He still couldn't figure out what the fuck she'd done to Karel.

They dragged him into a huge ballroom, vaulted ceilings, glittering crystal chandeliers. The tall windows that lined both sides of the room revealed a thick forest tossing wildly in the stormy breeze. The twilit sky was heavy with clouds. Lightning flashed on the horizon.

They dumped him face first onto the parquet floor. He rolled up into a sitting position. They lifted their rifles. He sank back down.

Thunder rumbled. A teeth-grinding eternity of seconds ticked by.

The door finally opened. Margot walked in, head high. Marcus followed her, holding a pistol on her.

His panther woman. Her eyes met his, bright with emotion. The makeup smudged beneath her eyes made her look feral. Untamed.

What a fucking waste. A woman so tough and brave and special, sucked into this black hole of greed and insanity. His gut ached with fear for her. He couldn't resist his feelings anymore. He had to face the truth, and truth was standing there in a slip and dirty sneakers.

Margot Vetter ripped his heart wide open and let all his monsters out. So be it. He let out his breath, and his resistance with it. The room was full of monsters. Might as well add his own to the crowd.

Snakey walked in, staring hungrily at Margot. His arm was bandaged, and he had gauze patches on his face, but he looked better than he had last night in the hotel room. His bloodshot eyes glittered with the vibe of a guy hopped up on some performance-enhancing drug that killed pain and quickened reflexes. Davy had run into those guys before. They were tough to fight. Sometimes they didn't even have the sense to know when they were dead.

Marcus gestured to one of his men to take out Davy's gag. "Mr. McCloud, you have a choice," he announced. "Faris wants to fight you. If you agree, I'll have your bonds removed. You will be covered by several gunmen at all times. If you attempt to escape, or do anything that I find objectionable, you will be instantly shot. Do you agree?"

"If I don't?" Davy asked, just out of curiosity.

"Then we'll leave you tied, and let Faris amuse himself with you while your lady friend watches. Faris is very talented with his needles."

Some choice. Davy shrugged. "I'll fight him."

"I've given Faris a little pick-me-up to compensate for the injuries you inflicted." Marcus looked smug. "Do you think that's unfair?"

"Yes," Davy said.

"You're right," Marcus agreed easily. "Life isn't fair, so why pretend? Rules are just a self-imposed prison."

Davy struggled to fathom the guy's reasoning, and quickly abandoned the attempt. "You think you're some kind of god, don't you?"

Marcus gestured for them to remove Davy's bonds. "We all are, but most of us are afraid to accept our own divinity. Not me. I've embraced my power. I'm completely free."

Davy struggled to his feet once they'd cut him free, and tried to flex his numb fingers. They wouldn't respond. Marcus's words echoed in his head, reshuffling as if he were trying to break a code. *Rules are just a self-imposed prison.* His brain was trying to tell him something, but he couldn't stop to ponder it. He wished he could tell Margot how beautiful and precious she was, but he didn't dare say it in front of these people. Anything he said could be twisted into a weapon to hurt her.

He tried to tell her with his eyes.

Faris walked into the center of the room. The black tank top and workout pants he wore showed off his thickly muscled body. He jumped up and down on the balls of his bare feet and stared at Davy, eyes burning with hatred. Feeling no pain.

Davy did a quick and depressing inventory of his own injuries. Swelling in the joints of his arms from being hyperextended for hours. Numb hands beginning to tingle. Eyes and throat burning from dehydration. The bruises and strains of the last two battles, a pounding head, a swollen, battered face. Days without sleep.

Whatever. It was as it was.

He loved her.

"Faris is actually a handsome young man when his face is not so battered," Marcus remarked to Margot. "You never saw him at his best."

That comment set Snakey off, and Davy barely parried a chop to his neck, twisting his arm around Snakey's and tossing him over his shoulder. Snakey spun several yards across the room, sliding on the slippery parquet, and bounded to his feet like he was made of rubber.

Back he came, with a blow to the gut, but it was a feint, and Davy barely changed course in time to parry the vicious kick to what would have been his groin, if he hadn't spun sideways.

He was thick, and slow, and hurting. And getting scared.
Rules . . . a self-imposed prison.

Sweat rolled, burning into his eyes. He was furious with himself. A lifetime of relentless training, and still he struggled with himself as much as with his opponent. He blocked a lightning fast volley of lethal blows while he contemplated the resistence inside himself. He'd tried so hard to keep it together, with all his rules and tricks and techniques.

But now he was dragging a shell of useless armor around. It was unwieldy, heavy. Weighing him down. It was killing him.

He was changing. Outside that rigid shell was a huge new world. He'd gotten too big to fit inside his own cage any longer.

He loved her. Something inside him let go, softening and shifting, and it all came into focus; the global awareness of every square inch he inhabited, the balance of yin and yang, the qi sinking lower in his chest with each deep breath, energizing him. *Right crane neck* fist parried a jab to his face. He dropped the crane neck down to block a punch to his ribs, hooked Snakey's arms, stabbed at the guy's eyes with a left crane beak. Snakey shrieked, jerked back, rubbing his eyes.

He loved her. His pain was gone. He sank down into horse stance, front leg ready to kick, sweep, exert force in any direction. He was the crane, the leopard, the tiger, the snake, the dragon.

Snakey struck at his throat. Davy's dragon's claw smashed into Snakey's face, trapped his hands and bore him to the floor. *Dragon swings his tail*, whipping from the waist, a spinning backfist to Snakey's temple, crushing the zygomatic arch.

Snakey lay on his back, blood flooding out of his nose. He coughed, began to choke. His eyes stared at the ceiling, unseeing.

Davy rose to his feet and backed away.

Marcus's face was expressionless. He walked slowly over and knelt next to Faris. He placed his hands on either side of his brother's face. "Failure is unacceptable," he said softly.

Faris's body jerked. He dragged in a labored breath and blinked up into his brother's face.

Marcus got to his feet and gestured imperiously to Davy with his pistol. "Finish what you started."

Davy stared at him. "Say what?"

Marcus's sigh was impatient. "You've broken him. Finish him off."

"But he's your brother," Davy said, unbelieving.

"So?" Marcus's face did not change. "Do it."

Davy wiped the sweat from his face and stared around at the guns that were trained on him. "I'm not your fucking gladiator," he said quietly. "Do your own killing."

Marcus shifted his aim until his gun was pointed at Margot. He smiled and let the barrel drop till it was aiming at her knees.

Suddenly Marcus gasped, and stumbled back, pinwheeling his arms. The gun went off. *Zing,* shards of plaster exploded from the wall.

Marcus toppled. Faris had hooked his leg through his brother's, and jerked him off balance. His finger stabbed into Marcus's groin. The man's shriek of agony cut off abruptly as Faris's other hand chopped down like an axe over the bridge of his nose. A hideous crunch, and Marcus's nasal bone and orbital socket fractured and collapsed.

In that split second of stunned disbelief, a shrill whistle pierced the air from outside the room. Two ascending tweets followed by a short, lower trill. Marcus's goons panicked and opened fire on Faris.

The guy jerked and twitched as bullets punched into his body.

Davy launched himself at Margot. "Get down!" He bore her to the floor beneath him, just inside the three-second window Sean's signal had indicated. They hit the floor so hard, they bounced.

All hell proceeded to break loose. Sean and Seth were spraying the room at chest height, or so he assumed. Glass shattered, shouts and screams of confusion and pain between thundering crashes of gunfire. One of the chandeliers crashed to the ground. Margot huddled beneath him, warm and trembling and alive.

Sensation crept back. He wished it hadn't. His shoulder ached as if it had been punched, but it was more than a punch. He knew that cold, sick feeling of an energetic hole. Blood pressure dropping. He was bleeding heavily. Nothing to do but wait for the storm to pass.

But by then he was already far away and fading.

Chapter
27

Margot squeezed her eyes shut and endured the huge noise. Even without Davy's weight pinning her down, it would have been impossible to breathe. His landing on top of her had knocked her breath out. She was squashed, strangled, forced from three dimensions to two.

Unconsciousness threatened. She fought it.

Her ringing ears finally registered that the noise had abated. She was just starting to drag tiny, hitching teaspoonfuls of air into her lungs when it dawned on her. Davy wasn't moving.

He was sprawled on top of her, and not moving at all. Dead weight. Something wet and hot was trickling over her back, over her arm, and pooling on the floor near her face. Crimson.

Panic and horror exploded inside her. "Davy? Hey! Davy, answer me!" She struggled beneath him, and it abruptly occurred to her to slow down, move gently. Any move she made could hurt him more.

She wiggled, slowly and carefully out from under his inert body, careful not to jostle him. His shoulder had a ragged hole in it, and was bleeding copiously. His face was grayish, eyes closed. Terribly still.

"Davy?" She looked around desperately for something that could serve as a bandage, and saw Sean galloping across the room.

He skidded to a stop on his knees next to Davy. "What the fuck have you done to yourself now?" Panic edged his voice.

"He was shot," she whispered.

"No shit. Seth, call an ambulance! Now!" Sean dropped the rifle in his hands to the ground and shed a pack from his shoulders, yanking a small kit out of it. He popped it open, pulled out a wad of gauze with the sharp, efficient movements of a man who knew what he was doing. Thank God for that, at least.

Margot finally noticed carnage around her. The lights had been shot out. The bodies of Marcus's men were scattered and sprawled around the floor, pools of blood of varying sizes around them. Some of them still moaned. Most did not.

Marcus and Faris were locked in a grisly, blood-soaked fraternal embrace. Broken glass covered everything, glittering like shards of ice. Gusts of cool, rain-scented wind blew into the room.

"Is he going to be OK?" Her voice felt like a child's whisper.

"He has to be." Sean said viciously, pressing down on the wound. "Or I'll clobber the bastard."

Seth crouched down beside them. "The bullet didn't hit any vital organs," he said to her. "There's a lot of blood loss, though."

She took Davy's uninjured hand and held it. Faris's bloodshot dead eyes stared straight across the room at her, a wide, accusing stare. She looked away, shuddering.

Davy's hand was cold and clammy. She clutched it tightly, as if she were in zero gravity, and if she let go, she would spin away into deep space. There was nothing holding her back. No other point of reference. He couldn't die, or there would be no point left in anything.

Just a cold, blank nothing.

A bunch of noise started up, after a while. A clamor of voices. People bustling around. They strapped Davy onto a gurney and took him away. She tried to follow him, but she was blocked by a guy who stuck his face in hers and started asking a bunch of loud questions. Something about blood. She tried to explain that it wasn't her blood, it was Davy's, because he'd saved her life, but they were taking him away, she was losing him, and they had to let her go with him.

She couldn't get the words to make any sense. She couldn't communicate at all. She tried to pull away. The medic held her back.

She started to cry in pure frustration. Davy was gone, Seth and Sean, too. It was all over. All lost, all gone. Someone gave her a shot.

She floated away, on a river of hopeless tears.

"I'm really sorry, miss." The woman behind the desk regarded Margot's bloodstained slip and mascara-stained face with fearful fascination. "It's not visiting hours, and only family's admitted. Are you OK? Do you need to go to the emergency—"

"I'm fine, thanks, and this is a special case," Margot said. "He took that bullet for me. I count as family. Believe me. I'm in the club."

"I'm sorry. I just can't break the rules—"

"Oh, never mind," she snapped. She turned her back on the suspicious cow and recommenced pacing up and down the brightly lit corridor. She wished she could disguise herself as a normal person, but even a desperate scrub in the hospital bathroom with stinky surgical soap and a wad of harsh paper towels hadn't made much of a dent in her scary look. Every time she caught sight of herself in a reflective surface, she almost yelped. Psycho raccoon woman on the rampage. No wonder the hospital personnel wouldn't let her anywhere near the poor guy. She wouldn't either, if she were in that woman's shoes.

At least she knew Davy was alive. That question had been torturing her ever since she woke up, all alone, in the curtained hospital bed.

On her fourth turn up the corridor, the bulldog who guarded the ward was talking with a nurse at the end of the corridor. All rule-breaking inhibitions had been burned out of her. She crept closer to the door. Someone punched the button on the other side and shot her a startled look as she sailed on through the automatic door, borne along by a tidal wave of lawless momentum.

Seth was lounging in a plastic chair in the corridor, his long body still giving the impression of coiled tension in spite of the relaxed pose.

He turned as she approached, and looked relieved. "Oh, hey. I was wondering where you'd disappeared to. You got lost in the shuffle when the medics came and did their thing."

"Somebody gave me a shot," she said. "I just woke up a while ago. I've been looking for you guys ever since."

His dark eyes slid over her, looking for injuries. "You OK? You look kind of puny."

"I'm fine," she said. "Davy?"

"Asleep. He'll make it. The wound is no big deal, he just lost a lot of blood. But Sean's all torn up about it. He thinks we waited a nanosecond too long for the cavalry charge, so it's all his fault Davy got shot." He shook his head. "McClouds are so high-maintenance," he grumbled. "Drop a pin, and they freak out. Go all emotional on you."

She thought about Davy's passionate anger, his protectiveness, his unbridled eroticism. "I know exactly what you mean. Can I go in?"

Seth grunted. "I'm not the watchdog around here."

She pushed open the door, and stared at Davy for a long

moment. It hurt her heart to see his powerful body so inert. An IV snaked into his arm. His battered face was pale where it wasn't bruised. The golden tinge of his skin had taken on a grayish tint.

Sean sat beside him, his face in his hands. He looked up.

She almost gasped at the change in him. His dimples were gone. His mouth was hard, eyes cold. All the humor gone from his face.

He looked like Davy. She'd never noticed the resemblance before.

It was an uncomfortable thought: that the way Sean looked when he was tense and miserable was the way Davy looked most of the time.

It made her feel guilty, for some reason. From the moment she'd met the man, she'd done nothing but give him trouble. Lying to him, provoking and goading and bugging him.

Still, he'd saved her life. Heroically, more than once. And he was brought to this for his trouble. Silent and gray-faced on a hospital bed, hooked up to a bag of fluid. Covered with bruises, full of holes.

Seth had nothing to say to her. His eyes flicked over her, checking for injuries as Seth had done. Evidently contenting himself that she was in one piece, he dismissed her and turned back to his brother.

"Seth said he was going to be OK," she offered timidly.

"So they say. He looks like shit to me."

She moved closer to the bed, and put her hand on Davy's big hand. Cool, so still. She gripped his long, graceful callused fingers. "He'll be fine," she said quietly. "He has to be."

Sean's short laugh was full of bitterness. "You think? Hah. The worst can always happen." He stroked Davy's arm. "I spend a lot of time staring at my brothers lying unconscious in hospital beds. Only thing that can be said for it is that it's better than staring at a coffin."

"I'm sorry." She felt helpless.

Sean shook his head. "I'm always lagging a couple of steps behind," he said. "I never get to fix things, or save anybody."

She struggled to think of something comforting to say. "But you did help. You came, and you saved him. You shouldn't blame yourself."

"Oh, yeah? Shouldn't I? I was the one who maneuvered him into hooking up with you in the first place. I thought he needed to get out more. I thought he needed to relax, get laid, have some fun. Hah. Would any of this shit had happened if I hadn't done that? It's the story of my life. One catastrophic fuck-up after another."

The cold knot in her belly tightened until the pain was almost unbearable. "I'm sorry," she whispered again.

Sean waved his hand. "Nah," he said. "You're not the one who shot him. It's not your fault the world is full of slime-sucking assholes."

But it was true. None of this would have happened if Sean hadn't nudged her into asking Davy's advice. Of course, if she hadn't, she would probably be dead, or worse.

That reflection was not a particularly helpful one.

"I should have known he'd react like this to you," Sean said. "Like that stripper he got mixed up with years ago, what was her name . . ."

"Fleur," she said. "His ex-wife."

Sean looked startled. "He told you about her? He's never told anybody about Fleur. Even Connor and I had to get him drunk to pry it out of him. And it's not easy to get that uptight bastard drunk."

"I believe you," she murmured. "I know how he is."

"He never lets down his guard," Sean said. "Not even with Connor and me. He's got to be the one who's always strong for us. You know about what happened to our dad?"

She nodded again.

Sean gave her a long, wondering look. "Huh. So he told you all his deep, dark secrets, then. He must be crazy about you."

"I do drive him crazy," she said. "That much is for sure."

Sean reached out to touch Davy's forehead. "He knocked himself out, trying to be our dad, our mom, and our chief commanding officer. Ever since he was fourteen. He hasn't given himself a break ever since. He just forgot how it's done."

Her throat was too tight to reply. She just nodded.

"And the harder you push him to loosen up, the worse he gets," Sean went on. "Stubborn tight-ass." He leaned his folded arms against the bed, pressed his face against them. His broad shoulders vibrated.

Margot touched his shoulder. He jumped, and she jerked her hand back. "Please, don't," he said dully. "Nothing personal. I just can't stand it."

"Sorry," she whispered. "I'll just, um, leave you guys alone, then."

She backed away until her shoulders hit the door, and wiped the tears out of her eyes so she could see well enough for one last look.

Then she walked out into the corridor. Or floated, rather, into deep space. Seth was no longer in the chair outside the door. She began to walk, she didn't know in what direction. She used the strips of reflected light in the middle of the shiny white tile floors to orient herself. When she came up against a blank wall, she turned until she found another strip of reflected light, another white corridor.

She couldn't stay here, a helpless parasite, glomming onto Davy McCloud and his family. She felt so empty and lost. She'd leaned her weight on him, and look what had come of it. She'd almost gotten him killed. She wanted to nurture him, but she was just a piece of flotsam in deep space, now. Nowhere to go. No one to be.

She didn't even know what had happened to her purse. She didn't have a tissue to blow her nose, or two quarters to make a phone call.

Not that she had anybody to call. Her eye fell on a clock high on the wall, which informed her that it was 3:45 A.M. Nine months ago, she wouldn't have hesitated to call one of her girlfriends to pick her up, but so much time had gone by. She was twisted out of recognition by unspeakable events. Jenny or Pia or Christine might not even recognize her. She might scare them. As if she'd become a criminal or a junkie. A human black hole, not to be left alone with the silver.

But she had to start somewhere. Use somebody's shower, crash on someone's couch. God, she missed Mom. She sniffled, her eyes blurring, and her leg bumped painfully hard into one of the plastic chairs. She sank into the chair, and let it take her weight.

She couldn't offer herself to Davy McCloud in this state. He deserved so much better. She had no center, no self. She was hardly a person at all. Just a piece of flotsam. She would have cried to relieve the ache, but she didn't have the strength.

The minute hand ticked around the clock. Time warped, light swirling and mixing with the water in her eyes, making bizarre shapes. Her eyes were so heavy. Like her legs, her heart. So damn heavy.

"Mag Callahan?"

Her chin jerked up from where it had been resting on her chest. Her neck ached from drooping forward. She'd fallen asleep.

She rubbed her eyes and focused on a tall, impeccably dressed black man. He held a cup of coffee. "Are you Mag Callahan?"

She nodded. Nothing to add. No curiosity, no fear, no hope. She gazed at him with dull eyes.

"I'm Detective Sam Garrett, of the San Cataldo Police Department," he said. "We spoke yesterday afternoon. Remember?"

"Vaguely," she said. "You'll have to excuse me. I'm kind of out of it."

"So I can imagine." He held out the coffee. "Sugar and cream OK?"

She took it. The hot cup nearly burned her hand. She welcomed the pain. It was a rope to cling to, a sensory anchor.

"Ms. Callahan, you promised me that if you lived through the night, you'd tell me what this is all about," Garrett said.

"Oh," she said. "So I did. I'm still alive, aren't I? Sort of." She tried to focus her eyes on his face, but he kept blurring and losing his shape.

"Do you feel up to making a statement?"

She thought about it. "Am I being arrested?" she asked, without much curiosity.

Garrett sat down next to her. "Not at the moment."

"Ah." She ruminated for a moment. Hmm. Making a statement. It would be something to do. A starting point.

She blinked, shook herself to clear her head, and took a gulp of the coffee. It hit her unprepared throat and made her sputter and cough. When she got herself under control, she nodded.

"Sure, I guess," she said dully. "Why not?"

Chapter

28

It was Davy's fourth pass around the block. He was getting self-conscious about acting like a lovesick teenager. Or worse, an obsessed nutcase. Truth to tell, he was just plain chickenshit.

He parked up the block and stared at the Victorian house. He'd pried Margot's contact number out of Sam Garrett, and some mucking around in public databases with Seth's laptop had yielded up her friend Pia's address. But he still wasn't exactly sure why he was here.

Mikey sat in the passenger's seat, panting cheerful gusts of hot dog breath Davy's way. Mikey was his excuse for hunting Margot down.

He hated needing an excuse, but she knew where he'd been for the past eight days, trapped in a hospital bed. She knew his cell number. If she wanted him, she could have him. Anytime, anywhere.

Evidently, she didn't. Maybe she wanted to forget everything that had happened, himself included. Maybe it had left a bad taste in her mouth. He could hardly blame her. His behavior certainly hadn't been exemplary. He'd been a dick-head with her most of the time, when he thought about it, which he tried hard not to do. It made him squirm.

And he could rationalize and justify hour after hour, and nothing made the hurt go away. She'd told him that she loved him, but that was before the shit hit the fan. How long was a statute of limitations on a declaration of love? Particularly one that had been first rejected by an ignorant, cowardly ass-hole, and swiftly followed by a bloody massacre.

Fuck it. He just had to see her. It didn't matter under what circumstances, on what terms, or according to what rules. He would do anything. He had no dignity, no pride left.

He'd been so sure in Marcus's lair that if they could just get through that nightmare intact, they would love each other forever, but after days of silence from her, doubts had dug in. Lots of people fell in love with people who didn't love them back. Or with people who then fell completely out of love with them, leaving them high and dry.

It was a common enough tragedy. Look at poor Miles.

He took a deep breath, and got out of the car. Mikey sensed his misery when Davy took him out, wriggling his body up over Davy's chest to lick at his jaw. He panted, blowing the heavy stink of canned dog food into Davy's face. Disgusting, but it still made him smile.

Ironic, that an aging dog was more talented than he was when it came to emotional communication. Mikey just let it all hang out.

He would just have to try to do the same.

Margot stared at the real estate listings on the computer screen, but she kept spacing out. She couldn't keep focused long enough even to finish a sandwich, or drink a glass of iced tea.

Davy had been scheduled to get out of the hospital yes-terday. She wondered where he was. How he felt. She wanted to see him so badly. She'd been fighting the compulsion for days.

But he'd done so much for her already. It didn't seem fair to fling herself at him and beg him to love her, too. He'd made it abundantly clear, several times, that he wasn't interested in doing so. All she had to offer was a weepy, clingy wreck of a woman who was sloppy in love with him. If he pushed her away for the umpteenth time, she would implode.

She buried her face in her hands and reminded herself that she wasn't always going to feel this fragile. It had to get better sometime.

The doorbell rang, and she bounced about a foot out of her chair. She sank back down, heart thudding, irritated at herself. There were no monsters on her tail anymore. Probably it was the FedEx guy, delivering samples for Pia, her friend the fashion designer. She padded barefoot to the door and peeked through the peephole.

Her breath turned as solid as stone in her chest.

Open the door, you idiot. Do it. Now. She opened the door.

He was thinner. The hollows beneath his cheekbones were deeper. His bruises had turned yellowish green. He was so beautiful, it broke her heart. Mikey yipped in welcome, struggling in Davy's arms.

"Hey, Margot," he said quietly. "Or should I call you Margaret?"

"My friends used to call me Mag, but it's funny. I've gotten so that I like Margot better now," she said. *Since that was what you called me.*

A luminous smile flashed across his face. "Good," he said. "I like the name. It was hard to think of you as anything else."

An awkward silence fell. He handed Mikey to her. She gathered the writhing dog into her arms, and Mikey flopped and whimpered in passionate welcome. "You look much better than you did," she said.

"You look beautiful," he said.

She blushed, and looked down at herself. She had on a pair of Pia's cutoff jeans and a brief white halter top. If she'd known Davy was coming, she would've raided Pia's fabulous wardrobe more aggressively.

As it was, she wasn't even wearing makeup, and her hair was all over the place. "Um, hardly," she murmured. "But thanks."

The somber intensity in his eyes was almost too much to bear.

"Thanks for bringing Mikey." She set the dog down on the floor, where he rolled onto his back and waved his legs joyfully in the air. "I thought he'd be so mad at me. The unpredictable twerp."

"I think he had a great time with Miles," he said. "They bonded, evidently. Two lonely males, deprived of their hearts' desire."

The silence after his words seemed fraught with importance.

Don't you dare project your wishful fantasies onto him, she scolded herself. She'd fallen into that trap before, and suffered for it.

"Are you going to let me in?" he asked.

She shoved open the screen door, flustered. "Of course. Sorry. I didn't mean to seem—"

"Don't worry about it." He walked in. They stared at each other as Mikey perched against her thigh on his hind legs. "You doing OK?"

She gave him a wan smile. "More or less. I've been trying to figure out how to put my life back together. But it's hard to work up any momentum. So much time has passed. I feel lost."

"I know what you mean." Davy touched her cheek with his fingertip. She jerked as if his finger had burned her. He let his hand drop. Damn. She wanted to grab his hand and put it right back.

She controlled herself, with difficulty. "Um, how about you?"

His mouth twisted wryly. "That thing with Marcus was good publicity for our new business, if nothing else. Calix wants to hire us. Priscilla Worthington was impressed with our teamwork. Go figure."

"So she should be," Margot said. "No problems with the police?"

Davy shook his head. "Seth's button recorded everything Marcus said. My ass is covered. They fixed it with the Seattle police, too, so Gomez is off my case, thank God. Garrett said we might even be hearing from the SCPD for some consulting work. We're the flavor of the week."

"Wow. That's great," she said. "And . . . your wound?"

"Fine. Healing. They let me out yesterday."

"I know," she said. "Garrett's been keeping me informed."

"Oh yeah?" Davy frowned. "He didn't tell me that."

"Probably because I asked him not to," she admitted.

"Why?"

The edge in his voice made her eyes slide away from his. Her reasoning seemed so cowardly, now that he was here in front of her.

"I'd already caused so much damage," she said. "People had died. You almost died. I felt like the kiss of death. This needy, crazy, freaked-out woman who caused chaos everywhere she went—"

"Margot. I've told you. It wasn't your fault," he growled.

She pushed on. "And in the end, I figured . . . I know you've got this thing about rescuing girls in trouble, and you'd already been so heroic, saving my life. It wasn't right to glom onto you and—"

"You've got it all backwards."

She lost her place in her monologue, and floundered. "Huh?"

"The freaked-out, crazy, needy person was me. Not you."

She stopped breathing. "Davy . . ."

"You shouldn't have disappeared on me like that," he said. "Not when I was shot up, in the hospital. That was cruel."

Cruel? "But—but I never thought of you as needing anything from me," she stammered. "I just didn't think I should lean on you anymore. God knows, I'd almost destroyed you already."

"So who the hell was I supposed to lean on?"

The question made the world spin into a new, confusing shape. She shook her head, tears prickling her eyes. "I didn't know you felt that way," she whispered.

"Well, I'm telling you now."

His cool tone sparked her anger. After all the evasive head games he'd played, the guy had the nerve to guilt trip her. "Exactly what are you telling me?" she demanded. "That you have needs? I know all about your famous needs. That's the one thing you've been willing to concede to me from the very beginning of our depraved affair."

"I'm not talking about sex." The words were ground out one by one from behind his gritted teeth.

Baiting him wasn't fair or smart, but it was such an ingrained habit, she couldn't help herself. "You're not? What a shame. So you're not going to make me another indecent proposal?"

"Would you accept it if I did?" he demanded.

The question caught her off guard, and the truth popped right out, no thought of pride or playing it safe. "God, yes," she blurted. "I would do anything for an indecent proposal from you."

A long, breathless silence stretched out. His eyes dropped. "How would you feel about . . ." He swallowed, and went on, his voice hesitant. "How would you feel about a decent one?"

She was utterly lost. "A decent what?"

"Proposal," he said. "As in, of marriage."

She didn't even have the presence of mind to close her mouth. "Marriage?" Her whisper was barely audible.

A muscle pulsed in his jaw. "I don't know if you still feel, uh, you know. The way you did when you said that you, uh . . ."

"That I loved you?" she supplied, when his voice trailed off.

He nodded. "I know a lot of crazy stuff has come down since then. Maybe you need some time to—"

"No," she said.

His face tightened. "I'm just asking you to think about it."

"No, what I mean is, I don't need any time," she said. "Not so much as a second."

He made a furiously impatient gesture with his hand. "So? What, then? For Christ's sake, Margot, haven't I suffered enough?"

She was dizzy. She put her hand against his heart. It throbbed, quick and hard. "Where can I grab you? I don't want to hurt you."

His arms encircled her, and he stroked the bare skin of her back. "My left shoulder is sore. Grab anything else you feel like grabbing. So? Are you putting me out of my misery, or are you stringing me along?"

"You're the one who's doing things backwards, now," she said.

He tilted her face up, frowning. "Don't be cryptic. I've been lying in a hospital bed feeling pathetic for eight days. Be nice to me."

She looked him straight in the eye. "Most guys don't propose marriage to a woman before they express their feelings for her."

Davy stroked the hair away from her cheekbones. "I figured all that gooey emotional stuff was automatically implied in a formal proposal of marriage." His voice was low and cautious.

She rubbed her cheek against his hand. "You could indulge me anyhow," she said. "That gooey emotional stuff wouldn't kill you."

He scowled and jerked her closer, his fingers twining into her hair. "Oh, for Christ's sake, Margot. What do I have to do to convince you? Chasing you all over hell and gone, duelling with maniac assassins, catching bullets, is that not dramatic enough for you? You know damn good and well that I'm crazy about you!"

She caught her breath. "You, uh . . . you could've done all that stuff for me just because you're a righteous, heroic sort of guy."

"Hah." His laughter was derisive. "Yes or no, Margot. Out with it."

He was in such distress, she couldn't bear to torture him any longer. "Yes," she said. "I love you, Davy. Always have. From the start."

His eyes closed. He let out an explosive sigh, wrapped his arms around her and hid his face against her neck. His shoulders shook.

They swayed, locked together, vibrating in perfect tune. She could have stayed there forever, if she hadn't been forced to fish some Kleenex out of her cutoffs and blow her nose. Niagara Falls was flooding down.

It turned into a two-Kleenex operation. She finished mopping her eyes and nose just as he pulled a small box out of his pocket and gave it to her. "I spent the whole morning in jewelry shops, but once I got here, I was so jacked up, I forgot about it," he said.

She opened it and stared at the beautiful square-cut emerald, glowing with soft light. It was surrounded by tiny pearls and baroque gold beads. "Oh, Davy," she breathed.

"I thought the emerald would look good with your red hair, once you grow it back out," he said hesitantly. "Is it OK?"

"It's spectacular," she whispered. "It's so beautiful. Oh, God."

Time for another Kleenex. She dealt with the mop-up operation with her right hand while he slid the ring onto her left. He pulled her hand to his lips and kissed it until her own knees almost gave way.

Davy hooked his finger into the loop of white bow that held the halter top closed under her breasts. The knot gave way, and he brushed the thing off her shoulders and stared hungrily at her body. "You said you were up for indecent proposals too, right?"

The look in his eye made her breathless. "With you, I'm up for anything. But aren't you sort of fragile and delicate right now?"

He ignored her question. "Will your friend Pia walk in on us?"

Margot glanced up at the clock. "She'll probably be out for another couple of hours, but I sleep in the studio in back if you'd rather—"

"Please. Yes. Now."

She took his hand, and led him to the studio, filled by Pia's fold-out futon bed. Mikey scampered after them, but Davy scooped him up and ruffled his floppy bangs apologetically. "Later, dude. Nothing personal." He put Mikey gently outside the door and closed it.

He pulled her into his arms, nuzzling her as his hands slid over her bare skin. He pushed her cutoffs and panties down with reverent gentleness and his fingers slid between her legs, teasing with a skill that brought an instant rush of damp heat to her sex. A ragged sigh jerked out of him when he felt her slick moisture on his fingers.

"Do you have any, ah . . ." Her voice trailed off as she remembered their last problematic condom conversation.

He shook his head. "It seemed presumptuous to come here with an engagement ring in one pocket and a condom in the other. Do you?"

She shook her head. Davy's warm lips brushed over her cheek.

"This is my reasoning," he said. "I don't want any woman but you. I want to marry you as soon as we can get it together, and I want to make kids with you. Now, later, whenever we get lucky. So . . . ?"

"Yes," she said quickly. "Fine. I'm right there with you." Her hands shook as she undid the buttons on his loose shirt. "Are you sure this is a good idea? We can wait for you to—"

"Don't want to wait. I'm starving." He shrugged his shirt off. "Besides, it's a chance for you to knock me over with your feather and ravish me. I won't be delicate for long. Go for it while the going's good."

He stretched out on the bed and tugged Margot down to straddle him. She stared at the bandage on his shoulder, starkly white against his bruised skin. "Oh, my poor baby," she whispered.

He placed a finger over her lips. "Not now. You can fuss over me later. I want to play out my new favorite fantasy. Laid out on the bed while a gorgeous panther woman uses my helpless body as her boy toy."

She laughed. "My turn to crack the whip, hmm?" She attacked the buttons on his jeans. "Tell me if anything I do hurts you—"

"Just don't leave me again," he said. "That hurts me."

She stared down into his somber eyes, trying to swallow around the lump in her throat. "I won't," she said quietly. "You couldn't drag me away." She pushed his jeans down and seized his stiff, hot penis in her hands. She caressed him as she positioned herself over his body.

It felt exquisitely right. She sighed as she sank down with aching slowness, taking him inside, dragging the precious moment out.

Davy grabbed her hands and brought them to his lips. "I love you, Margot," he said.

She collapsed forward over his chest. "I love you, too," she told him shakily. "Am I pressing on your sore spots? If I—"

"No. It's great. Therapeutic," he assured her. He pulled her tighter against his chest as his hips surged beneath her. "I love you. I love you." The words burst out of him, rough and impassioned, as if they'd been under pressure. "You're so beautiful. I'll always love you."

She was too overcome with feeling to respond in words, but he understood her kisses perfectly. From the beginning, their bodies had never lied. They twined together, fused by passion and delight that took them to a realm beyond doubts or games or even words.

They gave themselves up to trust, and endless tenderness.

Are you ready for
HOT NIGHT?
Here's a sneak peek at Shannon McKenna's
next romantic thriller,
coming in October 2006 from Brava . . .

Zan didn't come in, but just stood there waiting for her permission. Seconds ticked by. She flipped the kitchen light on to break the spell.

"Come on in." She aimed for nonchalant, but her voice came out too high-pitched. "I hope a check is OK. I didn't plan for this."

"A check is fine." He strolled into her kitchen, his eyes sweeping the place with discreet curiosity.

Sheba padded daintily over to the stranger's feet, sniffed his boots and began to weave a sinuous figure eight around his ankles.

Abby was startled. Sheba was the most snobbish, uppity cat she'd ever known. She never sucked up to strangers. She clawed strips out of the hands of anyone foolish or presumptuous enough to pick her up.

The locksmith picked her up.

"Careful," Abby warned. "She's twitchy. Don't let her scratch you."

"She won't. Cats like me." He stroked Sheba's downy back.

"Really?" she said wistfully. Her last would-be boyfriend, too long ago to calculate, had been violently allergic to Sheba, who was a constantly shedding ball of fluff. The affair had ended after a panicked trip to the emergency room. Cortisone shots really killed the mood.

"Never met a cat who didn't like me. They know I like them, too." He caressed Sheba's ears. She purred raucously and flung her head back over his wrist, baring her throat with sluttish kitty abandon.

The man's big hands tickled fur beneath Sheba's chin. The cat writhed in ecstasy. It was very distracting. Abby dragged her eyes away from the spectacle with some effort. "Thank you, by the way," she said.

He shrugged. "Just doing my job."

"No, not for the lockout. I meant for what you did with Edgar."

He looked uncomfortable. "You don't have to thank me."

"Well, too bad," she said. "Thanks anyway. It's a huge deal to me."

He gave her a brief, dismissive nod, followed by a long silence fraught with embarrassment.

"I, uh, have to pay you," she repeated.

"Yeah," he agreed, rubbing expertly behind Sheba's ears.

"What's your fee?" she asked. "And is a check OK?"

He looked faintly amused. "You asked me that before."

Abby discreetly tugged her neckline higher. "Did you answer?"

"Yes." His deep voice was as soft as silk. "I said a check is fine."

She let out her breath slowly, in a long, controlled stream, as her yoga teacher had taught her. "So what's your fee?" she repeated.

"Does your check have your phone number on it?" He stroked Sheba's fluffy belly. Her raucous purring seemed deafening.

"I can write my driver's license number on the back, if you'd like."

"I'd rather have your phone number."

Abby checked to make sure her hair was covering her cleavage. "I usually don't—that is, I prefer—I mean, why?"

"So I can ask you out." He grinned. His teeth were very white. He had a deep dimple on one side of his cheek. So lopsided and playful, it seemed out of place in that lean, dangerous face.

The hairs on the back of her neck stood up, and her toes curled inside her spike-heeled pumps, and a rush of shivery, breathless excitement tightened her chest so much she could no longer inhale. "I—I, um, thought this was a . . . a business transaction," she stammered.

"It is. I just happened to ask for your number in the middle of it."

Yeah, right. "Don't take this personally, but it's been a bad night."

"I know," he assured her. "That's why I'm not asking you out tonight. I'm just getting your number. I'll wait until a decent interval has passed before I call and ask you out."

Abby smoothed her damp, shaking hands down over her hips and tugged her skirt down over her thighs. "What's a decent interval?"

His grin widened. "Hadn't thought about it yet. Week? A couple days? Twelve hours? What do you think would be a decent inverval?"

She pressed her lips together hard. "Let's stick to business. How much do I owe you?"

He looked thoughtful. Sheba butted his hand with her fuzzy head. He stroked her obligingly. "That depends."

"On what?" she demanded.

"The client. If that guy had called me—what was his name?"

"Who?" She was so flustered, she could barely follow him.

"The dickwad in the red Porsche. Edward? Edmund?"

"Oh. Edgar Thornton. The Third."

He grunted. "Third, my ass. If it had been Edgar, I would've jacked up the price as much as my conscience would allow, which is quite a bit. Then I would have made him pay before I opened the door."

Abby was suspicious of the dimple that came and went in his cheek. He was making fun of her. "And why is that?"

He shrugged. "He could afford it. Plus, he'd been driving under the influence, which pisses me off. I take drunken driving personally."

"I'm not drunk. How do you know I wasn't driving?"

He rolled his eyes. "As if a meathead like him would let a girl drive his eighty-thousand-dollar penis substitute."

A smothered snort of laughter shook her. "You have a point. I tried to get him to let me drive, but the harder I tried, the faster he went." She shuddered. "Scared me to death."

"Hmm," Zan commented. "Truth is, I wouldn't have come out tonight if I hadn't liked your voice on the phone so much. I had to see who owned that voice. That sexy accent. Where are you from?"

Abby tried three times before she could make any sound come out of her throat. "Atlanta. But that's, ah, inappropriate."

"Oh, don't mind me," he said. "I'm just stalling."

"I see that." She grabbed her checkbook and opened it, scribbling down the date. "So how much do I owe you?"

"But as soon as you write that check, I'll have to go away." His fingers dug into the thick fur of Sheba's belly. Her tail lashed wildly.

Abby wrenched her gaze away from the sensual spectacle and realized she'd written the wrong date. She tore it out and started over. "Stop stalling and tell me how much I owe you, Mr. . . . er . . ."

"Duncan," he said. "Call me Zan. Here's my card." He dug a business card out of his pocket and laid it on her counter. "I could cut you a deal. I always cut my friends a deal."

Sheba nuzzled him with her fluffy head. Abby's heart pounded, and her face felt damp. A reaction to the adrenaline, she told herself.

Not the idea of being his, ah . . . friend.

"I appreciate your kindness, but I'm obligated to you already," she said. "Please, just tell me your fee right now. It's very late."

His eyebrows lifted. "No phone number?"

"No phone number." She poised the pen over the check.

He looked wistful. "OK. Make it for a hundred and twenty."

Abby's mouth fell open. She slapped the pen down onto the counter. "That's highway robbery!"

He blinked, with exaggerated innocence. "At least I didn't ask you to pay me in advance."

"You couldn't have! My checkbook was locked inside!"

"Never said I wasn't practical." His eyes gleamed with sly humor as he stroked her cat. She had abandoned herself in his arms, her fluffy tail dangling over his dark sleeve like a feather boa.

"One twenty is ridiculous!" she snapped.

The lines around his eyes crinkled. "I didn't mean to piss you off," he said meekly. "I thought you didn't want to feel obligated."

"There are limits!"

"I'll make a deal with you, then," he said. "Your lock is crap. I probably could have opened it with my bare hands. Let me replace it with something decent. A Schlage, maybe. Parts and labor, plus the lockout, two hundred bucks. It's a great deal."

She tried not to laugh. "You are an opportunist."

"One seventy-five, then. Parts and labor. I swear, you won't regret it. Call around, do a price comparison, if you want."

She rolled her eyes. "Get real."

"Don't be mad," he coaxed. "One-sixty? I swear, I'm losing money."

Sheba yawned hugely and stretched, in a state of utter bliss.

Abby scurried around the kitchen counter and flipped open her checkbook. This conversation had dragged on long enough, and it was her own damn fault for encouraging him. She wrote out a check for one hundred and twenty dollars. "Who do I make this stupid check out to?"

"Make it out to Night Owl Lock & Safe." He leaned over the kitchen counter, blocking her light.

"Step back. Don't loom over me," she snapped, signing the check. "Tomorrow I'm going to make some calls to see what the going rate is for a nighttime lockout."

"Be my guest."

"If I find that you've egregiously overcharged me, I'm going to call the Better Business Bureau."

"You do that," he said. "Then call me up and tell me what an evil, greedy, grasping bastard I am. Any hour of the day or night is fine."

She held out the check. "Take this. And put my cat down."

"But she loves me. Look at her. She's as limp as a noodle."

"That is irrelevant," she said tartly. "Thank you, and good night."

"It's true, what I said about your lock," he said quietly. "You need a dead bolt and a chain. And an alarm system."

"How much would it cost to install a lock that you couldn't get through?" she demanded.

He smiled again. "It would cost you a fortune to install a lock I couldn't eventually get through," he said. "I'm really, really good. Patient, thorough . . . tireless."

She broke eye contact, and laughed, nervously. "My goodness. You certainly do have a high opinion of yourself."

"Yes, I do."

She blew out a sharp breath. "Don't make fun of me," she said. "What a night. First Edgar, now you. Just take your check, please." She pushed the check across the counter at him.

Zan did not take it. When she met his eyes, his smile was gone.

"I am nothing like Edgar," he said. "I have nothing in common with that shit-eating insect."

His tone chilled her. "I'm sorry. I didn't mean to offend you," she murmured. "This is getting awkward."

"I don't want your apologies," he said.

She was at a loss for a moment. "Look, ah, thanks again for—"

"I don't want your thanks. Most of all, I don't want your check."

"So what do you want, then?" The words burst out, unconsidered.

The eloquent silence following her words made her feel like a total idiot. "Oh, wow," she whispered. "Duh. I set myself nicely up for that one, didn't I? Handed it right to you on a silver platter."

"A kiss," he said softly.

She blinked. "A . . . what?"

"That's what I want."

She put her hands over her hot cheeks. "Whoa. Back up a step."

"You don't have to kiss me," he said. "You don't have to do anything. You asked me what I wanted, and I'm telling you."

She was completely disconcerted. "I can't."

"I know. That's OK. I'll live," he said. "You're just so pretty. You smell wonderful, and your voice is so pretty, it makes shivers go down my spine. I'm talking about just a tiny, respectful, worshipping kiss. Like kissing the feet of a goddess. A sip of paradise. That's what I want."

Oh, he was good. Scarily good. She was entranced by those

magic golden eyes, that silk and velvet voice. Helplessly imagining how it would feel to be kissed like that; as if she were precious, unique. Loved.

She backed away, appalled at how tempted she was. "I'm sorry," she whispered. "I . . . I just can't risk that."

He nodded. "Of course you can't. I shouldn't even have said it to you, after what you went through tonight. Sorry. Don't sweat it."

Damn. If he'd been churlish, that would have broken his spell, and she could have showed him the door. Buh-bye.

As it was, his sweetness threw her into terrible confusion.

He placed Sheba on the floor, gave her a farewell stroke, and rose to his feet. He gave her a gallant nod that was almost a bow, and walked out. She stared at the rectangle of night beyond the open door.

The darkness looked so terribly blank.

A surge of unreasoning panic made her stumble out onto the porch, just to make sure he was real. Not just a feverish dream.

He was real. He was halfway down the steps. "Zan!" she called.

He stopped, waited a few seconds before he turned. "Yeah?"

She held out the check. "Don't you want this?"

He shook his head. "No. I'd rather dream about my kiss."

She started down the steps toward him. The expression in his eyes changed. She stopped on the step above his, and he was still inches taller than her. "That's not good business," she told him.

"I suppose not. I shouldn't have pressured you."

"Shhh." She put her finger against his lips. They were amazingly soft and warm. She felt the delicate contact throughout her whole body.

That light touch set her off, and there was no stopping the tears. She put her hands over her face. His arms circled her, and soon she was draped over him, leaning on his solid warmth.

She finally lifted her head, sniffling. "Sorry," she said. "Bet this service isn't in your fee schedule."

"I don't want a fee from you," he said.

"Take this, then." She took his face in her hands and kissed him.

It was a careful, tender kiss, charged with sweetness. She felt every detail so intensely; the warm fragrance of his breath, the different textures of his lips, the velvet softness of his full lower lip, the tiny moist sound as she pulled away, still hungry for another tiny touch.

She wanted to wrap her arms around him and just drink him in.

His head was tilted back, his eyes closed as if he'd received a divine benediction. His high cheekbones were stained with hot flags of color.

Her laughter came out a little soggy. "Zan? Hello?"

He smiled. "I'm in heaven."

"Oh, please." She swatted his shoulder. "Don't overdo it."

He opened his eyes, and she was lost in their complex golden depths. "I tasted your tears on your lips. It made me blush."

"Oh." She wiped her eyes, her cheeks, and discreetly blew her nose again. "I'm, ah, glad you liked it."

He took a step down the stairs. "I'd better go," he said. "I can't keep up this perfect gentleman act any longer."

So don't. She swallowed the words back. "So it's an act, then?"

He backed down the rest of the steps, mouth twisted wryly. "Since the dawn of mankind," he said. "Good night, Abby."

He disappeared into the bushes. She listened to his vehicle pulling away. Headlights rounded the curve, and he was gone.